# THE DARWIN ELEVATOR

"The best part about alien stories is their mystery... and I keep
................ g
c .......... ........ .......... .. Darwin Elevator delivers
both despair and hope, along with a gigantic dose of wonder.
It's a brilliant debut, and Hough can take my money whenever
he writes anything from now on."

KEVIN HEARNE, *New York Times* bestselling author
of The Iron Druid Chronicles

"Claustrophobic, intense, and satisfying... I couldn't put this
book down. *The Darwin Elevator* depicts a terrifying world,
suspends it from a delicate thread, and forces you to read with
held breath as you anticipate the inevitable fall."

HUGH HOWEY, *New York Times* bestselling author of *Wool*

"Jason Hough writes with irresistible energy and gritty
realism. He puts his characters through hell, blending a
convincing plot with heart-stopping action and moments
of raw terror as the world goes crazy in the shadow of
unfathomable alien intentions."

SARA CREASY, author of the Philip K. Dick
Award–nominated *Song of Scarabaeus*

"A thrilling story right from the first page. This book plugs
straight into the fight-or-flight part of your brain."

TED KOSMATKA, author of *The Games*

"Deliciously complex and satisfying... The story unfolds with
just the right balance of high adventure, espionage, humor and
emotional truth... As soon as you finish, you'll want more."

*ANALOG*

**ALSO AVAILABLE FROM JASON M. HOUGH AND TITAN BOOKS**

**THE DIRE EARTH CYCLE**
*The Darwin Elevator*
*The Exodus Towers*

# THE PLAGUE FORGE

### BOOK THREE OF THE DIRE EARTH CYCLE

## JASON M. HOUGH

**TITAN** BOOKS

The Plague Forge
Print edition ISBN: 9781781167670
E-book edition ISBN: 9781781167687

Published by Titan Books
A division of Titan Publishing Group Ltd.
144 Southwark Street, London SE1 0UP

First edition September 2013

1 3 5 7 9 10 8 6 4 2

*The Plague Forge* is a work of fiction. Names, characters, places, and
incidents are the products of the author's imagination or are used fictitiously.
Any resemblance to actual events, locales, or persons, living or dead,
is purely coincidental.

Jason M. Hough asserts the moral right to be identified as the
author of this work.

This edition published by arrangement with Del Rey, an imprint of The Random
House Publishing Group, a division of Random House, Inc.

A CIP catalogue record for this title is available from the British Library.

Printed and bound in Great Britain by CPI Group (UK) Ltd, Croydon, CR0 4YY

For my sons, Nathan and Ian.
The sky is not the limit.

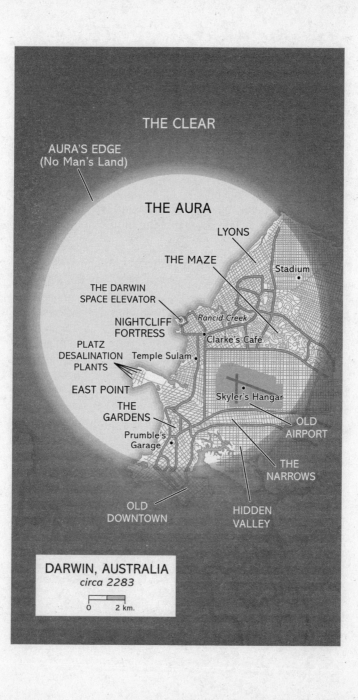

THE CLEAR

AURA'S EDGE
(No Man's Land)

THE AURA

LYONS

THE MAZE

Stadium

THE DARWIN
SPACE ELEVATOR

NIGHTCLIFF
FORTRESS

*Rancid Creek*

Clarke's Café

PLATZ
DESALINATION
PLANTS

Temple Sulam

EAST POINT

Skyler's Hangar

THE
GARDENS

OLD
AIRPORT

Prumble's
Garage

THE
NARROWS

OLD
DOWNTOWN

HIDDEN
VALLEY

DARWIN, AUSTRALIA
*circa 2283*

0      2 km.

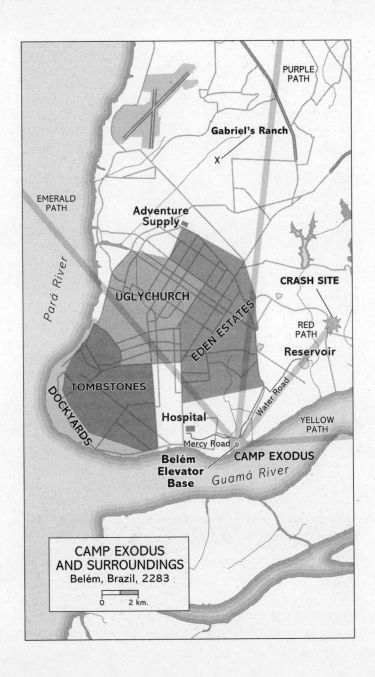

PURPLE
PATH

Gabriel's Ranch

X

EMERALD
PATH

Pará River

Adventure
Supply

CRASH SITE

UGLYCHURCH

EDEN ESTATES

RED
PATH

Reservoir

TOMBSTONES

DOCKYARDS

Water Road

YELLOW
PATH

Hospital

Mercy Road

CAMP EXODUS

Belém
Elevator
Base

Guamá River

CAMP EXODUS
AND SURROUNDINGS
Belém, Brazil, 2283

0    2 km.

I drew these tides of men into my hands
and wrote my will across the sky in stars.
Sister Haley, a verse from the Testament of the Ladder
(redacted—deemed plagiarized in 2292 from
T. E. Lawrence's *The Seven Pillars of Wisdom*, 1926)


After everything we've done to each other,
all the wars and shit, maybe this aura is the
Builders' way of telling our collective
asses to go to our room.
Without supper.
Skadz, 2280

# THE PLAGUE FORGE

# 1

## BELÉM, BRAZIL

### 20.MAR.2285

Seconds from collision the vehicle lurched.

Mud sprayed from knobby tires as the bulky truck whipped around and slammed back-first into the mouth of the tunnel. Dirt and rock clanged against the roof outside. The whine of electricity bleeding out from the ultracaps below Skyler's feet dropped off to nothing, allowing the clatter of heavy rain on armored body panels to fill the cramped compartment.

"All clear," Pablo said from his perch in the gun turret. "You're up, señor."

Skyler gripped the long chrome handle on the rear door with both hands. The full suit of body armor made him feel like he'd been dipped in concrete. Plates of carbon fiber were woven into thick ballistic fabric, even the gloves. He glanced back at Ana. She sat cross-legged in shorts and a T-shirt on the bench that ran the length of the compartment, an improvised explosive in her hands. The thin brick of wrapped plastique sported a hand-built receiver glued to one side. As he watched she stuffed the bundle out a murder hole, then smacked the portal closed with her hand.

The arming beacon lay on the bench beside her, safely in the off position.

"All set," she said. Then she caught Skyler's nod, leaned in, kissed him hard on the lips, and flipped his face mask down for him. "Good luck."

She'd been confined to a bed for the last few weeks after suffering bruised kidneys and some internal bleeding in Ireland. The camp medics, and Skyler, had advised against her going on this mission at all, but when her eyes had flared with dogged determination he'd known the argument was pointless. At least she'd promised to stay inside the vehicle.

He grinned. "You, too."

Ana returned his grin with a half smile of her own, then brushed a strand of hair from her face. In that instant she looked as lovely as she ever had, and Skyler glanced away. He couldn't quite explain why, and hoped against hope that Ana hadn't noticed his sudden distance. The truth was, ever since Tania had given him her air aboard that alien ship he had found himself in a strange sort of limbo. He turned back to the task at hand, focused. With both hands he yanked the door handle.

When the door swung open, Skyler found himself staring down the tunnel once again. A steady stream of dirty water ran down the center of the floor where, after all this time, a deep and erratic gouge had been carved. More water dripped and trickled from the curved ceiling and walls, making the inside of the tunnel appear to be engulfed in the same storm that pummeled the rainforest outside.

With all the dexterity his combat armor would allow, Skyler hopped out of the APC and raised his gun. He smacked the weapon's light on, and then did the same to the one mounted on his helmet. Already he regretted wearing the heavy suit. Sweat trickled down his back, and his legs felt like lead weights under the bulk.

The gun he'd chosen only made matters worse. The heavy assault rifle fired large-caliber rounds, regular from one magazine and explosive-tipped from a second. He could switch with a flick of his thumb. Mounted halfway down the barrel was a slightly curved steel plate that came up a few centimeters above the body of the weapon save for a small gap through which he could aim. The bulk of the shield descended from the barrel, which provided an extra barrier to anything that might seek to hit him in the chest. The protection might come in handy, but it made the weapon unbalanced and difficult to aim. Skyler had almost left it behind in favor of something smaller when Ana pointed out that he needed it only to get to the shell ship. Once he had the relic that lay within, he could ditch the bulky thing and run.

He glanced back one more time, some clever bit of reassurance on his lips. The words were drowned by a thunderous eruption. Pablo, on the roof-mounted rotary cannon. Individual gunshots could not be heard, only the steady hum as the weapon spewed bullets like a fire hose. It sounded like a pure bass note run through a stack of concert speakers. The vibration shook droplets of water from the circular tunnel around Skyler and made the plates of his combat armor chatter together.

The brutal noise vanished, replaced by the prattle of shell casings tumbling down the side of the APC and into the mud. Pablo fired the weapon for only a few seconds. Whatever had been his target, Skyler imagined it had been reduced to a few shredded bits of meat. He saw none of this, though, as Vanessa had stuffed the vehicle's rear end expertly into the maw of the tunnel, ensuring Skyler would not have to worry about attack from behind.

"Get moving!" Ana shouted at him. She stood crouched in the center of the compartment now, pistols in both hands, ready to move to murder holes on either side of the vehicle should anything get past Pablo's Gatling gun.

The plan required speed, and Skyler had not moved a step yet. He faced the tunnel again and started to jog forward, as if pushed by Ana's gaze at his back.

Skyler's breath fogged the inside of his face mask. Moisture from the humid air of the tunnel formed droplets on the outside. The thick sheet of clear plastic curved around in front of him and offered decent enough protection as long as he kept his chin down, visibility be damned.

He walked forward. The mud swallowed and sucked at his boots with each step. He moved farther to the outside of the curved passage, where the mud wasn't as deep, but walking along the steeper part made his footing awkward and forced him to use his left hand to steady himself. This meant he had to carry the heavy rifle and its huge shield with his right. By the time the crashed ship came into view his arm burned, barely able to keep the tip of the barrel from dragging in the rising water. Aim of any effectiveness would be all but impossible.

Pablo's rotary gun hummed again, strangely muted here at the end of the tunnel, as if the sound came rolling down the long tube and then canceled itself out where the space abruptly ended. Beneath the thrum came a rapid series of claps—Ana's pistols. Skyler forced himself to ignore it. They had their job; he had his.

Water pooled in the cavity at the end of the tunnel. Despite the time that had passed since Skyler had first come here, the water had not increased in depth, leaving the scarred vessel resting in waist-deep water. Visibility dropped the closer he came to it, and by the time his boots filled with water Skyler found himself surrounded in humid air that smelled and tasted vaguely of copper.

Movement in front of him.

A black shape, slipping out of the opening on the side of the craft and into the water, so smoothly no splash was generated. Instead a subtle ripple fanned out across the surface.

Skyler braced his feet and raised his weapon with both hands. Between the riot mask in front of his face, the swirling steam in the air, and the plate of shielding mounted halfway down the gun barrel, he could barely see anything. The thing that had slipped into the water had merged with the darkness around it, and his gun's light failed to illuminate anything other than the fine droplets of moisture in the air.

He held his breath and waited, counting silently. *Four . . . five . . .*

Something surged in the water, a bow-shock spray of dark liquid as torso and arms came up and lunged forward.

Skyler recoiled on instinct, felt himself tipping backward under the weight of his gear as the subhuman came fully out of the water, red laser light flaring from its eyes.

Some small corner of Skyler's mind kicked in during the split second it took for the creature to close the distance. He thumbed his weapon's clip selector, switching to explosive-tipped rounds.

He fired.

The bullet hit the creature square in the chest at the same instant its outstretched fingertips brushed Skyler's shield. A deafening crack, a blinding flash of light. Pressure on Skyler's own chest as the blast pushed the two of them apart. He fell backward into the water, had a strange awareness of cold seeping around his combat armor and into his clothing. His ears rang, yet he still heard the subhuman splash back into the pool and writhe there, thrashing in the water like an irritated alligator. Skyler sat up. He raised his gun from the water and aimed toward the splashing chaos a few meters away.

This time he held the trigger down.

A rapid series of small explosions lit the cave, as if someone had thrown a string of lit fireworks into the pool. Some of his rounds hit the back wall; others exploded on impact with the water around the creature, filling the space with a violent spray. Still more found their target, racking the augmented being with brilliant flashes of light, pushing it back.

The subhuman somehow found its footing, tried to dodge first left then right. Skyler gave it no relief; he kept firing even as he came to his feet. He swept the barrel of the gun in synch with the creature's movements and sensed the desperation there. It was hard to tell for sure, but Skyler thought he saw one of the creature's arms had been severed just below the elbow.

With a click the magazine of explosive rounds ran dry. The weapon automatically reverted to the main clip, and after only a split second the bark of gunfire filled the space again. Skyler had his legs under himself now, and despite the added weight of water that soaked his clothing, he found himself energized by the sight of a severed arm bobbing in the choppy water nearby. The creature could be hurt.

He focused his armor-piercing rounds on the subhuman's glowing red face, those strange traces of laser light that vaguely marked where its eyes used to be. The creature had backed up all the way to the far wall now and had nowhere else to go. The aggression seemed to drain out of it, and Skyler almost relented when the being took on a sudden, pathetic slouch against the rock and mud, accepting its fate.

Skyler kept firing until the creature slumped and slid down the wall into the water, disappearing below the surface. He fired into the water then, another burst just for good measure.

Then, silence.

Smoke wafted off the barrel of the gun. The water around him sloshed against his legs briefly before settling into an inappropriate serenity.

Skyler waited, breathing the gunpowder-scented air in voracious gulps. He focused on the space where the creature had been, and realized he could just see the top of its head above the water. The black armor had cracked like an eggshell, revealing matted, bloody hair beneath. Jagged bits of the exotic material floated nearby. The sight gave him enough confidence to yank the empty clip of explosive rounds out of his weapon, toss it aside, and slap in his only spare. He flipped the selector back to the more powerful ammunition and willed himself to be calm.

Ten seconds passed. Twenty. Another deep buzz from Pablo's Gatling reminded him of the urgency of their plan.

Emboldened, Skyler waded to the Builder ship. The surface of the hull seemed to drink in the light from his helmet and gun. Geometric grooves along the surface crawled almost imperceptibly as light and shadow played around them. Skyler stepped carefully, unable to see his feet or the tortured lumpy cavern floor below the pool's surface. He moved to the opening on the side of the vessel, gun raised and ready.

Nothing within. No subhumans, at least. Just the pedestal he'd seen before, and on top of it, the object.

Circular, with a single small half-circle notch along the edge. Red light rippled along the straight-edged grooves on its surface. It seemed to brighten as he came closer.

Skyler took one glance around the cavity, saw nothing moving, and set his rifle on the edge of the opening in the crashed ship. He placed his hands on both sides and hauled his waterlogged and armored self into the cramped space, groaning with the effort. Memories of what had happened in Ireland bloomed to mind, and he wondered for the hundredth time what would happen when he lifted this "key" from its resting place. He'd imagined all sorts of scenarios, the worst being a simple cave-in. Being buried alive was pretty fucking low on his list of preferred ways to die. Standing inside the ship might give him some protection if the cave's roof fell in, and at Ana's insistence he'd packed two days of food and water in his already overloaded kit. "I'll dig you out if I have to, no matter how many of those things try to stop me," she'd said.

The memory of her words urged him into action. Skyler gripped the alien object with both hands, his teeth clenched as he imagined himself being covered with that same black coating the object provided to the subhumans. Nothing happened, though. Perhaps it was his gloves, or his lack of SUBS infection. Either way, the object did not seem to have a taste for him.

He lifted it and braced himself for the worst. An earthquake, a shower of rock . . . anything. Again, nothing happened.

The alien object mercifully weighed less than the one they'd taken from Ireland. He found he could hold it with one arm, like clutching a sleeping child to his side. Skyler left his gun where he'd dropped it and hopped down from the ship.

He was halfway down the tunnel, grinning despite himself, when the rumbling started.

Clumps of dirt and rock began to pelt his shoulders as the tunnel shook apart. Skyler felt a sudden, deep affection for the helmet and riot mask he'd worn. Not so much for the bulk of his body armor and the steel-toed boots that sloshed with each heavy footfall.

Many years earlier, when SUBS finally reached Amsterdam, Skyler had seen an elderly woman running along a rain-slicked cobblestone street. She'd had high heels on her feet, a long dress tangling about her legs, and two bloodied knees flashing into view with each awkward stride. A bundle of clothing under one arm and a wailing child under the other. As the cave shook apart around him, Skyler thought that old woman would probably beat him in a footrace right now.

A man-sized clump of dirt fell in front of him, forcing him to dodge and traverse the curved side of the tunnel floor.

Somewhere outside, above all the noise, he heard Pablo's gun again. This time it hummed and stayed on, a sound so low and steady it seemed to loosen something in Skyler's gut. He clutched the alien artifact tighter under his arm and forced his legs to move faster.

A few steps later the back of the APC came into view, and Ana stood in the door, urging him to move forward with frantic gestures.

"Move back!" Skyler shouted at her.

She pressed herself against the sidewall instead.

He jumped as he reached the back of the personnel carrier, and turned and rolled as he did so. His legs flipped around and over him as he tumbled into the back of the vehicle, mud spraying from his boots.

Ana, unencumbered by any armor, leapt over him and reached out for the door handle.

A shape, a being, emerged from the gloom of the tunnel.

"Look out!" Skyler roared, fumbling for his pistol.

Ana didn't miss a beat. She simply grabbed the door handle and yanked it with such ferocity that even she wasn't prepared for how fast it swung. Her feet tangled with Skyler's legs.

The armored subhuman in the tunnel jumped, hands outstretched and flaring with bright red light. It hit the door, adding its own weight and momentum to Ana's pull. With a thunderous boom the heavy door slammed shut. Ana toppled over Skyler and hit the floor of the compartment, hard.

A second of silence passed. Then something pounded against the door, hard enough to rock the vehicle.

"Go," Skyler said. "Go!"

He heard the whine of electricity surging through the vehicle's four motors. The next sound filled him with fear. Wheels spinning uselessly in mud.

"Slowly, Vanessa," he growled toward the front, where the woman sat hunched over the steering wheel. "Let it get some traction."

Vanessa tried again, coaxing the accelerator this time. At first nothing happened, and then the wheels began to spin against the mud below again, gaining no purchase.

"It's not working!" Vanessa shouted back.

"Fuck, fuck," Skyler whispered.

Pablo's Gatling gun thrummed to life again. Skyler heard cries of pain from somewhere outside and wished he had a window.

Vanessa, in frustration probably, slammed the accelerator to full power. She was only digging them in deeper, Skyler knew. He needed to take the driver's seat from her, and was starting to rise when the armored subhuman in the tunnel slammed into the vehicle again. Even through the closed rear hatch, Skyler could see the flash of reddish light flare in through the tiny gap around the edges. The whole APC lurched forward from whatever weapon the subhuman had embedded in its hands. Lurched enough that the tires found a bit of purchase. Vanessa still had her foot firmly planted on the accelerator, and like a caged animal being freed the vehicle surged into motion.

Skyler saw Pablo turn around, heard the Gatling begin to sing its deep song again.

"The trigger," he said to Ana.

She nodded, went to the side bench, and picked up the small transmitter. It was a simple metal box, with a plastic bulge on the front that covered a tiny switch. Ana flipped the cover up and thumbed the switch.

On the drive into the circle of red aura towers, Ana had pushed bundles of explosives out of the vehicle every ten meters or so. Each had been fitted with a custom arming switch, cooked up by some of the techs in camp. The bombs would arm when they came in range of the trigger Ana now held. Once armed, when the trigger left their range the bombs would detonate.

Ana grinned mischievously when the first explosion went off, a grin that turned into a broad smile with the second, and third.

Skyler found himself smiling, too, until the APC hit a bump in the ground that sent him bouncing upward. His skull smacked into the ceiling, not hard, but enough to remind him of the danger they were still in.

"Take it easy up there!" he shouted forward to Vanessa.

"Bite me," she shot back.

More jostling followed as the APC barreled over fallen trees and rain-carved grooves.

Explosions continued to go off in rhythm with their departure. Skyler had no idea if the bombs would kill, or even harm, a single subhuman, but the hope was that it would keep them from following. At least until the APC reached the road.

"Low on ammo!" Pablo shouted down from his perch on the turret.

"Conserve it until we're back on the path," Skyler said.

"Almost there," Vanessa said over her shoulder. Then, "The towers are moving."

"Just as we hoped," Skyler said. "Get ahead of them if you can, and let Karl know to be ready." He got to his knees on the floor of the compartment and studied the object he'd stolen from the cave. In shape it almost reminded him of a giant wheel of cheese, thick and circular. At one position along the edge a small half-circular section had been carved out. Skyler wondered at the reason for that, but knowing the object would fit into a specific place inside the Builder ship seemed to answer the question: It would only fit in one position, like a puzzle piece. Or a key.

Skyler lifted it into a hard case, then closed and latched it.

Explosions trailed behind them, every two seconds.

"The armored one is following," Pablo said. "The rest stayed inside the mist."

Skyler glanced at Ana. "How far behind us is it?"

"Ten meters," Pablo said. "I can't get a good shot."

Ana read Skyler's face and knew his plan almost before he did. She moved to the rear and grasped the door's handle.

Skyler lifted the seat of one bench, revealing a compartment within. He pulled out another assault rifle and thumbed it to explosive rounds.

"Do it," he said to Ana.

She yanked the handle and pushed the door open.

Skyler stared down a "road" of flattened trees and crumpled foliage. To his left and right, enormous aura towers lumbered along in the same direction the APC headed, knocking over everything in their path as they made their way back to the space elevator.

Off center, but on the path, a black-armored subhuman sprinted toward him. The creature moved with inhuman speed, augmented no doubt by the strange material that coated its entire body.

One of Ana's bombs went off a few meters to its left, and the creature stumbled but hardly broke stride.

Skyler aimed, a pointless endeavor in the bouncing, jostling vehicle. He pulled the trigger anyway and held it down. The rifle chattered, followed a split second later by a myriad of small flashes around the feet of the creature. Some of the shots went high and exploded into the trees at the side of the carved road. Splinters of wood filled the air behind the subhuman like confetti.

Finally Skyler got the weapon under control and swung it back toward his target. A round exploded off a clump of dirt just beside the creature, and it dodged left.

A fatal mistake.

Just as it stepped, one of Ana's bombs went off, right beneath it. The subhuman cartwheeled into the air, limbs flopping with sickening lifelessness. It landed in a splash of mud, unmoving.

Ana hooted in victory and rattled off a string of words in Spanish that needed no translation.

Skyler kept the gun trained on the body until it faded from view. Two more of Ana's bombs went off before they passed the point where she'd started to drop them on the way in.

Vanessa weaved the vehicle around a few more aura towers, and then they were clear. The towers were all behind them, making their slow journey back to camp. Skyler guessed it would take them half an hour to reach the base of the Belém Elevator. The towers released when he'd picked up the object in Ireland were still weeks away.

He left the rear door open and set his weapon on the side bench. "Vanessa, let Karl know we're en route, and to get everyone ready on those barricades."

"Already done," she said. "He said the cord shook a few minutes ago, like before."

*The second object we've picked up, but the* third *time that's happened.* He didn't like what that implied.

The camp had drilled four times in the last two days for the possible return of the aura towers. Portions of the barricade around the camp had been placed on wheeled pallets, and the expected path to the center of camp had been cleared of structures, tents, and vehicles. No one wanted a repeat of the mess their departure had created.

Skyler leaned under the roof turret, squinting as he looked up. "Pablo, you all right up there?"

"Uh-huh."

"You can come down if you want."

"I'll stay. Just in case."

"Suit yourself."

A moment later Vanessa turned them hard left and gunned the motors. Teeth-rattling bumps turned into a gentle sway as the vehicle transitioned into the potholed road.

"Help me with this," Skyler said to Ana. He tugged at the heavy armor on his chest and Ana stepped across the cabin to assist. Together they lifted the bulky plated mass over his head and dumped it on the floor with a deep, dull thud.

"That's better," he said, and leaned his head back against the wall. The rush and chaos of battle behind them, Skyler's thoughts turned almost immediately back to Tania. The sacrifice she'd made so that he would have enough air to survive. The sight of her drawing that last tiny breath before her oxygen ran out.

He felt the sting of tears and willed them away. A familiar hollowness slithered into his gut, something he'd foolishly hoped would fade with the distraction of a mission.

Ana, uncanny in her ability to sense the shifts in his mood, took a seat next to him on the bench, folding her legs up beneath her and resting her head on his shoulder.

He took her hand in his, and together they watched the infinite blur of forest go by.


At Camp Exodus, Karl waved them in. He stood in the middle of a widening gap in the colony's wall, a bullhorn in one hand and a radio in the other. Colonists scurried about, pushing portions of the wall aside. Farther inside camp, more people worked to reposition the temporary structures that surrounded the base of the space elevator. A few forklifts assisted the effort, tracks coated brown with mud.

Rain pounded the entire area. It had been relentless for the last week, turning the unpaved areas of camp into muddy ponds and the rest into slippery patches if one wasn't careful.

Vanessa pulled to a stop next to Karl and they exchanged a few words. She coaxed the vehicle forward and turned hard left, moving them toward the river, well out of the path of the incoming towers.

Skyler could see almost nothing but a rain-lashed windshield; still, he knew the camp's layout like the back of his hand and could guess how far they'd driven. "That's good enough, Vanessa. Park here; we'll help them prep."

She obliged, rolled to a stop, and killed the current to the motors.

"Damn this rain," Skyler said once he set foot outside. The thick drops of water fell at an almost artificially steady pace. He left his body armor in the back of the APC, and offered Ana a hand down to the ground. She jumped instead, wincing slightly on the landing and probably hoping Skyler hadn't noticed. He pretended not to and pulled his bushman's hat from the pocket on his pants where he kept it. The downpour soaked the treated leather before he could get it on his head. "This is miserable."

Ana pulled her own hat on, a black baseball-style cap unadorned with any logo. She still wore her shorts and tee, but at least she'd pulled a combat vest on over the thin top. She flashed him a thumbs-up.

"Pablo, Vanessa, guard the . . . thing," he called out, and they set out.

They met Karl at the edge of camp. He stood on a scaffold that had been bolted to part of the wall there, allowing a kind of lookout. A metal ladder provided access, and Skyler climbed up. Ana, he noted, stayed behind. The lingering pain in her back must be flaring up again, but he knew better than to suggest she find somewhere to lie down.

Karl held a set of binoculars to his eyes. He lowered them as he made room for Skyler. "Can't see shit in this rain. Are half coming?"

"Just like Ireland."

"Okay." He turned and raised his bullhorn. "Control team, into positions!"

A portion of the camp had been cleared in a pie-slice section expanding out from the Elevator base, in the direction of the crashed ship out in the rainforest, plus a healthy buffer around the entirety of the disk that marked the cord's actual connection point.

"Think it's enough?" Skyler asked.

"Only one way to find out." Karl waved as a group of colonists emerged from the shelter of a camper some distance away. They rushed forward and swarmed into the cleared space.

Skyler noted that the rest of the colonists had also sprung into action at the command Karl had shouted, retreating far to the opposite side of camp by the university complex.

The "control team" fanned out and spaced themselves evenly in a line, halfway between Aura's Edge and the base of the Elevator.

Karl spun around and scanned the forest again. The path originally carved when the towers had left was still detectable if one knew where to look, but a remarkable amount of foliage had already regrown along the route.

Skyler heard the towers before Karl saw them. The crack of young trees being folded in half, the crunch of rock being pushed aside. Muted under the heavy rain, but there, and growing louder.

"I see them," Karl said.

Visibility in the rain was two hundred meters at best, one hundred at worst. What Skyler expected to see was tall, black towers pushing through the wall of rainforest that ran right up to the edge of Belém's slums. Instead he saw the foliage begin to whip and sway, as if a strong wind had suddenly risen.

Then the towers came.

Like an advancing army of siege engines from medieval times, the dark obelisks powered their way through the tree line. Skyler's heart leapt when those at the vanguard suddenly dropped as if falling into a pit, until he realized they were just crossing the steeply banked water channel that marked the border where city and rainforest met. The towers rose again a half second later as they reached the other side, a fine mist of water rising from where their bases touched the swollen waterway.

Still more came through, in a wider spread than Skyler would have guessed. One, a shorter tower whose tip sat well below the tree line, broke through close to where they stood, outside the cleared wall section. Karl saw it the same instant Skyler did.

"Hell," he said, "too close."

"Get to the ladder!" Skyler bellowed. He was closest and went first, taking the rungs two at a time and jumping the last three. His boots landed in the mud below with a splash, and he stumbled trying to make room for Karl. He braced his fall with one hand and whirled in time to see his friend slip on the scaffold top, still two steps from the ladder. The man landed hard on the wooden slats, one arm folded awkwardly underneath his torso. His binoculars tumbled over the edge and into the mud below. Wincing, Karl started to stand again and move for the ladder.

Then the wall wrenched and broke apart.

The scaffold heaved and tilted. Skyler had time to see Karl tumble off it and fall to the mud, before he, Skyler, had to move or be crushed himself.

Sheets of aluminum siding and chain-link fence crumbled as the tower pushed through. The scaffold walkway finally tipped and fell, slamming into the murk below with a tremendous sound and sending up a wall of milky brown water. Somewhere, underneath the broken remains of the wall and the ankle deep mud, was Karl.

Once the tower passed by, Skyler leapt forward. He hoisted a segment of fence away and tossed it aside. Someone else appeared next to him and lent a hand. Then two more people, shouting Karl's name and tossing chunks of debris aside.

Karl's hand grasped Skyler's and he yanked without a second thought. "Help," he grunted. The others around him converged, and then Karl came free of the mud. He was covered in the stuff, screaming and coughing in agony as his leg and foot came out from under a section of the collapsed walkway. The foot splayed out at an unnatural angle. "Careful of the leg," Skyler said to the three people helping.

They moved the injured man a few meters away and laid him on a patch of paved ground. Karl whimpered when they set him down, then spat, groaned. He swiped mud from his face and Skyler could see the intense pain on the man's face.

"I've got him," a nearby man said. "I'm a medic. Go help the others."

In the confusion Skyler had forgotten all about the rest of the towers. He glanced toward the center of camp in time to see the first of them reach the line of colonists who'd volunteered to try to stop them, an act of selfless bravery Skyler greatly admired. The men and women held their ground despite having just witnessed Karl's fall. The first of them, a stocky woman with short curly hair, held out her hands to an approaching tower, dug in her feet, and pushed.

The tower slowed, and stopped.

Skyler let out a sigh of relief, and turned back to help his fallen friend.

"Arm's broken," Karl said with a medicated slur. "The leg, too."

"Yeah," Skyler replied, kneeling down next to the cot in the infirmary tent. "I saw the way it was bent. Not pretty. Are you all right?"

"High as a kite."

Skyler grinned. "Thought we'd lost you when you went under the mud."

"How I had the presence of mind to hold my breath, much less keep it in, I have no idea." His eyes lost their focus for a few seconds, then he seemed to come back and see Skyler again. "I remember the snap in my leg, and then, then, waking up here."

The injured limbs were engulfed in thick spray-on casts, both propped to minimize swelling.

"How's it look out there?" Karl asked.

"You took the only wounds, you clumsy bastard."

Karl's laugh slid into an anguished grunt.

"Sorry," Skyler went on. "Twenty-two towers back, all safely in the yard. And one alien key, or puzzle piece, or whatever, ready to make the climb up."

"Who's taking it up?"

"I am."

"Good."

Skyler looked at the man's leg again, recalled the way his foot had been pointed the wrong way. He shivered despite the humid afternoon. *As if the slight infection of SUBS weren't already enough for Karl to deal with . . .*

The hammering of rain on the tent suddenly subsided, and then vanished altogether.

"You shoulda heard the twang of the cord when you picked that object up," Karl said. "Damnedest thing."

"Tim's coming down. Just to help manage things here, until you're up and about."

"You won't hear me complaining—*Fucking hell! Ow!*"

His leg had slipped off the stack of books that propped it up, landing with a thud on the thick canvas cot. Skyler winced, stifled a laugh without much success, and helped him get resettled.

# 2

## PLATZ STATION

### 22.MAR.2285

"How do you feel?"

"Like . . . like vomiting."

And so she did.

Skyler had imagined a number of reactions Ana might have on her first visit to space, her first time in weightlessness. This hadn't been his preferred outcome. Still, he'd prepared, had a plastic bag handy for her to use. He even had a handkerchief ready, and by the time they reached the climber port on Platz Station, Ana wore a wide grin and her eyes sparkled with an almost adolescent delight.

She bounded through the airlock with too much enthusiasm, drifting across the wide space beyond until she finally landed halfway up the far wall. He watched her drift in the microgravity, and laughed with her.

Ana pushed off with better aim on her second attempt, and he caught her, clasping a hand on her forearm as she did the same to him. She landed and slipped her other arm around him.

"This is better than swimming," she said.

"I prefer the water."

She punched him playfully on the shoulder. The motion made her body try to drift away, saved only by the fact that her other arm was around his waist. Skyler gave her a tug and pulled her back to the floor. She met his gaze, a silent thanks passing between them. Then he glanced down at the hard-shell case they'd brought up.

"I should probably—"

Ana spoke over him, saving him from an awkward conversation. "I think I'll stay in here for a while, if they'll let me. Learn how to, er, swim. Come get me when you're done."

*When I'm done. Right.* He didn't know if that day would ever come, but one thing he did know is that they would have to talk through the more complicated aspects of their relationship sooner than that. Skyler sighed and kissed her on the forehead. With that she pushed off the floor again and floated up to the ceiling.

He watched her for a few seconds, stalling, admiring her lithe form and the way her hair looked all tucked back in a tight ponytail. Finally he lifted the hard plastic case from the floor with one finger and pushed it ahead of him toward the cargo bay's exit—an alcove in the wall with a lift that went "down" to the outer portion of the station's central ring. He tucked the case under an elastic blue netting at the back of the lift to free his hands, then hooked his foot under a metal loop on the floor by the activation button. He tapped it, and waved to Ana as the cargo lift drifted slowly outward. He watched her perform a spiraling dive across the room and chuckled to himself. *A dancer at heart, no different than the first time I saw her.*


"Excellent work, Skyler," Tim said as Skyler approached the infirmary. He must have heard about the climber's arrival, as he seemed to be waiting.

"Thanks, Tim," Skyler replied. "Aren't you supposed to be headed below to fill in for Karl?"

"I'm taking your climber back down." Tim nodded once toward the case. "Is that what I think it is?"

"Can I go and visit?"

Tim's gaze lingered on the black container for a moment, then met Skyler's. He held Skyler's stare for a few seconds, then nodded and stepped aside.

Skyler couldn't quite decide why he treated the younger man with such blunt formality, such distance. Maybe it was just that Tim had an easy life up here, and unless Skyler was mistaken he'd yet to volunteer for any activity that would put him in harm's way. A desk jockey, through and through.

*It's none of my business,* Skyler thought as he pushed past the lanky man and into the medical section. He forced himself to think of Ana, somersaulting from wall to wall in the cargo bay. He'd made his choice, for better or worse, and Tania's heroics, as insane and remarkable as they were, wouldn't change that.

Dr. Brooks took one look at Skyler and pointed toward a curtained section at the end of the room. "Keep it to fifteen minutes," she advised after he'd passed her.

"Okay."

At the curtain he cleared his throat. He was about to call out when Tania drew the fabric aside.

She looked impossibly tired, her face thinner than he remembered. Had it been just a week? Ten days? Her raven hair hung loose and unkempt about her shoulders, a look he'd rarely seen, and it seemed to frame her face in a shadow that only served to accentuate her tired appearance. A pale blue hospital gown draped from her shoulders to her knees. Her feet were bare.

"I look that bad?" she said.

Skyler coughed once, rubbed the back of his neck. "No, no. I just . . . I'm glad you're awake."

"I look that bad."

"Awful," he said. "Awful . . . and, somehow, never better."

Her eyes brightened at that, the hint of a smile at the corners of her mouth. Skyler pulled her into a gentle embrace before she might catch any stray emotion in his own gaze, then let her go when he caught the scent of her hair. A slight hint of vanilla and cinnamon there that reminded him of their first meeting. She'd been disguised as a maintenance worker then, and full of the kind of confidence that can only come from almost total ignorance of what lies ahead.

She held him by the arms, studying his face. For an odd, uncomfortable second he thought she might be expecting him to lean in and kiss her. Instead she tilted her head, one eyebrow arching slightly. "Say something; this is getting weird."

"Um."

" 'Thanks for saving my life, Tania'? 'Thanks for the air'?" Her eyes narrowed slightly at his continued silence. " 'Glad you're not dead, Tania'? 'How's the food in this place'?"

Skyler shook his head. "I would have given you my air, had I known how to do that. Nice trick, by the way."

"Well, for once I was the one who had a survival technique up their sleeve."

"I . . ." He paused, trying foolishly to find the perfect thing to say. "You shouldn't have done it, Tania. I'm nobody. It was more important that you make it back."

"Stop," she said with a perfect mix of strength and finality. "First, that's bullshit. Second, what I did I'd do again without hesitation. You would, too, if you knew how, so if you're mad that I beat you to the idea . . ."

"I just . . ." He chewed his lip. "If you'd died—"

"I didn't, though. Okay, okay, technically that's not true."

"See?"

"Moot point; they found us in time."

"Barely."

"The fact remains. Dr. Brooks says I need to take it easy, and by that I think she means not to have conversations like this. So we'll table it, all right?"

"Okay," Skyler said. Absently he rubbed his shoulder. Old wound, old habit. "Well, um. I'm glad you're not dead. How's the food in this place?"

She laughed, and a bit of the vigor he'd seen so often before returned to her cheeks and her eyes.

A few seconds of silence passed. Tania sat there, studying her hands. Then she closed her eyes. At the same instant, her hands clasped together. "I have to tell you something, and there's no easy way to do it."

"This always leads to a fun conversation."

"Just . . . listen. And try to withhold judgment." She took

a breath, exhaled, and looked at him with absolute sincerity. "There's only one more Builder event."

He'd expected, well, anything but that. "Pardon?"

"After this ship's arrival, there's only one event left in this . . . sequence."

"How can you possibly know that?"

"Because," she said, and paused. Another deep breath.

Skyler felt a tingle ripple across his scalp and down the center of his back. The room seemed to go totally silent.

"It would appear," Tania said, "that Neil Platz knew more than he was letting on."

The tingle became an outright chill. Before he could ask the next question, she held up a hand and went on.

"He sent a note to Zane, just before he died. Literally, as Warthen's men were storming Platz Station. We only found it recently. According to the letter, Neil knew all along. Neil and my father."

"He—wait, your father?"

She'd closed her eyes again, and nodded solemnly. "Listen for a moment. I'm tired."

"Okay."

"All the note said, all I know, is that they knew. Somehow, they knew, because something happened *before* the Darwin Elevator arrived. An earlier event that, at least at some level, explained what was going to happen."

Skyler felt a flood of realizations pour into his mind from every angle, as if everything that had happened since the moment he left Amsterdam were disconnected pieces of the same puzzle, and Tania had just shown him a glimpse of the picture the pieces were supposed to form once joined. "He fucking knew?"

"Don't judge—"

"Don't *judge*? He knew about the Elevator and built an empire around it? Nightcliff and the water plants and all that. All those aerospace companies he bought up. He, Jesus, he fucking knew about SUBS and didn't warn anybody?"

"Stop."

Her voice hit him like a whip, snapping his mouth shut.

"You're not just talking about Neil: You're talking about my father. And we don't know what exactly they knew, except the number. Six events, Skyler, and we just experienced the fifth."

He had more to say. A lot more. But the look in her eyes, and the memory of her brush with death, pulled him back from that precipice. He stared into those eyes, the deep brown with flecks of gold, and felt one final revelation, one more piece of the puzzle, click into place. All of that business in Japan and Hawaii had been bullshit. Neil had already known what they would find; he just didn't want to expose that fact. No other explanation made sense. Which meant he'd sent Tania into mortal danger, and Jake to his death, to keep his secret. He'd known. It was, quite possibly, the most brazen example of insider trading in history, and like so many bankers and politicians before him, Neil had clearly gone to great lengths to cover it up. Only when faced with certain death or capture had he bothered to tell anyone. Despite the plea in Tania's eyes, Skyler couldn't bring himself to suspend judgment. He knew better than to tell her that, though.

"Thank you," he said, "for telling me. It makes things easier."

"How so?"

"A light at the end of the tunnel." Tania didn't look convinced, so he tried a different tack. "Can you imagine if Neil had said 'There's eighty-seven events, just eighty-two more to go!' No offense, but I probably would have thrown up my hands and walked away."

She was nodding as he spoke. "And I wouldn't have blamed you, Skyler. You're right. Knowing this somehow makes the task ahead seem worth the blood, sweat, and tears I fear will be required. It's like . . ."

"Like the surge of energy you get when you know the end of the race is just over that next hill."

Tania grinned at the analogy. "I've never run a race," she said. He laughed.

"I was going to say it's like piecing together a jigsaw puzzle, when you reach that moment where suddenly the pile of remaining pieces seems . . . manageable. A narrowing of possibilities."

"Your analogy is better," he said. Her smile at the compliment carried something more. An implied thank-you for swallowing his opinion of Neil. Skyler decided then that he'd keep his revelations to himself. It wouldn't do any good to point out to Tania what he now understood. She knew it, too, probably, and had enough on her mind already. Neil was dead. What was done was done.

"I brought you a present," Skyler said.

"Chocolate?"

"Er . . ."

"I'm kidding. A little. What'd you bring?"

Skyler stepped aside and watched her reaction as she saw the black case just behind him.

A split second of confusion crossed her face, then her eyes darted back to Skyler. "Is it . . . which one?"

"The red one. Belém. The circle."

She folded her arms across her chest. "And you're lecturing me about reckless behavior?"

"There was nothing reckless about it."

Tania rolled her eyes. "How'd you do it?"

"We just went in and asked. Nicely."

"Uh-huh."

"There may have been some explosives involved. A lot of explosives, actually."

"Perhaps you can share the details another time." She patted the sheets next to her.

Skyler sat, and they both stared at the case for a long moment in silence.

"I've been racking my mind," she said finally, "trying to imagine what possible motive lies behind all this. What the Builders are up to, I mean really up to."

"I think I've figured it out," Skyler said. "They're a race so advanced the only amusement left for them is to pull elaborate pranks on their neighbors."

She elbowed him. Then she stood and walked to the case. She ran a single finger along the surface of the thing, as if trying to feel some energy from the object within. "I suppose the more pressing question," she said with her back to him, "is what do we do now?"

"Tania," Skyler said, heat rising around his collar.

"Is it wise to install these things in the ship the moment we find them?"

"Tania."

"Or, should we hold on to them until we know more about their purpose."

"Um, Tania."

She glanced over her shoulder at him. "What?"

"Your gown is open at the back."

A high-pitched yelp rang out across the room. Tania whirled, clutched the garment tightly at her spine, and returned to her seat, all in the span of a heartbeat.

Skyler stared at the curtain next to the bed for a long moment. He studied the ceiling, estimated the sizes of the various pipes that snaked across it.

"Would you give me a minute?" she eventually asked.

He stood and walked away, heard the sound of the curtain drawing closed behind him. Skyler grimaced, stifled a smile, and crossed the infirmary to where Dr. Brooks leaned against a table, studying a slate. Skyler introduced himself formally and shook the woman's hand.

"How's she doing, really?" he asked.

"Tania? She's fine, but you don't need to tell her that. I've only kept her here so she can get some rest."

"She looks exhausted."

"You should have seen her a few days ago. She slept twelve hours last night, which is as much as she's been getting in an entire week lately. Now if she'd just eat."

"So she's okay?"

Dr. Brooks nodded. "We're always concerned about possible brain damage due to oxygen deprivation, and she was certainly in the danger zone in terms of time. But the tests are all negative. She'll be fine with a little more rest and a decent meal."

"When can she leave?"

The doctor shrugged, then nodded past Skyler. "Now, from the look of things."

He turned to see Tania emerge from the curtained area in one of her jumpsuits, a white one with blue stripes that ran from the neckline down the arms. She tied her hair back into a loose knot and gestured for Skyler to rejoin her.

"Thanks, Doctor," he said, and went back.

Before he could get a word out, Tania held up a hand. "We won't speak of it."

"Never happened," he agreed.

Her gaze went back to the container. "I guess we'd better decide what to do with this."

An hour later the alien object sat on a table in the cafeteria, a crowd of people around it. Someone had even brought a special microscope, the images it produced enlarged on a few slates that were passed around, eliciting excited commentary from those who studied them.

Skyler kept to the periphery of the group. He held his tongue for the most part, except occasionally when they asked him questions. Apparently Tania had been chastised for not allowing such an opportunity with the first object that was brought up. Somewhat hypocritically she'd also been criticized for allowing these alien objects aboard without careful decontamination measures. Tania defended herself, and Skyler, by explaining that in the excitement to explore the Builder ship she'd simply forgotten.

There'd been a time when such carelessness could not be explained away, or overlooked, so easily. But here, now, with everything at stake, her excuse earned scattered grumbles and more than a few sympathetic nods.

Food was brought in—a mix of fresh fruit and cut vegetables, some hummus, and nutrition bars likely brought up from the growing mountain of scavenged supplies in Camp Exodus. Someone even produced a bottle of cider, which lightened the mood in the room slightly.

Ana came in at one point, a sheen of sweat on her skin. She ate some food, said a few polite hellos, then begged off from the gathering of scientists to find a place to shower after her low-gravity antics. She didn't like being around the colonists much, especially the scientists. "They treat me like some kind of circus curiosity," she'd once said to him. He couldn't blame her.

When she'd gone, Skyler turned back to the group and caught Tania looking at him. She glanced away when their eyes met.

By late evening the people in the room had dwindled to what

Skyler assumed were the most senior scientists on station. Zane Platz came by, and Tim was there, too, hovering about Tania like a manservant. His affection for her was so obvious, Skyler found it amusing if a little boyish. To his surprise, Tania didn't seem too bothered by it. She even squeezed Tim's arm at one point, giving Skyler an unexpected twinge of jealousy.

A natural pause in the conversation gave him the chance to ask the question.

"Well, what do we do with it?"

They'd been debating just that all evening, but never with enough seriousness to call their conclusions a decision. Skyler asking the question served to crystallize it, and to his surprise they all turned to Tania.

"I think we should take it over there and install it," she said.

A few of the people present shook their heads. "Hold on," one woman said. "This thing has the ability to coat subhumans with some kind of weaponized armor. I don't know about the rest of you, but I'd like to understand how that works."

Others voiced similar ideas, concerns, worries. For his part, Skyler held Tania's gaze. He saw an apology there, and her eyes darted to the door and then back to him. "Outside," she mouthed.

He met her in the curved hallway, the sound of the animated crowd vanishing as the door clicked shut behind them. They stood an arm's length apart, dense red carpet at their feet. A few curious onlookers were milling about, probably hoping for a glance at the object. At the sight of them Tania moved off a few paces.

Skyler followed. He took in the bystanders and felt a sudden, surprising tingle on his neck.

"What is it?" Tania asked, sensing his sudden worry.

"Nothing. Well, just a . . . after what that woman Jenny did, I think we should post guards here. And anywhere people might gain access to a vehicle that could make it to the Key Ship."

"Guards?"

"Yes," he said under his breath. "That's a chunk of alien technology on the other side of that door, Tania. Jenny might not be the only closet Jacobite around here who can't resist the temptation to snatch it. Or destroy it."

"I really don't think—"

He pulled her farther from the people hovering in the hall. "Let's assume for a second that what we're supposed to do here is find these five objects and install them, okay?"

"Seems a fair assumption."

"Good. Can you imagine if we had to stop at four because someone walked off with the fifth and hid it somewhere? Or that we lost it? Maybe some experiment caused it to crack and fall apart?"

Tania glanced at the handful of people in the hallway with palpable suspicion now on her face. Then she turned her gaze to the doorway.

"I don't mean to make you jump at every shadow," Skyler said. "Paranoia won't help us right now, either. All I'm saying is that I don't think we should take chances with this. If we agree the task before us is to find and install these . . . keys, or whatever . . . then we should do that and *nothing more*."

She engaged in some silent deliberation, then took a deep breath. "You're right, of course. Okay, I'll give them until morning to study the object, but restrict their efforts to passive methods only. And I'll find some guards."

"Two outside, two inside."

She winced at the implication but nodded anyway.

"What about the ship?" Skyler asked. "We can't have any unauthorized visits to that room."

"Ah, well, we don't have to worry about that."

"No?"

"The outer door closed when Tim picked us up. A few of the scientists tried to go back and document the place, but apparently it won't open unless a 'key' is present. Well, a key or an immune, we're not sure which. Both, maybe."

"Interesting."

"We'll find out soon enough what the requirements are. I'll have a team, trusted people, take it over in"—she glanced at her watch—"twelve hours. You can observe from ops if you wish."

Skyler shook his head. "I think I'll get some sleep and head back to Belém. There's too much to do."

Tania nodded. "Well, if the door won't open, we'll need you or one of your comrades to assist."

He rubbed at the stubble on his jaw. "One of the others, maybe. It'd be good if I wasn't the only one with experience. Vanessa should be able to handle it. I can vouch for her, though you'll need to get her acquainted with zero-g."

If his suggestion disappointed her, she hid it well. "I'm sure she'll be fine. I'll make the arrangements." She paused, studied him. "Thank you, Skyler. For finding this, and bringing it in."

"Thank me when we've got all five." He turned to go. A few paces away, he stopped and turned toward her. "That reminds me."

"Yes?"

"There was a vibration that ran up the cord when we picked up that object."

"We felt it," Tania said. "Rattled the station. Even went as high as some of the farms. The same thing happened when you picked up the object in Ireland."

"It happened once before that, too," he said, and waited.

Realization dawned on her face a few seconds later. "I'd forgotten. Of course, yes. But that means—"

"One of the other keys has already been picked up."

Tania's gaze fell to the floor, as the possible implications percolated through her mind. Her mouth opened, then closed.

"Get some rest," Skyler said. "We'll talk again tomorrow."

# 3

## DARWIN, AUSTRALIA

### 23.MAR.2285

Despite the hour, and the citywide mandate against such things, a lively crowd filled the Chō-Han joint. Men for the most part, though Samantha could see a few painted women in the mix, arms draped around some of the players seated at the long dice table. The gathered audience for the game spilled out into the street in a rough half circle around the tiny gambling club.

A sake bottle passed between the onlookers. From her shadowed vantage point across the street, Sam couldn't see the contents but guessed it would be cider, being much easier to acquire or produce.

"Some balls these blokes have," Skadz whispered at Sam's shoulder. "Look at them, they're flaunting it."

"They better. I paid them to," Prumble said. He stood in the darkness on the opposite side of the alley.

Sam could barely see him, just a splash of wan yellow light on his round face. The cloak-and-dagger activity in the dead of night seemed to add a hardness to his features that she'd never seen before.

"Ah," the big man said. "Entering stage right, our pious and predictable Jacobite enforcers. Drawn from their station like moths to a flame."

"I'd rather be elsewhere," Skadz said. "As in now."

"Patience, patience. Let the kindling catch."

Whether the crowd pretended not to notice the approaching patrol, or genuinely didn't, Sam couldn't be sure. Their excitement at the game within the tiny storefront was realistic enough. Bets were placed. The shirtless dealer waved down the murmur and silence fell.

Sam could barely see the dealer through the crowd, but she heard him call out the result when the cups were flipped over. "Han!"

Roughly half the crowd roared in delight, loud enough to wake those in the cramped apartments above the street. Sam could already see a few candlelit windows above, shadows of worried faces looking down on the gathering in disbelief. Gambling and drinking in the open like this just wasn't done in Darwin anymore.

There was a flurry of activity as the bets were settled, and then the enforcer's whistle blew. The crowd turned almost in unison to face the approaching patrol. Sam held her breath in the brief silence that followed. Instinctively she appraised the Jacobites. A few held riot clubs; one had a wooden table leg studded with nails at the top. The leader, the one with the whistle, had a pair of pistols.

"Get ready," Prumble whispered.

Sam glanced at their destination. An alcove, diagonally across the street, where a steel-plated door that was rarely unlocked would now be having its dead bolt turned by Prumble's contact.

When the violence came it came quickly. A shove, one Jacobite fell. The swing of that nasty table leg and a spray of blood. Then chaos as someone in the gambling room killed the lights. Concealed weapons came out; the crowd fanned. The Jacobites were taken off guard, unused to anyone standing up to them as the consequences were well established.

"Go," Prumble said.

Sam did. She ignored the melee, ignored the cries of pain coming from both sides despite her natural instinct to step in and crack a skull or two. Instead she jogged across to the steel door at a half crouch, aware of Prumble behind her and Skadz bringing up the rear. Three paces from the door she saw it open and she kept moving straight inside.

And just like that they were in. The door closed without a sound, cutting off the light coming in from the street. A second later fluttering candlelight bathed the entryway. The glow revealed the face of an Asian boy, no more than ten years old, Sam guessed. He looked bored. "This way," he said with a heavy Malay accent.

Per some unspoken agreement, Prumble fell in behind him. The boy led them up a few flights of stairs, then down a long hall that ended at an open window. Without even a glance back, the kid stepped out the window and clambered across a ramshackle bridge erected between this building and another just a few meters away. The bridge creaked and swayed when Prumble stepped onto it. Sam decided to wait until he was across before stepping out herself.

She'd seen thousands of such bridges in the city, but never traversed one. They allowed buildings to join forces, or simply for commerce to occur, eliminating the need to risk the streets below. They also frequently collapsed, a tragedy made worse by the fact that children were usually the runners who made use of them. This one, mercifully, seemed sturdy, if Prumble's successful crossing proved anything.

More stairs followed. A lot more. The big man was barely breathing hard as he kept pace with the boy.

"Didn't you used to walk with a cane?" Skadz asked him, sucking wind.

Prumble shrugged. "Used to need one."

"What, healed, did you? Some kind of fucking miracle?"

The big man laughed. "Cured of the need to cultivate that particular myth, is all. Give credit to Blackfield for that."

Sam's thighs were on fire by the time the kid finally turned and went to a door. He stepped aside and used one foot to prop it open, holding out his hand eagerly. Prumble fished a candy bar out of his pocket and slapped it into the boy's tiny palm.

* * *

The woman in the room beyond looked like a brothel's couch.

She was enormous, larger even than Prumble, and draped in a gaudy mix of red velvets and patterned silks. Her puffy face hid under a veneer of white-powder makeup and purple eyeliner.

Two effeminate boys in garish makeup stood to either side of the madam, fanning her with broad, colorful antique fans like she was some kind of queen or goddess. The whole display was so absurd that Samantha glanced instinctively to the corners of the room on either side of the entry, anticipating a trap. She saw an armed man in each, hard-faced and well muscled. They showed no sign of taking any action, though.

"Oh, pooh pooh," the gigantic woman said. "I thought we had customers." She spoke slowly, in a gravelly voice that implied a lifetime of smoking.

"Greetings, Dee," Prumble said. "Delightful to see you, too."

Dee made a show of looking to either side of him. She took in Samantha and Skadz in turn, then smiled. "Perhaps they wish to partake, even if you don't?"

"Another time, maybe," Skadz offered. "Cheers, though."

Prumble quickly added, "We're on a schedule, I'm afraid."

The corner of the woman's mouth twitched. "You have the payment?"

"Of course," Prumble said. He pulled a thin case from the inner breast pocket of his duster and held it out to her.

Dee plucked it like one might pull a grape from the vine. She smiled slightly as she opened the box, and her eyes gleamed as she took in the contents. Sam hadn't thought to ask Prumble what this little venture had cost, but she guessed jewelry of some sort. Diamonds, or pearls, judging from the madam's fashion sense. "This is glorious," she breathed. "You've always known the key to my heart, Prumble."

"It's the keys to your comm I'm interested in."

"All business tonight, is it? You used to at least make an effort at a little foreplay." Dee shifted on cushions upon which she lay. Each movement made one roll of fat hide and another emerge from her silks. Sam fought to keep the revulsion from her face.

Prumble spread his hands in apology. "Sorry about that, Dee, but we have a link to make. Not my schedule. And with all these Jakes around . . ."

"Let's not talk about them," the woman said. "You know, Prumble, the only reason I'm entertaining this little bit of intrigue is because you said the bloody Jakes couldn't know about it. If you can't tell me who you'll be talking to on the comm, can you at least tell me if the end result will be to get rid of these prudish bastards, hmm?"

Prumble only shrugged.

Perhaps he just didn't want her to know something she might later relay, or perhaps he sensed a trap. Either option made Samantha's trigger finger twitch. She shifted her weight slightly to her left foot, in case she needed to draw and turn on the guard behind her.

"Relax, dear," Dee said, leveling a condescending gaze on Samantha. "These walls have no ears. I'm just starved for information in this cave. No one comes to visit anymore, to tell me stories or buy some pleasure. I used to count some Orbitals among my clientele, did you know that?"

Prumble cleared his throat. "Clock's ticking, Dee."

The big woman made a theatrical sigh and shooed them with one fat, jeweled hand. "Blake, show them to the comm. Give them privacy for twenty minutes."

One of the guards came forward. "Yes, madam. This way."

The comm room had once been someone's kitchen. Tiles had been chipped off the counters, leaving glue-smeared plywood underneath. A refrigerator still sat in the corner, though it had been turned to face the wall, all its guts ripped out through the back for spare parts.

On a rickety wooden table in the center of the room sat a serving platter dotted with lit candles, providing the only light. Next to that a dusty, antique comm waited for them. Cables snaked out the back, across the table, and over to the countertop before exiting through a boarded-up window. Sam guessed there'd be an aerial on the roof, well hidden no doubt.

Comms were rare in Darwin. Before SUBS, most everyone

carried a personal slate that relied on the global mesh for connectivity. That infrastructure vanished shortly after the city became *the City*. Looted equipment, failed power sources, and the hubs that ran the whole thing off in places like Sydney and Ho Chi Minh City. A comm, though, could make a direct connection with another comm over great distances. Private relays could be arranged. Corporations and governments used them to avoid the bottlenecks of a shared network. Rural homes and ocean vessels loved them for the range they provided. Criminals used them to keep away from prying eyes and ears.

Sam assumed this one had been stolen, probably during the chaos when the refugees started to pour into the city. There was writing on the side, Vietnamese, she thought, so it might have been brought there and bartered with. She wondered how many hours a man could have purchased in one of the rooms below for such a thing. Just one, most likely, ending with a knife in the back.

There were only two chairs at the table. Prumble moved one into the far corner, sat, and rotated the comm to face him. Skadz offered the other chair to Sam, but she waved him off and leaned against the counter instead. He mouthed "your loss" and sat next to Prumble.

While the big man waited for the comm to start up, he fished around inside his duster and produced a small pink box. He handed it over his shoulder toward Samantha without looking. "Set this on the counter there and switch it on, okay? Aim it at the door."

"Sure," Sam said. The pink device had the words SLEEP, BABY, SLEEP! written on the side. "What is it?"

"Infant sleep aid."

"I can read."

"It generates soothing sounds," Prumble said. "Like white noise, for example. A paranoid precaution."

Samantha didn't think it paranoid at all. They were about to make contact with the runaways, the first action they'd taken that Grillo would likely have them all killed for. If Dee had an untrustworthy bone in her body—and Sam guessed she had a lot of those—she'd record this supposedly discreet use of her precious comm. Once she realized the Jacobites would be very interested in the conversation, she'd either try to sell the information or keep it for bartering her way out of any trouble in the future. Given the nature of her business, such trouble was a virtual guarantee. Sam set the device on the counter and switched it on. Static came from the tiny speaker.

"Come stand behind us, Sam," Prumble said. "Keep your voices low."

Sam followed his command and moved around so she could see the screen. A ripple of excitement ran through her at the prospect of hearing Skyler's voice again.

Prumble tapped in some codes from a piece of paper, and waited as the words ESTABLISHING LINK flashed. Then the connection light went green.

"That's Kip," Prumble said, already tearing the slip of paper to shreds. A red circle came up around the green light. "He's started encryption, good. Now for the relay link through Anchor." He glanced at his watch, not trusting the time displayed on the comm's screen.

Kip had said he could get them ten minutes on the powerful antenna in Nightcliff while shifts changed in the control room, and route the signal up through Anchor Station to achieve the required strength. Anything longer than that would arouse suspicion.

A relay icon appeared, and then Skyler's voice came through, crystal clear. "Hello, are we on?"

"We are indeed!" Prumble said.

"Hello, Skyler," Sam said. She felt the sting of tears welling in her eyes and laughed them away. "Nice to hear your stupid Dutch accent again."

"Sam," he said laughing, his voice thick with emotion. "Damn it's good to hear your voices! I—oh, right. I've got some people here with me. Tania Sharma, Zane Platz, and Tim Jordan."

Introductions were made all around. "We have a surprise guest with us, too," Prumble said.

"Oy, Skyler," Skadz said. "What's the rumpus, mate?"

"My God. They let you back in the city?"

The grin on Skadz's face almost touched his ears. "For now.

And at least I stayed in Australia for a proper walkabout. You had to fuck off halfway around the world."

"All right, ladies," Prumble interjected. "Save the weepy reunion nonsense for another time. We have much to discuss. Skyler? Would you start?"

Sam listened with rapt attention as he recounted the last two years. How they'd fled aboard part of Anchor Station, and met up with Zane, who'd taken Hab-8, a facility supposedly still under construction. Skyler alluded to difficulties in getting the colony up and running, but didn't elaborate. She knew from his tone that there must have been some major problems.

Then he spoke of what they'd learned about the Builders. They'd put a space elevator in Brazil, but with a much more limited aura. Instead, the aliens had provided a number of small towers that created pockets of aura and could be moved around. Sam's mind immediately began to run through the possibilities that must have created. She forced the thoughts away when Skyler detailed how an errant explosion had somehow woken the towers and sent them off in four groups to various parts of the planet. He'd tracked one set to Ireland and found something incredible there.

When he described it, and how it made their space elevator vibrate when he removed it from where it lay, Sam spoke up.

"I found something similar," she said. "In Darwin's Old Downtown. When I picked it up it caused the space elevator to shudder for a moment, too."

A new voice, barely a whisper, broke in. "Hi. Um, hello. Kip here. That's happened again since. Just the other day."

"That was us," Skyler said, "both times. Found the one in Ireland, and another here in Brazil."

"This is great news," Tania Sharma said. "We knew there were five but only four groups of towers fled Belém. So Darwin was the fifth location, and you have it! That only leaves—"

"Hold on," Sam said. "I picked it up, but I don't have it. Grillo took it, and where it is now I have no idea. He never speaks of the thing."

The comment earned a few seconds of silence. A sudden sense of guilt swept through Sam, for not mentioning it sooner, and for not doing anything to stop Grillo in the first place.

"Grillo," Skyler said. "Yeah, we've heard about his rise, his alliance with the Jacobites. Um, Blackfield is with us over here. House arrest, and he's been talking."

Prumble cleared his throat. "In a few minutes this link will be cut. I suggest we make some plans."

"Agreed," Skadz said. "Let's keep it simple, though, all right?"

Skyler and Tania explained what Kip had already alluded to before. A new Builder ship, massive in size, had arrived in orbit a few weeks earlier. Inside it was a room that had slots for each of these objects. Keys, Skyler called them, for the Key Ship. Two were still unaccounted for. Skyler would lead a team to find one, and Tania the other.

"Hold on," Sam said. "What the hell are we dealing with here? What are these 'keys,' and why is an immune required to install them?"

"This is the Builders we're talking about, Sammy," Skadz said. "You'd have an easier time figuring out the bloody Jakes."

"But—"

"He's right," Skyler said. "No one knows, Sam. Tania tried taking the last one over and nothing happened. Vanessa, an immune we met over here, had to go along and help."

"Well, are they some kind of weapon?"

"At this point we simply don't know," Tania said. "We don't know what the point of the room is, why an immune must be present, or what will happen when all five objects are installed." She let that sink in. "But we've all talked through the possibilities and decided that we can't just ignore this. We can't wait. I have . . . information implying that the next Builder event, in just under a year, will be the last, and there's reason to believe we have even less time than that. Skyler, tell them about the dome in Ireland."

Sam listened intently. Hearing the tale from anyone else she would have chuckled with disbelief. *An aura that fucks with time, yeah right.* From Skyler, though . . .

"If either of the remaining objects is within such a dome," Skyler said, "we need to get to them now. Get them and get out as quickly as possible, or we may well be too late."

"Exactly," Tania added. "The nature of this room and the objects implies we are up against a timer now. We need to act immediately, not just wait around. The only sensible thing to do is gather these objects and install them as soon as possible."

"Sensible might not be the right word," an older man said. Zane Platz, Sam assumed. "Nevertheless . . ."

The implication of their words crashed down on Sam like a load of bricks. "You're saying we need to get that thing back from Grillo, like yesterday. Move it up to that Key Ship somehow."

Skyler cut in. "I think it might be easier to get it to Belém. We can haul it up from here."

"Oh, sure. We'll just nab it and pop over to Brazil. Easy as pie. We don't even know where Grillo is keeping it. He might have destroyed it, for all we know. I wouldn't put it past him."

"Er," Kip said, his voice a whisper. "I can help there. From what I hear the object is in Nightcliff. It had been in Lyons, but Grillo recently moved it here."

"Any particular reason?" Skadz asked.

"No idea, but I can speculate." When no one objected he went on. "Be aware that he knows there is more than one object, and of the large ship that arrived. A Sister Jennifer, I don't know her, reported this. I was listening in. She made no mention of this room inside, however.

"Since then there's been a, well, a schism of sorts, within the Jacobite ranks. A faction led by Sister Haley that now openly questions Grillo's rise, his motives and conviction. I'm not sure how much her faction knows, but they know he found something. I suspect he feels Nightcliff is the easier place to defend, should his detractors become more aggressive."

"Ah hell," Skadz said. When Sam looked at him he frowned. "The bloke's already worried someone's after the thing. That's going to make our task even more difficult."

Prumble urged him to silence with a wave of his hand. "Perhaps, perhaps not. Kip, do you know where in the fortress the object is? Can you get us in? Provide a map?"

"Secure storage. I'll do what I can, but the vault itself is beyond my capability."

"Leave that to me," Prumble said.

The rest of the plan came together so quickly that Samantha felt dizzy. It sounded too complicated to her, too many failure points. Exactly the type of thing she'd have called Skyler on had he proposed something similar for a scavenger job. And yet, given all the angles, and the distances involved, she saw no other solution.

"One minute left," Kip said.

Prumble let out a long breath. "Let me recap so we're all in agreement. Tania will be responsible for one of the missing keys, and Skyler the other. Skyler, once you've recovered yours you'll fly here, landing just beyond the aura at the old raceway in Hidden Valley. If we're ready, we'll meet you there."

"Yeah," Skyler said. "Minimal baggage, okay? It's a small bird."

"And if we're not there, you'll hike in and help us."

"Or finish the job, if you made a bloody mess of it." His words broke a tension Sam hadn't realized had fallen upon them. She snorted a laugh and out of old habit glanced at Skadz.

The other man, however, looked worried. "It's complicated, lots of ifs. In my experience that's rarely a good thing."

"Granted it is a complex task, and there's still one more if." Prumble paused long enough to let the words settle. "*If* we yet live, we'll all fly back to Belém with you and finish the job from there. Clock's ticking, everyone. I suggest we get started immediately."

"Agreed," Skyler said. Tania Sharma echoed the sentiment.

"Time's up," Kip whispered. Without ceremony or goodbyes, the link dropped.

# 4

## BELÉM, BRAZIL

### 27.MAR.2285

When the climber door swung open, Tania found herself staring at Ana, not Skyler as she'd hoped.

The day was clear and bright. Drops of rain still dappled every flat surface, shining like diamonds in the rare naked sunlight. Insects danced about, so many that they simply became part of the landscape.

"Welcome back," the young woman said. She wore khaki pants and a maroon tank top. Her brown hair hid under a silk scarf tied over her head. Mud caked the bottom halves of her brown hiking boots. She had a pistol strapped to one hip, and a small machine gun slung over her shoulder.

The outfit made Tania feel suddenly very unprepared for what lay ahead, despite all the training she'd been doing. Three times a week she brawled with old Beram in Melville Station's common room. Karl had told the soft-spoken, unassuming man to go easy on her, or so Beram said. She had suffered dozens of bruises and sore muscles that said otherwise, but the end result was worth it. Her body had changed as much as her mentality. When she stepped out of the climber, Tania could feel the change

53

in her own presence. The way she held herself, the way she walked tall and yet somehow coiled at the same time. She found herself appraising everyone she came in contact with, thinking how she'd block if they suddenly struck out at her, how she'd counter. The simple mental exercise made her look at everyone differently than before.

She thought Skyler must make the same calculations, only at a subconscious level, and she understood how it was that he always seemed in command no matter who was present.

"Hello, Ana," Tania said, her feet clanging on the metal ramp as she walked down. "It's good to see you."

The young immune smiled politely. "Skyler's not here," she said, reading Tania's face. "We don't expect him back until this evening."

Tania resisted the urge to ask where he'd gone, what he was doing. "Fine. We'll visit Karl first. There are a lot of preparations to make."

Ana squinted at her, glancing down briefly at the simple jumpsuit Tania wore. "You're going after Emerald wearing that?"

"Emerald?"

"The towers that went northwest had that color to their light."

"Of course. Yes. I mean, no. I brought an environment suit, of sorts."

"Oh," Ana said. "Of course, you're not immune. Forgive me."

Whether or not this comment was an insult, Tania wasn't sure. She decided to let it go and simply waited.

A thin, compassionate smile crept onto Ana's face. "Come to the armory after you speak with Karl. I'll help you pick out some gear."

"Thank you," Tania said, surprised. Between Karl and Beram she'd been instructed on how to break down, clean, assemble, and shoot just about every gun the colony had available, but there was an implied offer of tacit friendship in Ana's invitation that took Tania off guard. Skyler's lover had all but outright avoided Tania in the past. Yet she knew a peace offering when she heard it and accepted it gladly.

Tim stumbled out of the climber car behind her. He had a backpack in one hand and a briefcase in the other. He'd chosen to wear a jogging suit, comfortable on the space stations and in a climber, sweltering here on the ground.

"See you later then," Ana said, and walked away.

Tania watched her go while Tim swatted at mosquitos, a task made all the more awkward by the gear he carried. "Karl better heal quickly," he grumbled as he smacked the back of his neck, his backpack now lying on the black alien disk at their feet. He inspected his hand and frowned in disgust.

"Let's go find him," Tania said, and led the way to the infirmary.

Karl sat on the edge of his bed, his broken leg outstretched before him. "I'm not saying you're not ready, Tania. I just think it's unwise for you to go."

"Why?" she asked. "Not that I need your permission, but I've trained hard. Ask Beram."

"He's given me regular reports," Karl admitted. "I suspect you could break my other leg right now if you wanted to."

Tania shrugged, forced her voice to remain casual. "Waste of a strike; you're already hobbled. I'd go for the bones on the top of your good hand, which is exposed and in easy range, in case you had a gun or a knife hidden somewhere—"

"Jesus," Tim said. He stood by at her right.

"At the same time I'd kick Tim in the stomach and flip him on top of you. By the time you two even knew what happened—"

Karl held up that good hand in defeat. "Okay, all right. Beram's done his job well, obviously."

"Obviously," Tim echoed.

Tania smiled victoriously. She tried to ignore Tim's slack-jawed expression and kept her focus on Karl. "I think," she said, "Beram should start working with Tim next. He's the weak link now."

"No kidding. Sign me up," Tim said. "Wait, did you just call me weak?"

Karl winced, tried to scratch his leg, and gave up. "But this mission, it's not about training, Tania. It's about you not being here."

She'd expected this argument. Indeed, she'd already had it with Skyler, Tim, and Zane. "You guys are plenty capable of making decisions without me. Tim will be down here until you're healed, and Zane is improving every day. Besides, I'll be with Vanessa and Pablo, who've more than proven themselves in Ireland. Skyler can't be in two places at once, and with your condition I'm the next-best choice to lead the expedition."

He opened his mouth to speak but Tania waved him off. "We have no idea what we'll find out there. I'm a scientist, I've got experience in the field—Hawaii, and in the rainforest here—plus I've been inside the Key Ship. I know what we're looking for."

Karl frowned. A light rain began to tap against the tent above them, and the sunlight dimmed as clouds began to cross the sky.

"On a lighter note," Tim said, "we brought Russell Blackfield down with us."

A dark scowl crossed Karl's face. He shifted on the bed again as the news settled. "I suppose it's for the best. It's too easy to sabotage a space station, and down here at least he can be put to work." His focus moved back to Tania. "There's no talking you out of this venture into the Clear?"

"No."

He nodded for several seconds. "When do you leave?"

"As soon as a suitable aircraft—"

The sound of roaring engines drowned her words.


"Easy," Skyler said.

Vanessa tapped the stick with a gentle deftness, pushing the bulky aircraft back over the clearing just outside the colony's gates. "You can take over," she said.

"Your bird, your landing." He grinned at her reaction and studied the array of instruments before his co-pilot's chair just to be safe.

The aircraft, designed for coastal patrol and rescue, had ample storage and crew capacity, excellent range, a full medical bay with supplies, and even a winch to lift people or gear while hovering at one hundred meters. Skyler felt a little jealous, in truth. The Magpie's only advantage was top speed. Well, that and luxury, but Skyler had no use for the latter. Given the choice he'd take this craft any day, but given the circumstances he felt it better that he make do with the lesser aircraft.

He tested the intercom as Vanessa descended. "You boys okay back there?"

"Copy that," the one named Colton replied. The young man, one of the better scavengers Skyler had trained, spoke easily despite the thunderous noise around the craft. Out of necessity he'd worn an environment suit for the mission, and he had apparently figured out how to plug it into the intercom. "Some bits weren't quite secured, but Nach' and I have it all sorted."

They'd spotted the aircraft in one of the gigantic collage picture layouts they'd assembled of the city. A barge, run aground on the shore of the Pará just north of the city, had caught their attention. It was listing as it deteriorated, revealing a portion of the tarp-covered cargo it carried: the tail wing of an aircraft. It was a hell of a piece of scavenging work, he thought, and had told them as much. He could only imagine what kind of operation Prumble could run with these two geniuses working for him, and grinned at the idea. Maybe it would come to pass, if everything ran according to plan.

The aircraft rotated at a leisurely pace as Vanessa pointed the nose toward the colony's gate. Water and dust began to stir from the ground below, filling the air around them. Skyler saw colonists on the wall now. They held hats to their heads in the press of the powerful wind. He waved at them.

The craft had a similar design to the *Melville*, with four cap-driven engines out at the ends of four broad wings. Unfortunately it did not have the plating required for atmospheric reentry, an exceedingly rare feature given that it made sense only for people or parties with access to the space elevator in Darwin. Even on the other side of the planet, Skyler had only seen a few such vehicles in his years searching.

He could hardly complain, though. This bird had a larger cargo capacity, bigger crew compartment, and could even lift heavy loads. It was a boon.


The gun felt cool in her hand. Perfectly weighted, solid.

In a way, she could appreciate the art of it. The masterful combination of ergonomics, design, and engineering were beyond question. Tania had never cared much for guns. She'd seen them as a tool for killing, and she saw killing as something human beings should not be in the business of. Even after the subhumans arrived it had been easy for her, from her isolated, almost utopian place aboard Anchor Station, to take the position that there must be a more humane way to deal with the former people.

Her opinion had changed.

"That's my favorite," Ana said quietly.

Tania thumbed the clip release, pulled it out, and slapped it back in. "It's a Sonton?"

"SIG Sauer, actually. Not as common, but I like the way it feels and since the ammo is the same . . ." She shrugged. "No laser sight. I find those distracting. Of course, Skyler chides me for it, but—"

Footsteps on the stairs cut her words short.

"What do I chide you for?" Skyler stepped into the windowless room and paused to let his eyes adjust. Tania heard the reinforced door click closed behind him.

The armory had been set up in a storage room within the university that overlapped with the colony on the western side. A courtyard just outside served as the impound yard for the aura towers, and most of the rooms that fell within the subsequent protective aura were dormitory-style bedrooms, put to good use by the colony. This room, probably once for cleaning supplies, Tania guessed, was off an interior hall below a stairwell. Concrete walls kept it cool and dry, even at this time of year, and at some point a pair of metal plates had been welded to the door. A heavy lock had been installed, too, just in case. Tania thought it telling that Ana knew the combination and clearly knew the room like the back of her hand.

"Laser sights," Ana said without turning.

"Ah." Skyler offered Tania a bunch of bananas. He held one, half eaten, in his other hand. "Quite useful when shooting from the hip."

Ana turned finally. She waved off the bananas when Tania offered them. "I'm standing there trying to figure out where that stupid little dot is when I could just be shooting."

"Waste of ammo," Skyler said over a mouthful of the fruit.

Ana's eyes flared. In answer she gestured to the wall of boxes behind her. Boxes of every size, shape, and style of bullet.

Skyler took another bite, chewed. "All that matters is what's in the clip."

"You want to sleep outside tonight, *pendejo*?"

Tania, stuck between the couple with nowhere to go, turned her focus to peeling a banana. The girl's tone, playful and flirtatious, nevertheless had a note of challenge to it. She might be Skyler's lover, but she was also part of his crew. Tania didn't consider herself an expert, but she'd seen enough of the old romance sensories to know mixing business and pleasure was rarely a good idea.

Skyler just grinned, though, and looked to Tania. "The others are gathered in the *Helios*'s crew cabin. It's time to make our plan."

"*Helios?*" Tania and Ana asked simultaneously.

"Vanessa's name for the new aircraft. Something to do with her jujitsu." He said the words over his shoulder as he departed. Deep down, he probably felt more uncomfortable than Tania, though he did a good job of hiding it.

When his footsteps faded and the door clicked closed again, Tania turned back to the weapons. She picked up the SIG again, hefted it, and cracked a smile toward Ana. "I don't really like laser sights, either."

The young woman chortled.


A paper map lay splayed out on the crew compartment floor of the *Helios*, located just aft of the cockpit.

Skyler had marked the location of the Ireland object with an hourglass shape drawn in pencil. Similar markings noted the crash sites in Belém and Darwin where objects had been recovered.

Then he'd drawn lines out of Belém marking the two remaining paths taken by aura tower groups. At the extent to which they'd been explored, he'd expanded the lines into cones, indicating a best-guess search area for the ultimate whereabouts of the crash sites. One went north and west, toward the Gulf of Mexico and on up into North America.

"This one," Tim said, tracing a finger along the line Skyler had drawn east from Belém, "runs roughly toward where the key ship is parked in orbit."

Skyler frowned. "Roughly?"

Tim nodded and held out a hand for the pencil. Skyler handed it over, and the young man drew a box around a portion of the Sahara in northern Niger. "Right about here," he said.

The spot lay just below the cone Skyler had drawn. His guesswork on the spread of the cone had no evidence to back it up; it was really more optimism than anything else—something much wider would take months to explore even from the air. Still, the mark Tim made was close enough that it couldn't be ignored. Perhaps the Builders' mother ship had parked itself directly over one of the crash sites.

"Interesting," Nachu said after a moment. He and Colton had remained in the cramped room in case additional supply requests came up. At this point they knew the city better than Skyler himself.

Skyler glanced at the kid and was reminded of the university students he used to beat at cards back in Amsterdam. All the intelligence to take on the world, just enough experience to think they could pull it off. Only one in a thousand could stand out in a crowd like that, and this kid was one of those. Same went for the other, Colton. In another time they'd have been future Neil Platzes, waiting to happen. "What's interesting?"

"That spot." Nachu pointed to the mark in Niger. "It's due south of where they say the SUBS virus started."

Skyler looked closer. Tania and Tim both leaned in, too, and Nachu took the pencil. "They never nailed the exact place down," he said, "but it was somewhere around . . . here. This map shows it as forest and grazing land, but this is a historical map, see? A.D. 2100. Today that's all part of the Sahara."

The circle he drew encompassed parts of Cameroon, Chad, and Nigeria, and it lay right in the middle of the cone Skyler had drawn. He swallowed hard. It couldn't be a coincidence, and as he stared at the map a sudden chill made him shudder.

"Tania," he said.

She looked at him, eyebrows raised.

"What if . . ." He paused, considering his words. "Suppose that new ship *is* a weapon. Only, not aimed at us, but aimed at the disease."

Her nose wrinkled. "Why would they start the disease and then attack it?"

"Maybe it got out of control?" Tim offered.

"Or," Skyler said, thinking aloud now, "maybe they didn't start the disease." Everyone stared at him now. "Look at us. I mean, humanity. We're a mess. Our colony. Blackfield coming after us, Platz and the council, factions like the Jacobites. Grillo and all the other minor syndicates. We're fractured all over the place, but we've been making this assumption that the Builders are a cohesive whole."

Tania nodded slowly. "So, one Builder faction decides Earth should get a free space elevator. An opposition group can't stop it from being sent, so they decide to wipe us out instead."

"Exactly."

"Then," Tim said, "the first group somehow sets up the Elevator to offer some protection, the aura, until they can devise a way to stop the disease." He was smiling, but it turned to a frown almost instantly. "Doesn't explain the Belém Elevator, or the aura towers."

"Or these crashed ships, and that room inside the Key Ship," Tania said. "I mean, if it's a weapon, why not have it ready to go? Why scatter these bits across the planet and require us to reassemble it?"

Skyler shrugged. "How should I know?"

"Besides," Tania added, "it doesn't mesh well with the fact that Neil somehow knew exactly how many events would occur. Hmm . . ."

"It's just a theory."

Tania patted him on the forearm. "Relax, Skyler. We're scientists. Poking holes in theories is part of the job."

Nachu spoke up again. "Maybe this opposition group sabotaged the weapon in flight. They couldn't destroy the parts, but they could make them really hard to find, hard to gather. Buy time for the virus to do its job."

"Yeah," Skyler said. "How about that? I like this kid."

"Not bad," Tania agreed. "I'll admit it's probably the best theory I've heard yet, save perhaps for the insane space clown theory Greg and Marcus cooked up. But it doesn't change the mission. It adds urgency, yes, but the task remains the same." She gave him a serious look. "Are we agreed to the plan?"

The conviction in her eyes startled him. He'd hoped against hope she'd abandon the idea of joining the Emerald mission. "Look," he said. "I know you've trained hard, Tania. But you're not immune; at least it's highly unlikely that you are. Your presence on the mission is an unnecessary complication. I mean, it could last weeks."

"There's plenty of room for compressed air tanks in this plane."

"Air, sure, but how are you going to go to the bathroom?"

"Is this craft rated for high altitude?" she asked.

"Yes," Vanessa said. "Thirty klicks."

Tania nodded. "So, we keep the cabin sealed until we reach the aura towers, or get to half our air."

Skyler shook his head. "Too many things could go wrong. A leak, an emergency landing. Hell, you'll have to recharge the caps at some point."

"Um," Vanessa said, raising her hand. "Don't forget, on this aircraft the cockpit is a separate compartment. Pablo and I would ride up there, get out if we need to, all without breaking the seal on the cargo compartment."

"You're supposed to be on my side," Skyler said to her.

Vanessa shrugged.

"A third pair of hands," Pablo said, "could be useful."

Skyler looked at all of them, exasperated. Then he turned to Tania. "You'll be cooped up in here for days. Weeks, maybe."

"Skyler, I've lived on a space station for almost my entire life."

"Okay, okay. What about when the time comes to get out? How much help can you be in one of those environment suits?"

"I thought of that, too," Tania said. "I won't need one."

"Come again?"

She grinned knowingly. "Remember those spacesuits we wore over to the Builder ship?"

"Yes. I won't soon forget those."

"Well, I brought them. They'll work just as well in atmosphere.

They're sealed, and they have excellent mobility."

He grunted agreement. The suits were undeniably superior to any environment suit he'd ever seen. "You brought both? Why?"

Tania shrugged. "I thought you might want some help on your mission, too. Maybe one of these two," she said, gesturing at Nachu and Colton. The two young men glanced at each other, then back at Skyler.

He knew he'd lost the argument, probably before Tania had even stepped off her climber. The next hour was spent hammering out details, supply requirements mostly. He waited until the group had split up for the evening to tell Colton and Nachu that he thought they should stay in Belém. The colony would need them for any scavenging needs while the immunes were away.

He felt glad when both agreed. Though either of the young men would be a welcome addition, Skyler had a different sort of help in mind.

Two days later the *Helios* took off. Skyler watched the aircraft arch across the cloudy sky until it disappeared behind the city's dark downtown skyline. The Tombstones, so the colonists called the ghostly high-rises. The bleak structures moaned when the wind came up off the Pará and rushed through their broken windows. Usually rain would drown that sound. Today the thunderous roar of the *Helios*'s engines did the job, though that noise dwindled with each passing second.

"Everything's green here." Vanessa's voice, over the comm. "We'll see you soon, *amigos*."

"Godspeed," Tim said. He stood within the comm room, hunched over the lone terminal. Skyler had spied the young man wiping a tear away when the aircraft lifted off. He'd seen the way the man looked at Tania before that moment, too.

A cool sprinkle of rain whipped about him. Even now, with the *Helios* gone from view, he stayed just outside the comm room and ignored the playful spray of water. He tried to imagine the aircraft, putting himself in the pilot's chair as city gave way to the wide river, then rainforest, then the unknown. Nothing but a path carved almost two years ago to guide the way. And Tania, huddled in back, isolated, one small window to look out of. A pang of guilt rippled through him as he recalled the final words he'd said to Vanessa before she climbed into the cockpit: "Don't let her out until you know it's safe."

Vanessa had agreed, but her eyes held a hint of something that said otherwise. She'd been impressed by Tania, he saw the evidence of it in that look, and he couldn't blame her. Still, he had to say something, despite the fact that Tania would probably slap him again if she knew.

*She'll do worse when she finds out what I'm doing next.*

"Keep an eye on them?" he asked Tim.

"Will do," the man said, and smiled. "For as long as they'll put up with me."

"Good." He shook the water from his hat and studied the sky for a moment. "I guess it's the Magpie's turn, before this becomes a real storm."

Tim nodded. "Good luck out there, Skyler."

"Thanks. We'll be off within the hour."


Skyler entered the dimly lit room and set the duffel bag on the floor beside him. The prisoner's gaze darted to it for a split second, only the slightest hint of fear on his face. Then he glanced up, past Skyler at the woman behind him.

"Well, well. Skyler Luiken, we meet again," Russell Blackfield said. "Who's the tart?"

His words tumbled out with no real emotion behind them, as if some part of his mind had forced him to speak. The once-impressive man looked thin, haggard. Dark lines marred the skin under his bloodshot eyes. He had an uneven beard and his hair was matted. There were bruises around his wrists, likely from restraints applied too tightly. His lips were cracked from dehydration.

Skyler glanced away from him and focused on Ana, who stood in the doorway of the colony's only holding cell, arms folded.

"Well?" Skyler asked her.

She pursed her lips slightly, then gave a small shrug. "Yeah, I could do it."

"Do what?" Russell asked, a slight amusement in his voice.

"Kick your ass from here back to Darwin," Skyler said.

"Ah. No need for violence, young lady. I'm a lover, not a fight—"

"He gives me the creeps," Ana said to Skyler, ignoring the prisoner. "But I've met worse."

With a grudging nod, Skyler went to Blackfield and set a canteen on the floor in front of him. "Go start the preflight," he said over his shoulder. Then he waited until he heard the outer door click closed.

Russell picked up the canteen, removed the cap, and sniffed the contents before taking a swig. His eyes closed ecstatically as he swallowed.

"The water has a price," Skyler said.

Russell took another sip. "Put it on my tab? I'm good for it, thanks to this work furlough program they've planned for me. Digging ditches, my dream job."

"I want information."

The man paused. His eyes flicked to Skyler, then back to the canteen. "Is this going to be more bullshit about how my presence here is some kind of ruse? I'll let you in on a secret, Skyler. The only secret here: I am *not* that clever."

"Oh, I know."

Russell laughed once, raised the canteen in cheers, and took another sip.

"I want to know about Nightcliff."

The man lowered his hands, a flicker of doubt crossing his face. Then the bemused smirk returned. "What about it? No offense, mate, but I'm not running the show there anymore."

Skyler rubbed his neck, feeling a headache coming on. *I can't believe I'm doing this.* Still, if he could kill two birds with one stone . . . "Maybe not, but you know its secrets."

Blackfield gave a slight shrug. "Maybe. Some, yeah. I'm a bit curious why you'd care." His gaze went to the black duffel bag again. "Darwin's a lost cause, or hadn't you heard?"

"That may be true, but there's still people I care about there, and I'm going back for them."

"So? You're immune. Land in the Clear and hike in. As long as you keep your head low, I doubt the vigilant Jacobites will notice."

"It's more complicated than that, unfortunately." He'd debated all night how much to say, and he chose his next words carefully. "There's something we need, inside Nightcliff. Something Grillo won't want to lose."

Russell's eyebrows shot up, and Skyler knew he'd played the right card. Blackfield was a lot of things, but at his core lay a thirst for revenge. The slumlord-turned-ruler was currently atop that list, from the look on the man's face. "That so?" he said, mustering an impressive disinterested tone.

"You can help, Blackfield."

"How?"

"Patrol routes. Door combinations. Weapon storage locations. Medusa launch codes." Skyler saw a flash of interest in the man's face and went on. "How to gain access to the secure storage."

"Is that all?"

Skyler shrugged. "Anything else you can think of that will help, I'm listening."

Russell held up his hand and gave a thumbs-up. He held it there in silence for a long time.

A hot flare of temper began to course from Skyler's head down to twitching fingertips. He checked it, took a breath. "You'll want to start helping right about now, or this ends badly for you."

Blackfield raised his thumb higher. "I am helping."

Skyler drew his pistol.

"This," Blackfield said, wiggling his thumb. "Everything you asked for Grillo would have changed. He's smart, that one. But one thing he can't change is the biometric access for the locks. Those are keyed to my thumbprint."

"If he's so smart, wouldn't he have them re-keyed?"

"Sure. And he'll succeed, for the primary access. But I was there when the system was recalibrated. I bribed the contractor to use my print for the maintenance access. The fallback in case all other parties leave or die. He had to fly someone in from his home office in New Zealand on the same day SUBS hit, just to make that happen. On the down low, if you get me. Cost me a fucking fortune. Point is, Grillo won't be able to change that. He probably doesn't even know it's in there."

Skyler put his pistol away and removed a knife instead.

"A pulse is required," Russell said with a wry smile. "You can put that away."

He walked to the man anyway, and slipped the knife back in its scabbard easily. He dumped the duffel bag slung on his shoulder at Russell's feet, stepped back, and nudged it toward him with a toe.

"What's that?" Blackfield asked, rubbing his wrists.

"Open it." When he started to unzip the bag, Skyler continued. "I figured you'd try to turn this into a free ride back to Darwin, so I planned ahead. If that fits, you're coming with us."

Russell glanced at the elaborate suit in the bag. "And if it doesn't?"

"Hope that it does, Blackfield, because if it's your thumb I need it's your thumb I'll get. And honestly, dragging a subhuman version of you to Darwin might be less of a hassle."

The suit fit.

Half an hour later, Skyler led Russell Blackfield from his cell. Hands retied, and the prospect of returning home if he just kept his mouth shut, made him a cooperative prisoner. Whether or not Blackfield sensed the clandestine nature of his removal from captivity, Skyler figured it didn't matter as long as he said nothing and went where he was guided.

None of the colonists questioned the sight of Blackfield being led from his cell. Skyler had broad authority to do as he pleased inside Camp Exodus and beyond. The people he passed probably thought he was moving the prisoner to a more secure holding place, or perhaps taking him for questioning. For those who bothered to ask, he had a simple answer: "You don't want to know." Not exactly a lie.

*La Gaza Ladra* was already provisioned and charged when he led the prisoner inside and chained him to a seat. They'd stored enough air tanks for Russell to last forty hours. Plenty of time, Skyler estimated, to reach the circle drawn by Nachu on the map in central Africa and locate the "yellow" towers. They could refill the tanks there using a compressor, then worry about the next leg of the journey to Darwin. Skyler knew that distance was beyond the Magpie's range but figured they'd still have time to stop somewhere—Yemen, perhaps—and locate a thorium reactor to spool from for a few hours.

A lot could go wrong, which normally implied a bad plan. But here the net result was a 90 percent chance of death for Russell Blackfield. Or, maybe Skyler would get lucky, and the bastard would survive infection and become a subhuman with one very useful thumb.

*This started with a finger,* he thought, *and it'll end with one.*

Tania, Karl, Tim, Zane . . . none of them need ever know the outcome. He'd simply explain the reason he was forced to bring Blackfield along, and make up something plausible for the rest. The colony was better off with Blackfield gone, and Skyler figured if everything worked out and the man somehow did manage to help them enter the bowels of Nightcliff, well, that was simply a debt repaid. He could decide then if the man could live. He might just leave him in Darwin, alone and unarmed, hopefully still fostering a thirst for revenge against Grillo. Russell could certainly be a threat when he set his mind to it.

Or Skyler would just shoot him, and be done with it. The world would be a better place. He doubted Tania would understand, much less approve, of such an action. "So be it," he muttered to himself as the Magpie's engines roared to life. Maybe he and Tania could call a truce then, wipe the past away, and get on with their lives.

He took off with a terse goodbye to Tim and flicked off the comm before any questions could be asked about why the prisoner had been taken aboard.

# 5

## DARWIN, AUSTRALIA

### 28.MAR.2285

Approaching the mouth of an alley in the Narrows, Pascal yanked hard on the truck's steering wheel. Samantha winced as the metal side of the vehicle scraped along the brick-and-mortar wall of the building there, until she remembered the vehicle was borrowed.

The truck rocked as portions of the wall came free and went under the rear tires. The side mirror on the passenger side next to Samantha crumpled and tore free. Pascal stomped on the brakes and came to a sudden stop.

"Jesus," Skadz said from the backseat. "Take it easy."

"It has to be convincing," Pascal replied. "Go now. Go!"

Sam pulled the door handle and pushed. It didn't budge. Behind her the back door opened. She heard Skadz and Prumble slip out. "Help me with the door," she called to them.

Skadz's face appeared at her window. He motioned for her to lower the window, and when she did he grabbed the frame of the door with both hands and pulled.

Sam put her shoulder into it and pushed. Nothing.

"Hurry," Pascal said, "they're coming."

"Fuck it," Sam said. She yanked the seat recline lever and lowered herself instantly to a prone position. Then she pushed herself into the backseat and went out that door.

A cloud of dust from the collision filled the air. She grabbed Skadz by the elbow and urged him deeper into the alley as angry shouts began to drift in from the street on the other side of the supposedly crashed vehicle. The locals would be angry until the nearest Jacobite patrol arrived, which wouldn't be long.

Prumble was already at the first turn in the alley, coughing from the concrete dust in the air. Sam urged him around the corner and then forced herself to walk. Per the plan, Skadz ran ahead to the far end of the L-shaped lane. He glanced out into the street, looking left and right, then turned and flashed an a-okay.

"Clear," Sam said.

"All this to visit the tailor," Prumble replied. He moved to a door on the back of an unremarkable three-story building. A sign at eye level read PRIVATE. And below that, CUSTOMER ENTRANCE AT THE FRONT.

Prumble tried the handle, found it to be locked, and gave a sharp rap on the door. Sam drew her pistol and waited.

A muffled voice from inside answered Prumble's knock. Sam couldn't understand the words, but the tone was clear: *Go away*.

"It's Prumble. Open up, Jaya."

"Piss off." Sam heard that response clearly enough.

"You owe me, dammit. Open the bloody door."

The door swung open so fast Prumble almost fell backward. Inside stood a short, balding Indian man wearing a dirty white tank top that accentuated a round belly. Thick glasses were pushed high up on his bulbous nose, tape holding together the wire frames. "I owe you?! *I* owe *you*?! What the fuck—oh, hello, Sam."

"Hello, Jayateerth." She mustered her best apologetic smile and glanced into the room behind him. Though dimly lit, she saw reams of heavy fabric, enormous canisters of one chemical or another, and part of a machine. She saw no one else inside.

"Uh," the tailor said, suddenly confused. He scratched absently at the greasy, curly gray hair that ringed the bald dome of his head.

"We need your help," Sam tried. "Can we come in and talk, at least?"

He hesitated. Sounds of commotion came in from the mouth of the alley around the corner. "Heard a crash," Jayateerth said. "That you?"

"We needed a distraction," Prumble replied.

The tailor nodded solemnly, as if he'd just accepted the way the city worked now. In years past all the scavengers came to Jaya's shop for patchwork on their environment suits, and they paid handsomely for it. They still did, but under Grillo's watchful eye. There was only one reason someone needed an environment suit, and Grillo wanted total control over who came and went from the city. Word had come down months ago that anyone wishing to procure the services of one Jayateerth Laxman had to have their order approved by the Jacobite leadership. As far as Samantha knew, there was no one else alive who could be trusted to patch the suits. Certainly there was no one who could provide what they'd come for.

"Fine," the man said, and waved them in. When he turned to go back inside she saw a silver pistol tucked into the back of his pants. He drew it and stuffed it inside a cubbyhole on a shelf near the door.

Sam glanced to where Skadz waited. He gave her a single nod, and she returned it. They'd agreed he'd stay out of sight if possible. Jaya was known to be trustworthy, but if there were any Jacobite minders within it would be good if they didn't provide a description back to Grillo. Skadz had already tempted fate with his initial presence at the airport, but so far they'd been lucky. None of the Jacobite guards seemed to know who he was, and Sam had talked the other scavengers into silence. Walkabout or not, Skadz was one of them.

Sam followed Prumble inside and closed the door behind her, leaving it unlocked. The room stank of glue and fabric, electronics and lubricant. LEDs hanging from the ceiling provided the only light.

Environment suits of every size, shape, and color lay in stacks along one wall of the long room. Floor-to-ceiling shelves along the opposite wall contained all manner of supplies and spare parts, organized in a way Samantha figured only Jaya could understand. Mismatched tables ran down the center of the space, each covered with suits in various states of assembly or repair. Scraps of fabric littered the floor.

At the far end of the room was a closed door. Next to it, a scrawny child slept on a cot.

"Blink!" Jaya called out.

The kid, a girl of no more than ten, Samantha decided, rose immediately and stood on bare feet, eyes still bleary from sleep. She blinked rapidly.

"Go out front, girl, and make a ruckus if anyone comes in."

The child gave a nod, her eyes continuing to blink erratically. A nervous tic that had earned her her nickname, apparently. She turned and slipped through the door, briefly revealing stacks of cardboard moving boxes.

"All right," Jayateerth said. "I'm listening. What do you need?"

"An environment suit," Prumble said.

"This I know."

"For me."

"This is impossible."

"In two days."

"This is goodbye. Thank you for the visit. Nice to see you." He swept his arm toward the exit.

Prumble didn't budge. "You have to help us, Jaya. It's important. For old times, please."

"Old times?" The short man leaned against his shelves and folded his arms. "My recollection of old times is that you still owe me a lot of equipment. Things I paid for in advance."

"Blackfield blew up my garage! I've been in hiding!"

"Two years and you can't send a messenger?"

Sam sat on one of the tables, testing it first and deciding the wooden thing was sturdy enough. "C'mon, Jaya. Everything's changed. None of that matters anymore."

The man ran a hand over his face and stared up at the ceiling for a long moment. Then he turned to Sam, the look in his eyes profoundly sad. "I'm tired, you know? Tired of all this. I just want to tend my garden and watch the sun rise and set. I didn't want any trouble with Platz, or Blackfield after him. Especially not with these new fuckers." His voice dropped to something just above audible on the last word.

No one said anything for a long time. Then Sam tried a different tack. "Jaya, what's with the boxes out front? Going somewhere?"

He waved a dismissive hand toward the door Blink had used. "In a week, to a place over by the stadium. Something about consolidating essential services. Can you believe that shit? I've been in this building for sixteen years. Now I'm going to be stuck in some basement at Selby, surrounded by Jakes, Grillo breathing down my ass."

"Selby," Sam said. "That rings a bell."

Jaya nodded. "Selby Systems, Limited. The only remaining supplier of propellant for moving those stations around. They had an exclusive with Platz back in the day. Grillo's got the factory running again."

"That explains a lot of the lists Grillo's had me handing the crews lately."

"A lot of raw materials for that goop they produce, you know. And they've got it fired up to full capacity." Jaya ran one hand tenderly along the wooden table in front of him. Years of stains and scrapes marred the surface. He let his hand fall to his side. "Once I'm over there Grillo will have all his Orbital needs under one roof."

She glanced at Prumble, and he stared back at her. "One place to guard," the big man said.

"Yeah," Sam replied.

Finally, Jayateerth turned to Prumble. "What do you need a suit for, anyway? What business do you have outside that you can't just send her?"

Prumble fixed a hard stare on the man. "We don't plan to come back, Jaya."

"You're going to die out there? A bullet would—"

"There's another aura," Sam said. That stopped the man cold. "Another safe place."

"Ridiculous," he said. He wanted to believe her, though. She could see it in his eyes—a flicker of hope like a match being lit and settling into steady flame.

"Skyler found it."

He glanced between the two of them, then his gaze became distant. "Where?" he whispered.

"Make the suit," Prumble said, "and we'll tell you."

A light rain had begun to fall when Sam stepped back out into the alley. Skadz stood casually at the western end, one foot propped on the wall he leaned against, cap pulled low as if he slept. She glanced at her wristwatch. They'd been inside for just under an hour as Prumble's measurements were taken. Jaya had grumbled and moaned at the difficulty of making a suit that would fit, but in the end declared they could pick it up in twenty-four hours. The prospect of moving somewhere, anywhere, other than Darwin turned out to be a fantastic motivator.

Telling him about Belém was a risk, but one she thought they'd forgive at the prospect of having someone with Jaya's skills in their fledgling camp.

Sam whistled to get Skadz's attention, then pointed at her watch. The rendezvous was only minutes away. He waved and remained in position while she walked east to the bend in the alley.

The borrowed truck no longer blocked the alley entrance. *Good*, Sam thought. Pascal had done his job. Well, that or the vehicle had been stolen or apprehended by one of the street patrols. In a few minutes they'd know, one way or the other.

While Prumble waited in the middle of the alley, Sam walked around the bend and moved up to the gap they'd originally entered through. A pile of debris still lay in the road beyond where the truck had clipped it. A few kids were collecting the larger chunks of concrete onto a shabby wheeled cart. They scattered at the sight of her.

She looked both ways and waited. The street wasn't too crowded. None were, really, under this new regime. Nobody really knew what was allowed or frowned upon in the Jacobites' view, and even the obvious things were enforced erratically. Only one thing seemed certain: The cult, or rather Grillo's muscle behind it, owned the city now.

A vendor rode by on a rickety bicycle, mesh bags of jackfruit and some overripe durian hanging from the handlebars. He circled back, a salesman's grin forming on his weathered face, but which vanished when Samantha shook her head. The man completed his circle and continued down the road, his bike splashing through potholes.

"C'mon, Pascal," Sam muttered.

She heard the truck before she saw it. Pascal hadn't turned on the headlights, and with the near-silent electric motors he was only thirty meters away when she spotted him through the misty rain. She turned, nodded to Prumble at the elbow in the alley. He turned and nodded to Skadz down at the other end.

Pascal rolled to a stop across the wide street. When she met his gaze, he pointed back the way he'd come. Sam looked, and her heart sank. A street patrol of toughs in Jacobite colors jogged after the vehicle. There were six of them, which meant a seventh would be lurking behind. They often kept one member back, usually the one with a gun, in case trouble arose. Sam guessed that trouble to them meant drunken mah-jongg spectators who had yet to come around to the Jacobite way of thinking. A brawl might ensue, but one gunshot in the air would probably be enough to disperse such a crowd.

The way this group jogged up to Pascal's borrowed truck, however, brought goose bumps to her arms. They were fanning out. One even came to Samantha's side of the street, as if expecting Pascal to get out and run.

*What the hell are they doing?* Pascal was dressed in Jacobite garb, and a vehicle in Darwin said "don't fuck with me." Yet on they came, and they clearly weren't stopping to chat.

She glanced over her shoulder. Skadz stood behind her, gun drawn. He'd probably sensed the danger from her posture. Prumble lingered farther behind, looking more irritated than anything else.

"Something's wrong," she said.

Skadz nodded and pressed himself against the wall. Prumble took a few steps forward, craning his neck to see what was going on.

The Jacobites reached the vehicle and surrounded it, two of them moving around the front. Pascal could still drive away, but he'd kill or injure two of them in the process.

"Out!" one of the patrol shouted.

Pascal complied. His eyes darted to Samantha briefly, looking for guidance. "Easy," she mouthed.

The patrol surrounded him. The leader of the group moving right up to her pilot in a blatantly aggressive stance. He was saying something, agitated. Pascal started to argue something, but after a few seconds he just looked at the ground with his shoulders slumped.

The leader took a pinch of Pascal's poncho between two fingers and tugged at it.

*Fuck.* Sam drew her pistol, wishing she'd brought her shotgun. "Skadz?"

"I'm ready. Lay it out."

"Go around. The trailer with the gun."

"On it." He slipped away silently.

She watched him go, and held up a hand to Prumble, motioning him to remain in the alley.

When she glanced back around, she saw Pascal doubled over on the ground. The leader loomed over him, spitting words into his ear, still tugging on the improvised garment Pascal had worn.

Sam slipped around the corner, hands behind her back. She walked swiftly toward the truck, sizing up the group as she went. There were two outliers: Gun, down the street and about to meet Skadz, and the one that had come across to Samantha's side of the street. He looked unarmed and was thin. Their fastest runner, in case of chase, she guessed. She ignored him for now.

The leader was still crowding Pascal. She heard the word *pretender* and some pseudo-religious nonsense. He had two heavies just behind him, ready to move in and help if Pascal resisted. Their attention was fixed on the man on the ground.

The two who'd come around the front of the truck were closest, and they had their backs to her. She decided to start there.

A yelp of pain down the street, out of sight. Skadz had struck. One of the heavies heard it, looked back that way.

The one across the street by the wall finally noticed Samantha. "Oy," he snarled. "Piss off, whore."

Sam ignored him. The two in front of her were alert now but still looking the wrong way, confused. She closed the gap, raised her pistol, and shot the first in the back of the knee. His leg buckled and he started to go down.

Everyone jumped at the crack of the gunshot. The noise echoed down the streets like thunder.

Sam shifted her aim to the second and fired again. The round took him in the thigh, a bit higher than she'd wanted so she squeezed another around. But he'd moved, and she missed. Despite his wound, the man spun around and swiped at her, knocking her gun away.

The leader spun toward her, as did his two heavies, Pascal momentarily forgotten. One heavy carried a police baton. The other was unarmed. No, she saw the glint of metal in his hands. Her heart lurched. Two pistols? Then she realized the man was adorned with brass knuckles on both hands.

The one near her staggered when his swipe attack forced him to put weight on the wounded leg. Sam slugged him with a right hook and he flew backward, knocking his head against the front of the truck as he fell.

She glanced around for her gun as the two heavies came around to face her, putting themselves between her and the leader. The weapon, she realized, had slid under the vehicle. She'd never get to it in time. *Right.*

Movement across the street. The scrawny runner had come halfway across. Indecision flashed in his eyes—join in, or go get help?—and he hesitated. A huge shape emerged from the alley and loomed up behind him. Prumble. Sam winced. She'd wanted him to stay out of sight. Any onlookers would have a hard time describing Sam and Skadz, but Prumble's immense frame would be an almost immediate giveaway.

Pascal grabbed at the leader's leg. The man jumped back and then kicked the pilot in the stomach. Pascal groaned and curled into a fetal position.

*Better end this quickly,* she thought.

Knuckles stepped toward her. Sam grinned at him. He grinned back and swung. The meaty fist whooshed just over her, so close she felt the cap on her head shift as she ducked under the blow. In the same motion she yanked her knife free from the sheath on her calf, lurched forward onto one knee, and thrust the blade forward into his belly.

He screamed, twisted away. She lost her grip on the hilt of her knife at his sudden movement. Knuckles staggered, his scream turning into an inhuman wail. Sam clubbed him on the side of the head and he went down.

The runner in the street turned to go for help. He took one step and ran straight into Prumble. The big man lifted the poor kid up by his armpits, then slammed him down into a raised knee. Six meters away and Samantha still heard the jaw break. Prumble heaved the limp body up again and tossed it into the wall across the street.

At this, the leader broke and ran.

The second heavy with the police baton still seemed willing to fight. Samantha let him come to her; she raised her fists, her gaze dancing between his eyes and the black stick in his hand. The man moved in fast and swung in a controlled manner, surprising her with his skill. She was forced to dive backward and roll.

When she came up she noticed the leader, now fifteen meters away and fading in the gray murk of light rain. He skidded to a stop, and then Skadz appeared and tackled him.

Police Baton came at her again. She tried to duck left and her foot slipped on the damp ground. His blow caught her on the shoulder—the meaty part, luckily. It still erupted in pain and sent her to the ground.

Sam rolled twice, grunting each time her shoulder met the asphalt. She'd have a nasty bruise in the morning. Worse, if she didn't get up and finish this asshole.

She started to stand, and then Prumble was there.

The big man came at the heavy with surprising speed. Baton swung but his footing was wrong and he didn't get much behind the blow. Prumble blocked the riot stick with his forearm and the black baton flew from the man's hand. Then Prumble lifted one massive leg and kicked outward. His foot plunged straight into the heavy's stomach and pushed him a full meter back until he slammed into the door of the truck.

Prumble continued toward him, both arms held out, hands upturned, middle fingers extended.

The thug tried to run, but Pascal suddenly reached out and gripped his ankle. The Jacobite went down hard, landing next to Sam. She leapt on him and clasped her arm around his neck. "Finish them off," she said through gritted teeth. "No witnesses."

Thirty seconds later the truck drove away, seven bodies left behind in its wake. Sam saw pickers rushing out from a half-dozen nearby buildings before the whole scene faded into the distance. With any luck, they'd drag the bodies off the street before they stripped them clean.

Her heart hammered in her chest. This marked the first overt action they'd taken against Grillo, and in her mind leaving a trail of bodies did not equate to a good start. Even if they could get back here tomorrow, the place would be swarming with Jacobites—inner-circle types, probably—looking for answers. She'd have to hope the locals kept quiet or didn't see enough to describe them.

On the other hand, it only took one poor beggar to describe them—a fat man, a tall woman, and a black guy with dreadlocks—and they'd be blown. She cursed inwardly. They needed to be more careful, avoid trouble until the time was right.

Darwin didn't work the way it used to.

# 6

## MEXICO

### 29.MAR.2285

Tania sat cross-legged on the floor of the *Helios,* a map spread out in front of her, a pencil tucked behind her ear.

She took a small sip of instant coffee, winced at the cold temperature, and set it aside. A quick glance at her slate indicated eight minutes before she should check in with Vanessa for the next position fix to chart. She'd made a mark every twenty minutes since takeoff, hoping to find some pattern to the path the emerald aura towers had taken. Normally Tania would have used a slate for such work, but seeing Skyler's hand-marked map in Belém had inspired her to try the old-fashioned method. It turned out to be strangely cathartic, and the large size of the paper was somehow liberating.

The marks on her map traced a wavy line that swooped and turned, erratically if gently. She was beginning to suspect that the random nature of the path was deliberate, as if this set of towers for some reason didn't want to be found.

The sky outside her small window dimmed as the sun neared the horizon. Soon they'd have to land, having no way to track the path in darkness.

She stared at the curvy line again, focusing on the landscape over which it traversed rather than looking for some pattern in its shape. But there was nothing obvious there, either. The path seemed indifferent to the land over which it crossed. Twice they'd lost it when it went out over water, but luckily the curves the path took were not so extreme that it couldn't be extrapolated with reasonable accuracy for short distances. As of yet, the line had not left land for more than twenty kilometers or so. Tania had fretted about this as they'd flown up the spine of Central America. Anything more than about one hundred kilometers of water and she feared they'd lose the path for days, maybe weeks.

Her headset crackled, and Vanessa's voice came through. "Everything okay back there?"

Tania glanced at her timer. Five minutes left before they were due to mark another position. "Yeah, I'm good. Is something wrong?"

"We're going to need to land soon. I've been looking for a place on the path with power so we can top off, but it's pretty desolate below."

"Cap level?"

"Seventy percent, so it's not critical."

*Not yet.* Tania looked at the general direction the path took on her map. Although it curved erratically, the general direction was north. For all she knew it could end over the next hill, or wind all the way up to the North Pole. A frown tugged at the corners of her mouth at the idea of the path wrapping all the way back around and ending a few kilometers south of Belém.

"Hold on," Vanessa said. "Pablo's spotted something on infrared. Yes, there's a heat source to the northeast."

"Okay, let's mark the path here and go check it out. Any opportunity we have to spool the capacitors is worthwhile."

Vanessa rattled off a latitude and longitude combination. Tania confirmed the numbers and a few seconds after she felt the aircraft bank. The tone of the engines dropped.

"Tania?" Vanessa again. "There's something else I need to tell you."

The woman's tone gave Tania pause. "Go ahead."

"Tim contacted us a few minutes ago to let us know the Magpie has left Belém on the yellow path."

"Good to hear."

"He also said, well . . . look. Skyler and Ana took Russell Blackfield with them."

Her stomach tightened. "What? Tim allowed that?"

"Skyler didn't tell anyone until they'd departed. I'm sure there's a good reason," Vanessa said.

Tania forced herself to remain calm. Vanessa, though no doubt loyal to Skyler, was probably right. Skyler hadn't wanted to take anyone along, much less someone he despised. There must be a reason. But the fact that he'd done this without asking permission, or even telling anyone, meant he knew the action was ill-advised.

She thought back to when she'd first told him that Blackfield had come to Belém, hat in hand, asking for asylum. "Put him out the nearest airlock," Skyler had said immediately.

Could it be they'd taken the prisoner along just to dispose of him? She wanted to believe Skyler had a bit more compassion than that, but perhaps he'd seen his chance and acted rashly. Perhaps it had been Ana's idea. The girl had been known to do reckless things in the past, and maybe she held more sway over Skyler than he held over her.

*Stop that, Tania.* There must be a reason. Skyler's mission called for continuing on to Darwin to pick up the object Grillo held. Perhaps he felt Blackfield could be useful there. Maybe he intended to exchange the fugitive for the device. That plan seemed ridiculous to her. She knew nothing about Grillo, but if he saw the object as some kind of holy relic, she doubted he'd hand it over for a broken man like Russell.

No, there must be something else, something worth adding such a huge risk to their mission. Whatever it was, Skyler must think it's a long shot or he would have made his case to take the prisoner along.

"Are you there?" Vanessa asked.

"Thank you. I'll try to raise Tim once we land and get the details."

"Copy that. I would have patched him through, but he was in a rush."

"No problem." Tania clicked off transmit mode and set the

headset aside. Then she pinched the skin between her eyes to stem a coming headache. Too many pieces were moving at once. Too many variables, points of possible failure. She hated the feeling of not being in total control of a situation. More than that, she hated not having the luxury to analyze and plan. She lacked Skyler's ability to act purely on instinct and never look back. It was a characteristic he shared with Neil Platz, and she knew it was the reason she felt incomplete when he wasn't around.

Of course, it was also the reason she often felt infuriated when he was.

The *Helios* set down shortly after dark on a landing pad beside a dry lake. Tania found the location on her slate's map and, when switched to historical view, saw that there had once been a man-made body of water here, created by a dam. A hundred or so years ago the water had dried up, either by choice or due to a shift in climate. Hydroelectric power had all but vanished in the face of much cheaper and more flexible thorium reactors, so it made sense that the dam had simply been shut off. The lake had once again become a stream.

However, the electrical infrastructure in place would still have been useful, and what Pablo had spotted on the infrared turned out to be a large complex with an array of thorium reactors inside. The units predated miniature versions but were nonetheless reliable enough that electricity still flowed despite a lack of supervision for the last seven years or so.

Tania studied all this from the tiny porthole window on the aircraft's door. She longed to go outside, to stretch her legs and look around, but unsealing the cabin now would mean she'd be in her spacesuit for the duration of the trip and they still had no idea how much farther the search would take them.

So she remained inside and watched. Since landing she'd turned all the lights off in her cabin, allowing her eyes to adjust to the darkness outside. The buildings were simple cube-shaped affairs with metal stairwells and catwalks attached to the outside. Each was identical from the last, save for one that was roughly half the size of the others and had windows. An office, she guessed.

For five long minutes the immunes remained in the cockpit, studying the immediate area for movement or sound after the engines finally went quiet.

"All clear," Vanessa said. "We're going out."

"Okay," Tania replied. "I'll keep an eye from here and let you know if I see anything."

A few seconds later she saw the pair walk out toward the reactor complex. They carried their assault rifles casually. Vanessa took the lead and walked purposefully to a metal box the size of a refrigerator a few meters away from the landing pad. Pablo followed, constantly turning to scan the area around them.

"Cover me," Vanessa said.

Pablo walked a circuit around the charging station while Vanessa tried to open it.

"It's locked," she said after a short pause.

"Shoot it open?" Tania asked. She wondered if they'd brought any explosives, but then thought that might damage the unit.

"Too risky."

"Might be a key in that office," Pablo said.

Vanessa stood and looked toward the smallest of the six buildings. "We'll try that first. You okay, Tania?"

"Yes," she said despite a growing anxiety. She didn't want to voice it, afraid she'd sound weak. *Who cares?* she told herself. *You are weak. You're stuck inside here, isolated and helpless.* "Actually, no. Wait."

"What's wrong?"

"I . . ." She swallowed. "I'd feel better if you stayed with the aircraft, Vanessa. God forbid anything happens out there, but if it does, you're the only way any of us are getting home."

The pair walked back to Tania's window so they could see her. "If anything happens out there," Vanessa said patiently, "we're better off handling it as a team. But . . . you don't look convinced."

"I'm trying."

"Okay," Vanessa said. "I explained this to Pablo already but you should know, too. If something happens to me, suit up and get to the cockpit. There's an autopilot unit just above your head when seated in the pilot's chair, and before we left I set it to record our departure position. Tap the option to execute, then confirm, then power up. The *Helios* will fly back to Belém, no further action required. Just make sure they clear the landing pad, because it will set down exactly where we took off from."

Tania balked initially, but when the words sank in she found a surprising amount of comfort there. Her anxiety melted away. "Thanks, Vanessa. I understand."

"Good. Stay put, we'll be back in a few minutes."

They moved more purposefully now, reminding Tania of Special Forces teams she'd seen in dozens of action-thriller sensories. She noted how Vanessa always took point, her focus on the goal unwavering, while Pablo came behind, his gun and gaze sweeping in a circle around them, then up above, too. It amazed her that just a few years ago they'd been a lawyer and a farmer, respectively. Skyler had taught them well, and despite all the firearms training and the endless hours of Krav Maga sparring, Tania realized then she still had no idea what she was doing. Worse, she doubted she'd ever have thought to look in the office building for a key to the charging unit, yet Pablo had suggested the idea almost instantly. A scavenger's instincts, as if he'd been at it all his life.

She watched as they took positions on each side of a first-floor doorway. They were almost two hundred meters away now, but even from this distance she could see Vanessa count to three on her fingers. Then Pablo kicked in the door, causing a sudden distorted burst of sound in Tania's ear. He took a step back and Vanessa stormed inside.

Tania remained glued to her window, watching the door, listening to her headset. Other than breathing and the occasional footstep she heard nothing, as the two immunes were working as silently as possible.

*They're good. They're really good.* Skyler would know this already, but she made a mental note to tell him later. Skill like this deserved recognition.

"Clear," Vanessa said a short time later.

"Clear," Pablo agreed.

Tania let out a relieved sigh. She listened in silence to the sounds of them searching the building. In her mind's eye she saw them rifling through desk drawers and coat closets, perhaps knocking aside things that in any other circumstance would have been collected and returned to the colony.

A subtle movement caught Tania's eye. Something small crept along the edge of the landing pad. A cat? It was just a shadow in the darkness, bobbing along the lip of the circular raised platform. Then it stopped, and Tania went still.

An arm appeared over the edge, hoisting a rifle. The weapon was set down on the pad, and then she saw another arm. He or she placed both hands on the landing pad and thrust up on to it, one leg swinging over the side and then the other. The person picked up the gun and stayed crouched at the edge of the pad, studying the *Helios*. A man, Tania numbly realized. He had a catlike litheness to the way he moved, and he seemed to be staring right at her.

Tania tried to speak and couldn't. She didn't move, unsure if she'd been spotted. She wanted to duck away, to find a gun and wait in the corner. A sudden panic filled her when she realized she wasn't suited. If this intruder opened the cabin door from the outside, she'd be exposed. Her pulse pounded in her ears and her hands were shaking. Tania swallowed, made two fists, and squeezed. She took a deep breath and exhaled it.

"There's someone here," she finally managed to say. Her voice cracked, and sounded childlike.

"Repeat that?" Pablo said.

"Someone's on the landing pad."

"A sub?"

"No," Tania said. "An immune I think. He's got a rifle."

"What's he doing?" Vanessa asked, urgency in her voice.

"Just crouching there, looking at the aircraft."

"Okay. We're coming back. Pablo found a key ring."

The man on the landing pad stood and began to walk—no, creep—around the aircraft. It took all the willpower Tania had to remain still, knowing she'd killed the lights in the cabin upon landing, which meant her window would be dark. She moved back a little, just to be safe.

A sudden blinding light fell upon her, and she leapt backward. A flashlight, she realized with dread. She moved away from the door, stumbled on the water bottle she'd left on the ground, and almost fell. Her heart raced. Had he heard that? The light slid away, then swept across the window, then fixed on the window again. Tania willed herself to be calm. Maybe he hadn't seen her after all.

"We're coming out," Vanessa said quietly in Tania's ear. "What's happening now? Where is he?"

Tania gathered her wits and pressed herself against the wall by the aircraft door. The light became very bright and began to dart around the inside of the cabin. "He's right at the door. Has a flashlight. I think he saw me."

"Relax, Tania," Vanessa said. "Don't assume he means harm. He's just a survivor, probably saw us land and came to see what was going on. We might be the first people he's encountered since the virus swept through here."

The words made perfect and complete sense, or at least would if she hadn't seen the way the man moved. Curious didn't apply. Tania thought him more like a thief trying to find an open window.

"We see him, almost there," Vanessa said.

Once again the light shifted away from the window. Tania heard something soft and mechanical. She looked down to see the large door lever starting to turn.

"Oh God!" she exclaimed, and grabbed it with both hands. She pushed it back with more force than she'd intended. The man outside reacted a split second later, pushing from his side. Tania strained, squeezed her eyes shut as she leaned into the lever arm, and pushed with both arms. The lever remained caught between two positions.

Then, one horrid centimeter at a time, it began to move in his favor.

"No . . ." Tania grunted. She gave up a few centimeters to get better footing, then shoved with every bit of strength she had. Still the lever arm ratcheted toward open.

Vanessa spoke in her ear. "What is it?"

"He's trying to open the door." The words came out like an angry growl. A burning sensation began to rise in Tania's shoulders and at the base of her spine. For one fleeting second she wanted to laugh. Months of training and all of it worthless now. And yet she knew that was dishonest. A year ago she wouldn't have been able to push back on the handle at all. She'd been soft. Not anymore. "Hurry, dammit!" she shouted.

Through the strain she turned and glanced at the porthole beside her. Centimeters away from her was the gaunt face of a survivor. He had a shaggy beard and wore spectacles. His weathered skin was filthy, and as he strained to move the door handle she saw a row of dirty, uneven teeth in his snarling mouth.

She met his gaze. The man might be an immune, but his eyes had the same insanity that a subhuman's did.

"You! Step away!" Vanessa's voice.

The man ignored the command. Maybe he hadn't heard it; maybe he didn't understand English. The door latch clicked into the open position. One pull from the outside and the cabin would flood with contaminated air.

*I'm going to die. Or worse.*

"My suit," Tania said breathlessly. She shot a glance across the cabin, looking for the case. With horror she realized it wouldn't matter. The suit would fill with the same air as she put it on in, and there was no way she'd get it on before he opened the door. "No time." She turned toward the door instead, braced one foot against the wall, and pulled the handle toward her, hoping against hope she could keep it closed with the seal integrity intact. She only needed to last until the others returned.

The man outside started to laugh.

A distant gunshot interrupted him. Vanessa or Pablo had fired, the round ricocheting off the airplane's fuselage. The man returned fire, two booming shots. A split second her friends fired again. Tania heard a dull *smack* as a round pelted the porthole window. *God, be careful!*

Then silence.

"He's down," Vanessa said.

Tania realized she'd closed her eyes. With trepidation she stopped pulling on the lever. Somehow she had the presence of mind to yank it into the closed position again. Only then did she look out the window. Blood, and what she assumed was bits of skull, dripped down the clear surface. Through the red she could see Vanessa and Pablo, still only halfway to the aircraft and running hard.

"Is he dead?" Tania asked.

"Unsure."

Tania tried to crane her neck to see the body on the ground, but it was useless. She could only wait and watch through a lens of blood as her companions raced back up the steps to the landing pad.

Belatedly she glanced up at the light in the cabin that indicated the state of its seal. To her relief it still glowed pale green.

Ten agonizing seconds passed before Vanessa and Pablo reached the aircraft. Pablo went to the body, and Tania watched his face as he prodded it with his gun. His eyes then met hers. "It's over," he said.

"Thank you," Tania replied, her voice just more than a whisper. The post-adrenaline crash combined with the physical exertion made her arms feel like two dead weights. She let her death grip on the lever relax and slumped against the door. Of all the scenarios she'd played out in her mind, she'd never expected someone to try to force their way into the aircraft. She'd imagined subhumans clawing without effect on the fuselage, but this . . . As hard as she tried, Tania couldn't dispel the image of bone fragments sliding down her lone porthole. Nausea forced her to drop to a sitting position on the floor.

"Okay in there?" Pablo asked.

Tania inhaled through her mouth and let out the breath through her nose. "Shaken up a bit, I guess. That was close."

Pablo didn't reply. She heard rustling sounds through her headset. A moment later he spoke. "The guy was carrying a wallet. From Panama."

"That's a long way to go just to be in this dump," Vanessa replied.

"Mm. A notepad here, too," Pablo said. "There's a map, and drawings. Lots of them."

"Drawings of what?" Tania asked.

"Aura towers."

Tania caught herself nodding despite the empty cabin. "He must have seen them come through, and followed the trail this far."

"All that distance just to try to force his way inside the *Helios*?"

"From the way he looked," Tania reasoned, "I don't think he was entirely sane."

"Wait till you see these sketches," Pablo said. "Anyway, it's over. I'm going to try these keys now."

"Pablo?" Tania asked.

"Yes?"

"Before you do that, could you wipe the window clean?"


Vanessa slept while the *Helios* spooled her ultracaps off the platform's charging station. It took three hours to reach capacity, during which Tania dozed fitfully. She woke every twenty minutes or so and checked in with Pablo, who'd offered to keep watch from a second-story catwalk on the side of the nearest reactor building, fifty meters away.

Just before midnight Vanessa fired up the engines and flew them back to the last position they had marked on the emerald tower path. She landed there, in the middle of a vast desert, and shut down the engines again. They slept in total silence and isolation until the sun rose.

# 7

## OFF THE COAST OF LIBERIA

### 29.MAR.2285

Upon leaving Belém, Skyler had flown as high as he was comfortable with, visually tracking the path that ran almost perfectly east from Belém until it reached the ocean. At that point there was no reason to keep the land in sight, and so he'd climbed to a cruising altitude.

When the west coast of Africa appeared on his map, Skyler dropped the engines to zero and glided, letting gravity pull the Magpie down to a comfortable three hundred meters.

"We're going to need to land," he said to Ana. "Caps are already low."

She nodded. "Want me to check on him?"

"Sure. He'll say he needs to use the bathroom. Tell him to hold it."

She gave his shoulder a squeeze and climbed out of the co-pilot's seat.

"Better yet, just ignore him."

Ana flashed him a grin as she went aft.

\* \* \*

Escape was the furthest thing from Russell Blackfield's mind. Part of him thought maybe he should at least pretend to be trying, just to feed a little kindling to Skyler's paranoia. Something as simple as a guilty expression when the pilot checked on him would keep the man tense and provide a little amusement.

This time it was the woman, Ana, who came back. That was a change, at least. A welcome one.

She had a little swagger to her step, a confidence in her movement that he found undeniably attractive. When she ducked through the cockpit's door he craned his neck in hopes of a glimpse of cleavage, but the young woman's small, proud breasts were well covered by a buttoned-up shirt.

At least she was still wearing those khaki shorts. They left plenty of long, tan legs to study.

"Keep looking at me like that," she said, "and I'll blindfold you."

"Whatever you're into, I'm into," he shot back.

A few seconds later her bandanna was firmly tied around his head. *Dammit,* he thought. "I was just having a bit of fun," he said.

"Have some water instead."

He felt the cold rim of a cup press against his lips, and opened his mouth to sip. She gave him two mouthfuls, no more, just as Skyler had.

"Something to eat?" he asked.

"Later," she said. Her hand pressed hard against his shoulder, leaning him forward so she could inspect his bindings.

"I'm not sure what you two are so worried about. Where the hell am I going to go?"

"We're not taking any chances with you. Skyler says he knows you too well."

"He barely knows me at all," Russell said. "Look, I'm sorry for staring at you but you must be used to it. You're very attractive."

She leaned in close. He felt the heat of her breath on his ear. "Do you really think so?" she cooed.

"Yup."

"Well, Blackfield, everything you see"—she leaned in closer until her warm breath tickled the skin of his earlobe—"is Skyler's. Is that clear?"

He chuckled. "A bloke can look, can't he?"

In answer she tightened the blindfold.

*Touché,* Russell thought. "You could just take it as a compliment," he tried.

He heard her walking away.

"I need to use the head!" he called out. In response he heard her slip back into the co-pilot's chair. Some conversation he couldn't quite make out passed between the woman and Skyler, and then the two of them laughed.

He wanted to hate her, then. Wanted to tap into that well of rage that had always been ready and waiting, as long as he could remember. A thirst for vengeance when someone slighted him. Something had changed, though. The day he'd left Darwin some piece of him had fossilized. A buried fragment with Grillo's name on it, waiting to be unearthed.

For Ana he found something unexpected. Attraction, yes, but also admiration. Respect, even, he supposed. Instead of a burning desire to conquer her like a mountain summit, he could think only of that shared laugh with Skyler. The way she looked at him, as if they were a team. A multiplication rather than two opponents in the oldest game. No woman had ever looked at Russell Blackfield like that. Or if they had he'd never noticed.

Somehow Skyler had earned it. From this little tart and Dr. Sharma before that. How? What was he doing that drew such women in like moths to the flame? Perhaps it was all just that cocksure flyboy attitude, or maybe they just really dug his apparent total lack of ambition.

Russell slumped back in his chair and forced his thoughts from tan legs and selfless heroes to slumlords and priestly white robes.


"There's the path," Ana said, pointing.

Skyler guided the Magpie in low over the Liberian coastline. Where the Azores had mostly rocky cliffs for a shore, this part of Africa was dominated by kilometers of sandy beaches broken by the occasional river delta. A remarkable portion of the land beyond was still forest, and sure enough he could see a swath of flattened palm trees exactly where they'd predicted. After half a kilometer the towers had run headlong into Sinoe City, leaving a path of destruction exactly like those in Belém.

He knew little about Liberia, or much of the rest of this part of Africa. The area had gone through an explosion of investment and prosperity eighty years ago or so, when most of the continent had finally achieved a long-sought political stability. Foreign money came pouring in, mostly from China and India, resulting in gleaming new cities like Sinoe. The place reminded Skyler of Darwin in some ways—a chaotic forest of metal and glass towers, tall at the center and shrinking down to residential structures on the outskirts. Slums on the inland side, luxury homes and mansions along the coastal edge and lining the river that ran through the heart of the city.

"I've got four possible landing sites," Ana said. She'd been poring over maps in the Magpie's computer for much of the flight.

"I really need to piss back here!" Russell shouted.

Skyler ignored the outburst. "Our best bet is a military base. Preferably one with the lights on."

"I know, but the nearest is a hundred klicks north. I did find two commercial landing grids within the city."

"Nice work."

"Marking them for you now."

He flew over the first and didn't even bother to slow down. Skeletal remains littered the ground around a handful of crashed aircraft, a sight Skyler had come across all too often—everyone wanted to get to Darwin when the disease finally came, and when the mobs realized there wasn't enough room they took on an "If I can't go, no one can" mentality.

The second location proved better. A row of ten landing pads, all empty, in the center of a gated warehouse district. He'd scavenged dozens like it all over Southeast Asia. In crisis situations, for reasons Skyler couldn't quite fathom, people seemed to flock to grocery stores and the like to loot their supplies. Riots ensued and hardly anyone found what they needed, all the while the warehouses that supply such venues were left relatively untouched.

Blue landing beacons still winked on and off at steady intervals. Skyler picked the one at the end of the row and circled around so that the Magpie would be pointed down the rest of the row, making it easy to hop pads if needed.

"One of these days," he said to Ana, "I'll teach you how to parachute. I hate landing without someone on the ground first."

"Sounds like fun," she said.

*If only she had the patience for a sniper rifle,* he thought, *she'd be a perfect stand-in for Jake.* In time, perhaps, she'd get there, but time wasn't exactly an abundant commodity anymore. Besides, her strange mix of fierce independence and fierce loyalty was starting to grow on him.

Once safely on the ground, Skyler let the engines unwind and unbuckled his harness. "Watch for subs," he said to her. "I'll get our passenger suited."

"Yes, *sir*," Ana said. She winked when he glared at her.

He lumbered aft on stiff legs, chuckling to himself at the sight of Ana's impromptu blindfold tied across Blackfield's face. He yanked it off and tossed it on the seat across the aisle.

Russell blinked a few times, then leaned his head back against the seat. "Where are we?"

"Africa."

He frowned. "Big place."

"Yup."

"Last time I was here, Tania tried to kill me."

"I'd be happy to rectify that mistake." Skyler drew his pistol, and felt some satisfaction as Russell eyed the weapon. "You need to get suited up now, so we can open the door and recharge."

"Can I piss first?"

"Yes. Once suited, though, you'll have to hold it."

"Maybe you can scavenge up an adult diaper for me, Captain."

"I have an easier solution. No more food or drink until we find the towers."

That finally caused the man to shut his mouth. Skyler undid the bindings on Russell's wrists and stepped back toward the cockpit as the former Nightcliff security chief rubbed feeling back into his hands. Russell stood then, and rolled his feet in circles to get the blood flowing again.

"Head's over here," Skyler said, waving his gun at the aircraft's only bathroom. Despite the luxury appointments, the space was still tiny. "Leave the door open."

"Maybe you could swap places with Ana for this part?"

"Not going to happen."

"Ah, the overprotective boyfriend, is it?" Russell laughed. "Or maybe you play for both teams? I've seen you naked, so it's only fair I guess."

"Blackfield," Skyler sighed, "urinate, take a shit, whatever you need to do, just shut your damn mouth. If you're not suited in five minutes I'm opening the door anyway."

"You won't do that; you need me."

"Fine, then I'll club you until you're unconscious and suit you up myself."

Russell seemed on the verge of continuing his attempt at witty banter, then thought better of it. With a sigh he squeezed into the tiny bathroom and took care of his business.

"Now," Skyler said, "the suit."

The man went to the back of the cabin and unzipped the duffel bag. The spacesuit seemed a waste on such a pathetic person, but Skyler saw no viable alternative. A normal environment suit, while effective enough, was a bulky affair that made movement slow and awkward. Tania had managed to survive Hawaii in one, but only just, and there was no telling what dangers awaited her when she found the emerald towers. He'd rather Russell not slow them down, even if it meant putting the impressive suit at risk.

"What's this thing on the arm?" Russell asked. "Looks like a gun."

"A thruster. Before you get any ideas, it doesn't work unless vacuum is detected."

"That's okay. I can thrust just fine without help."

Rolling his eyes, Skyler turned and called out over his shoulder. "Any movement out there, Ana?"

"It's quiet."

"Good." Skyler stepped in to help Russell with some of the more complicated parts of the suit, recalling the fact that he'd needed two helpers when he'd suited up aboard Platz Station. Just before the helmet went on, Skyler held up a hand.

"Something wrong?" Blackfield asked.

Skyler shook his head. "Listen up, and for your own sake cut the snark for a minute. It could make the difference in your survival."

To his surprise, Blackfield said nothing. He just nodded once.

"Once that helmet goes on, a clock starts. If we don't find and secure those aura towers within the next twenty hours or so, you're a dead man."

"Twenty? I thought you brought all these tanks along so I'd have forty hours."

"I did. And it'll take us the better part of twenty hours to get back to Belém if we don't find what we're looking for." Skyler thought it best not to point out he had no intention of turning around just to save Russell's life, though the man would probably expect as much.

Russell said nothing, so Skyler went on. "I'm telling you this because I want you to understand: Every time you do or say something that delays us, it's your own life you're putting in jeopardy. I couldn't give a rat's ass if you live or die, so please, if you want to keep up the aloof-chauvinist act then be my guest. I'm happy to trade barbs if that's how you want to spend your time. And I guarantee you Ana will, too. She's much better at it than me."

In answer Russell fitted the helmet over his head. "What are we supposed to talk about, then? The weather?"

"I have a better idea," Skyler said, adjusting the fit and clicking the sealing ring into place. He tapped a button on the chest and waited.

"What are you doing?"

"Making sure we have integrity. This might be the first time in your life that word has been used on you."

"Ha-dee-fucking-ha. You know, mate, it's not fair if I'm supposed to be quiet and you can still blabber on like that."

The suit integrity light came on, green. "Clock starts now, Blackfield, and it's just an estimate. If you do nothing else, keep an eye on your air level and let us know if it drops below ten percent so we can refill the tank."

"Aye, aye, Captain."

"Ana, let's see if that charging port works," he called out.

She emerged from the cockpit a few seconds later, took in Russell's status with one glance, and started to open the cabin door.

"What was your idea?" Russell asked Skyler. "For what we could talk about."

"Grillo," Skyler replied. "I want to know everything you can tell me about Grillo. Now, outside."

"I'm not a prisoner anymore?"

"You're the manual labor. Get moving."

Russell couldn't help but be impressed by the suit he'd donned. Compared to the bulky outfit he'd been forced to wear during the Purge, and again when he'd made his first ill-fated trip to Africa, this suit was far more advanced. He could move almost as well as if he were wearing normal clothes, but the best part was the weight. The breathing apparatus, air tanks, and other systems were not all in one massive package on his back. They were spread out evenly across his body, and the net effect made them almost invisible. Other than the slight reflection of his own face in the helmet, he found within just a few minutes that he'd almost forgotten about the outfit.

As instructed, he walked behind Skyler at a comfortable distance of three meters. Ana trailed behind, her gun presumably trained on him. If the suit had one drawback, it was that he couldn't easily look backward. That he rectified a minute later when he found the HUD and began to explore the suit's menu of options. A rearview camera was built into the back of the helmet, and when he turned it on a small, widescreen view of the world behind him came into view. Ana, against the backdrop of the sleek aircraft, filled the image. Russell smiled. *I can look at her without Skyler knowing. Better yet, I have eyes in the back of my head.*

He found another menu, next. One that controlled the thruster built into the suit's right arm. He saw an option called "diagnostics," and within that another choice caught his eye. *Vacuum detection override?*

Russell Blackfield grinned again. He suddenly felt like a prisoner who'd been slipped a hidden shiv in his care package.

# 8

## DARWIN, AUSTRALIA

### 29.MAR.2285

The air inside was stifling and smelled of sweat. Though she did not enter as a prisoner this time, she remained an outsider, and Samantha received more than a few mistrustful glares as she circled the periphery of the dimly lit space.

A fight in the center of the room otherwise held the crowd's attention. They echoed the constant rhythm of landed punches and grunts of pain with a mix of enthusiastic cheers and sympathetic groans.

Sam noted one change to the room right away: Nobody was drinking. She wondered if bets would be settled once a winner emerged, and got her answer a few seconds later after the distinct thud of a body toppling to the ground.

Most of the crowd cheered, some grumbled. What followed almost made her laugh aloud. Quiet conversations started all around the room, forced smiles and polite handshakes across the board. They reminded her of extras in a crappy theater performance, pretending to be having real discussions at the back of a stage. Bets were being settled, she had no doubt, but it couldn't be done overtly lest they draw attention from the guards posted at the door.

That the league had been allowed to continue at all surprised her. It didn't fit with Grillo's way of doing things at all. It must have been a concession to keep morale up, just as he'd compromised on the rules laid out for the scavenger crews. Grillo certainly had a knack for giving his subjects just enough slack to keep them happy without drawing wrath from the Jacobite hard-liners.

Sam completed her circle of the room without any sign of Vaughn. In her mind's eye she'd imagined him leaning against the wall, arms folded, in exactly the same place he'd waited for her when she'd fought here. But no, he was not there, nor anywhere else. She turned her attention inward, toward the center of the room. Another match was starting. Sam pushed forward, scanning the faces of the audience. If anyone recognized her, they hid it well. She had to remind herself it had been almost two years since that night. Her performance in the ring had faded from memory, not become something of legend. She hadn't really expected that, but some part of her hoped for a flash of "oh shit, she's back!" recognition.

*Maybe I should go a few rounds,* she thought idly. *Remind them.*

The current bout ended almost as soon as it began. Sam hadn't been paying attention, but from the pained looks on the crowd's faces someone had just been dropped on the first or second blow. Another comically obvious stealth-settling of bets ensued.

It took her a moment to realize that the room had grown quiet and people were looking at her. No, not simply "people." Everyone.

Sam felt a slight rush of fear at the sudden attention. She half-expected to turn and see Grillo marching toward her, a slew of guards at his back, her murderous escapade in the Narrows exposed.

What she saw when she turned was Vaughn.

He stood in the center of the fighting ring and was pointing at her.

Calling her out.

Sam smiled. "You want a piece of me?" she said with a mock accent.

Laughs from the crowd.

In response he turned his hand over, held it flat, and then beckoned her with his fingers.

He wasn't smiling. That worried her. But she cracked a grin anyway and strode into the circle of onlookers.

She walked a circuit around Vaughn, studying him. He seemed leaner than last time, and he'd been naked then. Right now he wore brown shorts and a bloodied white tank top. If any of his previous opponents had landed a blow on his face, there was no bruising visible to indicate it. *Impressive,* she thought.

His lunge came out of nowhere. Two quick steps closed the distance between them and a meaty fist flew straight at her nose. Sam ducked on instinct and felt the blow graze the top of her head. In the same movement she lashed out with one leg, expecting to kick his feet out from under him. He wasn't there, though. He'd jumped, straight up, and landed hard on her thigh and calf.

Sam yelped and rolled, heard a roar of approval from the crowd. Her leg throbbed and she had to grit her teeth when she came to an awkward stand.

Vaughn was right in her face again. He punched and she parried this time. Another blow came right behind and she just managed to block it, the fist stinging her forearm.

*Fucking hell, what's his problem?*

Sam fought back. She slugged him on the jaw with a left, which seemed to surprise him. Her right hook took him just below the eye and sent him staggering.

A chorus of oohs and aahs erupted from the audience with each punch, as if they were watching a fireworks display.

"Miss me?" she asked.

"Something like that," he grumbled. She'd hit him hard—most would be on the ground now—but he'd already found his footing and now faced her with an expert stance, dancing from foot to foot.

"Aren't you full of surprises," she said, and took her own stance, bringing both fists up in front of her. Clearly the man had some pent-up aggressiveness, and Sam decided to let him deplete it.

In truth she didn't have a choice. He fought as well as she did.

They danced around each other for a good five minutes, each landing as many blows as they blocked or avoided. Sam had a split lip and a pounding headache when she decided enough was enough. Another few minutes would have decided it anyway, and although she thought she could beat him, she decided that letting him win in front of his comrades would be wise.

Sam let the next punch fall; she feinted away at the last instant so it didn't do much damage but still looked good. Vaughn's fist still stung. She closed her eyes, whirled with the impact, and collapsed to the ground.

Wild cheers erupted from the crowd. When Sam opened her eyes, Vaughn stood over her, sweat dripping from his chin onto the floor next to her. She blinked away the sparkles floating around her vision and held up a hand. A few seconds passed, and just as she thought he might not help her up, he clasped her forearm and she his, and he hauled her to her feet with one easy motion.

"Hello, Vaughn," she said, her face just a few centimeters from his.

He frowned. "What are you doing here, Sam?"

"Looking for you."

"I figured that part out."

Bets settled, the crowd shouted for Sam to depart the ring so that Vaughn could face his next opponent. When Vaughn waved them off and pulled her by the elbow toward the exit, they booed him, though she could tell it was mostly in jest. They hadn't even reached the door yet when another match had started and the crowd had forgotten them.

A strong wind whipped the clotheslines that hung between buildings outside, bringing with it the smell of coming rain tinged with the ever-present salt of the ocean. Lightning danced across the sky to the east; a bright full moon gleamed to the west. Somehow it all seemed to mirror the way Sam felt as Vaughn tugged her into the darkness between two buildings and pushed her against the slat wall. The bruises, blood, and sweat on her face suddenly forgotten, Samantha gripped his shirt in both hands and pulled his lips to hers. They were warm and urgent and tasted like battle.

* * *

Sam fumbled in the dark for the glass of cider and giggled when she almost knocked it over.

Vaughn's room was pitch-black, illuminated only in staggering flashes of white light from the thunderstorm to the east that filled the tiny space every few seconds. But sometimes a full minute would pass in total darkness. Sam found those periods of exploration only by the sensation of touch and taste to be intense, but there was something equally thrilling in seeing his naked flesh lit up by a lightning strike—on top of her, under her, behind her.

He lay next to her now, a sweaty sheet covering one leg and the rest of him exposed. She sipped the cider and watched, studying his form every time a flash of white filled the room. He'd been in decent shape the first time they'd slept together, and a passable performer between the sheets. That had been two years ago, and he'd changed. Whatever workout regimen he'd undertaken had hardened his form in all the right places. And, she suspected, he must have taken another lover or two since they'd parted, or perhaps found a good whore, because his skill in lovemaking had improved even more dramatically.

"I should have come back sooner," she said, running a finger along his thigh and up his chest.

"You probably shouldn't have left in the first place."

Sam had expected this, and had thought up a variety of responses. She'd been his prisoner before, and they'd fucked on the floor of her cell with such intensity that he'd fallen asleep almost as soon as she'd dismounted him. Exactly as she'd hoped. "I guess it doesn't matter in the end. Grillo was right outside, waiting for me. On his way to talk to me, in fact. What happened between us didn't change his plans."

"Not for you, no. And if you'd hung around for thirty seconds he would only have faulted me for shagging a prisoner."

The words hung in the air like silence after a thunderclap. Sam had to wait for a flash of lightning to try to read his face, only to find him staring blankly straight up at the ceiling.

"Vaughn, I—"

"Forget it. Ancient history."

"Part of my deal with Grillo was that you not be punished."

She heard him sigh, then sit up. "What the fuck did you tell him that for?"

This she hadn't expected. "I used you. I felt like shit about it, and . . . Jesus, Vaughn, I couldn't leave thinking you'd be . . ." She paused, remembering the man in the hospital, and the sound of Grillo's knife plunging into him. "Did he?"

"Did he what?"

"Punish you."

"No, Sam. No he fucking did not. That I could have handled."

*Don't be so sure.*

"Nah, I wasn't punished, I was rewarded. Of course both are just a matter of perspective, right? But they couldn't exactly leave me in my post. I'm too easily swayed by temptations of the flesh, you see?"

Sam swallowed, hard.

"Tonight being no exception."

"Hey," she said. "This was just a bit of fun. A lot of fun."

A complex lightning strike flickered through the room, long enough for her to see him turn to face her, the bedsheet covering his lap. "Really, Sam? No other shoe to fall?"

He'd caught her, of course. She swore, inwardly, at her stupidity. For some reason she thought he might be sympathetic to the cause, or at least willing to take a night off when the time came for action. She hadn't bothered to consider his perspective. She'd used him, marked him as a failure at his job, and left in Grillo's good graces.

"You should go," he said flatly.

"Vaughn . . ."

He lay back down and went silent.

Sam sat next to him for a long time, trying to think of something to say, some way to salvage things so that she could at least leave without him despising her.

In the end she rose and dressed, hating how clumsy the darkness made her now.

"Tell me one thing, Sam," he said while she laced her boots.

"Okay."

"Is this another test? Are you one of them?"

"One of who?"

"The Jakes. You're supposed to tell them if I declined your advances or not, right?"

She balked. "Of course not. Goddammit, no." Then she turned and sought out his face in the dark. "Wait, if you thought that, why'd you sleep with me?"

"Simple," he said. "I keep hoping they'll give up on me and leave me the hell alone. You can tell them that, when you report in. I'm sick of this."

Sam made her decision then. She went to him, sat in front of him, and found his face with both hands and gripped. "Listen to me, okay? I'm not with them. Far from it. And that *is* the reason I came here. I wanted to tell you to be ready."

A long, lightning-punctuated silence filled the room. "Ready for what?" he said finally. A whisper.

"I'd tell you if I knew, exactly. But something's going to happen, Vaughn, and soon. I didn't want you to be caught on the wrong side. That's all."

He started to speak and she kissed him, hard. At first he didn't respond, but after a while she felt the stiffness in his lips, his shoulders, begin to melt away. When she pulled away he leaned forward until their foreheads touched.

"Last time we shagged," he finally said, "you left me in a right fucking mess, Samantha."

"I'm sorry. I'm trying to make sure that doesn't happen again."

"You coulda just said something in the canteen."

"And miss out on this?" She gave him a squeeze and felt him stiffen. She pecked his cheek just below the eye.

"Somehow I get the feeling this right-fucking-mess is only going to get worse."

Sam didn't bother to deny it.

He pulled her back onto the bed.

# 9

## NORTH AMERICA

### 29.MAR.2285

The emerald towers had carved an unceremonious hole in the Great Border Wall before vanishing into the New Mexico desert. The path, now almost two years old, had succumbed to the dry, sandy expanse and disappeared.

"We'll keep searching until the caps are at sixty percent," Vanessa said, a hint of defeat in her voice. "If we haven't spotted a place to spool up by then, we'll have to backtrack."

Tania had all but given up on her tiny porthole. It only gave her a partial view of the western horizon, and anyway all she could see when she looked through it was the ghost of an insane man. Her thoughts often drifted back to that moment, which seemed like such an incomprehensible waste to her. That man had survived for years, and traveled thousands of kilometers to follow the towers, only to try to force his way into the aircraft and, perhaps, the woman within.

Instead she turned to her slate and asked Pablo to slide a video feed to her from the *Helios*'s landing camera. The resolution wasn't great, but at least it was a straight-down view from two klicks up. Channeling a bit of her old friend Natalie, Tania put together a program to pull frames from the video every quarter of a second and stitch the resulting stills onto a map. She even had the images rotated based on the compass heading at the moment of capture, and then resized slightly based on any shifts in altitude. Finally she configured a cycling sequence of filters that ran all the images through various color enhancement algorithms that should, she hoped, accentuate subtle differences in the ground below that might otherwise be missed. That last feature seemed to come from Natalie's voice in her head, and Tania, though delighted at the result, wondered if she was starting to go stir crazy alone in the cabin. She dismissed the concern by recalling all the long nights she'd spent on Anchor Station, poring over telescope images searching for tiny luminosity shifts. This was really no different. In fact, the nostalgia alone made the effort worthwhile. At the very least it took her mind off the tainted air that rushed past just outside.

"Vanessa, do me a favor?"

The pilot replied an instant later. "Sure."

Tania explained her improvised visualization and asked the immune to fly in a zigzag pattern—northwest, tight turn, southwest—with each leg of the pattern one hundred kilometers long. Until then Vanessa had been flying about somewhat randomly. "I'd rather do this in a structured way, if you don't mind."

"It's a great idea," Vanessa replied. Within seconds the aircraft banked sharply and began the pattern near where the path had disappeared.

Two hours later, when Tania had several rows of zigzag-pattern images laid out on her slate's map, she spotted something. They'd had two false alarms before that, both turning out to be portions of the same irrigation channel. This time, though, the width was just right and the depression quite shallow.

"Take a look," she said into her headset, feeding the images back to Pablo in the cockpit. She circled the places in question—the line went across two legs of the V flight pattern.

"Best one yet," Vanessa replied. "We're near our turn-back point anyway, so we might as well check it out."

"Agreed," Tania said.

The *Helios* banked hard and Tania felt her weight change as the aircraft started to descend. On her screen, the program continued to run, laying out images that marked the route of the aircraft perfectly. The pictures shrank as the plane lost altitude, so Tania zoomed her view in.

Her image filter pass cycled to negative mode, and there, with obvious clarity, was the path.

Vanessa's voice came over the headset before Tania could speak. "We see it!"

"Me, too!" Tania said, a wide grin on her face despite the solitude. "Are we okay to follow?"

"I wouldn't advise it. Pretty desolate out here, and we burned a lot of energy flying that pattern. If we turn back now we can make our previous landing site and pick this up again tomorrow."

Tania frowned. It would mean losing a precious day. She switched to her slate's map and mentally projected out a cone along this leg of the tower path. "What about Tucson, in Arizona? It's only a few hundred klicks and in the right direction."

"It's a risk," Vanessa replied. "This country was in bad shape well before the disease came, remember. I'd feel more comfortable returning to a known functional charging port. Trust me, Tania, for your sake—the last thing you want is to be stranded out here."

"Everything we're doing out here is a risk," she replied. "Skyler told me that. We have to press on."


The path turned north again forty kilometers outside Tucson, so Vanessa marked it and flew on to the city. She said nothing about the range left in the capacitors, and little about anything else. Tania began to wonder if she'd made a mistake in overruling her, not to mention throwing one of Skyler's lines at her to seal the directive.

Under the blazing noonday Sun, the fringes of the city shimmered at the horizon. Tania craned her neck to look below, but it was a fruitless exercise. She saw nothing but an ocean of cloned tract houses, shockingly wide expressways crammed with abandoned vehicles, and bleak patches of sand where the desert had reclaimed some of its former domain. Vast swaths of homes had burned at some point, leaving nothing behind but charred skeletons and blackened ground.

Even from this height she could see the grit and sand that blew through the dry, cooked city on stiff winds. Bits of trash and dry weeds drifted through the streets. A huge pack of feral dogs rested in the shade of plastic playground equipment, until the booming aircraft engines stirred them into a frenzy.

All of it blended together as the *Helios* stormed by. Tania's stomach began to sink at what she saw. This was a miserable, forgotten place.

She hadn't studied America much in her youth, other than what her coursework required. She knew the nation had once been the world's dominant economic engine, only to spiral downward over the course of the twenty-first century, finally settling somewhere in the middle of the pack. The city she saw out the window could just as easily be Mumbai.

"Tania," Vanessa said through her headset. "We've spotted something."

"What is it? The towers?"

"No. Going to bank so you can see this for yourself."

The aircraft banked hard, so hard, in fact, she had to grasp the handle by the door. She had a view of blue sky at first as Vanessa turned the craft to fly perpendicular to whatever it was they'd spotted. Then it leveled off before banking slightly in the opposite direction. Tania saw the ground come back into view, and her breath caught in her throat.

Aircraft, as far as the eye could see, covered the ground below. They were arranged in orderly rows, grouped by size and type in meticulous fashion. She saw everything from ancient jet planes and helicopters to more modern cap-powered aircraft with vertical flight capability. There were hundreds—no, thousands—of vehicles, all clearly military in nature. Excitement rippled through her at the find. This place could provide parts, even entire aircraft, to the colony for decades to come. Perhaps even weaponry.

Her enthusiasm dwindled as Vanessa took them lower and circled the sprawling grounds. The planes were all in various states of dismantlement and decay. Tania began to realize this was not a storage facility, but a graveyard.

"Do you think there's anything we can use here?" Tania asked.

Vanessa brought the *Helios* to a hover over a row of warehouses near the center of the field. "None of the aircraft look fit to fly, at least to me. These buildings might have parts we can use, but nothing we can't find in Brazil."

"What a shame."

"However," Vanessa said with a hint of the dramatic. She spun the plane a bit farther until Tania could see a low administrative building, circular in shape. Around the base of it, four landing pads were arrayed, and each had landing lights that happily blinked away.

By the time the caps were spooled again, Tania had begun to feel the side effects of being trapped in a box for twenty hours. It wasn't the lack of fresh air, or not seeing the blue sky above—she'd lived most of her life on space stations, after all. No, what Tania began to realize she missed most was real human contact. Her early morning chats with Zane and her afternoon inspection walks with Tim. Tim's plain, youthful face came to mind frequently during the long flight. His goofy grin and nervous laugh, which she'd found so quaintly awkward at first, and now so endearing.

Between the idle thoughts and the lull of the *Helios*'s engines, Tania drifted off for a time. She woke to a weak light coming in through the porthole window, and glanced at her watch. Five P.M., unless they'd crossed a time zone. She sipped water from her thermos and ate dried mango while studying the line of overlapping images her slate displayed.

The tower path had continued to swoop and curve in apparent randomness, including a stretch that ran through the heart of the Las Vegas metropolis. Tania frowned at that. She'd seen pictures of how it looked before, and dreamt of visiting just to experience the place. To her it always seemed like an unintentional monument to the American collapse. Her images were too low-resolution to make anything out other than a vast sea of crumbling hotel and casino skyscrapers.

From there the path turned back east, cutting a barely discernible swath through eastern Utah before finally reaching the foothills and then mountains of Colorado, where flattened trees made the path obvious. From the flight pattern, Tania could tell her pilot had not lost it once all the way to their present location, a few hundred kilometers southwest of Denver.

Tania set the slate aside and stretched. She needed to get her blood pumping if she was going to stay awake for the landing they'd need to do at sunset. So she did what exercises she could in the cramped cabin: a set of sit-ups and push-ups, shadow boxing, and a little yoga. Then she used the restroom and washed her face with cold water.

The routine helped, and when Vanessa finally called over the headset, Tania felt ready to face another landing.

"Lost the path," Vanessa said suddenly.

"Oh, no."

A few seconds later. "Hang on, belay that. Tania, you might want to get suited up."

Nothing Tania had done, not the exercise or the cold-water splash, set her heart racing like those words. She hopped to the window immediately. "What? What do you see?"

Once again Vanessa turned the aircraft to give her a better view. A small city filled her view—Boulder, if she recalled correctly from the map—and Tania swallowed. For some reason she hadn't expected the towers to stop in an urban environment. There didn't seem any point to such a long trek when they'd started in the much larger Belém.

But the *Helios* kept turning until the city lay behind them. A mountain range came into view, one so stunningly beautiful that Tania found herself speechless.

"What is this place?" she mumbled.

"Our nav calls it the Flatirons."

From deep green forests came massive sheets of flat rock that jutted upward at almost perfect forty-five-degree slopes. The sheer faces receded in a line toward the south, and almost glowed orange in the reflected light of the setting sun. Huge clouds, burning with the same color on their west-facing fringes, drifted lazily overhead. It looked like a painting, Tania thought. Perfect in every way.

Except for the aura towers.

They stood like sentinels in a circle at the base of the closest rock face. Half were on the ground in a clearing they'd made among the trees. The other half rested on the slanted rocky mass, each having carved a chunk of rock out at their chosen resting place so they could stand upright.

Somehow the towers were even more ominous than the red-glowing group she'd seen in the rainforest east of Belém. Those almost seemed like they wanted to hide, surrounded by their mists and the tall trees. This group, with their shimmering emerald-colored lines of light, were right out in the open for anyone to see. It was as if they were begging explorers to come and look around.

"No dome here," Vanessa said.

"Not one we can see at least," Tania corrected. "Can you get a little closer?"

"Sure."

The aircraft banked and Tania lost her view for a few minutes. She felt her weight decrease as they descended to just a hundred meters or so above the dark green canopy. Then Vanessa turned the craft again so Tania could study the site.

Her eyes went straight to the center of the circle. She'd hoped to spot a crashed shell ship there, exposed and waiting, another prize nestled inside.

Instead all she saw was a hole in the slanted rock. "Perhaps it's another tunnel," she said. "Like the one Skyler explored in Belém."

"Only one way to find out," Vanessa said. "But it's getting dark, and we need to find a place to land. I suggest we wait until dawn to scout it out."

Reluctantly, Tania agreed. "I'll suit up an hour before that, and then you two can come back here and get your gear ready."

Tania didn't sleep that night. Vanessa had landed the *Helios* on a plateau with a view of the towers. The fine traces of green light that rippled and shimmered along their surfaces cast the surrounding rock face in a ghostly hue, augmented by moonlight that grew and faded as the great clouds drifted by overhead.

A full three hours before dawn she left the window and began to prepare for vehicle exit. Tania took her time. She broke down her rifle, cleaned it, and oiled the few moving parts. She laid out her EVA suit and inspected it for any signs of wear, despite the fact that the outfit's own diagnostic system would alert her to any problem. Then she topped off the air and water tank built into the backpack. Satisfied, she stripped and used a dry-shower cloth to clean up a bit. It was no substitute for a nice hot shower, but it was all she had. She put on some clean undergarments and then a skintight leotard so the suit wouldn't chafe against her skin.

Finally, Tania slipped into the suit. She'd practiced putting it on without an assistant, but even so she had to squirm and strain multiple times just to squeeze into the outfit. The semi-rigid pressure webbing that snaked through the material would be useless here on the ground, but even at its most relaxed setting the veinlike substrate still made the suit almost impossibly tight. Tania had watched sensories set in Victorian times, and it seemed a staple of such programs for the heroine to have to squeeze painfully into a corset before invariably meeting the hero. She felt the same pain now, only over her entire body. And, she mused, there was no hero waiting outside to meet her.

Of course, the last time she'd worn the suit, Skyler had been there. This made her chuckle. Arguably she'd been the hero on that excursion. Then another darkly humorous thought came to her. Somewhere, right now, Russell Blackfield was probably wearing the suit Skyler had worn. She shook her head, still unable to fathom why he'd taken the man along. There must be a good reason. At least that's what she kept telling herself.

She didn't have her headset on, so Vanessa's voice came through the cabin intercom. "Good morning, Tania. Are you ready?"

Out the porthole she could just see the first hints of daylight on the eastern horizon. "Putting my helmet on now. Give me five minutes, then wait at the porthole for an a-okay."

The helmet weighed more than she remembered. Tania sat on the edge of her seat and studied it, fighting a flood of memories from her trip into the Builders' ship. As much as she tried to force the thought away, holding the helmet now seemed to crystallize, to amplify, the basic truth: She'd died in this helmet once before.

*Once is enough,* she thought, and filled her mind with one vibrant picture until it blotted out the rest. The circle of green-glowing towers, standing vigil at the base of that wall of rock. The Flatirons. She'd had to look up the term to understand the reference, and though she did agree the strange rock formation resembled a row of clothing irons jutting up from the ground, to her they looked like the walls of some natural fortress in the process of being pulled back into the earth.

Tania focused on that picture in her mind, and pulled the helmet over her head.

She walked between her two companions, Vanessa on point and Pablo trailing behind. Once they were within the trees all sign of the alien towers vanished, and Tania shifted her focus to where she stepped. The ground was a patchwork blanket of melting snow and long-fallen pine needles. Both crunched pleasantly under her boots but also presented problems. The snow was slick here. One false step and she'd fall, which under any other circumstances would be cause to laugh. But out here one tiny puncture of her suit carried terrifying consequences.

The pine needles were another matter. It surprised her to find they provided even less traction than the ice. Worse, they were centimeters deep in some places, concealing chunks of rock or small depressions, all of which could easily send her sprawling if she wasn't careful.

It made the hike a slow and tedious process, and it was only after ten minutes of walking that Tania suddenly realized she'd never seen snow before. Not in person, anyway.

"Hold up a sec," she said.

Vanessa immediately knelt in a defensive posture. "What did you see?"

"Nothing," she replied. "That's the problem. I'm so focused on my feet I haven't even looked up. I just need a second to . . . center myself."

The woman nodded and made a gesture to Pablo that Tania assumed meant "stay alert."

Though her suit told her the temperature was a cool 7 degrees Celsius, she felt perfectly comfortable. Even when she knelt and touched some of the snow, the suit's construction allowed none of the cold to seep beyond its outer layer. Tania frowned. It might as well have been a sensory. Even the forest sounds were piped into her helmet via external microphones, giving them a manufactured taint.

*At least when we get to the towers I can open the mask and breathe this air.* She'd never been able to breathe the air in Hawaii but imagined it would have been hot, sticky, and rank with decaying vegetation. In comparison, this place seemed crisp and pure, like a drink of cold water.

"Okay," she said. "Let's go."

"One moment," Pablo said.

She turned to look at him. The tall, thin man was crouched beside a tree, his hands cupped over his mouth. It took Tania a second to realize he was breathing onto his fingers to warm them. "Forget your gloves?"

He shook his head. Then he pointed at a patch of ice by the tree. "Tracks here. Human."

"Sub?"

"Yes. Unless some immune is going barefoot in this cold."

Tania backtracked to his position and looked at the footprints. They were fading in the melting snow, but unmistakable.

"Looks like it was standing by this tree," the man said, "facing our plane. See these two deep ones? Then it turned and went toward the towers."

Tania felt a chill then, the kind her suit couldn't compensate for. "It didn't just attack. I thought they always attacked."

"No," he said. He stood up and glanced around, sniffing the air. "The ones you see are the ones that attack, so it can feel that way. Almost as many just run."

"Remember," Vanessa said, joining them. "Subs are gripped by primal emotions and responses. Some are blinded with the desire to fight, others to flee."

"Fight or flight," Tania said, nodding. Her experiences had been so clouded by the battles around the colony that she'd forgotten the fundamental symptoms of the disease.

"Exactly. There used to be others, too. Those who wanted to play, or even love. As you can imagine, few like that survived more than a few days. This one looks to be the flight type. It probably became curious at the noise of our engines but ran when it saw us emerge."

Tania nodded. Still, she couldn't shake the feeling the creature was baiting them. She held her rifle at the ready when they continued.

The farther into the foothills they went, the more snow they encountered, and by the time Vanessa glimpsed the top of an aura tower through the trees, white patches blanketed most of the ground.

They crept the last hundred meters to the edge of the clearing the towers had created. Vanessa took up a position next to a tree, and Tania placed herself directly across from her at the trunk of another. Pablo crouched in the snow between them, visibly shivering. He rubbed his upper arms as they studied the scene.

Just like in Belém and Ireland, the towers were arranged in an almost perfect circle roughly half a kilometer in diameter. In Ireland there'd been a purple dome that somehow manipulated the flow of time, something Tania still found hard to believe. In Belém, the towers were cloaked in a humid mist that reduced visibility to almost nothing.

Here the entire circle of towers rested in plain sight, which somehow made the place more unsettling. Nearly half of the towers were positioned on the ground amid fallen trees and flattened foliage. The other half extended up onto the rocky face of one of the five Flatirons. Each had carved a small flat space upon which to rest, and hints of the violence used to do this were there in the form of rocks and debris that trailed down the rock face like tears.

In the very center of all this was a hole in the base of the rock. From the plane it had looked small, but Tania saw now this had been a deception. The opening in the mountain's face was ten meters wide and twenty tall. All jagged-teeth edges, too, as if the mountain had formed a mouth and screamed. If she'd seen it without the towers surrounding it, she might have thought it to be a cave, but somehow with the presence of the towers it seemed obvious to her this opening had not been here before the ship crashed. Perhaps it had been blasted open rather than carved, or perhaps the ship had somehow cracked into an open pocket in the mountain that previously had no exit here.

"We should test the air," Pablo said in a flat voice.

Tania swallowed and thought of Karl, who'd done the same in Belém more than two years ago. He'd been infected then but returned to the aura so quickly, the disease went into stasis before it had done any serious damage. And yet even that had resulted in a constant battle with raging headaches, and an addiction to painkillers. Over and over Tania had told herself she could live with the same if she had to, but standing here she found herself wavering. Only after remembering the urgency of their mission did she release the latches on her helmet, twist, and lift the glass away.

Her first shock came from the brisk air. The cold made her nose tingle, her earlobes throb. She inhaled and got her second shock. The air smelled of pine and something else she couldn't quite place—rock or snow, perhaps both in concert. It was the smell of purity, of cleanliness, and in all her life she'd never experienced anything like it. The frigid thin air caused a slight ache in her chest, her lungs unused to both the temperature and the low oxygen level. When she exhaled, she was delighted to see her breath rendered like a puff of smoke where hot air met cold.

"Well?" Vanessa asked.

"I feel fine," she said. She was either immune, a statistical improbability, or the towers were generating aura.

Her companions wanted to wait a bit, just to be safe. After two minutes with no symptoms, Tania attached her helmet to her belt and looked at the two immunes. "Let's go see what's in that cave," she said.

# 10

## SOUTHERN CHAD

### 29.MAR.2285

The instant Skyler saw the end of the yellow tower path, he killed the Magpie's engines and lights, gliding over the scene at an altitude of one thousand meters.

"What are you doing?" Ana asked, stirring from a catnap.

"I'm trying not to be noticed. Look at this."

Her head jerked up, alarmed by the dire tone of his voice.

The scene below bordered on incomprehensible. Dozens of open pits stretched out for kilometers in every direction. Some were shallow, probably dug by hand. Others were massive, dark depressions in the earth big enough to swallow a small city.

Dotted throughout the landscape between the open gashes in the earth were what Skyler assumed to be villages. Rows of single-story rectangular buildings surrounded by crumbling mud huts and patchwork shacks. Mining colonies.

Blanketing all the remaining available desert were what must be millions of strange, raised patches of sand all perfectly square in shape, all tilted toward the sky. It took Skyler a few seconds to realize what they were: an ocean of solar panels, coated with sand after years of neglect. They lined the rims of the craterlike mines and filled the unexploited expanses of ground far out into the Sahara, until their coloration made them merge with the surrounding desert.

And there was more. Pockets of destruction radiating out from the aura towers. Not caused by their arrival, but older. Skyler saw a crashed aircraft and many abandoned vehicles, most of which appeared to be military issue. They were coated with sand, having been sitting out here for years. He even saw the tattered skeleton of a large tent near the pit, shreds of material hanging from the structure like clothing on old bones. Inside, half buried by sand, were tables and shelves and lumps on the ground Skyler assumed were bodies.

All of this served to create the strangest landscape Skyler had ever seen. And yet it all paled in comparison to the additions made by the Builders.

"Skyler," Ana said, "I'm scared."

"Me, too," he admitted. He let the aircraft continue to glide.

Below, the path of the aura towers had carved an almost perfect line of destruction through the field of solar panels. They'd plowed through one of the villages and dipped through many of the pit mines. In the center of it all they'd formed not a circle but a square, perfectly spaced around the rim of a pit mine that was easily a half kilometer deep and wide, like an inverted pyramid.

Resting in the center of this pit was no mere crashed shell ship. What Skyler saw defied belief.

The structure filled the bottom half of the pit, making it hundreds of meters on a side. It matched the shape of the pit mine almost perfectly, rising up from the bottom in terraced levels. A pyramid within the inverted one of the pit itself. The surface of the structure looked like every other Builder construct Skyler had seen—a graphite-black coloration that seemed to soak up light rather than reflect it back, laced with patterned grooves of varying size and geometric properties.

Dotted across the structure's "rooftops" were deep, square-shaped depressions. When the Magpie flew above the structure Skyler tilted her, then strained against his seat harness to take in the scene directly below.

The holes in the surface of the building descended hundreds

of meters in some cases and glowed at the bottom in a bright yellow exactly like the towers that now ringed the crater. Without warning the Magpie lurched upward, hitting a pocket of warmer air directly above the facility. Ana yelped at the sudden jolt.

"Oy, mate!" Russell shouted from the back. "A little warning next time?"

"Shut the fuck up, Blackfield." Skyler reminded himself to turn off the man's suit speaker unless he actually wanted to hear him.

At the corners on the base of the structure, Skyler glimpsed what appeared to be openings that led inside.

Crowded around these were subhumans by the dozen. Milling about, as if patiently awaiting his arrival.

The loss of altitude finally forced him to look away from the insane building and focus on landing the aircraft with minimal noise. The landscape ahead was more of the same. He figured the solar panels would make a hell of a landing surface, and the mining towns were too visible. A pit mine would be perfect, though. Flat bottom, and below the horizon line to any of those subhumans milling about.

"What was that place?" Ana whispered.

"I don't know." He looked at her, and saw raw fear in her eyes for perhaps the first time. "Let's worry about landing for now."

"Okay," she said. She exhaled through her mouth and shivered slightly, banishing the gigantic building from her thoughts. "Do you have a plan? We're dropping fast."

"Look for one of the larger pits, preferably one we can make without spinning up the engines."

Ana leaned forward and studied the landscape on her side of the aircraft. "There," she said. "Two o'clock."

Skyler trusted her judgment and banked in that direction. The pit that came into view was perfect. Perhaps a hundred meters on a side, and only fifty deep, with a wide and flat bottom. Some machinery dotted the basin, but it was all off to one side. Skyler circled the location three times, bleeding out the last of their altitude. The Magpie was dropping like a stone now, and he sensed more than saw Ana grip the arms of her seat as they neared the ground.

At the last instant Skyler rammed the accelerator to full

throttle position, all engines aimed straight down for maximum hovering. His guts felt like they were going to be yanked right out of him as the aircraft went from falling to hovering in less than two seconds. He groaned from the g-forces tugging at him but maintained focus and heaved the accelerator back to almost zero as quickly as he'd ramped it up. The Magpie dropped the last few meters. Skyler gave one more short burst of half-power thrust to cushion the landing itself, then killed the engines entirely. The high-pitched electric whine died immediately, followed by the slower rush of air from the ducted-fan thrusters.

He felt a small rush of pride at the landing, and glanced at Ana with a grin on his face. She was staring straight ahead, breathing hard.

"Goddamn," she said between gasps. "You're crazy."

"I'll second that!" Russell shouted from the back.

He ignored them both. "Gear up. Desert camo. We need to make sure none of those subs follow us here."

"And after that?"

"What do you mean?"

She grimaced at his lack of understanding. "How the hell are we going to get into that place, Skyler? It's crawling with them."

"Offer Blackfield as a sacrifice?"

Ana frowned and fixed a glare on him.

"I don't know," he said honestly. "But I suspect it's going to involve guns."

In the passenger cabin Skyler walked straight to Russell Blackfield and turned off his external suit speaker.

Russell looked confused at first, and then his lips moved. When the suit, which piped in external sounds, did not reflect the man's voice, he began to shout. Realization that the effort would be fruitless came quickly, however, and after a few obvious expletives Russell sank back into his chair and stared at the seat in front of him.

"You're in luck," Skyler said to him. "We found the towers. That means we can scrub our air, and you'll get to live another day."

The defeated man mocked gratitude with clasped hands

and batting eyelids, like a bad actress in one of those sensory melodramas.

Skyler grinned and moved to where the gear was stowed. Ana joined him, and while she found and laid out their desert camouflage, Skyler prepped the weapons. He worked quickly, removing two pistols and a pair of silencers they'd found inside one of the APCs left behind by Gabriel. Skyler would have preferred something with more stopping power, but the noise of gunshots from their assault rifles would draw far too much attention.

The arsenal prepared, he stood between Russell and Ana to let her don the appropriate fatigues without unwanted attention, then she did the same for him.

Skyler checked Russell's bindings one last time, then nodded to Ana and went for the door. He stopped when she grabbed his arm.

"You should stay here," she said.

"What? No way."

"Let me scout it first. If you die neither myself nor Russell is getting home anyway, so it doesn't make sense for you to go."

"Ana," he said, "we're *both* going. Sooner or later we're going to have to face whatever dangers await us in that building. A few minutes of safety right now won't make any difference."

Her lips parted slightly, an argument on the cusp of escaping. Whatever she'd been about to say, Ana thought better of it and let go of his arm. "At least let me take point."

Skyler opened the door and motioned for her to go first. She did a mock curtsey and stepped out into the heat.

"Talk among yourselves," Skyler said to Russell, and followed her.

The air outside was dry as paper and scalded his skin.

A ramp wound its way up from the pit's floor to the rim, blocked at the base by a dilapidated rock-hauler truck and two bulldozers. Fine beige sand covered everything, and Skyler was happy to see a complete absence of footprints other than those Ana's boots left.

She moved with the urgency he felt, running to the abandoned vehicles and waiting there for Skyler to join her. When he arrived, he nodded to her and took aim at the crater rim while she raced up the first leg of the ramp. They repeated this pattern until the last leg. The last ramp they took in leapfrog fashion, moving more slowly since they'd have less warning if any subs crested the crater rim.

Finally, Ana reached the point where she could see over the top. She stood on her tiptoes for a few seconds, scanning the horizon in every direction, then motioned for Skyler to join her.

Other than a brisk hot wind that pushed loose sand about like swarming insects, nothing moved. The ground around them was dotted with metal poles roughly three meters high, each of which had a sand-coated solar panel on top. Half-buried electrical wire snaked across the ground, combining into larger trunks in various places and ultimately into metal junction boxes strewn throughout the area.

Skyler looked northwest toward the crater where the alien structure was, easily spotted by the ring of aura towers around it. He put the site at two kilometers distant. From ground level the jet of humid air rising from the place was much more obvious. The invisible plume made the sky near the horizon shimmer in a gradually expanding column.

"What is that?" Ana asked. "Exhaust or something?"

"Maybe it's a reactor." Skyler recalled the young scavenger Nachu's words, about the SUBS virus starting near here, and wondered what, if anything, this place had to do with it. He forced himself to focus on the situation at hand and shifted his gaze to the flat landscape between there and the pit they stood in. A small mining village stood roughly a quarter of the way, a few hundred meters off. Skyler continued to the rim of the crater and lay down at the end of the ramp. He waited until Ana joined him before removing his binoculars. "Keep an eye on the area around us," he said.

"I wish we'd brought the sniper rifle now," she said.

"Too loud. Besides, I don't see anything moving. I think we're safe, at least for the moment."

"We should scout those buildings for supplies," the girl mused.

Skyler set his binoculars down and grinned at her. "There's a good scavenger."

Ana flashed a smile, then blinked as a sudden gust filled the air with a fine powder of sand. "We need goggles," she said.

He grunted agreement. The sand forced him to squint, and blink constantly. Goggles would impede visibility, and for that reason he hated wearing them, but it would be better than this. He began to taste the grit, too, and spat. "I'm suddenly jealous of Russell's suit."

"Not me. Poor thing has a Russell stuck inside it."

Skyler chuckled, got the crude innuendo a second later, and barked a laugh. He clapped a hand over his mouth, but it was too late. The sound echoed slightly off the "ceiling" of solar panels around them.

For ten seconds he remained perfectly still, scanning the forest of raised panels, angry at himself as much as Ana for acting unprofessionally.

"Behind us," she said.

He turned. A lone subhuman, short and scrawny, zigzagged through the rows of metal poles, racing toward their crater. Blinded by rage or just lacking enough intelligence, the creature went straight over the rim of the pit mine and tumbled brutally down the sloped side. It rolled to a halt on the first terraced surface below, opposite Skyler and Ana's position and ten meters lower.

A cloud of dust surrounded it. Not willing to take chances, Skyler took careful aim at the body. The instant he saw it lurch back into motion, he fired twice. The first round sent up a plume of dust from the pit wall behind the body. The second caused the body to convulse once before going still.

For a minute they sat in total silence, waiting for more to come. None did, however. Skyler lowered his gun and let out a breath he hadn't realized he'd been holding.

"Sorry," Ana finally whispered.

"It's all right. Maybe we should save the jokes for later, though."

She nodded like a chastised child, looking much younger than she was for a brief instant before gathering herself and focusing on their surroundings again.

Unbidden, Prumble's voice echoed through Skyler's mind. "You treat them as equals," he'd said so long ago about the old crew, implying Skyler needed to boss them around more instead of treating the arrangement like a club. Sage advice to be sure, but he'd found it impossible to apply with Ana. Treat her like an equal and she thrived, until some invisible line was crossed and she strayed into recklessness. Correct her, sternly or otherwise, and she seemed to withdraw into herself to the point of being only slightly more useful than a deadweight. Point *that* out and the trouble would really begin.

The fact that she'd already returned to scanning the horizon meant something of an improvement, so Skyler decided not to say anything further and see if she'd find that balance that so far had eluded her.

"Let's go scout those buildings," Skyler said, pointing at the cluster of single-story structures that lay between their crater and the one the alien building occupied. "Maybe we can move Blackfield there, and lock the Magpie. I feel uncomfortable leaving it open like this."

"Okay," she said in a gloomy tone. It'd be an hour or two before she was back to trading innuendo, he knew, and said nothing.

Despite the blazing sun above, the darkness under the canopy of solar panels was nearly absolute. On closer inspection Skyler realized the square surfaces were mounted atop their poles on small gimbal motors to keep them pointed at the sun. Even coated with sand, enough sunlight filtered through to the surfaces for the motors to perform their only function: keep the panels fixed on the sun. One in ten didn't work, forever frozen in time, pointing to where the sun had been at the time of death. Otherwise, the sea of squares made a near-perfect ceiling that left a grid of centimeter-wide bright bands of sunlight on the sand below. Only the open patches of the pit mines and housing clusters broke the monotony.

With an unspoken change in the plan, Skyler took the lead now. He jogged through the maze of steel poles with his pistol in front of him in both hands, keeping it sighted at all times. Should any subs approach, he wanted to drop them before they could make a noise.

He stopped behind a junction box ten meters from the edge of the tiny village and rested his hands on top of the green metal container. Ana took a position next to him a second later, aiming around one side.

The place consisted of a dozen structures in all, arranged in a square with some sort of motor pool in the center. All of it baked in the furnace of the sunlight, which glared so intensely off the sand it made everything seem like an overexposed photograph. Skyler waited for his eyes to adjust before studying the scene with any seriousness. He could just make out the wheels and a door of a large rock-hauling truck, every horizontal surface coated in sand, every vertical surface scoured almost down to the bare metal. Some faded writing on the side indicated a Chinese origin. It made sense. There'd been a flood of Chinese, Indian, and European companies seeking to exploit the minerals left exposed by the continued expansion of the Sahara. Proxy wars had been fought in some places over newly discovered pockets of thorium and other rare elements. In other instances, such as here in Chad, the local government had managed to keep their international suitors in line, divvying up the sites in a way that would actually benefit everyone involved. Except the environment, of course. Skyler could smell faint hints of chemicals in the air, and kept eyeing a stack of barrels to the side of the village in front of him, labels of "toxic" and "danger" needing no translation.

"Skyler," Ana said.

"Yeah?"

"There's nothing alive here. Besides the subs, I mean. No insects, no plants."

He'd noted that himself, but only insofar as being relieved to be out of mosquito-ridden Belém. "And?"

She turned away from her vigilant aim. "How are the subs surviving out here? And in such numbers."

Skyler turned toward the plume of humid air rising in the distance. He squinted, hoping some explanation might come to him, a little embarrassed she'd noticed it first. "Good question."

"*Gracias.*"

He smirked, then turned and readied his gun. Together they moved into the sunlight. After the shade of the defunct solar panels, the naked heat of the sun bordered on painful. Skyler felt it on his neck and ears first, then, more gradually, like a weight on his shoulders and legs. He fought the urge to race to the meager patch of shade offered by the nearest building. The baked, sandy ground crunched and cracked under his footfalls, and he felt the heat on the bottoms of his feet then, too. For the span of two steps he imagined what it would have been like to work here, day in, day out, mining these enormous pits. A misery, no doubt, and probably one with shitty pay.

When he reached the rear wall of the nearby structure, Skyler paused only long enough to let Ana catch up. He nodded to her and moved when she nodded back. Silently, they crept around to the front. Other than a single, skeletal body in the driver's seat of the truck, there were no signs of human life. Most of the buildings had been left open, exposed to the wind and sand for years now. Skyler avoided those and jogged around the perimeter to the only one with a closed door. Another shared glance with Ana and he twisted the handle. She went in as the door came open, flicking on her rifle's light as she crossed the threshold. Skyler swept in behind her, standing tall to complement her crouch. He activated his LED, sweeping the beam across the left side of the room while she took the right.

"Oh God," Ana whispered.

"Stay calm, stay calm."

Lines of laundry were strung across the rectangular room. Men's shirts and pants, Skyler noted. After so much time each article of clothing had become brittle and started to fall to pieces, allowing the flashlight beams to stream through thousands of tiny holes. Bunk beds lined the perimeter of the space, three high. Almost every bunk contained a corpse, each still in the relaxed pose of sleep or, perhaps, sedation. Years of dry air and heat had parched the skin down to a horrible leather texture, stretched over the bone beneath.

In the center of the room, next to an overturned meal table, were two dead subhumans, also mummified by the environment.

Ana was breathing hard. Her light began to waver.

"Relax," Skyler said through his teeth. "The disease must have hit in the middle of the night, and those two survived infection only to lack the intelligence to open the bloody door."

"So they turned on each other," she completed.

"They're animals. Never forget that."

The girl shuddered, but the beam of her light steadied. "As much as I dislike Mr. Blackfield," she said, "I don't want to lock him up in here."

"Agreed," Skyler said. He forced himself to ignore the grisly scene and looked instead for anything that could be salvaged. There were plenty of backpacks and small lockboxes tucked under the bottom row of bunks. Personal effects, unlikely to contain anything they needed. Skyler filed the information away and hoped he wouldn't need to come back here. "Let's go."

The exposed buildings were dusty, crumbling affairs, with piles of windblown sand along the edges of their floors. One, which appeared to be a meeting room for whoever ran the place, at least had metal outer walls and heavy furniture inside. The main room had been left open to the elements, but a smaller closet inside was closed, and within it Skyler found a bar for hanging clothing that was bolted into the surrounding structure. The bolts themselves had been painted over. He tested the strength by hanging from the bar with both hands for ten seconds. Then he braced his feet on the back wall and pulled as hard as he could. The bar didn't budge. "This'll do," he said. "Let's go get our prisoner and the rest of the gear, and then we'll go take a look at the Builders' pit."

# 11

## DARWIN, AUSTRALIA

### 30.MAR.2285

The afternoon warmth had just begun to fade when Samantha heard the trucks arrive.

She knelt amid dappled sunlight beside a sack half-full of freshly picked jackfruit that still glistened with clinging raindrops from a brief morning storm.

From below came the rapid-fire sound of doors thudding closed. A dozen or so, she guessed, feeling her stomach twist into a knot. Grillo had brought the cavalry, which could mean nothing good.

An image forced its way into her mind. Seven dead Jacobites, facedown in that dirty road in the Narrows. What else could he be here for?

The idea of running, of sliding down the back of the hangar and loping off through the weeds and into the Maze, came to her first. A glance in that direction dispelled the idea as quickly as it had formed, however. Two outriders on electric motorcycles ambled along the fence line, rolling to a stop once even with the hangar. Their white Jacobite ponchos took on an orange hue that matched the perfect disk of the sun, now kissing the tops of the buildings to the west.

She stood with a groan, pressed one hand to the base of her sore spine, and drew the other across her sweaty brow. Briefly she toyed with the idea of pretending she hadn't heard them, of making Grillo climb up here to speak with her. This idea she also discarded. Every time he'd made a visit to the hangar she'd made it a point to meet him at the door. A change in behavior now might be exactly what he was looking for.

Besides, this could just be another spur-of-the-moment mission. Or perhaps he'd simply learned of her visit to Vaughn and had come to voice his disapproval. She swore under her breath at the thought of once again making him the subject of Grillo's attention. But this, at least, she thought she could argue her way out of. There'd never been any explicit order to stay away from the man.

Decision made, Sam left her spade and hand shovel where they lay and climbed down the ladder. It led to a door that entered into the hangar's second level. Inside, the cavernous room was very dark. A few lights were on near the massive sliding doors where her two constant guards had been watching a sensory. One was frantically trying to turn off the display while the other waited at the door control.

Neither had noticed her entrance, even as her boots hit the catwalk that ringed the interior of the building. It wasn't until she'd marched to the halfway point that one of them glanced up at her, relief visible even from that distance. One of them should have been watching her, and now they would appear to have been doing just that.

A vertical line of light appeared as the huge doors began to roll aside. Soon the shadows of a dozen people, cast long by the late afternoon sun, began to stretch across the concrete floor.

Sam hopped down from the catwalk onto a stack of wooden pallets, then to the floor itself. She gathered herself and forced the knot in her gut to one corner of her mind. Belatedly she realized her clothing bore fresh soil stains. Likely her face did, too. Not that Grillo had ever shown the slightest interest in her or anyone else's appearance. His own flawless presentation often came across as an unspoken demand that others do the same.

*Oh well,* she thought, and hoped her state of cleanliness would imply a casual, innocent state of being. She continued toward the center of the room as Grillo and his men began to file in.

It took every shred of willpower she had to keep walking as the group came into full view. Grillo stood just off center, and standing beside him was a man with a black hood covering his head. His faded gray T-shirt sported a dribble of blood right down the center.

Grillo had to urge the man forward. It became clear the hooded figure's hands were bound, and that he was in pain. Or, at least, the anticipation of pain. He walked with pure apprehension, as if being forced into a furnace.

"What's going on?" she asked. "Who's your friend?"

In answer Grillo stopped and yanked the hood from his captive's head. The black cloth settled to the floor between the two men in a tidy little heap.

"Do you know this person?" Grillo asked, voice level.

*Pascal.*

She should have known from the clothing, the posture. She swallowed, and hoped against hope Grillo had not seen the recognition on her face.

Stalling, Sam tilted her head. Dried blood trailed from both of Pascal's nostrils, giving the pilot the odd appearance of having a red mustache and goatee. Other than the bloodied nose, he seemed to be unharmed.

Sam's mind raced. Had he already talked? Had they interrogated him and learned everything? She knew what kind of violence Grillo was capable of. Pascal, though, she did not know terribly well. They were friendly, but Sam had no idea how far the man would go to protect her, or to hold on to the truth of what had happened on that street. Even if he did harbor the kind of loyalty that required, was he the type of man who could withstand the sort of interrogation Grillo likely employed?

Suddenly his inclusion in their adventure to the Narrows seemed ill-advised. Stupid, in fact.

Maybe no interrogation had yet occurred. Maybe this was about something else entirely. She tried to bury the flood of worries that coursed through her under a façade of calm.

"Well?" Grillo asked.

"Of course. Yeah. He's Pascal, one of the better pilots here on the strip. The blood threw me off. What happened, a brawl down at Woon's?"

"I'm afraid not," Grillo said. He released the pilot's arm and let one of the flanking guards take over the job of holding the prisoner. With calm, fluid motions Grillo removed a white handkerchief from his breast pocket and wiped his hands. He looked at Samantha very deliberately then, not breaking the gaze until her eyes had met his. When they had, he turned, and walked back out through the wide hangar doors.

Sam followed, as she knew he'd expected her to do.

When they were out of earshot of the others, he wheeled on her. "Are you aware of what transpired two days ago in the Narrows?"

There'd been some talk at Woon's. She'd listened like a spy to the conversations and all of it had the ring of rumor. The only common thread was that a Jacobite squad was ambushed. Some said in retaliation for the brutal crackdown on a Han game a few nights earlier. One drunkard claimed more subs had made it inside the aura and that they were only targeting the cult members. This had drawn howls of laughter.

Someone had even speculated that the vaunted, secretive private army of Prumble the Fence had finally reemerged to challenge Grillo. The guards had perked up at that comment, but it died out quickly. Prumble hadn't been seen in two years, and the scavenger crews had all but written him off as dead.

She shrugged. "Nope. What happened? And what does it have to do with Pascal? He's harmless."

His gaze bore into her like a scalpel. Sam met it and held it, barely.

"An entire patrol of guardians are missing."

"Jesus." She covered her mouth. "Sorry, I mean—"

Grillo's eyes narrowed. He worked his jaw for a moment before speaking again. "I'm low on patience today, Samantha."

"I'm just shocked. Again, sorry."

He pointed vaguely toward Pascal. "Your friend borrowed a truck from the gatehouse captain. The vehicle was seen in the area, and it's been in some sort of accident."

"You think he ran them over or something?"

Grillo studied her for a long moment. "What I think is irrelevant. He'll tell us exactly what transpired."

"I'm sure he will." The knot in Sam's stomach twisted with the cold realization that she meant it. She had to leave, she knew. Or silence Pascal somehow. She felt her pulse quicken. "Do you want me to talk to him?"

"You'll forgive me if I decline that offer."

She knew then, with absolute certainty, that Grillo knew more than he was letting on. But whatever he'd learned, it wasn't yet enough to simply walk in and execute her.

Grillo's thin mouth twisted into something approximating a smile. "Protecting your friend here, though understandable, is pointless. We have witnesses, on their way to Lyons now."

She glanced at Pascal, forcing herself to turn her head slowly, as if trying to recall a forgotten conversation. The pilot would not meet her gaze, and this unsettled Samantha more than anything Grillo had said.

"Samantha, I'm giving you one last chance here to tell me what you know."

Footsteps from the direction of the airport gate broke the tension. A boy of ten or eleven years strode up. He worked the cap spooler behind Woon's, and twice a day during lulls he would run requests from outside to the scavenger crews. Sam had given him specific instructions the prior morning. Notes of a certain color, left in a certain place, were to be brought directly and immediately to her.

The boy held out his hand, a folded piece of red paper pinched between thumb and forefinger.

"For me?" Sam asked.

The kid smiled, revealing a jumbled mess of teeth.

She plucked the paper, swallowing with difficulty under the intense stare Grillo had leveled on her.

The note was from Skadz. Not wanting to further risk word of his presence, and more to the point his immunity, reaching Grillo, he'd taken to passing himself off as a desperate swagman. He would approach the airport fence well away from the main gate and push messages for her into the chain link like all the other pathetic requests, using distinctive red paper and a crude code hastily worked out two days earlier.

This exchange occurred four times in the forty-eight hours following their battle in the Narrows. Skadz learned that Jaya's shop had been closed the day after the attack. The move to the basement at Selby Systems had been accelerated in the wake of the attack, apparently. Grillo might not know what happened, but he wasn't taking any chances.

The latest message was simple:

## 2AM COFFEE. SUNDAY BEST.

The words opened a door in her mind. A door that led to a decision.

"Thank you," she said to the kid. "There's jackfruit on the roof. You can take two."

"Three," the kid said.

"We're in the middle of a conversation here, young man," Grillo said. "Return later for your payment."

"Three," the kid repeated.

Grillo started to raise a hand.

"Three," Sam agreed. "But later, okay? After dinner."

The child, oblivious to how close he'd come to a savage backhand, nodded and darted away.

"Is everything all right?" Grillo asked her.

Sam folded the note and slipped it in her pants pocket. "Fine. Just a jilted admirer, trying too hard."

"Perhaps we could return to the matter at hand?"

She smiled at him now, finding confidence in the newfound clarity in her mind. "There's really nothing else to say. Please, though, go easy on Pascal. Good pilots are hard to find."

"That's entirely up to him," Grillo said. He studied her for a moment longer, then wheeled and went back to his truck. The entourage he'd brought followed suit. Pascal did not look at her as they stuffed him into the back of one of the vehicles. Within a minute the small fleet pulled away, scattering crews along the runway as they made their way to the gate.

She left the hangar after dinner, slipping down a ladder at

the back. The rendezvous was still hours away, but she had a lot to do. Forcing herself to look casual, she waved at the guards posted outside and strolled down the runway looking for an aircraft recently returned from the Clear. Only one fit the bill. Sam approached the ragged scow, dubbed *Radar Malfunction,* and walked straight up the cargo ramp like she owned the thing. The captain, a brute of a man with all the character of the run-down ship itself, was mopping the deck, his back to her. His sweat-soaked undershirt clung to a disturbingly hairy torso thick with muscle and rounded by a healthy appetite for cider.

"Cervantes," she said.

He stiffened, but didn't turn. "Jesus. What now? We just got back for fuck's sake."

Sam looked past him. The forward crew compartment appeared to be empty. The door to the head was open a crack, so she doubted anyone was in there.

Cervantes put the mop into a scarred white bucket, oblivious to the dirty water that sloshed back onto the bare metal floor. He wiped his hands on a towel slung casually over his shoulder as he turned to face her. "If you want to borrow Nguyen, she's down at Woon's with everyone else, trying to drink away the stench."

"Stench?"

He glared at her. "You can't smell it?"

Sam sniffed the air. She caught a faint chemical odor, like sulfur.

Cervantes shrugged. "I guess the worst of it aired out, but they were stuck back here with the load for two hours. Even through our suits we could smell it. I don't know what the hell Grillo needs all these chemicals for, but it's nasty work, Sam. It's a miracle no one yacked."

Satisfied they were alone, Sam punched a button on the wall and waited for the hydraulic door to close and seal.

"The hell is this?" the man in front of her said.

"Too many Jakes about," she said, allowing the slang for the sake of talking down to her audience. "I need a favor."

"Shit. Just my luck. What is it?"

"Pretty simple. You go into the head, shut the door, and wait for five minutes."

The squat man scratched at his shaggy beard and turned

slowly toward the bathroom door, then back to her. "The hell are you on about?"

"Trust me, the less you know the better."

"What's in it for me?"

Sam narrowed her eyes. She felt the words of a threat trying to escape and steadied herself. "The choicest missions for an entire week."

"A month."

"Done."

His eyebrows crept upward. Then he turned, walked into the small bathroom, and slid the door closed.

"Turn the fan on," Sam said loud enough to ensure he heard. When the whir of the ventilation fan came on, she knelt and took her backpack off. From inside she produced a nylon duffel bag, spread it out, and opened it. Then she went to the lockers on the sidewalls of the cargo bay and threw the steel doors open wide.

Samantha spent a minute studying her choices. Cervantes and his crew were known for their crude approach to things, a reputation reflected in the equipment they stocked. None of his people were ex-military, and though the etiquette was to avoid asking people about their life before SUBS, Sam had heard interesting things about enough of the crew to know there were criminal pasts there. The pilot Nguyen, in particular, had apparently moved drugs between Darwin and Hanoi under the guise of a private executive flyer. A sour woman, but capable enough that Sam had sequestered her on a few of Grillo's more ambitious actions.

Still, despite the lack of military-grade gear, they packed plenty of firepower. Four minutes later, Sam had her duffel filled with what she hoped would be enough to pull off what Skadz and Prumble had planned.

Finished, she went to the bathroom door and spoke loud enough for the occupant to hear. "I'm leaving now. I'm going to mumble some shit about borrowed tools when I go, and you'll respond 'No problem.' Got that?"

"What are you taking?"

"Again, best if you don't know. Suffice to say, I can't use my own stuff on account of the Jakes."

"My crew is going to be pissed."

"They won't be for the month that follows, believe me."

"Goddammit, Sam. Please don't take any of Nguyen's stuff. She'll flay me alive."

Sam turned and went to the door.

At the bottom of the ramp, Sam stopped on the tarmac and set her bag of borrowed gear down. She inhaled deeply, and a sudden wellspring of memories came sharply to mind. Hundreds of missions flown. Twice as many nights spent on a stool at Woon's trading stories of the Clear with whoever would listen. Stories of success and failure and death. Death dealt, more often than not. Years of her life spent cleaning, prepping, sleeping, and fucking away the time between the dangerous forays out into the wastes beyond Darwin. And all the camaraderie that came with it.

Then the last two years, in charge. Generally hated. Grillo's handpicked girl, dishing out orders to former friends who'd lost almost everything under the Jacobite's rule that made this dangerous, difficult life one worth living.

"Goodbye," Samantha whispered, unsure if she was about to ruin their lives utterly, or make things right.


"Oy," Skadz said. He hefted a small machine gun from the bag and turned it about in his hand. Tiny skull-and-crossbones symbols were etched into the side of the pistol-sized device. The magazine sticking out the bottom of the grip was longer than the gun itself. "What gang did you roll to get this kit?"

Sam glared at him. "Cervantes."

"Ah," Skadz said, the matter settled. "He always did have a flair for this kind of shit."

"I couldn't exactly unload the weapons locker at the hangar."

"Easy, Sammy. It was a smart play. This'll do fine. Besides, if all goes well none of it will get used."

Prumble eyed the selection. "You're sure about this, Sam? Maybe Pascal won't talk. You could be back in bed before dawn if you returned now."

She shook her head. "You weren't there. Grillo knows

something, and he'll find out more tonight if he hasn't already. No, it was time."

"Once they realize you're missing . . ."

"I left a note for Woon, saying I'd decided to follow in Skadz's footsteps and explore the Outback for a while."

The black man slapped a clip of ammunition into his gun. "Brilliant idea. It really clears your mind, if you smoke the right leaves."

Sam tried to smile but found she could not.

"It'll make you look guilty," Prumble noted. "Persona non grata."

"Yeah, but Woon and a few others will say they saw me go, carrying a heavy backpack with all my belongings, headed for Aura's Edge. Even if Grillo thinks I left just to save my skin, he'll still think I left."

"Unless you're seen tonight, or in the days that follow. Maybe you should remain here, Samantha."

From a zippered pocket on her thigh she removed two items. A pair of scissors, and a packet of black hair dye.

"That won't disguise your stature."

"You're one to talk."

Prumble groaned before offering a grudging, defeated nod. Then he returned his focus to the weapons laid out on the table. He hesitated for a few seconds before settling on two simple pistols, the kind people would buy for basic home defense. He stuffed them in his leather duster along with a handful of spare clips. Lastly, the big man grabbed three antique hand grenades. He winked at Sam as these disappeared inside his coat pocket.

Once the two men had made their choices, she removed the sawed-off shotgun she'd picked out for herself and loaded it with slugs. The barrel had an attachment for holding ten extra rounds, which she filled as well. On a whim she grabbed the last two grenades, returning Prumble's wink. She gave one to Skadz and hooked the other on a belt loop before pulling her shirt back over the gear.

"Right," Skadz said when she zipped the duffel bag closed. "Here's what I had in mind . . ."

\* \* \*

Selby Systems Ltd. was a dull gray building four blocks south of Grillo's stadium-turned-airfield. The four-story structure had a manufacturing floor at the bottom and offices above, along with an assortment of chemical storage spheres at the southern end. The metal spheres, which varied in size from just a meter in diameter to almost ten, were all piped into the facility via a spaghetti maze of steel and plastic conduits. Scattered along these pipes were valves and welded junctions, some of which dripped fluid or vented gasses. A razor-wire fence surrounded the entire area.

Lights were on inside the building and throughout the supply apparatus. From the vantage point Skadz had found atop a nearby abandoned office complex, Sam could see Jacobite guards at every entrance. At least two patrols were covering the facility: one that circled the entire perimeter and another that focused solely on the spherical storage units.

Sam frowned. She'd heard from both Skadz and Jayateerth before him that the place was well guarded, but this seemed beyond paranoid. What, she wondered, was Grillo so worried about? A knot formed in her gut when a possible answer arose.

"Do you suppose he's got the object here?" she asked.

Skadz held up a finger. He had a pair of binoculars pressed to his eyes, and his mouth moved in a silent count of seconds passing. "A bit over three minutes for the main patrol to circuit," he said. "What, Sam? No, Kip says the object is in Nightcliff."

"Maybe Kip's wrong."

Skadz shook his head. Sweat gleamed on his dark skin. "I don't think so."

"So why so many guards here?"

"Protecting his assets," Skadz said. "If what we heard is true, he's got a bunch of space stations that have been moved around a lot recently, something they don't normally do. This is the only place in Darwin, which is to say the only place left on the whole damn planet, that makes the fuel they need. If they're not resupplied soon they might never be."

"And now he's got Jaya working here, too," Prumble added. "A lot of eggs in one tidy basket."

Tiny droplets of water began to pepper the roof around them.

Sam felt the warmth as the light rain began to dapple the back of her neck. Far to the north the sky lit up with a scattershot of lightning flashes, a storm just over the horizon. *If only it had been down here,* Sam thought, *we'd have some cover.*

As if he'd heard her, Skadz opened the black briefcase he'd hauled along on their walk through the city. He hadn't said where he'd acquired it, or explained the contents, but when Sam saw the telltale reflection of light off graphene fiber, she knew.

It only took Skadz thirty seconds to assemble the rifle.

"Jake would have liked to have that," Sam said, admiring the high-end weapon. It looked brand-new.

"Not true," Prumble replied. "I offered it to him, but when he declined I found a place to store it until he changed his mind. One of the few little prizes I hid around the city that was still unmolested."

"Jake loved that big old stick he carried," Skadz added with more than a little nostalgia. "I swear you stand that thing on its end and it'd be taller than you, Sammy."

She grunted, realizing the truth in both their words. This gun, though much more modern, was barely half as long. Where Jake's had a scope the size of a wine bottle, this one had a beer-can-sized sight. "I guess it's time to decide who's on sniper duty," she said.

They all looked at one another, hoping someone else would volunteer.

"It should be you, Sammy," Skadz said. "Grillo still thinks you're the tea and biscuits. If one of us gets caught, you don't know us. You can still carry on with this madness."

She shook her head. "I'm a terrible shot. Prumble should do it. He's slow and fat."

Skadz winced.

Prumble threw a hand across his brow. "You wound me. I merely have delicate feet and a family of lemurs living in my coat."

"Well, you two work it out," Skadz said. "As a man of color I'm gifted with stealth and speed, among other advantages."

Sam rolled her eyes, then stared at Prumble until he reluctantly picked up the sniper rifle and snapped the targeting legs into locked position. He began to position it on the edge of the roof.

"Let's go, Sammy," Skadz said.

She clapped Prumble on the shoulder and followed Skadz to the fire escape ladder they'd used to reach the roof. On the street below she took point, keeping to the shadows only when confident no surprises awaited. A quarter-moon near the horizon provided plenty of dark places, but the terrain was unfamiliar and she knew a trip and fall would be just as disastrous as being spotted.

Ten meters from the fence she ducked behind a low planter wall. Weeds choked the narrow basin, providing ample cover. She moved in far enough to let Skadz take the place at the end of the wall, and watched him. He leaned out, his attention split between his wristwatch and the active factory.

Sam could hear sounds of activity from the building clearly now. The rush of chemicals through pipes, the venting of pressure or excess gas. Electricity hummed through the apparatus, flowing up from a mini-thor somewhere below. Skadz had discovered when he scouted the site that the facility had originally relied on public power sources, and when it switched to a thorium reactor the private source had been routed into the same junction. A cheap and effective way to leave the public grid, with one nasty drawback: a single point of failure.

Skadz turned back toward Prumble's vantage point and winked his flashlight twice.

Prumble fired the sniper rifle four seconds later. One single deafening *crack* and the street went dark.

"Go, go," Skadz said.

Sam was already moving, letting adrenaline take over in a familiar addictive mental state she'd craved for so long. She'd felt it the day before on that street in the Narrows, but this was different. This was an assault on a guarded facility, not a sudden street brawl. It wasn't hard to pretend she was somewhere outside Darwin—in Japan, or Israel maybe—pushing in on a choice site crawling with subs, Skyler at her back and Jake watching them from some distant perch. For the first time in months, she felt absolutely in her element, and she reveled in it.

Sam rounded the corner and surged forward toward the fence line. Cries of alarm were already echoing off the flat surface of the factory. Off to her left she saw the power junction box, a lick of flame roiling up from a hole in its side. Flashlights began to play across it. Two or three guards were already there, calling for a fire extinguisher. With any luck, they'd assume the crack of the sniper rifle had actually been a failure of some component within. Though Sam didn't think it would take them long to notice the puncture went inward and not outward, a few seconds was all they needed.

She raced toward the southeast corner of the fence and looked for the stone Skadz had placed there the previous night. *There*. She angled toward it, lowered her shoulder, and burst through the fence in one swift motion. Skadz had cut the chain links in a perfect vertical line, then arranged the two sections of fence so they still appeared to be whole. Someone would have noticed eventually, but for their short-term goals the ploy worked perfectly.

He'd chosen the best possible location for their entry. Two rows of tall, rectangular steel boxes formed a passage of sorts. Sam moved more slowly now, having only the reflected light of the guards' flashlights to illuminate her path. Cables as thick as her arm snaked around on the ground. She didn't make any effort to quiet her footfalls with all the guards running about, but the footing was still treacherous.

At the end of the aisle was a simple maintenance door. Sam gritted her teeth as she approached, hoping to find it unlocked. She'd never find out, because three meters from the door it opened from the inside. Sam pulled up so fast that Skadz plowed into her back. If not for the nearby steel box she used to steady herself, they both would have fallen.

In the darkness it was hard to tell for sure, but she thought the person who emerged from the door was a factory worker, not a guard. She saw no hint of a gun or any weapon for that matter, just an average-sized man. His focus was on the electrical fire, and after only a short pause he rushed out toward it.

Samantha leapt forward and caught the door just before it clicked closed. She yanked it open, letting Skadz hold it so it wouldn't swing shut against her back, and went inside.

When Skadz came in behind her and the door did close, the space went completely black. "Flashlights," she whispered, turning on the one she'd attached to her shotgun with black electrical tape. Skadz held his in one hand, the miniature machine gun in the other.

A long hallway ran north, closed doors in regular intervals along each side. Down at the far end she saw a sudden flare of warm yellow light. A match being lit, then the glow of a candle.

"Stairs," Skadz said. He gestured toward a door to their right. "Jaya said the basement."

The door handle turned when she tried it. Sam pulled it open and cringed as the hinges creaked. She went in and down, two flights to the end of the stairwell and a lone door. This one was locked. "Shit," she said.

"Kick it in," Skadz said. "They'll be on to us any second."

"Can't. It opens this way." There was only one other choice. She leveled her shotgun at the handle and braced herself for the noise about to come. Her finger tensed on the trigger.

Then she let up.

"What—"

Sam placed a finger on Skadz's lips. "Listen," she whispered. "Footsteps."

The shuffling sound of shoes on carpet, and getting louder. She pushed Skadz back a few steps and pressed herself against the wall behind where the door would open.

When it did, Sam grasped it and pushed back slightly, raising her shotgun in the same motion. In the heat of the moment she'd forgotten to turn off her flashlight, a realization that came too late. The person who'd come through the door stopped on the first step of the stairwell and turned around.

Sam was about to fire when she recognized Blink.

"I know you," the girl said, bewildered and half asleep.

"Where's Jaya?" Skadz asked.

"He went home." Her facial tic began to manifest as she became fully awake. Hard, reflexive blinks.

"Good," Skadz said. "Do you know where the special suit is? The big one he's been working on?"

"*I've* been working on. I made it."

Sam smiled at the doe-eyed child and gripped her by the shoulder. "Tell us where it is, honey."

Blink pointed at a door a few meters down the hall, a flicker of fear starting to show on her face. Sam knelt down in front of her. "Do you know where Jaya lives? Where he's staying?"

Her face became stern, as if suspecting a trick. "They gave us some space at the stadium."

"Go to him now," Sam said. "Don't look back, okay?"

The girl stared at Sam until her blink reflex broke the spell. She nodded once, shrugged out of Sam's grip, and took off down the hall like a spooked cat.

In the room she'd pointed out they found the custom-made environment suit laid out on a work table. The outfit was a patchwork of different-colored materials—yellow, red, black. Sam had to stifle a laugh as Skadz loaded the suit into a backpack. Prumble would look like an overweight parody of some lesser comic-book hero when he donned it. She could hear his protests already.

"Let's go," Skadz said, hoisting the backpack's straps over his shoulders.

Sam took point again and retraced their route back to the first floor. Power to the building had yet to be restored, but she heard much more activity above as they climbed the steps. The first-floor hallway was well illuminated now by candles and LED lanterns as people moved about. Their hushed voices and urgent pace meant they now suspected foul play. On the last few steps Sam turned off her own flashlight and readied her gun.

She opened the back door just as a guard was coming through. A skinny man, Pakistani, she thought. His eyes went wide when he saw her. He started to yell something, the sound choking off when she slammed her forehead into his nose. A feeble gargling sound escaped his lips as he fell backward. Samantha immediately surged out into the yard, her focus on the gap in the back fence.

"There!" The cry of alarm had an odd tone. A youth to it, a feminine pitch. Strange enough that Sam glanced right as she ran forward, and there was Blink. The girl was on one knee, her hair caught in the fist of a Jacobite guard. Four, no, five others stood around. The child looked terrified, the guards full of wrath.

Before Sam could react, Skadz fired. His tiny machine

gun hummed, dispensing rounds so fast it sounded like one continuous expenditure. Sparks and tiny explosions of dirt flew from the pipes around the guards. The one holding Blink dropped to his knees, then toppled over to one side. The girl, smartly, lay flat on her stomach and covered her head.

The other guards dispersed. One more had been wounded, but not so bad that he couldn't move. Skadz's gun could rain bullets, but their small caliber had little stopping power. Sam, on the other hand, carried the opposite. She hefted her shotgun and fired at the nearest guard. He'd partially covered himself behind some pipes. Her slug burst the tube in a spray of yellow liquid, then continued on into the chest of the man. He slumped. Sam pumped another round into the firing chamber.

A crack of thunder boomed from down the street, and another guard fell. Prumble, a better shot than he'd let on. Sam grinned as she fired again, missing. Skadz moved behind her and then, on her left now, sprayed the rest of his clip in the general direction of the guards. When the hail ended Blink suddenly got up and sprinted away. *Good,* Sam thought. She didn't want the girl caught in the crossfire.

"It's that pilot!" someone shouted. "The immune!"

*Oh, fuck.* She couldn't place the voice; it sounded farther off. She saw someone running off into the maze of pipes and machinery, fired in that direction, and missed badly. *Fuck, fuck.*

Finally the guards started to shoot back. Sam heard a bullet whiz past her head and dove for the cover of the corridor of metal boxes that led to the fence.

"We're nicked," Skadz said.

"Plan B," Sam replied, hefting a grenade from her vest.

"Oh, bloody hell," he replied. He was up, then, sprinting for the fence.

She pulled the pin and hefted the explosive around the corner. Every ounce of suppressed disgust she'd felt working for Grillo the last two years seemed to flow out her fingers with that toss. Her sense of captivity, the constant guilt she felt when facing her comrades at the airport, her shame for having helped Grillo earn his position of power. All of it melted away as the grenade sailed into the air, unstoppable, a point of no return. She'd be her own woman again. She'd be free of the glorified slumlord and his flock. Free, and hunted relentlessly.

Sam ran.

The grenade exploded.

Something *else* exploded, too.

One of the chemical storage tanks, or one of the pipes. She had no idea. All she knew was she was off her feet, a blinding wash of heat searing her right side as the shock wave threw her into a steel box on the left. Her shoulder took the brunt of the impact. Sam stumbled, used one hand to steady herself and push back up, and then she was running again. Skadz waited at the back fence, holding it open with one hand, the other clamped tightly on a primed grenade.

She dove through the hole in the fence as a third, smaller explosion rocked the supply yard. People were screaming now. There was sporadic gunfire mixed in there, too, but they must have been shooting at shadows because no bullets fell near her as she rolled on the asphalt beyond the fence and came up.

Skadz's grenade exploded between the back door of the building and the aisle of metal boxes. Sam shielded her eyes and felt the punch of the explosion in her rib cage, then she raised her shotgun and unloaded the remaining rounds she had in the chamber.

"Go!" she shouted to Skadz, and he did. He raced past her into the darkness. Sam threw the spent shotgun to the ground and drew her backup pistol. Movement caught her eye, on the street outside the fence. Jacobite guards, a patrol maybe, running around the side of the building toward her. She ran perpendicular to their path and kept going when she cleared the edge of the fence. Pistol raised, she pulled the trigger as she ran across the street, firing for effect as her gaze fell squarely on a dark alley. They were shooting back, bullets peppering the side of the building that formed one side of the alley's mouth. Something tugged at her leg but no pain came with it. She barreled into the alley's mouth running full speed, hoping in the total darkness that nothing would trip her.

Light filled the space, sudden and bright as the sun itself. She heard the explosion—no, explosions—a split second later like a rapid drumbeat. More chemical tanks going up. Or maybe Prumble's three grenades. All of it at once? Even around the corner and five meters into the alley, she felt the heat of it on her back. *The whole damn place must have gone up,* she thought.

Every instinct she had told her to keep running, but she stopped anyway and dropped to a knee. A fire consumed the Selby Systems building, providing enough light for her to reload her pistol and check her leg. The bullet had passed through the back of her pant leg. In one side, out the other, without so much as touching her skin. Sam realized she'd been holding her breath and exhaled. Her hands began to shake, the impact of everything that had just happened collapsing on her all at once. She sucked in a breath as if trying to pull courage from the very air itself.

"Run, Sam. Fucking run," she muttered through clenched teeth. She'd taken an alley at random and had no idea where she was. Skadz and Prumble were fuck-knows-where. Through sheer force of will she rose to her feet again and moved farther down the alley.

It was a dead end. A block concrete wall with a happy face spray-painted on it. She looked at the single-story buildings to the left and right, hoping for a ladder and finding none.

"There!" someone shouted from the mouth of the alley.

Sam reacted instantly. She ran the last few steps toward the wall, threw her pistol over the top, and then jumped. Her fingertips just managed to gain purchase, and she grunted with effort as she pulled herself up and over, not even looking at the ground on the other side as bullets began to slap against the concrete where she'd just been. Her feet hit something soft. A pile of dirt had accumulated against the wall on the other side. She hit it and toppled forward into a lame attempt at a roll. The soft mound had cushioned the fall, but it had also swallowed her gun like a rock thrown in a pond. She took one step back toward the pile, struggling to see now with a wall between her and the light of the fire.

Voices came from the alley she'd fled. Sam gave up on the gun and ran into the night.

Into the Maze.

# 12

## THE FLATIRONS, COLORADO

### 30.MAR.2285

The cave entrance had a rough oval shape, ten meters wide and twenty tall with plenty of irregular indents and outcroppings to imply a natural origin. Tania didn't entirely believe that, but at the very least she figured portions of this pocket in the mountain had existed for millions of years, and the rest formed when the shell ship arrived.

Runoff water dribbled down from the cave mouth in a series of tiny frigid waterfalls, splashing against a pile of gray rubble that had accumulated around the base of the entrance. Spiderwebs ringed the ragged opening and flapped in a gentle breeze that shifted in and out as if the mountain itself breathed. A sudden rush of sound made Tania's heart lurch. Tiny black birds scattered from the cave, rushing around her head so close she felt the air displaced by their fluttering wings. She glanced left and right, somewhat embarrassed at being startled, hoping that either Vanessa or Pablo had felt the same way. Both the immunes wore hard expressions, though, and held their weapons halfway raised with a finger on the trigger. The sight of this reminded her of all the training she'd undergone, and the fact that she was, for better or worse, the leader of this expedition. She forced the nervous grin from her face and turned back to the cave mouth.

Sensing her desire to proceed, Pablo took point and stepped into the darkness. The pile of rubble that led down to the cavern floor was slick with runoff water and loosely piled. Each treacherous step he took created a small avalanche of rocks and pebbles that made so much noise she doubted any creature within the cave remained unaware of their presence. Despite that, he couldn't bring himself to abandon a slow and quiet approach. Tania followed, stepping where he had to minimize further noise. By the time she reached the bottom, Pablo had moved off a few meters and busied himself sweeping his flashlight across the cave's interior.

Instead of joining him, Tania moved to a position roughly opposite his and studied the dark cavern with her own beam while Vanessa trudged down the steep gravel mound.

Though no expert, Tania decided the bulk of the cavern was indeed natural, a vaguely spherical pocket within the mountain that had probably never been discovered or explored before now. The shell ship, assuming that was what had landed here, had punctured the face of the majestic Flatiron mountainside and then continued inward. A similar-sized hole exited out the back of the pear-shaped space into a tunnel that went back and down fifteen meters before curving out of sight. The walls of the tunnel were decidedly different from the walls of the cavern— smoother, rounder. There were no other exits Tania could see, although some of the crevices in the ceiling and floor looked deep enough to possibly be natural ways in or out. There must be some way out, as water had not pooled on the floor. She wished she'd studied more geology, but she knew enough to recall that most cave systems were carved by the flow of water over countless millennia. Other than the water dribbling in the entrance, she saw no signs of running liquid inside. No stalactites or stalagmites, no smoothed surfaces. Perhaps, she thought, there'd simply been a pocket of rock here more brittle than the surrounding material, and the shell ship had somehow targeted it, knowing it could crash through and burrow within.

*Worry about it later,* she told herself. "Only one way to go," she said, careful to keep her voice just above the sound of the trickling water. "Pablo, take point?"

He nodded and began to move, setting the pace at a patrol-like walk. His flashlight was attached to the barrel of his rifle, which meant whatever he illuminated was also where he aimed, so Tania made an effort to keep her own focus elsewhere, complementary to his. Vanessa, again bringing up the rear, added no light to the effort. Tania glanced quickly back to see why, and saw that the woman was keeping her focus entirely on the way they'd come. In that moment Tania felt a sudden sense of oneness with her "crew." They were working together instinctively and it felt good.

The tunnel curved left and downward, a slow, graceful curve as if the solid mountain rock had been nothing more than moist soil. She tried to picture the shell ship burrowing through here like a worm. Other than a light dusting of rocks and gravel on the tunnel floor, there was no real evidence of its passage save for a somewhat regular pattern to the shape of the rock walls around them. The surface resembled churned water frozen instantly, and when Tania allowed her eyes to defocus slightly in order to take in the entire space, she thought she could detect a slight corkscrew pattern on top of the vague waves.

Heat and humidity began to climb, the farther inside they went. At first she welcomed it after the thin mountain air outside. But twenty paces in she found her breaths coming in conscious draws, and an uncomfortable sheen of sweat began to make her formfitting suit itch anywhere it was slightly loose.

Ahead of her Pablo came to a stop. He didn't look alarmed, but something had given him pause. Tania pressed forward until she saw it, too. A fork in the tunnel.

"I didn't expect this," Pablo said when she came even with him.

She managed a nod, leaning against the wall so she could catch her breath. The first dull pain of a headache began to build behind her eyes. The elevation, she told herself, and then the rapid shift from cold to hot. It was too much. "Ugh," she muttered.

Vanessa's hand was on her arm. Light, then a fierce grip. Tania felt herself falling, being pulled backward, dragged by both arms. "What's happening?" she asked. She thought she asked, for her own voice sounded distant. The floor of the cave scraped against her suit's air pack. *Don't damage that,* she thought dizzily, *I might need it.*

Her headache subsided as quickly as it had come on. Her breathing, too, seemed easier. Pablo and Vanessa were leaning over her. "What happened?" she asked.

"Sorry, it's my fault," Pablo said. "I didn't think . . ."

"We walked beyond the aura," Vanessa said. "Are you okay?"

"I'm infected?"

Vanessa nodded. A shiver flickered across Tania's entire body; panic welled in her gut like water rushing from a broken pipe, filling her from the center. *The aura. How easy to forget.* Her hands shook despite every effort to still them. She'd been stupid, in a situation where it could mean her life. *Focus, dammit.*

"Keep calm," Pablo said. He looked at Vanessa. "Take her back?"

"Good idea—"

"I'm fine," Tania said. "Just . . . give me a minute."

She concentrated on her breathing and did her best to ignore the dull pain in her skull. A sense of grief began to rise in her with the realization that she'd have this for the rest of her life. Just like Karl, SUBS was in her now, held in stasis by the aura but by no means cured. She'd have to take pills every day for the headaches, pills that weren't easy to find. There might not even be any on the *Helios.*

Tania groped through her mind for the last time she'd been truly calm, and a scent came to her. Chai. With it, inexorably linked, came Tim's face. His twinkling eyes and goofy smile, his *calm.*

"I'm okay," she said. "It's manageable."

"You'll have to stay here," Pablo said.

"No," Tania replied, sitting up. "I just need to put the helmet on and reseal my suit. Go back to breathing scrubbed air."

"I mean," Pablo said, "we'd understand."

Vanessa helped her to a stand. "He's right, we can scout the tunnel system."

Tania waved them both off. She slipped the helmet off her belt loop and pulled it back over her head. The seal back in place, she waited for the HUD to indicate the breather met operating parameters and flipped on the external speaker. "Really, I'm okay. I got careless there and started thinking I was one of you, I suppose."

Her crew mates exchanged a glance. Whatever silent exchange passed between them, apparently it came out in her favor because Pablo resumed his lead and Vanessa motioned for her to follow him.

At the fork in the tunnel he went left. Soon, though, the passage narrowed until it became clear it would taper down to an end. Pablo backtracked and tried the right passage. Tania followed, the dull ache behind her eyes no worse than a fading hangover now. As long as she had other things to occupy her mind the pain was barely noticeable. And yet, despite it being manageable, she could feel the apprehension in her step that hadn't been there before. The brush with infection somehow focused every possible hazard like a laser beam that slowly burned away her resolve. Here she was, thousands of kilometers from the safety of Camp Exodus and the Elevator, in an unexplored cave deep below a wilderness, a thin suit standing between her and the worst plague in human history. Violent creatures, fueled by that virus, could lurk around any corner. They could even be armored, transformed into efficient killing machines instead of just primal subhumans.

The gun in her hands suddenly seemed a pathetic joke in comparison.

"Hold on," Tania said, stopping.

Pablo spun in an instant, the beam from his light almost blinding her before he corrected the aim. "Problem?"

"I just," she paused. "I just need to make some tweaks to the suit's configuration." A lie, but better than telling them she'd suddenly become terrified. She pretended to study the HUD for a moment, while internally she forced herself to do what had worked just minutes ago: summon Tim's face. He was like a rock that represented her normal life. A life of science, logistics, and the occasional political row. Up in space, with him and Zane and everyone else, she never felt like she was pretending. She'd trained to be there just like she'd trained to be here, but she knew now that this was merely a role she had to fill. It wasn't what she was meant for.

But she had trained. She could do this. She would.

Tania might be isolated from the environment in a suit, but she could turn that into an advantage the others didn't have. Belatedly she remembered her suit had position tracking sensors. They logged her movements automatically, and with a few tweaks could be made to display a 3-D map of her route. Not very useful in space save for post-mission review, but here it could mean not getting lost. She felt mildly ashamed that she hadn't turned it on earlier, but they'd only made one right turn so far. That should be easy enough to remember.

On the HUD she also saw an option to adjust the suit's audio. She selected it, then ramped up the gain on the external microphone to nearly maximum. "Keep very still," she said.

Her companions stopped fidgeting.

Somewhere ahead, below, came the sound of what could only be a power source. Constant and deep.

"We're going the right way," she said flatly. "I'm tracking our path now, so we can find our way back out. Keep moving."

The tunnel went on and on. Pablo always kept to the right unless a splinter tunnel in that direction ended.

Compared to the hot humid air within the tunnel, Tania found the processed, computer-controlled air of her suit's breather unit a marked improvement. Each step beyond the aura came more easily than the last, and after nearly thirty minutes of walking she finally felt comfortable again. The winding, forking tunnel had led them almost two kilometers from where she'd begun tracking. The path followed no pattern she could discern, but it had an organic feel to it as opposed to just a random collection of curves and branches. She began to suspect the path followed some route through, or around, a particular composition of rock within the mountain, like a mine that followed a vein of gold.

She heard the scraping sound before the others.

"Pablo," she whispered. Then, realizing her mic hadn't picked up the word, she said his name again, albeit with a low volume setting.

The immune dropped to one knee immediately. His light illuminated a curve in the tunnel ahead, silhouetting him. He glanced back at her.

Tania moved up next to him and lowered her volume to the minimum. "My suit is picking up something ahead. Sounds. It could just be a bat or something."

He nodded. For the first time she noted signs of fatigue on his face. Sweat drenched his skin and clothing. Noticing her concern, he took a sip of water from his water bottle and offered a reassuring smile. Then he put a finger to his lips and continued deeper into the cave.

At a sharp turn in the tunnel Pablo stopped cold. Tania crept up to join him, crouching and aiming her weapon only after she'd leaned out past him.

Ahead, a subhuman stood next to the rugged cave wall. Man or woman Tania couldn't tell. It had long hair that hung in matted, filthy strands. Its body was barely more than skin and bone. Naked and filthy, the figure reminded Tania of horrifying photographs she'd seen from the Holocaust. It stood with shoulders slumped and head down. Despite being illuminated by Pablo's light, it did not turn to face them. Instead it walked into the cave wall, bumped into it forehead-first, stumbled back a step, and then repeated the process. Again, and again.

"What's wrong with it?" Vanessa asked, moving into position next to Tania.

Pablo shrugged. "What isn't wrong with it?"

"It looks half dead already," Tania noted. "Maybe it's blind. Or exhausted, mentally and physically."

Vanessa shifted so she could keep her guard up on the tunnel behind. "What do we do?"

"We kill it," Pablo said.

His tone left no room for debate. Tania wanted to suggest they try to walk past it, but she knew the danger was too great. Once it noticed them, if it had the strength left it would try to attack. "It'll make a lot of noise, shooting it."

"No point in wasting a bullet," Pablo said. Then, "You might want to back up." He stood and slipped his rifle over his shoulder. Face hard with grim determination, he stepped out from the corner and closed the gap between himself and the creature in three quick steps.

Tania couldn't bring herself to look away. She watched Pablo step in behind the creature. In one swift motion he gripped it by the right shoulder, reached around its head with his left hand, and at once pushed and twisted. The body counterclockwise, the head clockwise. There was a sharp crack, then the subhuman went limp. Pablo held on, keeping it upright, as if the thing weighed no more than a backpack of clothing. He eased the lifeless body to the ground and laid it on its side.

Tania swallowed hard, willing away the lump that had formed in her throat. Try as she might, she simply couldn't let herself see the beings as anything other than human. When she caught a glimpse of Pablo's face, what she saw surprised her. Grief, anger. He felt the same way she did; he'd just somehow figured out a way to bottle it. It was there, though, in his narrowed eyes, the thin line of his lips.

Pablo came back to them, pulled the rifle back down from his shoulder, and looked at each of them in turn. "Not much farther now."

"How do you know?" Tania asked.

"That thing was trying to get to the end, too. It was drawn here, and it knew it was close or it would have lain down and died already."

His voice held a certainty that invited no argument. "I hope you're right," Tania said.

They looked at her.

"If they were drawn into this maze, few must have made it to the end. Perhaps none have and we won't find any like those transformed by the ship near Belém."

They both continued to stare at her, as if waiting for the punch line.

"A girl can hope," Tania offered.

Pablo grunted. "Only one way to find out."

# 13

## SOUTHERN CHAD

### 30.MAR.2285

Skyler placed his finger on the switch that controlled Russell's external speaker, and held it there. "You're going to want to stay very quiet," he said in an even voice. "Understood?"

Russell nodded once. He looked pale, and not from fear of the surroundings. No, Skyler suspected the man was growing hungry and probably really did need to relieve himself. He carried himself differently than before. Slumped forward, shoulders turned in, head tilted down.

"We're going to move you," Skyler said, finger still resting on the speaker's switch. "There's a village, a few hundred meters. Can you walk it?"

Blackfield thought about it for a second, then nodded. A single shift of his head, as if it was all the energy he had. He seemed a shadow of the man who'd once confronted Skyler on the landing pad in Nightcliff, but then again he'd been a prisoner aboard Melville Station for weeks leading up to this. Besides, Skyler reminded himself, he'd lost everything before that.

Skyler flipped the switch. "Once we secure the aura towers, we'll move you in range so you can eat something and take care of any personal business."

"Let's hurry, then," he said. "Enough talk."

"Fine with me."

Ana took care of guiding Russell so that Skyler could carry the gear. He filled two duffel bags with what seemed like an obscene amount of weaponry and ammunition. Two assault rifles with several extra clips. A sniper rifle, as Ana had suggested. And a mortar tube with two explosive rounds. Skyler had almost forgotten about that last device. They'd found it a long time ago but never had a situation in which to use it. Placing it in the bag now, the beginnings of a plan began to form in his mind.

Outside, Ana guided Russell by the elbow. He moved like a kid walking to school on the day of a test. His feet scuffed the dirt; his head remained down. But he cooperated, and that was all Skyler cared about.

The weight of the duffel bags had Skyler's shoulders burning by the time they reached the village. He dropped them in a room adjacent to the one where Ana took Russell. Rubbing his neck, Skyler left the arsenal on the floor and went to help her secure the man.

His assistance wasn't needed. When Skyler entered the meeting room, Ana had already attached the cuffs to Russell's wrists and looped them over the metal bar in the closet. Blackfield sat on the floor, back against the wall, eyes closed.

"He asleep?" Skyler asked.

Ana shook her head and led Skyler from the room. "I think he's sick or something."

"SUBS?"

She shook her head. "The suit shows green. But maybe he caught something in Belém. It's not like SUBS is the only ailment around, and there're so many insects there."

Skyler glanced at Russell with new interest. He crossed to him and gave his shoulder a gentle shove. "Hey. You awake?"

Russell mumbled something inaudible and turned away, slumping against the back wall of the closet.

"Exhausted is my guess," Skyler said.

Ana wrinkled her nose. "Maybe. Suppose he doesn't survive to Darwin?"

Skyler shrugged, leading her from the room to where he'd left their weapons. "I don't much care. He might not even be able to help us if he does make it, and I'd rather not be towing him around with us when we arrive."

"How can you say that? He's a human being. He's in our care—"

Skyler placed a hand on her cheek and forced her to look into his eyes. "Would you say that if he was Gabriel?"

Her mouth clicked shut. A few seconds later she shook her head.

"See him as Gabriel," Skyler added, "and you'll see him as I do. At the first hint he can't help us accomplish our goal, his life is over. I don't have the patience for anything else."

The words tumbled out with more vitriol than he'd intended. She searched his face for something, found it, and said, "All right. All right."

He gave her a quick half smile and turned his focus to what waited for them outside.


They found the first corpse just a hundred meters outside the village.

"A scientist," Skyler noted. "Or a doctor."

The half-buried body was clad in a long white coat, and looked as if it had fallen shortly after infection, as most did. A black patch on the breast pocket of the garment had Chinese lettering.

Thirty meters farther toward the circle of aura towers they passed an abandoned troop carrier, the doors still open. Nearby lay a cluster of bodies. Soldiers, save one who looked like a civilian. A miner, perhaps. There'd been a struggle, evidenced by the way the bodies had fallen. The civilian had rushed them, Skyler thought, and been shot. Yet still the soldiers had all died. A picture of what had happened here began to crystallize in Skyler's mind.

"I think Nachu was right," he said.

Ana looked up from the grisly, if faded, scene. "In what way?"

"The disease started here." He glanced back toward where the scientist lay. "They came to investigate that giant building, or ship. Whatever it is. I'm guessing they tried to keep it secret. Then the infections began, spreading faster than news of the virus."

"Why keep it secret?"

Skyler shrugged. "A giant alien vessel thing in the middle of your vast mining operation? They would have had soldiers, technicians, all that here already. But they would have also had businesspeople. People who'd seen how Platz capitalized on the Darwin Elevator. Is it so hard to imagine they'd want to keep it to themselves?"

Ana looked at the scene with the new perspective, and visibly shuddered.

"They probably cut communications first," Skyler said. "Maybe even rounded up the miners and forced them into the barracks."

"Those bunks we saw, all full."

"Yes. Exactly."

Ana let out a long sigh. "Sometimes I think we deserve what happened. Our species, I mean."

"Maybe." He thought back to what Tania had told him about Neil and what he'd known. He'd pondered it many times since then, imagined what would have happened if Neil had given the world some kind of warning. Would things have been any better? Or would the panic that spread like a bow shock in front of the disease have just started earlier? Perhaps Neil, armed with whatever knowledge he actually possessed, had done the right thing. Despite that possibility, Skyler knew the man's reputation and found it hard to believe that he hadn't kept the knowledge to himself for personal gain. He looked at Ana. "Greed played a factor, along with all our other legion of faults, but the way this disease spread . . . I don't think any improvement in us would have made much difference. It's not like anyone knew Darwin was safe at that point, and even if that realization had come out earlier, the city would have been worse off if more people had made it there. You didn't see it in those early days, Ana. I did."

"What was it like?"

"Another time," Skyler said. "It's not an easy story to tell, and this isn't the best time. We have a rendezvous to make, remember? The important thing right now is that we find what we came for."

She tried to hide a frown, and failed.

"On the flight to Darwin I'll tell you the whole, sordid tale. Okay?"

Despite all the dangers that surrounded them, Ana moved up next to Skyler and rested her head against his shoulder. He felt her arm slip around his waist, as natural as if they were on a beach stroll. When she spoke, her voice was tender. "Okay."

He tilted his head and inhaled the scent of her brown hair, somehow sweet despite the acrid odor of exposed minerals that clung to this place. "Good. Now, let's focus, hmm?"

"Yes." All signs of the frown had vanished.

Skyler took point again. The most direct path to Builders' Crater, as he'd come to call the depression where the giant structure waited, required traversal of a narrow strip between two identical pit mines. The sides were steep, the bridge of land between no more than four meters wide at the top. Even this tiny bit of land had a row of solar panel installations running right down the center. Skyler tried to imagine a team of workers placing the equipment in such a perilous place, until it occurred to him that they'd probably been there before the pits.

The bridgelike strip of packed sand ran a hundred meters in a straight line toward their destination. Beyond, with most of a kilometer still to go, more pits of varying sizes waited, lined by the surreal rows of solar panels. The sun lay low in the sky now, and the panels that still functioned were tilted steeply to drink in every last photon.

A pushcart lay in their path, just before that first long bridge, its handles and wheels half buried in accumulated sand. Skyler moved next to it and hunkered down.

Ana slipped in next to him, peering around the side opposite his. "Why are you stopping?"

"Notice anything different here?" he asked, jerking his head behind them and up.

She looked back for a moment, then shrugged her shoulders. "There's almost no sand on the solar panels now."

Her gaze went to the objects and her brow furrowed. "Why not?"

"Good question. It's not why I stopped, though. There's not much cover on these ridges, and it's almost dark. So let's wait a bit. Maybe you should switch to the sniper rifle now."

As Ana worked on changing her gear, Skyler continued to study the landscape around them. The longer he looked, it seemed, the more bodies he spotted. The more abandoned vehicles and equipment. The majority had Chinese lettering, but there were some in French and Russian, too.

Most, he noted, were pointed toward Builders' Crater, lured in like ants to bait. They must have been racing to be the first to claim the alien object for their company or nation. Perhaps some were motivated for personal reasons. The first person to set foot inside a Builder . . .

*A Builder what?*

Skyler still couldn't quite come to grips with the structure he'd seen from above. Was it a reactor? Or some kind of temple, purely without function?

Movement caught his eye. Above the horizon, stretching in a golden line from west to east, was a cloud. A cloud of sand.

"Ready," Ana said.

"Change of plan," he replied. "Look at that."

Ana gasped when she glanced where he pointed. The coming sandstorm bore down on them from the vast Sahara like a tidal wave, and visibly grew larger and closer with each second.

"Forget the rifle," Skyler said. "Visibility will be—"

The ground beneath them rumbled, cutting off his words. It started small, as if caused by the approaching sandstorm itself. But as the vibration grew Skyler knew it was something mechanical, something below the ground. The shaking grew with linear perfection, as if punctuating his theory. Sand began to shower down from above, shaken loose from the vast grid of solar panels. *There's one mystery solved*, Skyler had time to think.

At that instant, the structure inside Builders' Crater erupted.

A dark gray plume of gritty smoke shot upward from the pit like the initial belch from a long-dormant volcano. A single, enormous roiling ball of ejecta propelled high into the sky, stretching out as it went into one long smear. With its release the ground stopped shaking.

Skyler watched, mesmerized, as the dark cloud rocketed upward, slowed, and expanded. Then, as if pushed by some invisible hand, it started to stretch to the south. Propelled by the invisible bow shock of the sandstorm, he realized. He'd forgotten about that, and the wave of oncoming sand was almost upon them.

"Goggles," he growled. "Bandannas."

He tied a bandanna around his mouth and nose first, then fumbled for his goggles. A new sound began to grow, like a thousand rusty-hinged doors opening in sequence. The solar panels, caught up in the rush of wind and sand, were being spun away from the sunset. Skyler urged Ana to move to the south side of the tiny pushcart they'd hidden behind, and followed her, hunching over her as he had when the snow had fallen from the dome in Ireland.

The sound of it hit them first. In full force the noise bordered on deafening. The line of solar cells along the ridge flipped from west to south in almost perfect unison as the cloud of grit and sand rushed over them. Skyler felt his clothing tug in the rush. The cart offered meager protection, but there was nothing else, and anyway it was too late. He felt dry particles whip into his ears, his hair, and down his open shirt. All Skyler could do was press himself farther toward the ground, poor Ana below him screaming not from pain but surprise at the sheer ferocity of the maelstrom.

As quickly as it had begun, the storm weakened. Not entirely. No, Skyler still felt the rush of wind in his hair, against his clothing. Sand still spattered against his exposed forehead. But it weakened enough that he thought they could move. Perhaps find better cover, if not actually proceed with their mission.

He chanced opening his eyes and found that the air glowed.

A dim, pervasive yellow light enveloped the area around him. His stomach lurched from the fear that someone, or something, had found them. But as his eyes adjusted he realized what had happened. Mounted under each solar panel was an LED. They must, he thought, come on automatically when the sun sets, probably so the miners could keep working. And work they could have, for the light was bright and everywhere, save for within the pit mines themselves, which now stood out for their darkness rather than the bright spots they'd been under the furnace of the sun. It was like the world had reversed itself.

The lights in turn illuminated the fine sand that filled the air, creating glowing yellow orbs around each pole that held a solar panel aloft. To Skyler's eye it was all bizarrely romantic.

He helped pull Ana to her feet as he rose. "Come on."

"Shouldn't we go back?" Her voice sounded distant under the constant buffeting of wind.

"We can use this to our advantage. Come on, it's not that bad."

The row of poles along the narrow earthen bridge acted as perfect guideposts, and the deep pit mine to their right tempered the gale, sucking the wind down into its depths and then pushing it back up the steep side next to where they walked. Halfway across, Skyler found he didn't even need to hold the poles, so he increased his pace without complaint from Ana.

The landscape became a maze of such bridges, all lined with those glowing yellow orbs that constantly swirled and shifted. Visibility ranged from fifty meters down to just a few, and twice Skyler had to stop when he couldn't see the ground at his feet. The skin on the side of his face felt caked with sand, dry as flour.

As their goal drew closer, Skyler noted more and more evidence of what had occurred here. Scenes of confusion, chaos, and violence marked the landscape. Half-buried bodies of laborers, soldiers, and scientists. A crashed flyer, no pilot inside. Just two dried-out corpses in the back, a man and a woman in business suits. "Fly us out to see the object," Skyler could hear them saying.

One body wore a familiar outfit. A blue jumpsuit, like the kind Tania and so many other Orbitals favored. The corpse, a woman by the fine blond hair, lay faceup. Mummified as she was, Skyler thought he saw a smile there. He grimaced and moved on.

More and more the bodies he passed were subhuman. He'd seen enough over the years to know that they'd been in that state for some time. Hair grown long and wild. Thick shaggy beards on the men. Yellow, uneven fingernails and toenails caked with dirt. These had come here well after the *event,* as if drawn by some latent migratory instinct.

A few wore the clothes they'd been infected in. Skyler even saw one woman in a formal gown. He doubted there were any weddings or fancy dinners happening within a hundred kilometers of this nightmarish place when the disease hit, so she must have come from a long way. A broken high-heel shoe still clung to one filthy foot.

Most were naked, or at most wearing a few tattered remnants.

While the soldiers and scientists were well on their way to being buried under the wind-driven sands, the subhumans spanned a range from there to just a light coat of the yellow powder. Their skin hadn't dried to the point of leather yet. Fresh corpses. Recent arrivals.

Skyler swallowed down the growing lump in his throat. This, he thought, was an evil place.

When the yellow glow of the aura towers finally cut through the swirling sands, Skyler turned back to Ana and pulled her close enough that he could whisper. He tugged the bandanna covering his mouth away and cupped one hand over her ear.

"Visibility sucks," he said. "Might work to our advantage."

"I was thinking the same thing." If she was scared, she hid it well.

Skyler pointed toward the nearest tower. "I'll move up first. Stay just close enough to keep me in sight; keep your gun ready but don't fire unless there's no other choice."

She nodded, pulled down the bandanna that covered her mouth, and kissed him. Her dry lips tasted like the sand. "Be careful."

"You, too."

Skyler turned away from her and crept forward toward the row of alien pillars in front of him. They were spaced about twenty meters apart. The pillar in front of him was one of the taller versions, its tip mostly obscured by the maelstrom of sand. The two to either side were just vague columns of shifting golden pulses.

Near the lip of the mine he began to hear the sounds of activity below. The pit itself looked like a giant inverted pyramid, though he had to mentally fill in the picture of it from what he'd seen during their initial flyby. The sandstorm prevented him from seeing even a quarter of the way to the other side. But he could see all the way down. The artificial crater was largely sheltered from the windblown sands above, and what did make it down into those depths was pushed right back up again by the warm air that vented from the strange alien structure in the basin.

Again the ground shook. A low rumble Skyler felt in his

gut, building to one he felt in his teeth. At the crescendo the sound of it released in a booming *sha-coom* sound. In that instant, the hundreds of sunken cavities on the topside of the building spewed material into the air. The oily black smoke reminded Skyler of the footage he'd seen as a child illustrating the pollutants factories used to release into the atmosphere. The inky puffs quickly merged and rose. Near the top of the pit mine the winds of the sandstorm caught the rising cloud and pulled it into long, arching tendrils. Vortices of black and tan that snaked up into the sky with dizzying speed before melting together.

Skyler had lain down at some point, he couldn't exactly remember when, on the edge of the pit next to a tower that rippled with glowing yellow patterns. Ana lay next to him, a look of terror and amazement on her face that mirrored how he felt. "What is it doing?" she asked.

He shook his head, though in his gut he knew. The kid in Belém, the scavenger, had been exactly right. SUBS had started here, only that wasn't all. It was being perpetuated here. This place, this . . . forge, was pumping the manufactured virus into the atmosphere, letting the swift Saharan winds propel the material into the upper atmosphere, where it could fall like volcanic ash across the planet.

And directly overhead, the massive Builder vessel had parked itself. Fifth in a series of six events, if Neil Platz had accurate information.

*One more to go.*

A crazy thought entered his mind. Like the virus being thrust upon the world from the building below, the thought spread through him like a cloud and wouldn't go away. Somehow, someway, he had to destroy this place. Even if it took months of hauling explosives in, he had to blow it up. If there was even a chance it would end the disease, he had to try.

*Do I? Would it matter?*

He suddenly doubted blowing up the structure would make any difference. The virus replicated just fine on its own. This place probably still functioned because that's what it had been programmed to do.

At that moment the storm subsided. The howl of wind became

a rush, then a whisper. Then sand began to fall from the sky like snow. Thick at first, but even that abated with astonishing speed. Within ten seconds Skyler could see the entire pit as clear as day. The LED lights under the solar panel field were their characteristic white now, forming a gleaming band between the yellow ground and the blood-red remnant of sunset.

Skyler didn't know how long the calm would last. "Now or never," he said to Ana.

There was no hint of confidence or bravery in her face until she looked directly at him. When their eyes met, she seemed to drink his courage in. Courage he hardly felt himself.

With the air clear, Skyler assessed the pit in an instant. The mine had a square footprint, with steep sides that plunged down a half kilometer before becoming obscured by the Builder structure set within.

There were entrances, or what looked like entrances, at the corners. Shifting yellow light came from within, spilling out in bright pools onto the sloped sides of the open mine. Subhumans loitered at each. Some moved in and out as if carrying out tasks, though what they could be doing Skyler had no idea. Others just stood around. Some lay on the ground, unmoving. Dead, or sleeping.

A sloped ramp provided the only way in or out of the pit, just like the one they had landed in. It entered on the side opposite where Skyler and Ana lay and ran in a wide, flat path around the perimeter of the mine. Surprisingly wide, in fact, until Skyler realized the need to haul debris from the pit as it was dug. In evidence of this, on the side to his left about halfway down to the alien structure, a massive rock-hauler truck sat abandoned. Each of its massive tires was as big as a military APC, and the Magpie could have fit in the huge bin that made up the vehicle's bed were it not already piled high with boulders and crumbled earth. The vehicle had been on its way out when it stopped years ago. The side facing inward on the pit was all charred, likely from the violence of the alien structure's landing. Its driver had probably been cooked inside the cab, a mercy considering what followed. The huge tires, caked with sand, had almost melted away. They practically dripped over the precipice of the sloped road, causing the massive truck to list heavily toward the pit's depths.

An idea formed. A crude plan. "Keep an eye out for a minute," he said to Ana as he began to rummage through their gear.

"What are you going to do?"

He grinned at her. "What Jake would do."

Ana raised one eyebrow, confused.

"Sorry," he said. "Haven't told you that story yet, I guess. You're going to cause a diversion. I'm going to capitalize on it."

When he removed the sniper rifle from the gear bag, Ana figured out the plan. She pulled her sunglasses and bandanna off and took the gun, a hint of mischief playing at the corners of her mouth. It took her a few seconds to screw on the bulky silencer. Then she settled into a sniper's lie with practiced ease and pulled the lens cover from the scope. "Which one am I aiming for?"

"None of them, actually," Skyler said, removing the mortar tube from the bag. "Go for that dump truck, somewhere that will make a lot of noise. Get their attention. The side of the bed should get a nice loud bang. It might even rattle around inside."

She studied the decrepit vehicle through the rifle's scope, then flexed her fingers. "One of the rear tires is still inflated. I could pop it."

"Perfect." He unfolded the mortar's two stabilizing legs and locked them into place, turning the launch tube to face roughly in the same direction Ana sighted. Once in rough position, he thumbed wheels on each leg, fine-tuning the setup until the sight's leveling bubble came to rest in the center.

"Tell me when."

Skyler dialed in the primitive sighting system, adjusting the launch angle and hoping his estimates for elevation would be close enough. "Once you shoot, ditch the gun and be ready to move on foot."

"Okay."

"Fire when ready."

She did. A dull *thwick*. Sand on the ground near her barrel hopped into the air as the round flew.

There was no pop of the tire. Instead Skyler heard a crack, like a boulder splitting in half. Exactly like a boulder splitting in half, in fact. Ana cursed. She'd missed, her round slamming into the compressed earth just below the rear tire. Rocks began to slide down the sloped side of the pit mine as she took aim again.

"Wait," Skyler said.

The rock slide grew. With total fascination and more than a little horror, he watched the back of the vehicle dip suddenly. Then the giant machine groaned, an anguished sound louder than any exploded tire could have achieved. The groan of tortured metal grew as the vehicle began to list more and more toward the drop-off. Larger rocks began to tumble loose from beneath its tires. And then, in one violent instant, the whole section of access road collapsed.

The massive truck tilted and rolled into the depths, spilling the contents of its hauling bin in the process. Below, the subhumans closest to it began to spew agitated shouts, unaware of the catastrophe about to befall them.

Skyler all but forgot about the mortar. His hand rested on the trigger as his focus remained utterly transfixed on the tumbling morass of metal and rock that rolled down the side of the pit toward the alien building below. The subhumans there had lost the part of their minds that could evaluate a threat and know when to run. *Get the fuck out of the way!* Skyler's mind screamed. His mouth remained closed.

The dump truck, which Skyler thought must weigh twenty tons even unloaded, actually left the ground and tumbled over in the air when it cleared the last strip of road. It slammed into the crowd of subhumans and then the side of the Builders' structure with a noise as loud as any explosion. A split second later the avalanche of rock, sand, and boulders followed, extending the sound like a thunderclap and throwing up a cloud of haze around the point of impact. A good thing, too, for the toll on the subhumans Skyler knew would be gut-wrenching to look at.

"Oops," Ana said, when the sound died out.

"Indeed."

A new sound grew as those subs not near the point of impact began to swarm, still thinking there was some entity there they could fight. Dozens poured out of the corner entrances to the building and converged on the cloud of debris, disappearing into its murk.

Skyler remembered the mortar then. It took only two seconds to adjust the aim. He almost felt guilty as he dropped the high-explosive round into the tube and pulled his arm quickly back. He'd felt the same thing when he'd fired an RPG into a church tower what seemed like a lifetime ago. There was no pleasure in killing the defenseless. No honor. It was just . . . business.

The launch tube emitted a soft *voomp* sound. A few seconds of strange silence followed before the explosion came.

His aim was uncannily perfect.

A yellow flash right in the center of that dust cloud flung rock and limbs outward in equal quantity. The pressure wave hit Skyler a heartbeat later, a single deep pounding noise that overloaded his eardrums and left them ringing. It was a small explosive as such things went but produced exactly the desired effect. Subhumans poured from all sides of the facility now, tripping over one another to reach the supposed conflagration.

Skyler saw one being stumble out of the fiery cloud only to be mistaken as an intruder and tackled by two of the new arrivals. Others actually tried to pull them apart. He'd never seen behavior like that before.

"Time to go," Skyler said. "Are you ready?"

Ana had been busy while he sat there and stared at the riot below. As instructed she'd set aside the sniper rifle and readied her machine gun. He saw in her eyes a look he knew well by now. First from Samantha, now from this young lady. Bloodlust. "Ready," she stated flatly.

"Stay close," he muttered, picking up his own rifle.

As the last of the subhuman "guards" trickled out of the entrance below their position, Skyler hoisted himself over the rim of the artificial crater and jogged down the steep side in a barely controlled fall. Each step produced a small avalanche of sand and pebbles. Ten meters below he hit the narrow road that spiraled along the mine's walls. He tucked and rolled, came up running, and went over the edge again. This process repeated six times before he cleared the last bit of road. At the bottom of the next piece of sloped wall was the Builder facility, ten meters away now. He'd been angling toward the nearest corner entrance on the way down, but it was still a good twenty meters off to the right.

The small avalanches created by his and Ana's descent reached the building first. Rocks and pebbles clattered harmlessly against the side. The sand just pooled, adding a millimeter to an accumulation that Skyler assumed would be many meters deep by now, if this place had truly been here since SUBS began. He tried to slow himself before hitting the wall, with only a little success. In the end he did the only thing he could: turn his shoulder and wince. He smacked into the side of the building and felt a tingle rush up and down his arm from the elbow.

Ana came to a stop with much more grace, using an outstretched hand to blunt her impact and then twirling so her back hit next, leaving her in a tactically sound position, rifle raised. He felt a mixture of pride and, oddly enough, competition, whenever she did something better than him.

She jerked her head at the elbow he was frantically rubbing the numbness from. He waved off her concern and turned toward the opening. A dirty yellow light spilled out from somewhere inside. He saw no movement but thought he could hear some coming from within.

A few subhumans lay just outside. Dead, or maybe just too weak to move. That worried him until he recalled Ana's observation about the lack of food or water here. They'd come here, called by this place perhaps, or simply drawn to it by some migratory instinct. Smart enough to get here, too far gone to survive. And the building, he thought, didn't care. The Builders didn't care.

He felt heat pulsing off the alien structure, as if it had a heart within. A ripple of fresh fear cascaded down his spine. The rhythm of that pulse reminded him of the chanting subhumans he'd found in the rainforest near Belém. That unsettled him somehow more than the swarm of creatures in the pit with them. Despite the anxiety that now gripped his own heart like a fist, he felt his feet moving toward the opening. He went slow, gun aimed directly ahead. With every step he glanced back at Ana to convince himself she was still with him, still okay. She was, of course. Her face had become the very picture of a warrior. Serious, focused, and deadly. He hoped she couldn't see the fear in his eyes. If she looked she might have, but her gaze was like a searchlight now, sweeping in rapid bursts—behind, above, in front, behind—with her gun matching in perfect synchronicity.

A dancer's perfection.

In his mind's eye he saw her as he first had, twirling in a white dress. He saw the fabric flare out, her bare feet on the courtyard tiles, and his anxiety melted away.

At the corner Skyler paused and took a deep breath. This time when he looked back Ana's eyes did meet his. There were beads of sweat on her brow. She gave him a single, confident nod that served to remind him of the urgency. The diversion they'd created was like a countdown timer, ticking rapidly away to zero.

So he turned the corner, raised his rifle, and went inside.

# 14

## DARWIN, AUSTRALIA

### 30.MAR.2285

The storm front fell upon Darwin like a blanket thrown over a corpse.

Wind began to whip little daggers of water through the streets of the Maze, clearing what little foot traffic would be found at such an hour.

The fire at Selby Systems had grown significantly, engulfing the surrounding structures now. Sam couldn't be sure how much damage had been done. All she could see when she glanced back was an orange glow reflecting off the purple bruise of rain cloud that roiled above the city.

She'd been through plenty of bad storms during her time in Darwin. Even two typhoons. This one, she thought, would rank near the top.

*Perfect.*

Occasionally she heard shouts behind her, echoing off the broken buildings and shuttered window frames. Jacobites, fanning out into the labyrinth. Had they found Skadz? Prumble? Impossible to know. She ran and ran, fighting the wind with every step, squinting when the blown rain lashed at her face.

The narrow alleys all looked the same. Gray concrete, armored doors, broken windows all boarded and barred. Exposed pipes and bundles of electrical wire snaked everywhere. Some of the cables, the few that still carried a current, sizzled under the barrage of droplets.

Three minutes away from the inferno and she was utterly and completely lost. The space elevator provided her only beacon for navigation. A single lonely climber was visible just below the cloud layer, like a lantern on the peak of some great mist-shrouded mountain. The vehicle hadn't quite beaten the storm, and she could only imagine the turbulence it would face as it climbed up through those angry clouds. In years past, before all the upheaval, the cord would have been cleared well before a storm like this hit. A more experienced staff in Nightcliff would have known better.

Her foot caught on a loose bit of concrete and she went down, landing hard on her shoulder. The impact sent a jolt of pain that seemed to rocket straight to her brain. For a moment she lay there in the street, blinking away the flurry of water that sprayed into her eyes.

"Get up, Sam," a voice said. It took her a second to realize it was her own.

She stood and walked on shaky legs to a small alcove. In any other storm it would have meant a welcome respite from the rain, but when the wind hissed through narrow streets like this there seemed to be no escape. Still, it was dark. Very dark. She leaned against a wet wall and rubbed her shoulder. A burst of lightning produced flickers of white-blue light across the city. Shadows danced and parried up and down the alley. Movement above caught her eye. A candle in a window, high above, grew and faded. There were others, too. Pulsing yellow squares like ships on a dark and turbulent ocean.

Footsteps caught her attention. Someone was jogging down the alley.

Sam took a chance and glanced out of the alcove. A distant flicker of lightning gave her a glimpse of a thin, lone Jacobite heading in her direction. She waited. Timing was everything. She waited as long as she thought she could and then stuck out her leg.

The thug jumped it, deftly.

*Shit,* she thought, and went at him with a fist. In the heat of the moment she'd forgotten about her throbbing right shoulder. The punch produced a stab of pain and forced her to ease off, leaving the thrown fist with no weight behind it.

It wouldn't have mattered. The Jacobite—a woman, Sam now thought based on the curves glimpsed in another flash of lightning—dodged easily. She ducked and kicked out, her foot a smear of gray motion.

Sam leapt upward, the attack scraping her shin. At that instant the lightning hit a lull and the alley went almost pitch-black. Sam landed on something soft and her assailant yelped in pain. The limb—arm or leg, Sam had no idea—yanked out from under Sam's foot. She reached for it, caught it, and twisted. Another cry followed by a vicious chop that took Samantha on the back of her neck.

The sting of it produced swimming stars in Sam's vision. Somehow she'd managed to hold on to the Jacobite's limb—an arm, she knew now. Sam turned and ducked, putting her enemy directly behind her. She gripped the woman's forearm with both hands and pulled while at the same time thrusting herself upright.

Her attacker flipped over Sam's shoulder. *Lithe and light, easy to flight.* Skadz had said that once when she'd thrown a scrawny subhuman the same way. In that instance Sam had let go, tossing the scowling sub over the side of a building. Here, now, she held on with both hands, pulling downward as the woman came back toward the ground. There was a double smack sound as her feet hit the wall of the alcove, then a whoosh of breath being forced from her lungs as her torso slammed into the ground.

Sam wasted no time. She knelt, held on with her right hand, and rained blows with her left. Four punches to the face were all it took to convert the thrashing, terrified opponent into a lifeless mass.

"Nice to fucking meet you, too," Sam muttered as she searched the body. The white Jacobite robes were soaked through and clung to the skinny woman. In the dark Sam found it frustrating to try to move the ridiculous garment aside to look for pockets beneath. She gave up, patted the body instead, found nothing.

* * *

Ten minutes later Sam ran straight into a dead-end alley. Wind whistled along the buildings that lined the narrow lane until the last little boxed-in corner, where it then vaulted upward in a swirling vortex of debris.

She cursed the blocked path and turned back, only to spy two Jacobites entering the alley. They were just shadows in the dark city street, and she knew she would be, too, so she flattened herself against a wall between two thick pipes and hoped they hadn't seen her.

When they were two meters from her position she coiled. There'd been no time, nor anywhere near enough light, to assess them for size or weapons. So she'd take the closest one first, perhaps shove him into the other and send them both sprawling. If only the crumbling brick wall across from her had an alcove of its own, with Kelly tucked within. She'd worked so well with the nimble woman on Gateway during that week of constant cat-and-mouse. It had never been Sam's style before then, until Kelly had shown her just how effective it could be.

"I wonder where you are now," Sam whispered. "I wonder . . . shit." She hadn't wondered one critical thing until this moment, as the two patrollers drew near. *What will happen to Kelly once Grillo hears of my actions tonight? Does he still believe she's important to me? Is he still skeptical of her loyalty?*

Sam cursed herself for having considered none of this before the evening's events. She should have found some way to send her friend a warning. Be ready to run, or something like that. Anything. Instead she'd warned Vaughn, and only marginally, so she could get him in bed again.

The crack of two gunshots cascaded down the alley. Prumble, or Skadz? Likely. She hoped they were the ones doing the shooting. The two Jacobites halted at the noise. Sam half-expected to hear their bodies topple to the asphalt, but sounds were weird in the Maze, their distance all but impossible to estimate. A street vendor's call could seem a block away only to be a kilometer distant, channeled through the alleys in just the right combination. Neither of the Jacobites fell. Instead they both turned and ran, shouting cries of alarm and rally. They probably had as much idea as she did where the shots originated, but all that mattered was that they'd left. Sam ducked out of the dead-end alley and moved on, thankful she didn't have to leave any more bodies in her wake.

When the high fortress wall of Nightcliff finally came into view, she felt better. Tired, hungry, dead thirsty, and aching from half a dozen places, but still better. She knew where she was, and the café wasn't far. On top of that, the storm had passed, leaving in its wake ten million balconies and windowsills dripping water onto the surfaces below. That sound would go on for a long time, she knew, but at least the wind had died.

When Clarke's finally came into view, the lights were off. This didn't surprise her, given the predawn hour. Sam took one last glance behind herself, saw no one, and strode forward into the small square in front of the storefront.

"Wouldn't do that," a voice said. Just a whisper. Prumble.

She turned, couldn't see anyone, and stepped back into the shadows anyway. "Where—"

"Here."

A movement in a nearby doorway. Sam jogged across the street and slipped into the dark space. "Are you okay?" she asked. She couldn't see him but felt the girth of his belly press against her own in the tiny alcove.

"They're inside, waiting."

The words alone were bad enough, but when their full meaning hit her Sam felt a cold despair, like a dead bolt clicking into place. Not only were the Jacobites one step ahead, they knew where to fucking go. She thought they'd been careful. Perhaps they had and someone talked. She shuddered at that idea and buried it deep. "How do you know?"

He jerked his chin upward. "Second-story window on the left."

Sam looked. It was hard to see in the darkness, but on a small sill that extended out from below the window was a white bucket. This was not unusual in Darwin, where it rained almost constantly for half the year and external sources of water had all failed. Sam glanced farther up the side of the building, and nearly every window and balcony had similar containers out now that the winds had died down.

"Renuka's signal to me that the café is not safe," Prumble explained.

"Where's Skadz?"

The big man shrugged. "Aboard still, I hope. If he's in there we have a big problem."

"Another big problem, you mean."

"Quite. Problems seem to be breeding like rabbits this evening, don't they?" His last word ended strangely, as if he'd just stepped on a thorn.

"Are you all right?" she asked.

"Bit of a scratch. Took a knife to the gut. Relax, it's not deep and I have ample padding."

She slipped a hand into his coat and prodded until her fingers found a wet, sticky spot. He grunted when she put pressure there.

"We need to stitch you up."

"That's the least of your worries. Soon the sun will rise, and I don't exactly blend in, Sam."

"Nor do I. We need to get off the streets."

"Not without Skadz," he said.

Sam grinned at that. She'd been on the verge of saying the same thing.

A minute later, Skadz found them.

She heard him first. Rapid footfalls on the tortured streets, echoing off the vertical man-made canyon walls. He raced into the square in front of Clarke's as if he intended to burst through the door. Sam was about to call out to him when Prumble's finger curled around her arm.

Skadz ran past the café and kept going. He had the bulky duffel bag that contained Prumble's environment suit slung over his shoulder.

Another set of footsteps grew. Four people, maybe five, giving chase.

Before Samantha could even think what to do, Prumble moved. His speed was remarkable given his girth, his wounded belly. He ran into the square toward the abandoned wreck of a food cart. Every useful part had been yanked off the thing, leaving just a skeleton behind. A rat skittered from beneath it as the big man approached.

Prumble lowered his shoulder at the last second and propelled the metal and plastic carcass into the path of the oncoming Jacobites. His timing had a poetry to it. The first thug into the square yelped in surprise and smashed into the thing, toppling it.

Three others followed into the pileup, unable to slow themselves on the wet asphalt. An object clattered across the square and slid to a stop near Sam. She knew the sound of a pistol being dropped and went for it.

Prumble was on the newcomers in an instant. He lifted one into the air and tossed him into a nearby concrete wall. The others were scrambling to their feet. One ran. The other went at Prumble's midsection, as if he had some hope of knocking the giant man over. Instead he stopped as if he'd rushed into Nightcliff's fortress wall. Prumble grunted, his wounded belly no doubt on fire.

Sam hefted the gun, flipping the cold metal around in her hand to get the grip right. It was a small thing, an antique police-issue type, she guessed. Glock, maybe. She just hoped it was loaded and not a showpiece.

Skadz emerged from her left, coming back after no doubt hearing the crash of the food cart. Prumble was tangled up with two Jacobites, his body preventing Samantha from getting a clear shot. She was about to whistle for Skadz's attention when the door to the café flew open.

Sam hesitated long enough to see the flash of a gun barrel and the hint of a Jacobite robe behind it. She fired without sighting, letting the sparks that erupted from the side of the building refine her aim as she continued to pull the trigger. The first Jacobite out the door smartly dove to the ground. The one behind him froze, fell, and toppled in a heap. There were shadows of more behind that one, but they retreated as Sam's clip ran empty.

The one on the ground rolled to the side and took aim. She ducked back into the alcove just in time as the machine gun barked thunder. A short burst, professional. The ones inside the building were trained, then. Elite. She wondered with dismay if they'd been there since before or after the explosion at Selby Systems.

Another burst of fire slapped into the far side of the alcove, suppression fire. Between bursts she heard footsteps. The gunman was moving toward her.

Then he cried out. Surprise more than pain. She heard bodies tumbling and chanced a look around the corner. Skadz had tackled the man.

Sam rushed forward, tossing the empty pistol aside. She reached them as both men got back to their feet. The gunman was readying to shoot Skadz when she drove her foot into his groin from behind. She kicked so hard that he lifted a few centimeters off the ground, yelping like a dog. The effort made her slip on the still-wet ground and she toppled back, cracking her skull against the ground.

Skadz must have followed her kick with one of his own because the Jacobite thug was pushed backward, off his feet, toward her. She raised her arms and caught him as he landed on her; she clasped her hands around his neck and rolled to get on top of him.

More gunfire. Sam winced at the sound, expecting the worst. Then she realized it was Skadz. He'd managed to yank the machine gun away as he'd kicked the man she now held. Skadz concentrated his fire on the open doorway of the café. As for Prumble . . . she had no idea. *No such thing as a fight without chaos and confusion,* she thought as she choked the life out of the enemy under her.

The man squirmed. He got an arm free and clawed at her eyes, muddy fingers clouding her vision. She tightened her hands and let the anger pour into that hold. He gagged, gurgled. Something in his neck gave in and crushed under her grip with a sound that made her stomach lurch, but still she clamped down.

A hand was tugging at her shirt from behind. "Let's bounce!" Skadz shouted. He fired again and the rifle finally clicked, empty. "Now!"

Sam released her hands and surged to her feet. She blinked but it was useless. Frantically she swept her arm across her face but it only made the situation worse. Skadz was pulling her and she didn't bother to argue the direction. In four steps they were in an alley again and running as best they could. She could hear footsteps in front, heavy. *Prumble, good.*

"This way," the big man said. Skadz shifted direction and Sam allowed him to guide her as she tried to wipe her face clean with her shirt. There were shouts coming from behind them, but they sounded distant already.

A door opened somewhere ahead. Sam tried to look but the world still resembled a bad watercolor left out in the rain. Skadz didn't slow, though; he went in. There were steps going down, and the smell of sewage.

Sam asked no questions for the next half hour. She just ran, between the bulky confidence that was Prumble and the lithe paranoia that was Skadz. They were outlaws now. No doubt about that.

They'd gone underground and Samantha wondered if they'd ever come back up.

# 15

## DARWIN, AUSTRALIA

### 30.MAR.2285

An hour later Sam found herself in an underground bunker. The walls of the tiny room were lined with shelves and cabinets, mostly empty. A table—no chairs—dominated the center of the space. Spread out across that surface were the contents of a white first-aid kit Prumble had pulled from a shelf. The duffel bag that contained his environment suit lay on a high shelf near the back.

Skadz leaned against the far wall, sitting on the floor cross-legged and eyes closed, though she knew he was awake.

Prumble paced, his face scrunched up in concentration. The bottom half of his shirt was soaked with blood, but he seemed in no pain at all. When they entered the room he'd simply sprayed it with some bonding anesthetic and slapped a bandage over it. Then he'd started to pace.

He stank, they all stank, of sewage and sweat. Finally, after a long silence, the big man spoke. "I'll be back," he said, and left the way they'd entered. It was the only way in or out, save for a hatch on the roof.

She watched Skadz for a long time, hoping his eyes would open with some kind of bright, lightning-bolt revelation. A plan, a way forward, something she could follow without having to think for herself because that would require using her brain, and that lump of gray meat wasn't up to the challenge just now.

Her eyes drooped, slipped closed. She must have slept, because when she opened them again Prumble was back and he was eating. Fish stew, from the pungent smell of it. A staple of Darwin's ground dwellers that she normally shunned due to the often dubious ingredients. Here and now, though, it seemed perfect. Her stomach growled so loudly that Prumble turned to face her, spoon hovering halfway to his lips. "Top of the morning, Sam. Breakfast?"

"Please," she said. The word barely escaped her dry throat.

The first-aid kit had been tidied up and returned to its shelf. On the table now, she saw, was a chipped red Dutch oven resting on a camp stove, curls of steam wafting up from the edges of the lid. Next to it was a thermos, a few bowls, and mismatched spoons. She went to the table and scooped a bowlful of the stew from the cookpot, inhaled the salty aromas, then grabbed a spoon. "What's in the thermos?"

"Coffee."

"You're a magician."

Prumble shook his head, chewing on a piece of stubborn meat. "I'm a scavenger just like you, Sam. Only you work the Clear, and I work the city. Usually I find buyers, but sometimes it's necessities. Like coffee."

She smiled at him. "Those days are over, I think," she said with as much sadness and nostalgia as she felt.

He glared at her with mock incredulity, gesturing to her bowl and the thermos. "You're the one lazing away in this palace while I forage." At her wrinkled nose his expression became more serious. "You're right, of course. Still, the day I can't scrounge a cuppa is the day I'll consider myself unworthy of the Builders' filtered air."

The stew tasted wonderful. Scalding hot broth thick with chunks of fish that must have been hauled in recently near Aura's Edge, not by the coast where the waters were filthy. But the soup paled in comparison to the coffee. It was like drinking liquid focus. Each swallow chipped away at her exhaustion and the fog it brought. "Holy hell that's good."

Skadz stirred. A sharp intake of breath, followed by a catlike stretch of his arms. "Do I smell what I think I smell?"

Prumble spoke before Sam could. "Better hurry before it's gone, mate, because we've still got a job to do."

"Bollocks," Skadz said. He hauled himself to his feet and came to the table, going for the coffee first. "Cloak-and-dagger time is over. If Nightcliff wasn't already locked up tight as a Jake's ass, it will be now. The streets up there must be full of—"

"The streets," Prumble said, "are a powder keg. And about"— he glanced at his wrist—"twenty minutes ago I lit the fuse."

Samantha glared at the big man, impressed despite herself at the smug satisfaction on his face. "Prumble? What did you do?"

His grin grew wider. "Do you recall what our good friend Jaya said about the current landscape of Jacobite politics?"

She grimaced. "Er. Not really."

"Tsk-tsk, Samantha. Luckily I was paying attention. Jaya spoke of a growing rift. Grillo on one side and Sister Haley, the so-called girl who talks to God, on the other. And while it's true that the three of us are at the top of the most-wanted list, a rumor will be spreading like wildfire through Darwin today that we've holed up inside Temple Sulam, under the protection of our dear friend, the lovely pariah herself, Sister Haley. Eyewitnesses will swear they saw us enter to open arms."

The room went so quiet that Sam could hear the flow of runoff water in the sewer main ten meters outside the door.

Skadz wiped a hand across his face, as if trying to banish his own smile. The effort failed. "Bloody. Brilliant."

Prumble's face lit up at the praise. He rocked from foot to foot in his excitement, his fingers twitching with nervous energy like a drummer tapping out a mentally composed riff. "With any luck," he said, "by nightfall Grillo's forces will have the temple surrounded. Haley will deny our presence, of course, but she'll never let Grillo in to search the place because she fears he'll never leave. Meanwhile . . ."

Sam leaned forward now, her hands on the table. "Meanwhile, we go after the object."

"Precisely," the big man said.

His tone implied he had a plan for that, too.

* * *

Prumble led them through more sewers, his bulky form lit by dancing shadows cast by an LED camping lantern he held before him. They had no other light, nor a functional weapon between them. The gun Skadz picked up during the brawl with the Jacobites was empty, and the prospects of finding more ammo were slim.

Samantha stepped carefully. Every surface was slick with humidity and stank with an intensity that made her eyes water, yet the others didn't complain, so she kept quiet. Short of flying across the city at altitude, this was undoubtedly the best way to reach their destination without being seen.

Ahead, Prumble gestured at a branch in the tunnel. "That way leads to Nightcliff. Skyler took it when he had to sneak in, and they collapsed it a week later."

Sam couldn't see much in the dim light. She tried to imagine Skyler's trek through this dismal place. He'd somehow saved the Elevator from total failure, though only a few people knew it. Her captain had pulled it off and moved straight on to orbit, seeking to save her and then Dr. Sharma. Never once had he asked for thanks or praise. Few in Darwin knew how close the city had come to total collapse, or who their true savior was.

Prumble walked on, taking the branch that led west. After what seemed to Sam like a thousand kilometers the tunnel began to slope upward until it finally, blissfully, ended at a locked gate, bars as thick as her arm. Prumble, of course, had a key. Beyond was a disgusting stagnant pool near the ocean. Sam heard waves lapping against rocks, along with the creaking of hundreds of small boats. She gagged at the addition of rotting seaweed odor to the still-pungent reek of sewage. The big man seemed not to notice. Instead he just clambered up the large gray rocks piled around the mouth of the tunnel and continued on as if out for a morning hike. The rocks soon gave way to a barely visible path through shoulder-high reeds. The sun, though still low behind the city's skyline, already made the air uncomfortably warm and thick with flies.

The path led up onto an embankment that ran along one side of the artificial cove. Occasionally she spotted ragged camping tents nestled within the reeds, heard the sound of snoring from one. Once they were high enough on the inlet's side the ocean came into view. Boats and rafts of every size and condition clogged the waters out to a few hundred meters from shore. Those nearest the open ocean were in the best shape, either coming or going in their effort to catch fish. With no room for livestock in any appreciable quantity, Darwin relied on these boats as much as the farms high above to keep people fed. The placement of the Elevator on Darwin's coastline, either on purpose or otherwise, left almost half of the protective aura covering open ocean. This left fishing as an option, but the coast was so clogged with the watercraft that swarmed Darwin in their flight from the disease that it had become an ecosystem all its own. Fishermen came back to the edge of the flotilla with their catch, trading the haul for whatever supplies they needed, and so began a byzantine process far too complex for Samantha to comprehend. The net result was that some fish made it to shore, but not much.

Prumble halted their march here, overlooking the cluttered bay. He studied the flotilla for a long time.

"Oy," Skadz said, "big man. Why've we stopped? And isn't Nightcliff way the hell back that way?"

"Tell me something," Prumble said, as if he hadn't heard. "What's the one thing we possess of value?"

The question left Skadz speechless. Sam as well.

"Knowledge," Prumble said.

Sam smirked. "Okay . . ."

"We know, for example, that Darwin is not the only place on Earth people can live. We know there's another option. That's valuable."

Samantha put her hands in her pockets and shrugged. "So what? Hardly anyone could get there."

"Mate," Skadz said, "if you're proposing to sell seats on Skyler's bird, don't bother. He said it would barely fit us."

In response Prumble raised one hand and pointed out to sea. Sam had to stand next to him and sight down his arm to see what he was looking at. Even when she found it, she didn't understand. "That black square?"

"Indeed."

"What is it?"

Prumble grinned. "The *Vadim Zorich*. A Russian submarine, thorium powered. She surfaced here a full six months after SUBS hit. The last refugees, and the only people other than you immunes or the suited scavengers who can leave the aura."

Squinting in disbelief, Skadz said, "And in all this time the crew didn't bugger off?"

"Many did, yes, but there's still enough of them left to operate the craft. They go out for months at a time, just because they can, I suppose. Luckily for us, they're here now."

"Prumble," Sam said, "we've already got a ride. What's the point?"

"We have a ride, yes. People who can assist us in entering Nightcliff do not, and I'll bet they'd like one very much."

With that he turned and continued his march, his pace reinvigorated. They crested the embankment and left the stench of the shore behind. Prumble guided them through a junkyard of abandoned, crushed vehicles, through two chain-link fences, and finally out onto the strip of land that led to their goal.

"Best to conceal that rifle now," Prumble said to Skadz without looking back.

Ahead, perched on the shore of East Point, were the six functioning desalination plants. From a distance the huge buildings blended together into one massive industrial complex. A confusing array of pipes and storage tanks.

People, kids mostly, trudged along the crumbling road that led out to the facilities from homes nearer the coastline proper. They carried buckets, bottles, even mixing bowls—whatever would carry water. Empty going out, full going back. Their path took them through a gauntlet of street vendors hawking everything from fresh fish to reasonably clean undergarments. Plant workers weaved through the throng as well. Those carrying water parted for them, and the peddlers treated them as if invisible. They were something akin to an upper class in Darwin, though not quite on the same level as the roof dwellers. Payment being a rather dubious reward in the city, Sam had heard these people kept the water plants running mostly out of a sense of duty, not for the rewards they received. They were a small and dwindling brain trust, something Platz, Blackfield, and now Grillo all realized. So they had choice living conditions within the safety of the peninsula, food provided, and of course all the fresh water they required.

Prumble moved quickly through the crowds. At the far end of the narrow road, in front of the industrial buildings, were guards in both Nightcliff and Jacobite garb. They were checking paperwork as the workers shuffled in.

"Used to be all Platz people out here," Prumble said. "A lot of the bits and bobs you fetched over the years came this way."

"I recall," said Skadz. "Paid handsomely, too."

"It did at that." He hunched a bit as he weaved his way past a pair of merchants selling some kind of groundfish cakes, and then kept going down the embankment on the other side.

The reeds here were taller. Dry, tough things that snagged on any piece of loose clothing available. Unlike the side of the peninsula they'd entered from, there was no worn path here. The going was slow, and the day grew hotter with each step. All signs of the previous night's storm were gone, leaving nothing but a brilliant blue sky and a glaring heat lamp of a sun.

"On occasion," Prumble said in a low yet conversational tone, "I used this route when the items I needed to fence were, um, personal in nature." He came to a chain-link fence topped with razor wire. The barrier ran well out into the ocean. Multiple signs warned against trespassing. Prumble moved to a spot in the fence under one such sign and pulled a section aside. He waved Skadz through first, then Samantha.

Beyond, he took the lead again as the landscape turned from reeds to rocks once more. Sam could see the tips of giant exhaust stacks above the lip of the embankment, though no visible steam or other emission came from the towers just now. A steady noise began to build, a sound she assumed was the by-product of superheating ocean water over a nuclear furnace.

She was sweating profusely and her throat felt dry as paper when they came to a meter-high pipe that ran half buried down the rocky slope and out into the ocean. Sam placed her hand on the cool metal and felt the vibration of water flowing within. Prumble followed the pipe from there, surprisingly steady in his pace despite the distance they'd come in such heat. His trademark leather duster flapped behind him, snapping in the stiff ocean breeze.

When the main building of the desalination plant came into view, Prumble stopped. He leaned against the pipe, and sighed in relief as the cold metal chilled the back of his neck. Skadz mimicked the posture and so Sam did, too.

"Have the next bit figured out yet?" Skadz asked.

Prumble didn't look back. Instead he just raised one hand and waggled his fingers, urging quiet.

Skadz turned to Samantha instead. "Holding up, love?"

"Nothing like a brisk stroll to start the morning."

He smirked. "Wish we had some weapons."

Prumble did a half turn and hissed at them. "Silence."

"They can't hear us over these pipes, man," Skadz shot back.

"I don't care if they can hear us. I'm trying to listen."

"For what?"

Prumble held up one meaty finger, his eyes darting upward toward the sky. "Aha. Here we are, like the Tranz on a Friday afternoon at beer-thirty. Right on time."

"The hell are you on about?"

Sam gripped Skadz by the arm to quiet him. She heard the noise now, too, and nodded at Prumble. The wail of vertical thrusters grew from a whisper to a rushing gale as the water hauler came in from Nightcliff. The aircraft flew low on a curved approach that kept it well away from the coast, a route likely chosen to minimize any chance of being shot at. Darwin was full of people with little hope of improving their lives. They snapped all the time, and an aircraft hauling water for the "bloody Orbitals" made as good a target as any when the desperate needed to vent some frustration.

"Get ready," Prumble said.

As the aircraft slowed and descended to its landing pad, the engines began to howl in their battle against gravity. The noise became painful. Just before it peaked, Prumble moved. He went with laserlike focus, never bothering to pause or even look around at the bevy of guards stationed around the complex. His focus lay squarely on a carefully chosen path, one he'd probably perfected over the years. Or, Sam thought, perhaps it was a path he'd stumbled upon on his first visit and never wavered from. Whatever the case, she followed. First he led them along the pipe as it crested an earthen berm and began to descend into a depression behind the complex. At one point Prumble seemed to duck low, then Skadz did the same a second later, and she realized they'd dropped into a shallow pit. Who'd dug it, or when, she couldn't know, but soon she found herself hunched over and moving under the big pipe. The metal dripped with condensation. Cold drops that splattered on her head and down the back of her sweat-soaked shirt. It felt wonderful, and ended all too fast. The "tunnel" ran only three meters before exiting on the other side of the pipe. She had to haul herself up on the other side, with help from Skadz's outstretched hand.

Now they were between two identical pipes. These converged until parallel, with just a meter separating them. Prumble squeezed between and surged forward. When Sam took a second to look up, she saw a few guards standing on a loading dock at the building's rear. They'd stopped patrolling to watch the aircraft land. She could see their contorted expressions as the noise and wind generated by the plane buffeted them.

And then they were out of sight. The sky became obscured by a network of smaller pipes overhead, and then blotted out entirely. Her eyes struggled to adjust to the sudden darkness. Behind and above, the aircraft's engines began to power down, and their noise was replaced by the now-amplified drone of water rushing through the pipes to either side of her. From the volume Sam suspected there were dozens of such pipes converging here.

Prumble stopped at a metal door with a submarine-style circular handle. He gripped it with both hands and wheeled it easily until a wet ripping sound like almost-dry glue came from within. The thick hinges squealed when he yanked the door open. Soft yellow light spilled out from within. The big man climbed inside.

When Sam stepped in, Prumble wheeled his index finger around, his gaze on the door behind her. She closed it and wheeled the handle back into the sealed position. The cramped room went totally silent, save for the labored sounds of her breathing. An aroma hit her—salt and metal and stagnant water. The dimpled steel floor was grimy and dotted with pockets of damp, dark sand.

"We're inside," Prumble said, an expression of satisfaction on his face. Sam realized he'd been expecting some kind of confrontation or alarm.

Skadz laughed. "Sorta noticed that. The question is, how do we get on that water hauler for the return trip into Nightcliff? That is your plan, right? Can't fight our way on. Even if we succeeded, they'd be waiting for us at the other end."

"Agreed," Prumble replied. "I had something more subtle in mind."

"We're going to sneak aboard?" Sam asked.

"No. We're going to ask."

He stepped through another junction, the shape of which again reminded Samantha of a submarine. Oval, a good five centimeters off the floor, and thick. The entire basement was riddled with the odd things, and every third had the same wheel-handle door. Sam realized it must be some kind of spillway, the rooms meant to baffle rushing water. She imagined the doors could be opened remotely, probably by computer if the equipment still worked.

She hoped they would move on before high tide, and Prumble did not disappoint. After just three more of the raised doorways, he led them into a stairwell. There was a similar bulkhead door at the top of the first flight, and the big man opened it with extreme caution. When the seal made its little pop, he pushed the metal plate up just a centimeter and peered through, a band of light shining across his eyes. He waited for a few seconds, his gaze tracking something in the space above.

Sam felt a familiar surge of adrenaline. All extraneous thought melted away, leaving behind a pristine focus she loved.

Prumble raised the hatch and moved up, holding it as Skadz rushed up the steps. Sam went last and took the weight of the thick door so Prumble could resume the lead. He nodded to her, his eyes exhibiting the same focus she felt. She realized with sudden certainty that she'd underestimated him for years, either due to his size or his jovial nature. He was *good* at this. *It was that damn cane he always hobbled around with. A myth, he'd said at Dee's. Goddamned long con.* Perhaps she'd known it since last night, but she'd been too shell-shocked to really comprehend.

Sam lowered the hatch until it made a soft clank, then gripped the wheeled handle but changed her mind. If they needed to exit in a hurry every second would count. Better to leave it open.

More stairs led up in flights that zigzagged back and forth, reminding her of similar spaces in Japan and then Hawaii. She'd left Jake's body near the bottom of one there. The memory of his placid face, his distant, unblinking gaze ripped her from the state of adrenal euphoria she'd found moments before. Sam grasped the railing beside her and stopped for a few seconds, letting the image of her friend fade and the singular focus return. When she moved again Skadz was looking back at her, his unvoiced question clear. "You okay?"

She gave him a nod and waved him forward.

Despite his size Prumble took the steps silently. That was no small feat in Sam's book. She had to keep her footsteps to the sides, knowing a step in the center would send a reverberating clang up and down the enclosed space. It was only the ever-present vibration of machinery in the building that kept her from moving at a snail's pace.

They went up eight flights—four floors—before stopping at a more traditional door. Here Prumble transformed into his usual self. He stood up straight, turned the handle, and went through as if he owned the place.

Skadz glanced back at Sam, shrugged, and did the same. She followed, finding herself on a catwalk not unlike the one that ringed the hangar back at the airport. Only this one was much higher, overlooking the entire interior of the building.

Two huge machines dominated the floor below. She could feel the heat pouring off them even from this high above. Dozens— no, hundreds—of pipes fed into the behemoth devices, all but covering the actual floor of the massive room. She saw a few people moving about on narrow catwalks that rested atop the pipes in a grid, apparently inspecting the equipment below.

Prumble strode to a door at the middle of the catwalk, turned the handle, and moved silently inside. Again Skadz followed, tossing a single quizzical glance back at Sam before he entered. Sam shrugged at this and moved through the door, pulling it closed behind her with a soft click.

They were in an office. A big one, yet somehow not pretentious. There was a desk at one side, covered with a handful of slate terminals and a few old-fashioned clipboards. On the wall behind it, a map of the water processing plant was dotted with green, yellow, and red lights. Most were green.

On the other side of the space were three love seats, facing one another around a rectangular faux-wood coffee table. The layout reminded her of Grillo's office in Nightcliff, only larger and without the sterile cleanliness.

A man and a woman were standing near the couches, clearly surprised at the intrusion and perhaps, Sam thought, caught in the middle of a lover's tiff or marital argument. Given their apparent age, Sam decided it was the latter. The woman's face had tracks of tears running in two parallel lines down her cheeks. Her eyes were raw and red.

Skadz stood at Prumble's right shoulder. Sam dutifully came to his left, drawing herself to her full height, realizing suddenly that the three of them must look like thieves or a hit squad. She waited for something, anything to happen, but the pregnant pause only went on. Five seconds.

Ten.

"Do you know these people?" the woman asked out the side of her mouth. She'd balled her fists, Sam realized. Her eyes were squarely on Prumble.

"It's okay, honey," the man said. "They're old friends." Despite the words he still put his arm out protectively, urging her to move a step behind him. The woman did so reluctantly. Her hands remained clenched at her side.

"Arkin," Prumble said. "Sorry to drop in like this."

"Prumble," the man replied. "It's been a long time."

Prumble took a casual step farther into the room. Sam kept her gaze on the woman. Her bloodshot eyes darted briefly to Arkin, then to the comm on the desk, then to the far corner of the room. Sam stole a glance in that direction and saw a small safe embedded in the wall.

Out of instinct Sam turned and locked the door. Then she took in the room again, looking for anything that could become a weapon. Two sturdy umbrellas in a bin by the desk, a cricket bat mounted on the wall. Nothing substantial, then. Next she glanced about for another exit and found nothing.

*Not good.*

"Prumble?" the woman asked. "He's Prumble?"

"Not now, dear," the man named Arkin said.

The big man bowed to her. "I see my reputation precedes me. Does she know about the last time I was here? When you had a hood thrown over my head and hauled me in here at Neil's beckoning?"

Arkin cleared his throat. "She does, actually. There's no secrets between us." He hesitated, his stiff posture relaxing slightly. "Sorry about how that went down, by the way. It couldn't have been avoided. Platz didn't need to know about our little side arrangement."

"Forget it. A lot has changed since then."

"Yes," Arkin said. "I thought . . . well, everyone thought . . . you were dead. Or locked up."

Sam kept her eyes on the woman, saw her flinch as if jabbed at the mention of captivity. Their eyes suddenly met, and the woman's expression changed. Suddenly she was evaluating Sam, as if trying to gauge her weak points.

"On the contrary," Prumble said, "I've been busy."

The woman raised her chin. "Why are you here? Sneaking around, interrupting—"

"We need your help."

Arkin motioned his wife to silence with a curt wave. He took a deep breath and addressed the trio now, not just Prumble. "You can't stay here. You shouldn't even be here. I'm sorry, it's just—"

Prumble waved him off. "That's not what I meant. But we've interrupted you in the middle of something important, obviously. My apologies. Is there somewhere we can wait, at least, until you can talk?"

"We can't help you."

"Hear us out, at least."

"I'm sorry, but I insist you leave. If they found you here—"

The woman cleared her throat. "Maybe they can help us, dear. Perhaps their presence is a sign, or gift."

Arkin glanced at his wife now, studying her even as she studied the three intruders.

Suddenly Sam understood that appraising gaze. The woman hadn't been assessing danger, but opportunity. The question was . . . "Help with what, exactly?"

"You first," she replied.

Prumble took a small step farther into the room. "We need to get inside Nightcliff," he said. "And, ideally, back out again. Quickly and quietly."

The couple stared at each other as Prumble spoke, some silent conversation passing between them.

Prumble went on. "Grillo has something that doesn't belong to him, and we intend to get it back."

"Sweetheart," the woman whispered to Arkin, her gaze locked on his. "They can help us. We must act."

"June," Arkin said, turning to her now. "June, my dear, we'd put all of our lives at risk. Hers most of all."

"Mind telling us what you're talking about?" Skadz said. "'Cause we've got a clock and that bitch is ticking."

Sam shot her friend a look she hoped would produce an apology, or at least silence. Skadz just shrugged at her.

The woman, June, seemed unoffended. She turned abruptly from her husband and looked at the three of them in turn. "Our daughter is in Nightcliff. Our little girl." Her lip began to quiver, fresh tears welling at the corners of her eyes. When she spoke again her voice was thick and full of forced strength. "Grillo has kept her there since the water strike. A willing member of his flock, he claims, but we know the truth. She's a prisoner, plain and simple. A pawn, something to keep my husband in line and the water flowing."

Arkin looked down at his feet.

June went on, oblivious. "And it's *working*. We haven't seen her in a year. She could be . . ." June's voice cracked. She paused, gathering herself. "I hear terrible things. And she's little more than a child. . . ."

A shiver ran up Samantha's arms.

"I keep telling my husband we must act. Something bold. Sabotage the plant and threaten the others unless our little girl is returned."

"To what end?" Arkin said. "Suppose we get her back? Then what? Do you think Grillo will just leave us alone? That he'll let things go back to how they were? No. Impossible. We would be fugitives, and he owns this city now. Where could we hide that he couldn't reach? It's not like we can go anywhere else."

"We've been over all this a thousand times," June snapped, her voice growing in intensity. "I don't care anymore. I'd rather risk that, or death, than let our child endure one more day with that monster!"

Sam opened her mouth to speak. Skadz beat her to it.

"We can help," he said. "Right, guys?"

"Perhaps," Prumble said.

"Not perhaps. We'll help them. Simple as that."

Arkin shook his head. "I won't risk all of our lives just so we can hide in some hole in the ground."

Skadz leaned to his side and whispered something into Prumble's ear with a vehemence that matched what he'd said a moment before. The big man winced, then nodded. Skadz kept talking but his eyes, Sam realized, were on her. Looking, it seemed, for backup. Or at least for a shared conviction.

The memory of something he'd said to her months ago flashed into her mind. The girl he'd failed to save, whose name he'd forgotten along with the medicine he was supposed to find for her. Skadz had found his chance at some kind of redemption and latched on with both hands, and Sam found herself unable to argue. She'd been on the verge of offering to help before her friend had spoken, for the simple reason that she knew what Grillo was capable of, what he'd done to Kelly, and what he'd threatened to do. Threats he might well make good on, given the events that transpired the night before.

Prumble crossed the room. He gripped Arkin's shoulder and eased him down to the couch. June sat, too.

"Suppose there was somewhere else to go," Prumble said. "Somewhere safe. Not a hiding place, Arkin. I'm talking about a city. Far from here."

"Impossible. There's nothing outside the aura—"

June leaned forward, cutting her husband off. "What other city? You are sure that such a place exists?"

Prumble nodded. "We're going there, once we have what we need from Nightcliff. And never coming back. Zane Platz is there. I assume you know him?"

"Very well," Arkin admitted, his eyes lighting up at the mention of the younger Platz's name.

"He'd be happy to have you there, I'm sure. They could use someone with your knowledge."

June stilled her shaking hands. "Assuming we believe you, how do we get to this city? You have an aircraft?"

"We do," Prumble said, "but it's not big enough. There's another way, though."

Arkin and his wife stared expectantly at the big man.

"Have you ever been aboard a submarine?"

# 16

## THE FLATIRONS, COLORADO

### 31.MAR.2285

The trail of bodies grew thicker.

It seemed that the farther, the deeper Pablo went, so too did the number of subhumans who had tried and failed to make the journey increase. Initially Tania found the corpses at once depressing and terrifying. But as the true depth and complexity of the cave system revealed itself, and still the body count climbed, she found a strange grudging admiration for the creatures. To have come so far into this pitch-black world without equipment or, hell, the ability to think clearly, all for whatever single-minded purpose it was that drove their diseased minds.

The cave, which had grown quite warm, began to cool. Her suit, designed for use in space, kept the internal temperature strictly controlled but a display within her face mask summarized the conditions outside. The temp readout had blinked as it dipped below 10 degrees Celsius. Shortly thereafter she began to see visible puffs coming from Pablo every time he exhaled.

The tunnel began to straighten and level off, its walls here shiny with moisture.

"Hold on a second," Tania said.

"Another sound?" Vanessa asked from behind.

"Getting some static, actually. Weird." She scanned the readouts on her HUD and saw nothing out of the ordinary. Something in the rock, interfering with her systems? That made no sense, though. Perhaps the object they'd come for?

"Wait," Pablo said. "I hear it, too."

"How could—"

"It's . . . not static. It's a river."

He continued on, his pace increasing with the prospect of a change in scenery. Sure enough, with each step the sound of rushing water grew, and not a minute later the tunnel entered a large underground grotto.

The expansive space was eerily lit from below in emerald green. It took no imagination to guess the source of that light, yet Tania still found herself breathless at the beauty on display before her. Wave patterns danced lazily across the uneven ceiling, reflected off the rushing water below.

The river flowed in from Tania's right, cascading down the center of the cave. In places it appeared to be only centimeters deep as it flowed over smooth rock and around larger boulders that must have fallen from the ceiling millions of years ago. She based that estimate on the way they appeared to be melting into the floor.

In other areas the water pooled into imposing dark patches of a depth she couldn't begin to guess. Here the black liquid flowed more slowly, growing to its widest point almost exactly where their tunnel had bisected the grotto.

Directly in front of where she stood was a bridge of sorts. Ejecta from when the shell ship had bored through the cavern wall lay in an uneven line, piled as high as a meter above the surface of the river. The water flowed around the new obstacle with visible churning, its ancient route suddenly obstructed.

At the end of this bridge was the shell ship, nose half buried in the pile of rock it had propelled into the cave. It had come to rest at an angle, allowing Tania to see most of one side. The surface of the vehicle held deep scars—grooves spiraled around the front half in a corkscrew pattern.

Near the center was a gap in the fuselage, just like the one

Skyler had seen in the tunnel near Belém. The emerald-green glow that so beautifully illuminated the room came from within.

Caught up in the grandeur of the view, Tania almost failed to notice the lone subhuman corpse. It lay facedown in the black waters that gurgled against the upstream side of the land bridge. "Looks like at least one made it this far," Tania said, pointing.

Pablo had been about to step out onto the first clump of debris, but paused at her words. "All the way down here, only to slip and drown." He shook his head.

He also didn't continue toward the ship, Tania noted. She understood the hesitation, too. Each of the other objects had been protected, as it were, by a challenge. In Belém, thick mists had blanketed the area and concealed subhumans transformed into armored killers. In Ireland, Skyler had found a dome that manipulated time itself, and subhumans that seemed capable of utilizing that advantage. She didn't know what the woman Samantha had faced near Darwin, but she had heard in her tone the implication of similar dangers.

*So what is it here? The cave itself?* Could the challenge of navigating such a place be what the Builders hoped would serve as protection? She thought . . . maybe. Her eyes glanced at the 3-D route her suit was automatically generating as they moved. Maybe the Builders hadn't counted on such technology. Or perhaps that was the point. This would have been a nearly impossible task just a few hundred years ago. Maybe this was all some way to assess a planet's technical capability. Prior to first contact, as she still stubbornly hoped, or prior to invasion, as Neil had theorized.

Yet the presence of subhumans that had tried and failed to reach the thing disquieted her. Perhaps the aliens planned for something more, something deadly, but their material source— subhumans—had not made it. Not yet, anyway.

Pablo went to one knee and began to rummage through his backpack. He pulled out a coil of climbing rope and began to tie one end around his waist.

"What are you doing?" Vanessa asked him.

"The water. It makes me uneasy." He walked to Tania and looped the rope around her waist twice, then handed the rest to Vanessa. "I had a . . . vision, I guess. Slipping on that bridge, pulled down by an undercurrent and swept into darkness."

"A very wise precaution," Tania acknowledged. She looked at the water with more concern now. Before it had only registered with her as a pure liquid, an erosive fixture in this ancient place made dark only by the underground location. Now the obsidian-black rippling surface seemed alive. The entity the place had been missing. An enemy to focus on.

"I'll go first," Pablo said. "Tania, only come out as far as you need to."

His tone left no room for debate. Vanessa moved to stand beside a large boulder that had rolled to a stop at the lip of the river. She walked behind it and dug in her boots, positioned so the rope had to wrap around it. Satisfied, she nodded at them to proceed.

Pablo took each step with almost maddening care. Probing, testing. A little weight, then more, then a shift in stance to place himself exactly halfway between this step and the last. More probing, and then the final movement. Tania tried to focus on his foot placement, to spot for him and remember where he'd stepped so she could follow exactly, but the shell ship kept pulling her attention to it. The more she stared at that steady green glow, the more she thought it had a pulse to it.

"Whoa!"

Pablo stumbled, breaking her semi-trance with his voice and sudden movement. Instinctively she gripped the rope tighter, braced herself for the worst. Suddenly she imagined him going in the water, pulling her with him. This made her realize with horror that she wouldn't drown. No, her fate would be something even worse. The suit would keep her alive for hours as she drifted down the underground river until the water pinned her against a wall in some deep, dark place, until her air ran out and she suffocated. Tania slammed her eyes shut and forced that vision away. She thought of the avocado grove on Space-Ag 12, the sound of the artificial breeze rustling the branches, and Neil. Her pulse dwindled.

The man in front of her laughed, nervously. It had only been a loose rock, she saw. The gray object rolled into the black water and vanished. Pablo paused for a moment, gathering his courage again before trying another position. Tania waited, found herself focusing on the green glow again.

Finally Pablo reached the crashed vessel. He placed his hand on it for support without any apparent concern that the contact might cause something to happen. Tania wanted to shout to him, tell him not to jostle the thing, not to wake it, but his hand was already resting on the scarred surface and nothing happened as a result.

She let out her breath. He was five meters away, just a dozen steps or so. Tania moved toward him and felt the rope tug against her waist. She looked back and realized that the maximum length between herself and Vanessa had been reached. "This is as far as I can go," she said. "Can you move up?"

"I'd rather not," Vanessa replied.

"It's okay," Pablo said. "There's enough slack. I can make it. Stay put and be ready to go back."

And just like that, he stepped into the opening on the side of the alien ship and out of Tania's view. All she could see was the long blurred shadow he cast on the ceiling and walls of the cavern as he blocked out some of the green-hued light coming from within.

The rope that linked her to Pablo started to pull taut. Just when she began to think it might not be long enough, he called out.

"It's here. I'm going to pick it up . . . right . . . now."

The emerald-green glow vanished, plunging the cave into darkness. Tania gripped the rope in a fist so tight she felt her nails dig into her palm. Something pushed against her. A force, like a concussion wave from a nearby explosion. She almost fell. The display inside her helmet flickered once, then vanished. The static sound of the river coming through her suit's speaker vanished with it, as did the ever-present background noise of her . . .

. . . of her air processor. Gone.

A wave of anxiety swept over her. She slipped again, and in her rush to grab hold of the rope she let her gun drop. The splash of it in the water sounded far away, muted. Her heart pounded. Despite the lack of sound coming in she could hear her own terrified breaths, amplified in the confines of her helmet. She could smell her own fear, hear her own movements, but from the outside world . . . nothing. No scents. No light at all. Sounds were barely perceptible. Even her sense of touch was only what sensation came in through the protective suit.

All sensation from the outside world, gone.

She screamed for help, the noise of it deafening and yet, she thought, possibly inaudible to Pablo or Vanessa. Tania did the only thing she could think of and crouched down, suddenly feeling like she was on some tightrope over a deep, deep gorge.

Her panic faded enough to allow a single cold realization in: *The air processor has stopped.* Her suit was dead, all the electronics shut down, possibly fried beyond repair. It took a singular force of will to release one shaking hand from the rope and fumble at the control panel in the center of her chest. She tried to picture the layout of the buttons in her mind, and couldn't. In her panic she began to punch them at random. Nothing happened. She began to pound her chest.

*Calm. Get a hold of yourself.*

She hadn't even realized she'd let go of the rope. Utterly blind, she patted the slick rocks around her for it. Nothing. She extended her hands and felt a subtle change as they entered the water. Coldness bit into her fingers and for a fleeting second she thought the liquid had entered her suit. But no, it was just the outside environment no longer being held at bay by heating elements built into the fabric of her outfit. She splashed around in the water, felt something round, and gripped. The rope. She pulled it from the river and only then realized it was still wrapped around her waist. The realization that she could have found it easily by starting there seemed to stem the growing fog of panic in her mind.

Both sides of the rope were slack. She began to haul in the portion that led to Pablo. Or had, at least. If the rope pulled in without him at the end, or Vanessa at the other—

She couldn't allow herself to think that. Tania shouted again, at herself this time. *"Think!"*

There were patterns before her eyes, like the bizarre shapes that appeared on the inside of her eyelids if she stole a glance at the sun. Her foot began to feel cold and she realized it had slipped into the water.

Tania pulled in Pablo's side of the rope first, and to her horror it kept coming easily, just as she feared. Any second she expected to find the end, dangling loose. Then something—someone— bumped into her. She fell, a hand caught her. One strong hand, gripping her by the upper arm. Pablo or—

A demon's face emerged from the darkness before her, at the edge of her perception. Faint, stark hints of cheekbone and jawline. Haunted eyes like two emerald stones. The scream she'd been on the verge of letting out died in her throat at the sight of those eyes. They were terrible and beautiful and . . .

*Pablo's.*

He was shouting at her. At first she recoiled, sure he'd been transformed somehow by the alien vessel. But no, she realized, he was simply lit from below. Faintly, yes, but that was all it was. She looked down and saw an object cradled in his other arm. Glowing green lines a hair's width across covered the surface, emitting so little light, the ground at her feet was still nothing but inky blackness. The triangular object was perfect save for one missing tip, matching exactly with the receptacle she'd seen aboard the ship in orbit.

Pablo squeezed her arm and shook her. He was still shouting. Tania reached up and pulled his head to her visor, turning him so his ear pressed against the glass. "I can't hear you! My suit has failed!" Tears welled in her eyes as she said the words.

The immune nodded and guided her by the arm. She had to move one slow step at a time, tapping around with the toe of her boot to find a solid place for her weight. Twice she slipped and almost went down, and each time Pablo's grip—painfully tight—kept her from spilling into the water. Her proximity to spending the rest of her life in a weightless, frigid oblivion forced her to concentrate.

She felt a tugging at her waist and remembered that Vanessa wore the other end of the rope. Tania gripped it and gave it a tug in return. A second later she felt two quick tugs, which she returned. A signal that all's well. It added to her confidence and she took the next few steps more assuredly. Just like that, her feet were on solid ground. Pablo guided her a few meters onto the pile of rubble that served as a shore and eased her to a sitting position.

To her surprise he plopped the alien artifact in her lap and then vanished into the darkness. Checking on Vanessa, she supposed. Tania ran one hand over the surface of the triangular mass, watching as the silhouette of her fingers obscured the laserlike green lines.

The rope at her waist tugged from Vanessa's direction, and then the woman was next to her. She crouched beside Tania, probably thought she was in shock. Tania repeated the technique she'd used with Pablo and pulled Vanessa's face down to her helmet, pressing her ear against the glass. "I'm okay! The suit is off-line."

Vanessa cupped her hands against the glass and shouted back. "Understood. We need to—"

Red light exploded into the cavern. Tania jerked back in surprise as a single, fiery point of light began to float before her in odd lurches. She could see smoke curling away from the red fire and sparks dripping down from it.

A flare. An emergency flare, held aloft by Pablo. He'd pulled it from the backpack he'd left on the shore before venturing across. So their flashlights had failed, too. Anything electronic, she guessed, due to some kind of electromagnetic pulse unleashed when the object was picked up.

The man came to them and handed a second flare, unlit, to Vanessa. Tania saw his lips move. Whatever he'd said, Vanessa nodded back and slipped the spare light source into a pocket. The two of them then launched into a rapid-fire conversation. An argument? No, she thought, just frantic planning.

Tania tugged at both their sleeves and pulled them close. "My air processor is off. I don't know how long I can breathe this air. We have to get to the towers." Her voice came out steady, even confident, belying how she felt.

Pablo nodded once. He said something to Vanessa, who responded with a lengthy sentence.

*God*, Tania thought, *if the* Helios *was affected, too* . . . The thought pushed her toward an emotional cliff of sheer panic. It took all her will to pull back from it. All that mattered was reaching the aura towers. She could camp there if necessary while Pablo and Vanessa found another aircraft in Denver.

All of a sudden the two immunes jumped to their feet, guns

drawn, pointed somewhere behind Tania. The tunnel mouth, she knew. Tania rolled to her knees so she could see. She started to rise and felt Pablo's hand on her back, pushing her low. A flash of light above her, along with a deep *whump* sound she felt more than heard. A gunshot. He was shooting. At what?

Vanessa fired, too. A rapid pulse of white light like camera flashes. In that burst of illumination Tania saw their target. A subhuman, running on all fours toward them. *Toward me,* she thought. Could that be right? When the gunfire ended the creature was in shadow, Pablo's flare somewhere on the ground behind her. Pablo fired again. How he could still see the thing she couldn't fathom, but in the burst of light from his gun she saw a bullet hole appear on the left side of the sub's forehead. Tania moved to her right to let the light from the flare pass her, just in time to see the creature collapse into an unmoving heap just a few meters away. One of its hands—a dirty, scarred thing with jagged fingernails—was outstretched toward where she'd been.

*No,* she thought. *Not where I'd been. Where the object had been.*

Vanessa's cupped hands were on the side of her visor again. "Where's your gun?" Then her hands went away, replaced by an ear pressed against the glass.

"I dropped it when the lights went out, into the water." Tania searched the woman's face for a reaction to that and saw nothing. The immune whipped her focus back to the tunnel mouth. Her lips were moving. Talking to Pablo again. The lack of sound from the outside wasn't quite as terrifying as the absolute blackness had been just minutes before, but it was close.

With no gun in hand the task of carrying the alien object fell to Tania. Pablo emptied nonessential gear from the bag he'd left onshore and gestured for her to place the triangular mass within. She did so, then zipped up the bag, pausing only for a second to soak in those green angular filaments of light.

She hoisted the bag on one shoulder and saw Pablo was already moving. She followed, up the sloped tunnel through which they'd entered, leaving the shell ship behind them, perhaps forever. Tania tried to imagine recreational cavers exploring this place a hundred years from now. What would they make of the empty ship? The skeletons they'd find? She tried to picture the confusion on their faces if they searched hard enough and found her gun at the bottom of that river. This place would have to be marked, perhaps even made off-limits if the world ever recovered enough to worry about such things.

Ahead, Pablo had reached the first junction in the tunnel. He whipped his red flare in one direction and then the other. Then he whirled on her, shoulders up and hands turned out in a silent question: *Which way?*

Tania shrugged. *How the hell should I—*

*Oh, shit. The map.*

Stupidly she tapped away at the controls on her suit again. Of course this changed nothing. Her HUD was blank. No clean little 3-D trail marking their path, no reassuring display of her remaining air. Nothing. The electronics were fried. The caps would need to be replaced. Firmware, reloaded. Even then it might not work, and anyway it didn't matter. It was entirely possible there was no repair capability left on Earth, much less someone with the knowledge to do the work. Like most complex things that broke, it would be tossed, and the scavengers tasked with finding a replacement. Good luck, on a suit like this.

*Focus!* she screamed at herself. Tania strode up to Pablo and pulled his head close again. "My suit's off, I told you. No map!"

He opened his mouth, closed it, then shut his eyes in frustration. When he opened them, a bit of calm had returned to those eyes. "Try to remember," he said patiently. He couldn't cup his hands to channel his voice into her helmet, so he'd simply pressed his cheek against the glass. It worked well enough.

"I . . ." Tania paused. She simply couldn't picture it. She hadn't been paying attention, not beyond referring to the glowing line whenever necessary. She'd been relying on the computer to handle the task, and that, she supposed, was exactly what the Builders' . . .

The thought hit her like a thunderclap. Puzzle pieces, slipping into place as if finally viewed from just the right angle.

Can we retrieve this without electronic aid?

Could we fetch the object in Ireland under the accelerated pressure of time?

In Belém, could we overcome the augmented warriors? Could we fight and win?

She didn't know what Samantha had faced in Darwin, but it had sounded bad. And she couldn't fathom a guess what Skyler would find in Africa. It would be tough, no doubt, and doubly so with the presence of Blackfield.

*Maybe we're just inmates,* she thought. *Earth our prison, and all this just a test of our mental faculties.*

"Well?!" Pablo shouted into her helmet. There was no malice in his tone. No, the opposite was true. He'd no doubt mistaken her suddenly contemplative gaze and assumed she was recalling the map in her mind.

"It's gone, Pablo. It's gone."

She half-expected him to swear, to fly into a rage. There was no basis for that; he'd been nothing but patient before. A kind, quiet man.

Sure enough, he just closed his eyes and nodded. Disappointment, frustration, yes, but also understanding. He looked like her own father had when she'd failed her first test in school. "You'll have to try harder next time," her father had simply said. She'd felt like a child then and she certainly felt the same way now, only here there was no "next time."

Tania Sharma took a deep breath and forced all this from her mind. She was a scientist; she needed to think that way. The map was gone and so it was irrelevant. A data source that couldn't be used. What else did she have? Tania glanced at the cave itself, first looking for anything she could remember. It was useless, though. The tunnels all blurred together.

Something on the ground caught her eye. She moved past Pablo and knelt down. There, in the space between two clumps of rock on the floor, was a partial footprint. A hint of boot tread, actually. Tania pointed at it. The man nodded, slowly at first and then a bit faster. He said something, and though she couldn't hear it she thought he was chastising himself for not having thought of the same thing. Tania gave his arm a little squeeze and smiled at him. He didn't smile back, but the corner of his mouth twitched and Tania thought that was good enough.

"Let's go," he mouthed.

# 17

## SOUTHERN CHAD

### 31.MAR.2285

Skyler pressed himself against the wall and waited for Ana to move in behind him.

He trained his rifle in rapid sharp movements on the likely places enemies would be. Alcoves on either side of the room, the corners to either side of the entryway, that dark Y-shaped passage that exited out the back with one path leading up and the other leading down.

When no subhumans presented themselves as fodder for his firearm, Skyler took in the details of the alien place. The walls were constructed of the same material as the towers, or so their appearance said. The now-familiar black surface that had no shine to it, interlaced with geometric grooves. The patterns were bigger here, though, and not as intricate, nor were they glowing from within.

The walls were not vertical, but instead slanted inward slightly. Whether on purpose or not, the effect left Skyler feeling like the place was about to collapse in on him.

The floor had a slight undulation to it, further upsetting his equilibrium. Individual hexagonal sections perhaps three meters across were themselves flat, but they were not all on the same plane. The slight variance made the floor look vaguely as if a gentle wave had run underneath and then frozen in place. The sections differed from the walls in a material sense, too. Black, of course, but textured, reminding Skyler of the spray-on coating that lined the cargo bed of many trucks.

The ceiling consisted of much smaller hexagonal tiles, black as night. All of the yellow light within the space came from a narrow, glowing band that marked the gap between floor and wall, illuminating everything from below.

Every few seconds a warm breeze would push against him from within, then turn and pull inward again, as if the building breathed.

Movement to the right caught his attention. He'd been so transfixed on the architecture around him that he'd half-forgotten about the mission, the danger. Ana had slipped inside and was in position directly across from him, crouched down on one knee and sweeping the alien room with her rifle as he had. He caught her eye and pointed at himself, then pointed forward. She nodded.

Skyler moved along the wall, rolling his feet to keep them silent. He checked the alcove across from him first, saw it to be a meter deep and empty, then he stepped out from the wall and spun around to look into the alcove next to him. Empty as well. He took a position in it and motioned for Ana to move up.

Once she'd taken the alcove across the room, he stepped out again and continued to the back wall. Outside he heard a sudden eruption of chatter among the subhumans who'd swarmed on their diversion, reminding him of the dingo packs that roamed the canyons south of Darwin. Sometimes in the night he could hear them fall upon some unsuspecting animal, even from as far away as the airport hangar.

He waited for a second, aiming toward the entrance and expecting the pack to return, but as quickly as it had arisen the sound died out. Skyler shared a nervous glance with Ana and continued to the back of the room.

A wide gap in the rear wall served as the only exit. The hallway split in a Y just a few meters in, one section diving downward at a steep slope and the other going up at an identical angle.

He paused as another unnerving waft of warm air pushed against him, stronger here in the narrow mouth of the hallway. The "breath" carried a faint chemical odor he couldn't identify. As he waited for Ana he heard sounds, too. Barely audible, baffled by the layout of the building, no doubt, but there. Movement, chatter, and the underlying drone of some kind of machine.

Ana came to the wall on the hall's opposite side and glanced at him.

"Up or down?" he whispered.

"Down," she said, sounding only half sure of her quick answer.

*As good a choice as any,* he thought, and moved into the narrow space. Narrow compared to the room outside, but still spacious by human standards, he felt. Three meters across, wide enough for one of those hexagonal floor sections. The tunnel, like the room that fronted it, had the same undulating floor and sloped walls lit from below. The ceiling remained a narrow band of black, at least five meters above the floor. Skyler wondered for a moment what this might say about the Builders themselves. Were they twice our height? Perhaps walking on four crablike legs that spread out below them to support a heavy torso? He almost laughed at himself, for the thought conjured an image in his mind right out of some sensory shooting game.

*Focus, focus.* He mentally banished the visual. Let Tania and the other scientists theorize.

"Careful!" Ana hissed.

Skyler froze. In the gap where two hexagonal tiles met was a chute that went straight down into inky darkness. The toe of his boot dangled over the space, and his next step would have taken him in. Slowly he stepped backward and knelt. From a meter away, with his focus on the hallway as a whole, the floor looked entirely solid. But if he stared at the section while standing right next to it the gap became obvious. The illusory effect was nearly perfect. He swallowed, studying the rest of the slanted tunnel before him, to no avail. It was impossible to tell one section from another until standing right over it. He wondered how many subhumans had slipped into the pit, and if the bottom was full of their broken bodies. The hazard made one thing clear: He'd have to slow down drastically or risk falling in.

And yet any minute now the subhumans outside would likely give up on the diversion there and return to guarding the doors, assuming that was what they'd been doing in the first place. It certainly seemed to be the case.

Skyler sat down, set his gun on the floor, and started to untie his boots.

Ana glared at him from across the hall. She kept her voice a whisper. "What are you doing?"

Better to show her, he decided. He pulled one boot off and tipped it over, placing his other hand beneath it. Yellow sand spilled out into a neat pile on his palm. More than he'd hoped for, in fact. He stood, centered himself in the hallway, and tossed the handful of sand like a bowler in a cricket match.

The particles flew out in a cone before him and made their own whisper as they hit the floor. Thanks to the slope of the hallway, the sand rolled and bounced many meters ahead, coating the hexagonal tiles and the gaps between, except in two other places where darkness remained.

"There," he said, "and there." Skyler emptied his other boot and shoved the handful of sand into one of his pockets. While he relaced the long black shoestrings, Ana sat down and repeated his action. She thrust two handfuls of sand into her jacket and grinned at him when they were both ready to go again.

The tunnel evened out after twenty meters. By now the sounds of subhumans outside had vanished completely. Either they'd given up on the burning truck, or Skyler and Ana were simply too far inside now to hear them. Skyler hoped for the latter, or else getting out would be a bloodbath.

Where the hall flattened another junction loomed. Straight ahead an upward-sloping hallway mirrored the one they had just traversed. Skyler assumed it led up to one of the other corner entrances. A symmetrical layout made sense, though part of him wondered if that might just be a human peculiarity. To his right, another hall led down toward the center of the facility. The regular breaths of warm air were coming from that direction.

In the exact center of the T intersection lay a body. A woman, Skyler judged from the long hair.

She was clad in a white lab coat and black slacks. A gas mask covered her face, the plastic visor cracked and lacerated with claw marks. Her skin had dried into a leathery drape that covered the bones beneath. Her hands were outstretched in two claws, as if she'd been moving on all fours, which Skyler figured was exactly the case. A subhuman when she'd died, then.

Ana slipped along the wall toward the gap that led downward. She peered within and then turned back, giving Skyler a nod that said "clear."

Instead of joining her he moved to the body, ignoring the questioning look Ana gave him. Skyler knelt and began to rummage through the pockets of the woman's slacks. He found nothing, then rolled her onto her back. The corpse weighed almost nothing and felt like a loose bundle of kindling. Underneath the gas mask, her face was twisted in a snarl that, despite or perhaps because of the mummification, made his stomach flutter. Skyler forced himself to focus on the stained white coat. He fished through the two oversized pockets on the front and found what he'd hoped for: a terminal slate. As he stood he saw something else—an identification card around her neck. Skyler grabbed it and yanked, the fabric lanyard that held it in place disintegrating in the process.

Finally he stood and moved to the hallway entrance where Ana waited, eyebrows raised.

"What is it?" she asked.

"Hoping for a clue as to what happened here."

Ana nodded, her face determined, yet impressively calm given where they stood.

Skyler flipped the ID card over in his hand first. It had a picture of a young Asian woman. The title across the top was in English: CHINESE CENTER FOR DISEASE CONTROL AND PREVENTION.

He'd expected the logo of a mining company, or perhaps some military organization. But this made sense, too. The raw minerals exposed in Africa as the Sahara expanded were exploited by every major nation, China chief among them. So either they'd sent a team here after the first reports of the SUBS virus came in, or perhaps they'd even had a team stationed nearby for all the other wonderful ailments Africa offered. Either way, they'd not only explored this facility but also had known to send a virologist in. Skyler felt a surge of anger with that realization. No such news had ever been released that he knew of. Certainly the presence of an alien facility where the disease started would have been all over the press and the HocNet. No, the Chinese and whoever else here knew about it had kept it quiet, no doubt wanting to own the alien object and whatever benefits it would reap, as Platz Industries had done in Darwin.

Skyler handed the card to Ana so she could read it for herself, and turned on the slate. It worked, but the operating system and text displayed were all in Chinese. He slipped it into his inner vest pocket for now, in case someone at Camp Exodus could read it, or perhaps figure out how to switch it to another language. He doubted it contained anything useful, but it couldn't hurt to find out.

"Let's keep moving," he said.

"SUBS didn't just start here," Ana said, lost in thought. "This place is still churning it out."

He nodded. "So it would seem."

Her eyes darted back and forth. In Skyler's experience that usually meant something mischievous would be said next, and she didn't disappoint. "When this is all over, we should get your friend Tania to drop a space station on it."

Skyler grinned, happy that she'd reached the same conclusion he had. He saw no reason to debate the outcome of her suggestion now, deciding instead to wait and see if she made the next logical jump on her own.

Ana threw a handful of sand down the hall. Two more sections of floor proved missing, on opposite sides from each other, leaving only a narrow section in the middle upon which to walk. Skyler didn't like being forced down the center of the hall like that, but there was no other way. He went first, crossed without incident, and waited until Ana did the same. On a whim, while he waited he turned on the light affixed to his rifle and aimed it down into the pit. The void stretched farther than his beam could illuminate, and Skyler felt a chill course through him. How deep did this place go?

The next handful came from his pocket. Skyler released it a bit at a time now, as if he were sowing seeds. Coated such, the floor crunched beneath his boots, but not so loudly that their stealth would be spoiled by it. He hoped not, anyway.

Below he could see the hallway's end. The floor there was different. Much smaller hexagonal tiles, each glowing with a brightness that ebbed and flowed in synch with the warm breeze. Skyler slowed their pace to a crawl as the next junction came into view. Only it wasn't a junction this time.

Revealing itself with each step like a curtain being raised, a vast room began to appear. The floor first, which resembled a crime scene. Bodies lay everywhere. Dried blood scarred the glowing floor. Pools beneath some bodies, long trails where a few of the dead had been dragged from one place to another. Splatters and arcs of spray, all dry, marked almost every available centimeter, as if the space had been painted on by a child given red finger paint and a blank canvas. On top of all this the artist had thrown hundreds of shell casings. The little brass cylinders gleamed like gems.

The corpses were legion. Two dozen, Skyler guessed, his mind reeling from the carnage of the scene. Many wore the same lab garb as the woman one floor up. Others showed signs of paramilitary gear—black fatigues, high-end rifles. Despite the horror of the view, Skyler took in these details with a practiced scavenger's eye. One soldier had a pair of grenades on his belt. Another carried a rifle-sized revolver, probably loaded with tear-gas canisters or smoke grenades.

Skyler paused one step from the room proper and let the whole place sink in. He heard Ana's crunching footsteps grow slower as she approached, then a gasp escaped her lips. She began to whisper rapidly, sounding like a frightened, superstitious child. *"Santa María, Madre de Dios, ruega por nosotros pecadores, ahora y en la hora de nuestra muerte. . . ."*

"Knock it off," Skyler rasped at her. Too harshly, from the way her eyes flared at him. "I need you to stay focused."

After a few seconds she relented and began to study the room like a warrior.

Skyler's suspicion of a symmetrical layout to the structure seemed accurate. Four tunnels converged here, entering from the middle of each side of the square room. The bodies lay in a rough circle around a dais in the center, which hung suspended over a hexagonal hole that dropped out of sight below. A small walkway—it had to be a walkway—extended from the room's floor out to the dais. The body of a dead miner draped across the narrow bridge, arms dangling over one side and legs over the other. *A miner?* Skyler had seen nothing but soldiers and medical personnel until this body.

*Maybe he got here first.*

The dais held a structure that reminded Skyler of a gazebo. Intricate supports rose from the base, alive with traces of yellow light that writhed within. Each pillar was different from the other, some thin and straight, others bulbous and curved. They all angled inward near the top, joining together in a sort of conduit that continued up toward the high dome-shaped ceiling. There the thick twisted cord branched out into a hundred smaller cables that weaved and snaked their way up into the top of the space, forming a cone-shaped area around a gaping hole in the center of the roof. Sections of the ceiling were peeled downward, as if the thing below had made an abrupt and violent entrance.

"It's a shell ship," Ana whispered.

He glanced at her, saw her gaze lay on the gazebo-like structure. He looked at it again and saw the truth in her words. The gazebo was actually two halves of a shell ship, the pillars between the two more like stretched material that still clung from one side to the other despite the craft having been pulled in two.

"It landed exactly in the center?" she asked.

"Pretty good aim," Skyler agreed.

Across the rest of the dome were hexagonal holes of varying size. Lit from the floor below, the whole thing made Skyler think of honeycomb. It was as if he stood inside a beehive, and the idea unsettled him further.

A waft of warm air pushed against him, rising and falling like the breath of a slumbering beast. The gentle wind came up from the massive hole in the floor, carrying a fine black particulate. As the dusty plume rose through the room toward the dome it accelerated, sucked into the myriad of gaps.

He began to walk—slow, careful steps over the corpses that

dotted the floor—toward one of the fallen soldiers. He motioned Ana to follow and then instructed her with a hand signal to cover him while he looted the body. He ditched his machine gun for the much more advanced model carried by the dead man, after checking the clip to make sure it still carried bullets. It did, .45 caliber even, and there were two more magazines in his black vest. Skyler pocketed those, too. The gun had a holographic sight that still functioned. It was a risk, he knew, to switch to a weapon he'd never fired before in the middle of an op, but this didn't have a scratch or scuff anywhere on it.

He hefted the gun to a get a feel for the balance, then pointed toward another dead soldier. "Get that rotary gun," he said to Ana. She did, and gladly, slinging her own weapon in favor of the much more fiendish device. She strained under the weight of it at first, but adjusted quickly enough. Then she set it down on the floor and detached a bandolier from the man's torso. A dozen canisters were held in black nylon sheaths along half of it.

She studied the ammunition. "It's all in Chinese," she said.

"Trial and error then, I guess," he said.

Ana grinned at that. She checked the weapon itself and found it to be fully loaded. Whatever had happened in here, the dead solider hadn't fired a single round. "Whatever will be, will be," she said with a shrug, and gave the gun a little upward jerk. The front half clicked back into place.

"Right," Skyler said. "Cover me?" At her nod he crept up to the narrow bridge that extended out two meters over the deep pit in the center of the room. The bottom hid in darkness, far below, exactly like the silos below Nightcliff and Belém. Odd that those were both below space elevators, but this place had no such feature. *Perhaps the Builders sank pits like this for some purpose unrelated to the facility above,* he thought. Heat dissipation or something. He wondered, belatedly, if such a pit existed below the site in Ireland, too. There'd been no evidence of such a thing, but they hadn't really stuck around to find out, either.

Faced with the abyss, the slim bit of floor that led out to the dais suddenly seemed dangerously narrow. Skyler tested it with his toes, pressing lightly, then progressively harder until his entire foot rested on the surface. He gritted his teeth and shifted his weight outward, over that foot. "You bastards couldn't put a handrail on this, for fuck's sake?" he muttered. He took a full step now, over the thin body of the miner that lay draped across the narrow surface.

The bridge held. More than that, it felt solid, like it had been carved out of the same slab of material as the room. The thought gave Skyler a sudden pause.

"What's wrong?" Ana whispered. She stood at least seven meters away, but her voice carried well here.

"Just . . ." He paused. "Thinking." The bridge's width almost perfectly matched that of his shoulders. The hallways they'd walked through to get here, while tall, were certainly comfortable for a human to traverse. The objects they'd already recovered from Ireland and Belém, though bulky and quite heavy, were still within the limits of a human being to carry.

*Are they so similar to us? Do they know our physiology, our capabilities and limits? Or did we somehow tell them?*

He recalled again the news Tania had dropped on him: Neil knew. What exactly he knew, or how, seemed a detail he'd taken to his grave. But he'd known something, and perhaps, perhaps, he'd told the Builders something as well. An exchange? A goddamn conversation?

"We should hurry," Ana said.

Her voice brought him back to the moment. Skyler balanced himself one last time, then traversed the bridge in two quick steps. He glanced over his shoulder at the strip, then at Ana. He smiled at her. In response she made a shooing motion with her hand. "Okay, okay," he said.

In the center of the dais, which was actually the bottom half of a shell ship, lay another of the objects. This one radiated yellow light from the fine grooves along its surface. It was oval in shape with a wavy portion along one length, matching exactly the slot he'd seen aboard the massive Builder ship that hung in orbit above.

Skyler slung his new rifle over one shoulder and stood over the artifact. A meter wide and roughly half as tall, it would require two hands to carry. That wouldn't do, he decided. He couldn't have Ana the only one ready to shoot, given the swarm of subs that waited for them above. He unzipped one of the pockets on his jacket and slipped out a folded backpack made of ballistic nylon. It would be a tight fit, he thought, but should do the job. He unzipped the bag and laid it on the ground next to the alien object. Then he braced his feet on either side, crouched, and placed his hands on either side of the oval. The material felt cool to the touch. He flexed his fingers. The thing lay perfectly flat on the platform floor. If it was much heavier than the objects from Ireland and Belém, he'd need a pry bar to lift it, and that was one thing he'd not thought to bring.

In Ireland, lifting the object had triggered the release of subhumans trapped within what could only be called time bubbles. Near Belém, a localized earthquake had almost shaken the cave down upon his head. "Ana," he said. He made sure to lock eyes with her. "Something will happen when I lift this."

"I know," she said. "I'm ready, I think. Just do it and let's go."

"Right then." Skyler heaved. The object didn't budge. He adjusted his hands and tried again, emitting a grunt that turned into something of a shout by the time he gave up and relaxed.

"Let me help," Ana said. She stepped forward.

"No, no. Stay back, I mean it."

He saw the flash of an argument in the way her eyes narrowed, but she pursed her lips into a thin line and took one step backward.

Skyler adjusted his hands again, this time placing both hands next to each other. He dug his fingers into the edge of the object until the tips turned white, then red.

Something popped and the artifact lifted from the floor so abruptly he almost fell. Ana let out a little yelp of surprise from behind him as Skyler shoved one hand under the object and moved his other hand around to grip the opposite edge. The bottom of it must have formed a suction bond with the tile below, because now that the oval had lifted it weighed very little—less than half what the one in Ireland had weighed, he guessed. Skyler slipped it into the bag easily, zipped it up, and turned around.

Ana shrugged at him, a grin playing at the corners of her mouth. He returned the shrug and pulled the backpack on, again surprised at the relatively light weight of the object.

Skyler took the narrow bridge in one quick, long stride. He turned to Ana again. "Let's—"

She had a finger pressed to her lips, her eyes cast upward at the ceiling.

"What is it?"

After a second she shook her head. "I don't know . . . something's different. I'm not—" Then her eyes widened. "The breathing. It's stopped."

# 18

## DARWIN, AUSTRALIA

### 31.MAR.2285

In the end Arkin had offered to pilot the hauler himself, rather than risking the involvement of one of his pilots in the whole endeavor. The short hop across the water, undertaken many times per day and largely automated, was one the plant manager had taken upon himself to learn over the years. "Don't have the luxury of hiring young pilots out of the air force anymore," he'd said. "The only good one to come up since the plague hit took off to join one of the scavenger crews, and that was a couple of years ago."

He'd meant Angus, Sam realized. She'd said nothing, and neither had Skadz.

Twinkles of fading orange sunlight glinted off the water below. The flotilla of boats, barges, and improvised rafts that crowded Darwin's aura-protected shore lifted and fell as a gentle surf pushed beneath them.

"It's a bit sad, isn't it?" Sam asked, not speaking to either man in particular.

Skadz looked at her with mild annoyance. He always hated starting an op without a real plan.

Prumble, though, seemed relaxed, even happy, feet propped up on the duffel bag that held his custom-made environment suit. "Hmm?" he asked.

"All these boats, stuck here," Sam explained. "I mean, the life of a sailor is all about the freedom to travel at will, to enjoy the open water, you know? It's bad enough to have to live your life trapped in one city, but to do so while living on a perfectly mobile vehicle . . . It's depressing."

Skadz rolled his eyes and went back to staring at the roof of the cabin. No doubt he was playing out scenarios in his mind, trying to win the chess game before it started.

"There she is," Prumble said, his face suddenly pressed against the window. He was looking at the ocean below.

"What did they decide?" Sam asked.

"Take a look for yourself." He leaned back in his seat so she could see past him. Below she saw the edge of the flotilla. Despite the fact that nearly half of the precious aura generated by the alien cord covered water, the ships that had made it to Darwin mostly clustered together along the shore for the simple reason that they had to get supplies just like any other dwelling. Fish and rainwater would only go so far. A few boats, though, anchored farther out. Some were abandoned, already listing steeply and soon to be relics for the ocean floor. Most were fishermen, scavengers in their own right trying to bring in a haul of protein for the hungry city.

Prumble's thick finger pointed at a dark mass beneath the waves, lurking just a few hundred meters from the flotilla's border. A white shirt tied to one of the antenna masts that studded the bridge indicated the crew had voted to go along with the plan. Arkin and June, seated side by side in the cockpit, both turned and smiled at Prumble, though June looked decidedly more enthusiastic.

She forced her attention back to the submarine. "It's . . . gigantic."

"Alexander class," Prumble said, "incredible machine. With minimal crew it can stay out at sea for almost a year without surfacing."

"Wow," Sam managed to say. "How often do they go out?"

"More than you'd think. Her captain once showed me pictures

they take of coastal towns through the periscope. I think he was hoping I'd buy them, the pictures, as recon for scavengers like you."

"Why didn't you? They could have been useful."

Prumble shook his head. "The resolution was very poor, the images from too far out."

Skadz held his hand out near Prumble's face and snapped his fingers. "Oy, mate. Can we focus on the bloody plan? This tub is going to land soon in the belly of the beast."

The big man stared at the craft below for a few seconds longer, lost in thought as the ocean slid past. When he turned to face Skadz and Sam, his expression had hardened. "Arkin drops us off and stays with the plane with June. The three of us will make contact with Kip. Once we know where secure storage is, and how long it will take to get inside, we'll enlist him in locating Arkin's girl."

"If he can't," Sam said, "I may know someone who can." Whether or not she could find Vaughn was another issue entirely, but she let that detail slide.

Prumble nodded. "If possible, I think Kip should find the girl and deliver her to the aircraft. He may have the clout to do that without raising any eyebrows. We'll meet him back there and all fly out together."

"I don't know," Skadz said, tapping his chin with one finger. "I'd feel better if I was with him. In case a little force needs to be applied. I don't think Kip is up to that."

"An understatement if there ever was one," Prumble said. "Sam, your thoughts?"

"I'd prefer we stick together." She met Skadz's gaze and saw the plea there; whether he'd meant to hide it or not, she knew he needed to do this. "But I think Skadz is right. Kip seems like the type who would bail out at the first sign of trouble, and if he comes back empty-handed Arkin may not fly us back out."

"Fair enough." He still seemed unconvinced, frowned even, but let it go. "Afterward, Arkin will drop us at Aura's Edge near the valley, then join the *Zorich* crew for their trip to Belém."

Sam nodded. Skadz did the same.

"Now," Prumble said, "on the off chance we're unable to rendezvous with Skyler—"

Sam slugged him on the shoulder. "We'll make the fucking rendezvous."

"On the off chance Skyler is unable—"

"Skyler will make the fucking rendezvous."

Prumble sighed. "It's another option. I'll leave it at that."

"All right, you magnificent bastard," Skadz said. "This is all bloody fascinating, but what about the vault? I wouldn't mind some sort of plan for *that,* and we've got roughly zero minutes to cook one up."

Prumble shrugged. "We'll figure something out."

"Kip said it was impenetrable; you said 'leave that to me.' "

"Did I? Heat-of-the-moment thing, I suppose."

"Prumble . . ."

"I'm kidding. Yes, the vault. I can get us inside the vault."

Samantha folded her arms. "How?"

He flashed his mischievous grin again. "I've done it before. Twice, as a matter of fact." At their incredulous stares he held up his hands. "No, I didn't break in."

"Then how?"

"I was invited. First time almost eighteen years ago, when I was merely an apprentice installer with Novak and Sons Security out of Wellington. Top-notch operation, mind you. World-renowned. The second time was, oh, seven years ago."

"About when SUBS hit," Sam noted.

"To the hour, as it happened. Uncannily good timing, you'll note. I was, um, perhaps *freelance* is the best word? Use your imagination. Someone needed access to that vault in a hurry and flew me in for the job. It's a long and sordid tale, and the reason I was even in Darwin at all when the world went pear-shaped. Nice bit of luck, eh?"

"Yeah."

"Point is, I've got the level-one originator's fail-safe code burned into my brain. Can't be changed. If we can get to the damn thing, I'll open it."

The note generated by the aircraft's engines spiked as it adjusted course for the approach to Nightcliff. Below, the sprawling fortress came into view. The morning was bright and warm, but Sam noted there were few people about.

Other than the impressive wall that surrounded the place, and the giant tower that surrounded the Elevator cord itself, she thought the whole place looked fairly bland. A spread of buildings small and large. A residential area, even the gaudy mansion that Neil Platz himself used to live in. She'd seen all this many times when, on occasion, she'd taken the co-pilot's seat in the *Melville* on the return leg of a scavenger outing. But she'd never paid it much attention until now.

Her eyes gravitated to one of the converted high-rise hotels, the one where Vaughn now occupied a meager room on the third floor. The room where she'd slept with him just a few nights ago and warned him.

She wondered what would happen if they ran into him while inside. There were only two choices, really, and though she suspected her visit had swayed which side he'd come down on, she still had no idea which side that would be.

"Here we go," Skadz said. "Prumble? A plan, my good man?"

Instead of answering he leaned forward and poked his head into the cockpit, where Arkin oversaw the hauler's automated descent in toward the assigned landing pad. Prumble cupped one hand against the man's helmet and said something to him. Arkin replied. They conversed in this way for thirty seconds or so. Finally Prumble clapped him on the shoulder. Then Arkin leaned across the cockpit and pulled a slate from a pocket near the base of the co-pilot's seat where June sat. No, not a slate, Sam realized, an old-fashioned clipboard with a single laminated sheet held under the clip. Arkin took a grease pen from his breast pocket and scribbled something on the top sheet, signing it with a flourish.

Prumble leaned back heavily into his seat again and grinned with satisfaction.

Across from him, Skadz waited for an answer. Sam realized she wouldn't mind hearing one herself, but the smug grin on Prumble's face was one she knew well.

"Not funny, mate," Skadz said. "Give me something here, I mean it."

Prumble held up the borrowed object and tapped it. "Have clipboard, will travel," he said brightly.

* * *

"Flank me," the big man said.

As they had done when walking into Arkin's office at the water plant, Sam took the right shoulder and Skadz followed at the left.

"Don't brandish your weapons," Prumble added. "But don't attempt to conceal them, either. Squint a lot. Look both bored and alert."

Weapons. Sam wanted to laugh. Skadz had taken one of the umbrellas apart and kept the central shaft. He'd offered her one as well, but Sam thought it would snap on the first skull it came down upon. Instead she had the shorter half of a broken broom handle stuffed into her belt at her lower back.

Skadz snorted a laugh. "This is perhaps the most ridiculous thing you've ever done."

"Which is why it will work."

"I think on my tombstone I want the words 'It's the fat man's fault.' Sam?"

She considered. "Mine will say 'Had clipboard, died miserably.'"

"Enough," Prumble snapped with uncharacteristic impatience. "Focus now. Time to fool the fools."

He strode from the aircraft like a lion loose in a zoo. Absolute confidence wafted off him and seemed to flow straight into Sam's own psyche. Prumble selected a target and marched straight up to her. The woman seemed to be supervising the crew that had come out to unload the hauler. She glanced up just in time to see Prumble looming over her. Her eyes widened. "Who the—"

Prumble held the clipboard before her and tapped it with his index finger. "Who the hell am I? I'm the one you promised a new skid for the one your idiots cracked. That was a month ago. A month!"

"I . . . I promised?" she stammered.

"Not you *specifically*," Prumble said. He glanced at the clipboard, which Sam saw held some old flight operations checklist. "Osmak. Kip Osmak. This is his signature right here, is it not? I refuse to let that water go until he comes out here

225

and personally fits a new skid to this bird."

Sam realized that Prumble had chosen his mark perfectly. The woman had probably been recently assigned, and though she was no doubt a fine little Jacobite, she had no experience or real authority out here on the landing pads. The woman withered under Prumble's loud, angry tone. He stood at least a half meter taller than her and easily that much wider.

"Just a second," the woman said. She fumbled for a handheld that was clipped to her belt, almost dropped it, then dialed it on and brought it to her lips. "Could someone find Kip Osmak and put him on, please?"

A long twenty seconds passed, Prumble tapping his foot impatiently to mark the time. Behind them, the engines of the water hauler dwindled down to zero. The yard became silent save for the sounds of people working. There were few people about, Sam realized, and then she remembered it was Sunday. Maybe they congregated in the mess for prayers or whatever it was they did. Idly Sam wondered where Sister Haley's famous book was. Grillo's breast pocket seemed the most likely answer.

"Uh . . . ," a static-laden voice said. "This is Kip?"

The woman eyed Prumble as she spoke. "There's some people down here from the water plant; they said—"

Prumble snatched the radio from her. "Kip, you'd better get down here and make good on your promise. Otherwise I swear I shall take this to a higher authority."

His response came out like a squawk. "You're here? I mean. Yes, of course. Um. Meet me in the lobby in five minutes."

The big man grinned, shoved the radio back into the still-cowering woman's hands, and said, "You . . . deserve a promotion. Thank you." The change in her facial expression came instantly. The quivering lip and wide, terrified eyes vanished in place of something like awe.

"Where's this lobby?" Prumble asked her.

She pointed to the centerpiece of Nightcliff's grounds—the Elevator tower.

"Of course. Again, my thanks. You might as well give your crew a dinner break while we sort this out."

With that Prumble snapped his fingers at Sam and Skadz,

turned, and marched toward the massive structure. Sam kept on his heels, fighting to suppress her own grin. Skadz shot her a sidelong glance and gave a little shrug. "Have clipboard, will travel," he mouthed.

Halfway across the yard Sam felt the ground move beneath her feet. Not enough to make her want to dive for cover, but more like if a large lorry had rumbled by. A queer sound like a cable being twanged followed. She glanced up at the source of the noise—the space elevator.

"Someone's found another object," Skadz said.

"And if it was Skyler," Prumble replied, "he could be here in a matter of hours."

Sam couldn't see the cord vibrate, but the noise unsettled her. It seemed louder than the previous instances, though of course she hadn't been standing right under the thing then. Certainly it went on longer. The initial noise seemed to trace a quick path up the cord's slightly tilted length. Then, a few seconds later, it rippled back down. It reminded her of the highly stylized sound effects often heard in sensory shows about starships and laser weapons, not of anything a real-world object could generate.

She glanced down at her feet, trying to imagine the generator somewhere below that Skyler had visited. Had it initiated the vibration? Some change in state or perhaps, more unsettling, had it shut off? Sam nudged Skadz and leaned in to whisper to him when he turned to her. "Keep an eye on Prumble," she whispered. "In case that noise was the aura shutting down."

His eyebrows arched.

"It happened a few times, before you came back."

"I heard about that."

Sam glanced downward, pointedly. "Skyler said the generator was down there, somewhere."

There were no guards stationed in front of the lobby, and the wide sliding doors were fully open. Prumble breezed inside and then halted, looking about for the man Osmak.

Samantha took in the vast room. The ceiling soared more

than twenty meters above them. Made of glass and supported by thin metal rods, it had once no doubt provided a nice view straight along the cord. For reasons she'd never understood, the thread didn't go precisely straight up, but rather at a slight angle that tilted toward the equator. Eventually the path of it leveled out, but from here at the base the effect made her feel slightly off balance. The tilt made sense, no doubt, from a physics standpoint, but from here she thought it looked ready to topple over.

She turned her gaze to the lobby itself. Two curved staircases wrapped around a wide central shaft that no doubt concealed the Elevator cord, for it, too, rose at that slight grade. The stairs ended at a second-floor balcony that looked down over the main floor where she stood. People milled about, some running in or out, most talking in urgent tones. Only one was a guard, for he wore the maroon helmet, but he also had on the white Jacobite garments over his ad hoc uniform. He was staring up at the Elevator tower, one finger pressed to his ear. *The vibration on the cord has them all spooked,* Sam thought.

On the main floor there were four square areas evenly dispersed, with low couches facing in toward coffee tables. It had no doubt once been very slick and high-end, but not anymore. The couches were grimy, with tears in the upholstery either covered in tape or simply left exposed.

Around the perimeter were doors. Sam noted signage for men's and women's bathrooms, plus one for families. Platz probably thought this place would act like an airport terminal when he'd funded it, she mused.

Toward the back wall, behind the stairs, she saw the sickly form of Kip Osmak. He peered out from a shadow like some kind of back-alley drug dealer, all hunched over and eyes shifting. Stringy hair clung to both sides of his hollow face.

"There," Sam said, nodding toward him.

Prumble strode across the nearly empty floor and made to say something, but Kip shushed him. He stood, Sam realized, at the top of a stairwell that led down.

"Uh, Prumble. Hello," he said. "And your friends, too. Wasn't expecting you." He stole a glance at a small slate he held in his right hand. The hand, Sam saw, was shaking.

"Well, we're here," Prumble replied, "and time is short. Can you take us where we need to go?"

The frail man chuckled nervously and retreated a step toward the downward stairwell. "I'll try." He glanced at the slate again.

"What's wrong?" Sam asked him.

He glanced at her. "Ah. Uh, just waiting for the changing of the guard. Five minutes."

"Can we get out of the lobby, please?" Skadz asked.

"Of course, of course. Um, this way." Kip descended the steps half turned, as if he needed to be ready to run back up at any second. No, that wasn't it, Sam realized. He moved more like a host who'd just let guests into a house he was embarrassed to display.

At the bottom of the stairs there was a wide, square landing that fronted a pair of gray double doors. A sign stenciled on both said AUTHORIZED PERSONNEL ONLY—NO VISITORS BEYOND THIS POINT.

Kip pressed his thumb on a reader adjacent to the entry while simultaneously leaning down to stare into a retinal scanner. A second later a sharp click emitted from the doors and he pulled one open for them. Sam noted sweat on his brow as she passed him into the corridor beyond. "Relax," she said.

His response came as a feeble, nervous laugh.


The subfloor below the Elevator tower lobby had none of the grandeur of the space above. Grimy tile floors that had once been white matched the walls and ceiling as well. Sam had explored enough buildings outside Darwin to know the drill: rooms for janitors, maintenance crews, property managers, and various closets for a litany of supplies. Perhaps a small break area for those types of employees someone like Neil Platz would generally prefer didn't mingle with visiting dignitaries.

Kip led them to a dismal space lit by a single LED bulb embedded in the center of the ceiling. He pulled the door closed behind them and stood next to it, his gaze fixed on the slate in his hand.

Prumble cleared his throat. "Secure storage is just at the end of that hall. Once Kip here gets us past the biometrics, I'll spring the safe. It may not trigger alerts anywhere, but we'd best conclude our business quickly."

Sam nodded.

Skadz turned to Kip. "Do you know a girl named Eileen Arkin?"

"Err, no," Kip said. "Sorry."

"Can you look her up? She's here in Nightcliff somewhere, and I need to find her."

"Why?"

"Can you look her up or not?"

Kip fumbled with his slate, almost dropped it, then started to tap away at the screen. "Um . . . okay, yes. Royal—the old hotel—room 3636." His eyebrows raised. "That's a prison floor."

Skadz gave Kip a single, sharp nod. "Once they're in the vault, you take me there."

"I . . . Okay, if you wish."

The air tasted stale and smelled of mold. Sam was about to push for a change of scenery when Kip finally broke the uncomfortable silence. "Almost time," he said.

Sam eyed him. "You haven't even asked what the plan is. I mean, what happens after this."

He paled and then shrugged. "I figure you'd get what you came for and . . . leave."

"That'd put you in a fix, wouldn't it? Grillo would know you helped us. Especially with the prisoner."

Kip looked at the floor and his head bobbed.

"Come with us," Prumble said. "You've helped me enough over the years, I owe you that. All you'd need is an environment suit, but I suspect most any would fit you just fine."

Kip almost—almost—looked up at that. It was no doubt an option he'd considered but assumed impossible. Still he kept his head down, strands of sweaty gray hair dangling in front of his face.

*This is one sour son of a bitch*, Sam thought, and felt sorry for him.

The slate in his hand beeped. He glanced at it and turned to the door. "Um. Follow me."

Outside the long hallway was empty. Kip glanced both ways

and then hustled to the far end, where another fingerprint and eye scanner graced the wall next to a black door. He performed the unlock procedure again and held the door open, motioning them inside.

Sam was about to comment on the stupidity of leaving the room unguarded during a changing of the guard, but before she could speak another voice rang out.

"That's far enough."

Prumble froze in front of her and she, right on his heels, plowed into him. She fumbled to ready her broom handle.

"I wouldn't do that," the voice, a woman's, said. "Hands where we can see them."

Kip clicked the door closed behind them. "This is all of them," he said.

"Excellent work, Kip."

Samantha shut her eyes as she recognized the voice. A cloud of emotions rattled in her head. She stepped back from Prumble, her hands outstretched, and took in the scene.

Six Jacobite guards were fanned out in a half circle in front of the vault door. Each carried a machine gun, save for the leader in the center, who brandished a Sonton pistol. Unlike the usual improvised poncho, she wore a clean robe that seemed custom tailored. It covered her from head to toe, until she pushed back the hood.

"Kelly," Sam whispered.

"It's Sister Josephine, remember?" She glanced left and right. "Bind them," she said. The guards to either side began to circle around.

Sam stared at her former friend, wondering what had happened, wondering how this remarkable woman could have been so completely transformed. She thought back to that day on the roof above Grillo's office, the first time she'd seen Kelly in the robe. Her onetime friend had entrapped her, tricked her into talking about the very object they'd now come to steal.

Her thoughts turned to Kip. The slimy little weasel with his stringy hair and sullen face. She wondered if she could strike him in the throat, crush his Adam's apple before anyone could stop her. He'd been on the goddamn comm when the whole plan had been discussed, and probably relayed the whole thing to Grillo, too.

"Traitorous bastard," she said with a snarl at the pathetic, sickly man.

What little color his face had flushed away. "We all make our choices. We do what we need to do to survive."

Kelly narrowed her eyes. "How right you are."

She lifted her pistol, aimed, and fired.

# 19

## THE FLATIRONS, COLORADO

### 31.MAR.2285

Two wrong turns left Pablo baffled and Tania completely disoriented. If not for the scratches Vanessa made at each turn with the tip of her rifle, they would have been hopelessly lost. She'd even thought to X out the dead-end choices.

Tania had just started to feel confident again when she realized the effort her breathing now required. And while it may have been her imagination, her head also felt light. The feeling soon grew into a headache like a champagne hangover. She considered saying something to the others, but what could they do? Pablo was moving as fast as the party could go. To stop them now would only delay the one thing that would help her: fresh air.

The tunnel took a sharp upward slope and narrowed slightly. Tania remembered this part; she'd almost slipped down the incline coming in. At the point where the slope began to rise a narrow, natural tunnel broke off to Pablo's right. The opening was a full meter up on the side of the tunnel wall and barely wide enough for one person to fit through. He glanced in as he passed but kept going straight, remembering the way as well.

He came to the top of the incline and paused just as Tania reached the bottom, holding the flare out behind him to help light the tricky slope. Rocks and pebbles still rolled down from his climb, leaving tracks through the patches of loosely packed dirt.

The shadows around Tania swam abruptly. She glanced up and saw that Pablo had whipped the light around in front of him. He was moving it about in rapid jerks, each time sending the shadows around her in a lurch to new angles.

A hand on her back, Vanessa's, pulled her. Tania glanced behind her to see the woman's face in the shifting light. Her eyes were cast upward at Pablo, her mouth a tight line. Tania felt the now familiar *whump whump* of gunfire coming from above. Vanessa was saying something, urging her backward. Tania went, letting the woman pull her back the way they'd come. Ten meters, maybe more, before she shoved Tania to one side of the tunnel and brought her gun up.

Tania looked at the slope. The red light grew as Pablo came back down. First she saw his feet, moving backward down the incline. Then his legs, torso. All the while bright flashes of white light erupted from ahead of him. His gun. She thought there must be a lot of subhumans up there because he kept shooting. Soon enough his whole body was visible. He took a knee at the bottom of the ramp and quickly reloaded. As he did so, a subhuman—muscular, compact—raced past him. It ran straight toward Tania. Silhouetted against the red flare it looked like an ape, except only the head and chin had hair.

Vanessa shot the former human twice in the chest and it crumpled in a heap a few meters in front of Tania. The gunshots were so close she could hear them through her helmet, like the sound of snapping fingers. Tania hardly had time to feel helpless when she saw Pablo's flare move again. He'd tossed it aside so he could aim with both hands. A subhuman body rolled down the incline before him, forcing him to step aside. Another came down, running on all fours, again trying to slip past him rather than fight.

Pablo turned to shoot it as it passed, putting his back to the narrow side tunnel. He fired into the creature's side. She saw it react as if merely swatted at. One hand went to cover the wound, and the other continued to act as a leg as the creature rushed toward them. Vanessa finished it off.

*Pablo must have told her to retreat, and shoot any that got past,* Tania realized.

A shape, a blur, exploded out from the side tunnel. It leapt onto Pablo's back and the two went down in a cloud of dust. Kicking. Flailing limbs. A flash of gunfire.

Tania screamed, pointless even if anyone could hear her. She heard more gunfire from her left. Vanessa, firing into that confused mess? Too risky! Tania moved to stop her and realized she wasn't shooting toward Pablo: She was shooting behind them. She glanced back to see, but the tunnel was pitch-black. Each time she fired a small spark would erupt off the rocky walls behind them, giving Tania a brief glimpse of shapes moving toward them.

*Trapped. Oh God.*

The light Pablo had dropped faltered. Dirt, or rock, kicked on top of it. Tania dropped the pack that carried the alien object and rushed forward without another thought. Churned dirt and dust filled the tunnel now, giving her only a few meters of visibility. She saw movement. Feet, kicking—no, convulsing. Booted feet, Pablo's. The creature was on top of him, swinging wildly down where his head must be.

Her combat training took over. She kicked, and though she'd taken the correct stance her suit made the motion stiff, awkward. She'd aimed for the thing's head but hit it in the back of the neck. No matter, she had its attention. Tania followed up with a punch that landed perfectly on the sub's throat. She felt the Adam's apple shift under her blow, even through the thick glove of her suit.

The creature fell back, gasping, clutching at its throat. Tania stomped down on its abdomen, forcing the air out of it. It might not die, but it would be down for a while, so she shifted to Pablo. His face was a bloody mess, and he wasn't moving. His eyes were open, staring upward.

*No. No!*

She slipped her hands under him, lifting him by the armpits and dragging his heavy, limp form. Pablo's boots scraped two horrible trails along the floor of the tunnel. Subhuman bodies littered the ground, their blood mixing with the churned dirt. Tania could only see a meter in any direction, so thick with dust the air had become. It probably tasted dry and tinged with brass, but Tania would gladly breathe it right now if she could. The air in her suit wouldn't last much longer, of this she had no doubt.

She pulled Pablo's body around a fallen subhuman. All the while Vanessa kept shooting, ahead and behind. The half-buried red flare sputtered one final gasp and then the tunnel plunged into absolute darkness. With the black came a strange serenity. Tania groped around until she found Pablo's neck. She felt no pulse, but couldn't be sure if she would feel it through the gloves of her suit. So she pressed her fingers to her own neck.

The vein below her skin pounded against her gloved fingers.

Pablo was dead.

Tania slumped forward, clutching the quiet man to her, not caring now if her own supply of oxygen would run out as she wept. Another life, another good person, sacrificed to whatever these goddamn aliens wanted. She wanted to take that triangular slab of exotic material and throw it into the cold dark waters below. Let all the subhumans jump in after it. If they wanted it so badly, maybe they should have it.

Vanessa lit the extra flare and Tania found herself staring into Pablo's eyes. His face was a horrific mess of blood and deep gashes, but the eyes . . . his eyes were perfect. Strong, intelligent, calm.

*No.* No, she couldn't quit. Even if the others succeeded, failure here would make their efforts mean nothing. She couldn't let that happen. She wouldn't let this man's efforts go to waste. With one gloved hand, Tania reached out and drew his eyelids closed.

She felt a hand on her shoulder. A second later Vanessa collapsed on the ground next to her and fell over her friend's body. The anguish on her face knew no equal, Tania thought, and though it hurt to admit it, she felt glad in that moment that she couldn't hear the woman's cries.

Tania stood then. Something inside her ignited, brighter than the flare, brighter than the fucking sun.

She picked up the bag that held the alien object and hurled it toward the slope in the passage.

A second later two more subs came down the incline. Instead of rushing at her, they fell on the bag, clawing at it to reach the artifact within. Tania picked up Vanessa's gun and walked calmly forward. In the hazy red light it became easy to forget these beings had once been human. She put a single bullet into their heads from point-blank range, ignoring the sick way they convulsed, the fine spray of blood that dotted the glass of her helmet. Then she leaned against the wall and waited for the next. She shot that one, too. When the fourth came the gun clicked empty. Tania tossed it aside and threw her arms around the creature's neck, covering its mouth and nose as she'd been trained to do. The animal—that's what it was, an animal—began to claw violently at her arms but she held on until the body went slack against her. Tania let go. The body collapsed at her feet.

She stepped back again and waited, but no more came. Then something brushed her arm and Tania wheeled, lashed out, only to see Vanessa next to her. The woman raised her hands defensively until Tania relented.

The tears Vanessa had cried for Pablo ran in two vertical streaks down her dust-coated skin. Yet her expression held no sign of grief now. She reached out to Tania, grabbed her helmet, and twisted.

*So this is it,* Tania thought. *We kill ourselves, like Jake did, rather than let them get us.*

There was no hiss of air when the seal broke and the helmet came away. Tania ignored that and sucked in a breath of gritty air. She almost coughed, but somehow managed to choke it down. "I should have saved a bullet for each of us, I guess," Tania said.

"Don't say that," the woman replied. "We need to run now. Can you do it?"

"My helmet," Tania said numbly. "You—"

"The suit is torn," Vanessa said. She lifted one of Tania's arms and showed her. The material had been raked to shreds by the subhuman she'd strangled. "Take this knife. I'll carry the . . . thing."

"It's hopeless," Tania said, watching the immune shrug the bag that held the alien artifact onto her back. Her head pounded; whether it was from the near asphyxiation or the tainted air she now breathed, she had no idea.

Vanessa gripped her by the shoulder and growled her words. "It's not. We're going. The towers aren't far, Tania. We'll fight our way and finish this for him. Do you understand?"

Tania stammered.

"Go!"

She went. Up the slope, knife held before her pointed downward from her clenched fist, a style that allowed her to punch and slice rather than risk burying the knife into something and losing it. By the time she reached the top of the incline her head pounded. SUBS, already working its way into her brain. The first symptom, the headache, she knew lasted anywhere from one minute to as much as ten. Ten minutes, if she was lucky, to get to the aura and suppress the virus with nothing more than a pain in the skull to deal with. She'd be like Karl, popping painkillers with every meal, forever. If the disease progressed beyond that, she'd likely be killed on the spot by the collapse of her mind. If she survived, Vanessa would either kill her or leave her here in the wilderness.

The immune still held the flare, running a few paces behind Tania. The red light's jerky motion made Tania's own shadow sway, grow, and shrink in front of her as if she were trying to catch up to a demon.

Her head felt like it had been clamped in a vise. Vision began to blur. She stumbled, righted herself just as the tunnel turned and angled down, then up. Another turn. Something was running toward her. For an instant she thought it was a dog or wolf, until she saw the human—vaguely human—face. It was going to run past her, again going for the artifact. Tania struggled against the crushing force inside her head and dove right as the creature passed her. She knocked the thing from its galloping stance, for it weighed almost nothing, and pinned it against the wall, lashing her fist across its throat at the same time. A sharp black line appeared across the throat and fluid began to spill out.

*Good enough,* she thought, and ran on, using the brightness and motion of the light behind her to make sure Vanessa was still with her.

Light ahead. The vaguest gray highlights on one side of the tunnel. A flashlight?

No, she realized. Sunlight, glinting off the rock. "Almost there!" she shouted. The woman behind her made no response, but Tania could hear the pace of her footfalls increase.

The entrance to the cave was a glowing white oval, so bright it blinded her for a moment. When her vision returned, Tania took in the expansive space that marked the cave's entrance. She half-expected to see a crowd of subhumans standing there, waiting to ambush them. The space, however, was empty.

"Catch your breath," Vanessa said. "We should be in the aura now."

Tania hadn't realized it until then, but the headache had dwindled back to something manageable. Still, she wanted nothing more at that moment than to get back to their aircraft and find a packet of ibuprofen. The first dose of many to come, she thought bitterly.

Pablo's motionless face rose unbidden to her mind, dispelling the thought. Popping some pills was nothing compared to the sacrifice he'd made. Tania swallowed, accepting the pain as an eternal reminder that she still lived.

Vanessa stuffed the flare into a pile of dirt, killing its brilliant red light. Tania met her gaze and held it. She wanted to say something, anything, but no words came. The other woman broke eye contact first and glanced back down the tunnel through which they'd fled. Her lips moved in a silent goodbye, and one more tear rolled down a cheek that had seen too many already. She drew her arm across her face and let out a sharp breath. "He didn't talk much." Her voice was wistful. "Still, I felt like I knew him better than anyone."

"I'm sorry," Tania managed to say. The words sounded feeble, but the other woman nodded.

"Let's go," she said, "before the grief catches up with me."

Tania glanced down at the bloody knife in her hand, tightened her grip on it, and started up the pile of debris that served as a ramp to the mouth of the cave. Her now-permanent headache began to flare again, forcing her to squint and hold up one hand to block the brightness of the daylight that spilled in.

Her headache grew. *It is the brightness, isn't it?*

Another explanation came to mind, along with a cold

revelation. Tania began to tremble all over. "Something's wrong," she said, her voice a miserable, shaky mess.

Vanessa called up from behind. "What is it? Do you see something?"

At the mouth of the cave Tania froze, and heard Skyler's voice in her head—the last words he'd said before leaving Ireland. "There's a bunch of aura towers coming back. . . ."

To the south, Tania could see the last of the emerald towers vanish into the tree line, headed for Belém.

*No. Half should have stayed. Like Ireland and Belém. Why change the rules now, you bastards?*

She dropped to her knees, watching the source of the aura disappear. She would die here, or become something . . . less. There was no way to scrub the air inside the *Helios*.

The teeth that had wrapped around her skull bit down.

# 20

## SOUTHERN CHAD

### 31.MAR.2285

A violent wind roused Russell Blackfield from his fitful sleep.

The walls of his little prison shook with the force of the gust, and despite the closed doors a fine spray of powdery sand whipped in and coated everything. The winds outside dwindled as he became coherent.

He had no idea how long he'd been out. A wave of exhaustion had come upon him back in the aircraft. Lack of food, probably. Or depression. Whatever, the sleep had helped. He felt almost himself again.

He tried to move, only to find his hands were cuffed together, the chain going up and over a metal bar above his head. Some sort of closet, he guessed. The bar was thin but looked pretty solid. Two bolts held it to the wall at either end.

While he estimated his depleted strength versus those bolts, an alarm within his helmet caught his attention. It had been there since he'd woken, he realized, but only then did it occur to him that it mattered.

The oxygen meter read 3 percent. As he digested this the closet shook.

Russell felt more than heard what sounded like an explosion, though it came from far off. The uncomfortable floor beneath him trembled. His eyes never wavered from the tiny display projected onto his helmet.

## OXYGEN LEVEL CRITICAL

Still he waited. They'd probably just tossed a grenade to clear out some lingering subs and would be back any minute with one of those aura-generating towers in tow. He'd be able to open his mask, breathe air that didn't carry *eau de flatus,* melt Skyler's smug face with the thruster attached to his suit's arm, then . . . then he could focus on that little nimble-bodied mouse, Ana. Make up some stories about how Skyler had been bullshitting her from the start, how he—Russell—was the real hero.

More time passed. He tried to slow his breathing, and it might have helped a bit, but the air level still dropped. Two percent now. He figured he had ten minutes.

He felt a drop of sweat trickle down his spine as the possibility that they wouldn't come back at all started to feel more and more likely. How much time would he need to get to these aura towers, assuming they were even still around? Even if they were still here, they could be kilometers away. He might have already screwed himself by waiting this long.

The ground shook again. This time it felt different. No explosion, more like an earthquake. When it ended he heard a series of strange popping sounds at the edge of his perception, as if a hundred doors had slammed shut.

What could make such a sound he had no idea, but it couldn't be good. Then what could only have been a shock wave of air rattled the entire shack around him.

It was time to fucking go.

Russell navigated away from the oxygen readout and found the menu again that would allow him to override the thruster's "vacuum only" default. He had no idea how long he could run the thing for, or how much heat it would generate, but one of the things he'd spent the last hour mulling was his target. He figured he only had enough fuel for one shot at this, and so he'd spent considerable time weighing his options.

The thick chain they'd secured him with looked new. The bar they'd hung it on, however, did not. He'd seen Skyler test it with his own weight and a few tugs, but compared to the chain it looked thin and showed signs of rust through the sloppy coat of paint. He guessed it would be iron underneath.

The warning beep from his suit, which he'd hastily shut off earlier, came on again. This time the pitch, volume, and pace were all increased. One fucking percent.

"Right, then." Russell aimed his wrist at the bar above his head and fired the thruster. He felt his arm pushed by the little motor and saw a tiny yellow glow light up the spot on the bar he'd chosen.

Then the smoke started. No wonder the bloody thing should only be used in a vacuum. Whatever the fuel was, it apparently reacted with atmosphere like a trash fire. A gray-black cloud enveloped him in seconds, making it impossible to see anything behind the glass of his face mask. Russell swore, tried to hold his arm still. He thought he'd kept it pretty steady, but after a short thirty seconds the hiss of the thruster dwindled and died with no satisfying snap of the bar.

He reached up and gave it a tug. Solid as the moment he'd started.

He stood at a crouch and pulled, straining until he thought his eyes would pop out of his skull. Nothing. He was breathing hard now, a luxury he didn't have. The air in his suit started to taste thin. The warning beeps continued.

"Skyler!" he shouted, like a feeble idiot.

They weren't coming back. He had to act. Better to risk going subby than to sit here and suffocate. He had to at least try to make the aura. And besides, even a subhuman Russell Blackfield could still have a chance at hunting down and killing Skyler Luiken, even if only as payback for leaving him chained up like this.

He saw no other option, and so he turned as best he could and threw his face into the wall.

Again. Again. Again. On the fifth try a tiny crack appeared before his eyes. Russell felt faint, couldn't get a breath. He reared back and thrust his head forward with all the strength he could muster and . . .

The glass cracked. A long, jagged white line all the way across his field of view. He tried to laugh but no air came and his vision started to blur. *Fuck, too late,* he managed to think as he felt his body falter beneath him.

He fell, face-first, and that did the trick.

A chunk of his mask fell away and clattered inside his helmet. He drew a breath and almost gagged on the smoky air, which only made him involuntarily suck in more of it. A coughing fit followed and didn't end until his eyes were watering and his lungs felt coated in chalk.

The smoke had finally dissipated when Russell got his breathing under control. His head pounded, and he supposed—hoped—that was from the lack of oxygen and not a SUBS infection. He knew that took a few minutes on average to kick in, and so Russell set to work on the bar. He moved the chain so that it was right against the wall where the bar had been bolted in place, and then he started to jump. He kicked his legs out and let his chained wrist break the fall.

On his seventh such jump, his wrist numb and raw, the bolts pried away from the wall. Just a millimeter, but it was better than nothing. Skull throbbing, Russell jumped four more times before the bar tore away from the wall and sent him tumbling to the floor.

He welcomed the pain. Pain meant he still lived. He rolled, pulling his still-chained arms free of the broken iron bar, stood, and ran from the room.

Outside he pulled the shattered helmet from his head. It left a curved line in the sand as it rolled away. Seeing clearly, breathing evenly again, he studied the chain between his hands. Russell glanced around and saw a small rusted signpost jutting from the ground near the building, maybe a meter tall. The sign itself had fallen off, but it didn't matter. He lumbered over to it and put the chain over it, pulling it tight against one of the squared edges. Leaning back, one foot pushing against the old metal rod, Russell pulled his arms back, grunting with effort.

Nothing. But in his thrashing he'd exposed a concrete base the signpost jutted from. Kneeling, he set to work clearing the sand around it. The weathered bulb of gray stone came free easily, smaller than he'd hoped. He'd wanted to use it as a crucible. Now he realized it could be a sledgehammer.

Russell took the improvised tool back inside and knelt on the hard, flat floor of the building. Sand brushed aside, he gripped the concrete ball with both hands, with the chain of the handcuffs wrapped underneath the ball. Careful to keep his elbows still, Russell thrust downward with both hands. The chain hit the floor, then the ball of concrete on top of it. Sparks flew. Chips of concrete danced away.

He grinned against his headache and brought the hammer down again. And again. A dozen times, maybe more, before finally the link snapped.

The chains dangled from his wrists as he emerged from the building. Russell shrugged out of the rest of the now-useless suit as well. Then he took stock of the situation.

Russell stood in the middle of a desert mining town, somewhere in Africa, with nothing but his underwear, a raging headache, and a full bladder.

Bladder, yes. He'd been holding it so long he'd almost forgot. Russell stood over the suit that, without a helmet that worked, was never going to be used again. Skyler could scavenge another one.

Business concluded, Russell studied his surroundings. There were several low buildings around him arranged in a rough square, with a rotted-out old vehicle in the center. The air tasted horrid, like a . . . he struggled to think of anything similar and gave up. A chemistry lab, he guessed, though he'd never been in one.

Russell ignored all of it and studied the landscape beyond. To the south he saw the receding cloud of sand as the storm continued its trek. West, the sun hung in the sky and stabbed at his eyes with brilliant daggers. Fuck that. He had started to turn north when something caught his eye. A pulsing glow near the horizon illuminated a plume of smoke that rose above the strange roof that had been constructed over most of the landscape.

"And you will know us by our path of destruction," he said with a dry chuckle. The voice barely sounded like his own.

Where he'd heard that line he couldn't quite recall, the storm inside his head had apparently shaken it loose. A song, or some schlocky old sensory adventure. Trying to pinpoint it sent little jabbing pains through his mind. He gave up.

His feet took him west before he'd even thought to go, a trail of shallow footprints in the freshly deposited sand. Shoes might be a good idea, he realized, but he couldn't seem to stop himself from walking west.

"Feet," he said, looking down. "Stop, you twats. We need boots."

Thinking felt like trying to decipher a dream when still dreaming, all while someone ground away at his skull with a jackhammer. He kept walking west with no apparent control over his own limbs, as if some distant gravity source had grabbed hold of him. *That's not good.*

Only one explanation made sense. Admitting it felt like opening a door he'd never be able to close.

*SUBS,* he thought, and snorted. *Fucking perfect.*

He wondered what emotion the plague would bring out in him, assuming he survived at all. Most didn't.

For his legacy's sake he hoped for fight over flight. It wouldn't do to run like a frightened schoolgirl when he finally found Skyler. Worse, maybe he'd be nice to the guy. Fawn over him like Ana, even. *That would be the way to go,* he thought. "For my legacy's sake!" he shouted, laughing. What goddamn legacy? He racked his mind for a single accomplishment anyone would remember him for with respect, much less fondness. Nothing came to mind. He couldn't even think of a single person who would remember him, the person, well.

*I haven't a friend in the world—*

Movement to his left. Russell glanced that way and saw . . .

"Holy shit," he gasped. There were dozens of them. Scrawny, savage things. They worked their way along what appeared to be man-made crater rims to either side, moving in the same direction he did. Some ran, most lumbered. A few even dragged themselves along by their hands like some old shitty horror sensory.

*Goddamn,* he thought. *Do I look like that? Am I one of these pathetic animals? Are they my goddamn friends?*

He glanced down at himself. His body was clean. Muscled and

well fed, a few scars here and there. He didn't look anything like the filthy, shaggy monsters that now flanked him on both sides. He wore only the pair of underwear he'd had on under the environment suit. On a whim he yanked them off and threw them aside. The sight of his own manhood swinging lazily from side to side as he marched gave him a surprising respite from the fog that had settled over his mind. The headache didn't go away—in fact it felt worse—but somehow now he seemed able to think *around* it.

One of them caught Russell's eye and snarled at him. He glanced away, back down at himself. His legs still moved as if on autopilot, forcing him along in the same direction the creatures moved. They were the same, he and them. He'd joined their pack, which in a way he thought was good because it lowered the chances that one of them would bite his face off. But then again, it meant he'd dropped down a few rungs on the food chain. Russell Blackfield, primal edition. Perhaps the disease had actually improved him. The idea produced a rolling chuckle from his belly, along with a blinding sting of pain in his skull.

When that agony faded he found something odd in its place. Disappointment. Regret.

With an effort of will he forced one foot to remain on the ground. It did, but only for a fleeting instant. Whatever fate awaited him, he apparently had no choice but to meet it head-on. All he could think was, *This is it, mate. Last chance to leave a mark.*

Ahead the ground sloped away sharply on two sides of an earthen bridge barely two meters wide. The pit walls that joined to form the narrow passage descended down into identical holes a hundred meters deep or more. Open mines, he realized.

He passed a corpse. A scientist or doctor from the tattered clothing. He walked on, not that he had any say in the matter. Even if he could stop and search the body, it didn't look like it held anything useful. A few paces later he came across another dead form, this one wearing remnants of camouflage—green, for jungle use. *Wouldn't desert gear have been a better choice, fool?* This corpse he did search, fighting his body's desire to keep marching the whole time. He found no gun, but there was a single hand grenade on the dead man's belt. He snatched it, enjoying the weight of the explosive in his fist.

Emboldened, Russell focused ahead of himself and . . . *where were they?* He'd seen these aura towers before, in Belém and even in the secret video feed from that ill-fated rescue aircraft Tania had sent in. They were tall, and should have been visible by now, but he saw nothing.

Maybe they'd descended into one of these pits. Yes, that would hide them well.

A subhuman crawled on the ground in front of him. Gray hair hung in strands across the animal's haggard face. Russell couldn't control his own feet, not really, but he could move his hands. On a whim he reached down and pushed the creature as he passed, rolling it into the steeply walled pit mine. The thing went over the edge without a sound, rolling in a cloud of sand and dust.

There'd been no malice in it, no ill-will meant. He simply wanted to prove to himself that he wasn't one of them. Not yet. Not entirely.

He half-expected the other subs around him to fly into some kind of rage at this assault, but they didn't react at all. They viewed him as one of their own, even if the feeling wasn't entirely mutual.

"Goddamn that hurts!" he shouted, fists pressed against his temples. His head felt like a bucket full of thumbtacks, shaken vigorously. The coherent thoughts, those that seemed to slide around the jagged edges of pain, were infrequent but not totally gone. In fact the headache seemed to have stabilized. There was time yet. He could still leave a mark. Something none of them would expect.

He was Russell Fucking Blackfield, striding naked toward his destiny, and he could still vary the pattern.

# 21

## SOUTHERN CHAD

### 31.MAR.2285

"The breathing," Ana said. "It's stopped."

She had it right. The rhythmic ebb and flow of warm air had vanished. At that instant, as if on a dimmer switch, the yellow glow emitted by the floor began to fade.

"Shit," Skyler growled. "Run."

Even as Ana turned, Skyler saw the barricade iris in around the tunnel through which they entered. Three plates, hidden in recesses around the passage, slipped silently into place. He glanced left and right, hoping against hope, and saw the same thing.

"No. No, no, no," Ana was saying. "This is not good."

The light continued to fall until it vanished completely. The room didn't quite go pitch-black, though. Dull gray-blue light still spilled in from the hole in the ceiling above the dais.

A series of booming thuds shook the entire room. The sounds came from above.

"What is that?" Ana asked, breathless.

"I've no idea, and I don't like it. Not at all."

"Skyler," she whispered. She was looking past him, toward the dais.

He turned and saw . . . nothing, at first. Then it registered. A yellow glow where there'd been none before, coming from the depths of the pit below the shell ship. The light grew brighter as he watched, then seemed to stabilize.

The deep, reverberating thuds from above continued. Explosions? No, they weren't violent enough, he thought.

Skyler strode back to the precipice and looked down. Deep below, a half a kilometer or more, he guessed, a circle of blinding yellow light had appeared. It reminded him of looking directly at the sun, and of the silo below Nightcliff where he'd fallen through an iris floor into . . . something indescribable. Something that had saved him and not the creature that chased him there.

"Sky!" Ana shouted.

He whirled.

A shaft of light had appeared near the edge of the room, coming from a newly opened section of the ceiling. Shadows danced on the floor below and then something fell through. A body hit the floor with a grunt.

Skyler swallowed hard and aimed.

The lump on the ground moved. Hands stretched out, then it began to push up, revealing eyes that glowed with yellow laser light. It came to its full height, illuminated from the opening above like an actor on a stage. He could see it look from him to Ana, then back. At the same time the armored subhuman coiled and spread its arms out.

Without warning the light that shone down on it vanished as the portal in the ceiling closed, leaving just a pair of yellow eyes glowing near the edge of the room. The two glowing orbs hung there, unmoving.

His wits returning, Skyler slipped his finger over the trigger of his gun and began to squeeze.

Ana fired first.

He heard the *vump* from her launcher, saw the trail of smoke in the darkness between her gun and the creature's chest. It staggered backward a step from the impact, slamming into the wall behind it. Skyler braced himself for an explosion, but none came. Instead a cloud of smoke began to hiss from the small canister that now lay on the floor. White smoke, so white it almost glowed in the shadows. Tear gas.

"To me!" Skyler shouted to her. The gas he guessed would have no effect on the creature. It might be human, but that coating over its body he figured had to be akin to an environment suit, not merely armor.

Ana kept her body pointed toward the thing as she danced around the corpses on the floor. When the creature moved away from the wall again Skyler squeezed off a salvo aimed at its head. His aim was true; he saw the head jerk sideways. But the subhuman shrugged this off like a bothersome fly and turned to face him again, its glowing eyes like two stars in the growing cloud of tear gas.

Another shaft of light lit up the room off to his right, and another body fell through. Skyler spun and saw a third behind them, already up and surveying the room before it.

"Oh, hell," he muttered. They were trapped, good as dead.

"What do we do?" Ana asked, her voice high with fear.

"Try the other canisters—just fucking shoot!" He fired as well, clicking the weapon into fully automatic and pouring bullets into the same creature he'd already shot.

Ana's launcher took on a rhythmic pace as she emptied the remaining five rounds—two toward the right and three at the creature behind.

White gas began to fill the perimeter of the room. More shafts of light appeared. A fourth, a fifth. Soon there were seven of the armored creatures.

"What are they waiting for?" Ana shouted over Skyler's gunfire.

*Overwhelming odds,* he wanted to say, but a new sound cut off his reply. The noise began as a low rumble but quickly grew to skull-shaking volume, like standing near an aircraft that had suddenly ramped its thrusters to full power. The floor beneath him vibrated. Indeed, the whole building shook.

"What's happening?" Ana shouted, her hand suddenly gripping his forearm as she almost fell. She righted herself and, impressively, began to slip a new set of canisters into the chambers on her gun.

"Nothing good," he said back. His gaze remained on the

creatures at the edges of the room. Their posture implied they were just as awed by the noise as he and Ana were.

Then it ended. Gone in a heartbeat, absolute silence in its wake.

Skyler began to feel his eyes itch, a slight burning sensation building as the gas began to fill the room.

The creatures stepped forward in unison and Ana fired again.

This time, though, she did not aim at the enemies surrounding them. She aimed at one of the barricaded doors instead, and the cartridge she fired exploded in a brilliant flash of fire and smoke. Chunks of debris rattled against the walls, the floor, the ceiling. One of the black-clad subs toppled sideways, limp. Struck in the head by shrapnel maybe. A shock wave of air pushed against Skyler. He winced as the heat of the blast pulsed across his face, pushed him backward a step. Chunks of material skittered past his feet and into the deep pit.

Something grabbed his arm. No, someone. Ana. She yanked him toward the explosion, running hard. His legs lurched into motion as if by their own free will as Ana pulled him toward the cloud of smoke and fire. His eyes were burning. How she could see anything he had no idea, but he ran.

The floor beneath him changed, sloped upward, and he knew they'd made it out into the hallway through which they'd entered. At the top of the corridor Ana let go of him, turned, and fired. A ball of fire and heat erupted from below. Then another, and another. Ana pulled the trigger as fast as the bulky weapon would allow, turning the portal through which they'd run into a morass of fire, smoke, and rubble.

Her launcher clicked empty. She started to reload, the expression on her face a mixture of anger and grief. The grief was an illusion, though; the way she squinted and the streams of tears rolling down her cheeks came from the tear gas. Skyler grabbed her, turned her. "Save it, keep moving."

He took the lead, his weapon more appropriate in the tight hallways. The sensation of having needles piercing his eyeballs faded to a mere burn. He followed the same path they'd taken on the way in, hoping he remembered it correctly, but given the symmetrical layout he hoped it wouldn't matter. The tunnels, now mostly dark, all looked the same, though. It didn't help that his vision kept blurring, that he had to keep squeezing his eyes shut against the chemical agent. It occurred to him suddenly that the occasional holes in the floor were no longer there. Either that or he'd been extraordinarily lucky not to have tumbled into one as they'd run. He'd completely forgotten to watch for them.

"Wrong way," Ana blurted, halfway along a narrow corridor.

"It's this way. Right up ahead."

"No." She pulled against him. "We missed a turn or something; we haven't been here before."

He started to argue, then swallowed it. She was right. A dim light came from ahead, showing a pristine floor. Behind, he could see the evidence of their footsteps on the slightly dusty surface leading to this spot.

Skyler turned and went back down. The room below he'd rushed through without much of a glance. He studied it now and realized it was the same room they'd originally entered through, only the wide entrance had vanished. A wall like any other had replaced it.

"Open it," he said to Ana, glancing down at her gun.

She pushed back as far as possible, guiding Skyler to stand around the corner of the hallway. He let her push him, focusing on reloading his rifle. Last clip.

She took a place next to him, leaned out, fired, and ducked back. A flash of yellow lit the hall, followed by a rush of smoke and hot air. The sound buffeted his eardrums, already ringing brightly from the fight below.

He waited next to her, and while the smoke cleared Skyler took her hand in his. Ana turned and drew his mouth down to hers, pressing her warm mouth against his own with fierce urgency.

"I love you," she said.

"I lo—"

A subhuman's piercing howl interrupted his words. Skyler stepped past Ana and brought his gun to bear on the hole she'd created to the outside.

In the cloud of smoke that hung there he saw a half-dozen forms moving toward him. Some upright, some down on all fours. As he aimed the air in the room changed, almost pulling him toward the creatures. The smoke suddenly lurched in unison, rushing upward into hidden ventilation crevices in the ceiling.

The creatures took no notice of this. They saw him clearly now and began to move. Skyler fired at the two closest and dropped them easily. He adjusted his aim. The next pair showed no sign of fear.

More came in from the opening Ana's grenade had created. Only . . . had the hole become smaller? Skyler fired but his focus had split.

Indeed, as he watched, the outer wall changed. The ragged edges spawned by the explosion smoothed out as the hole shrank. A slow, almost imperceptible movement at first, in the span of seconds it became obvious, then astonishing. The last few meters closed in the space between two gunshots.

Just like that, the hole had vanished. Ana raised the grenade launcher again, but paused when Skyler rested a hand on the thick barrel.

"Save it," he said. "We're trapped."

# 22

## THE FLATIRONS, COLORADO

### 31.MAR.2285

The white-hot pain dug into Tania's skull like a thousand nails.

"Kill me!" she shouted. Or, she tried to. Had the words formed? Reality and imagination seemed to smear together.

She could do nothing except rock back and forth on her knees and try, try, try to focus. Focus on something, on anything. The pebble by her hand. A nearby clump of grass. Each time her eyes found something that might draw her to reality, a lance of agony would crush the world under its spiked boot.

There were sounds. Close or, perhaps, very distant. Gunshots and snarls and . . . birds. That was a new addition. Songs of birds. No, cries. Alarm. Thousands of birds, far off. Tania tried to look and was rewarded with a hammer blow to the center of her mind. The subhuman in her trying to break free. Her sanity, shattering.

"Something's happening!"

Who'd said that? Who had shouted? Natalie? No, Nat had died. Collateral damage in a failed assassination. *Oh Nat—*

The coherent thought was set upon by the virus, crushed, wiped away like a deleted file.

"Tania!"

A hand grabbed her arm. She pulled away, heard herself actually growl. But the voice, it was . . .

Vanessa. Yes, a friend. The woman's arms enveloped Tania from behind and forced her to the ground. Sheltering her from something.

All the while the birds screamed. Louder and louder until—

The wave hit. A pulse of something. Not air or water but . . . energy. Tania felt the shock wave slam into her not physically but mentally. A concussive force that rammed headlong into the thorns that gripped her consciousness, fracturing them, turning them to so much mental dust in a single, all-powerful strike. And then . . .

Clarity.

Quiet.

The pebble by her knee. The clump of green grass sprouting through a crack in the packed dirt. Vanessa blanketing her, sobbing.

"I'm . . . ," Tania said. She had to swallow first for the word came out as a croak. "I'm okay. I'm okay. I'm okay."

The woman who lay on top of her shifted, rolled to one side onto her knees. "I thought you were . . ." The words caught in her throat and trailed off. "I was about to shoot you."

She had a pistol in her hand, dangling from tired fingers. It fell to the ground in a dull thump. Numbly Tania noted the lack of a knife in her own hand. She glanced around, saw no obvious sign of it, and decided to accept the fact that she was unarmed.

Tania tried to rise, but despite the apparently stalled disease her head still pounded. She rolled partially onto her back instead, her air pack prevented her from going all the way over. She stared at the blue sky above. Birds were everywhere, floating in lazy circles, searching for the nests they'd just fled. Singing, now, or just silent. "What happened?" Tania asked. "Is the thing making its own aura?"

The idea made some sense. The object certainly resembled the material the towers were made of, yet clearly it hadn't been helping her when the towers left. Maybe their departure had switched it on. Maybe its aura was only a few meters in size.

"I've no idea," Vanessa said, picking up the gun again, "and I don't care. You're alive and talking clearly, and we need to go. Now."

Tania glanced up at the sudden urgency in her companion's voice. "Why?"

In answer she pointed. Along the tree line where the aura towers had powered their way south, Tania saw movement. People racing toward her. Some ran, some loped, others stumbled and staggered.

"God," Vanessa said. "They're everywhere. Tania, you have to get up."

She tried to stand. Her head still swam with the lingering pain of the disease's grip, but she managed to get to shaky feet and, holding Vanessa's free hand, ran with her.

They sprinted toward the *Helios*, visible on a low rise just beyond a swath of forest to the northeast.

Tania stared at the plane as she ran. *Please let her fly. Please.*

The aircraft seemed so far away, and even in that direction Tania could see the shady forms of subhumans rushing out from the trees toward them.

Something had changed about the creatures. No respite, not like Tania was experiencing, but something else. They were deathly silent. Their faces, even from this far off, were the very picture of stoic concentration, like a sprinter eyeing the red tape at the finish line, or a lion closing the last few meters on a fleeing, tired antelope. No anger now, no rage, just the focus and certainty that went part and parcel with the clarity of a goal. Something had changed them, and she had no problem believing it was the same pulse of energy that had all but banished the pain from her own mind.

The distance closed between them and the creatures. Vanessa raised the pistol she still carried and fired. A single clap from the handgun, so loud it distorted in Tania's already ringing ears. One of the creatures fell. The next sound from the weapon was a quiet click, and Vanessa uttered a curse in Portuguese as she tossed the gun aside.

"Slow down a bit," Vanessa said through heavy breaths.

Tania glanced at her. "Are you kidding?"

"We can't stop to fight them, so we need to . . . just, trust me, okay?"

Tania slowed her pace to a jog, matching Vanessa. The tactic seemed ridiculous, yet what else could be done? She had no weapon now. The knife, the bloody knife, she'd dropped somewhere without even remembering.

What she had was herself. Her training, over the last year, in an Israeli street-fighting technique. A year of welts and bruises and a hardening of body. Tolerance for pain, instinct for inflicting it. And she had Vanessa, who'd spent decades studying jujitsu.

The immune angled them toward the space vacated by the one subhuman she'd shot. Those to the left or right still rushed onward, and that gap Tania suddenly realized had become a corridor.

"Now," the woman said, "run!"

She surged ahead and Tania did her best to follow. She wished she'd ditched the entire suit and not just the helmet. Though formfitting, the material had a weight to it, a stiffness that made her feel lethargic. Compounded with the intense exhaustion she already felt . . . *no, no. No excuses. Run, dammit. Keep up. Survive.* She simply had to. For Pablo and Jake. For Skyler. For Zane. For Karl and everyone else that had fled Darwin to follow her toward a goal even she did not quite grasp.

And for Tim. Big-eared, goofy Tim, who'd been there every time she needed someone to be there. *Run.*

She ran, ignoring the beings in front of her. Only now they were beside her. Then, behind. Tania felt a rush of adrenaline as she realized Vanessa's simple tactic had worked. They'd increased their pace at exactly the right moment, and the simple-minded animals couldn't turn fast enough. Some even slipped on the snow and fell. Others tripped on those and went down, too. Most stayed on their feet, though, but ended up behind, adjusting and losing ground in the process.

The forest loomed ahead like a dark curtain of brown and green. She followed Vanessa as the woman plunged into that cold place, not daring to look back. She and Vanessa might have run the gauntlet, but she could still hear the beings behind them, and of course there were those already chasing from that direction. The subhumans were close, a dozen meters, maybe less.

Tania ducked under a branch and around the trunk of a pine, leapt over an exposed root, and raised her arms to protect her face as she crashed through the branches of two adjacent saplings. As complex a path as she could manage.

There were subhumans in the forest. Shadows glimpsed through the gaps between trees. Hunched, silent, and driven. On an instinctual level Tania knew they were all, every last one of them, after her. Or rather, the object Vanessa carried so awkwardly on her back.

*I could die here,* she thought. This thought she'd had many times already, but this time it came more as an inappropriate bit of self-introspection. *I could die for this slab of graphene circuitry or whatever the hell it is. I should be dead already, or at least one of these creatures, chasing Vanessa instead of running next to her.*

A shadow in front of her.

As she tried to dodge her foot snagged on a root. She fell as a snarling face, teeth bared, emerged before her. Tania tucked in her shoulder and rolled on instinct. She crashed into the being's knees and heard it huff in surprise as it hit the ground behind her. Tania came up in a fighting stance and her breath caught in her throat. There were so many, all rushing toward her.

The one she'd knocked over stood, bared its teeth, and struck a stance so savage, so animalistic that she could no longer see the human it had once been. She just saw a creature.

It stepped forward and reached for her.

Vanessa leapt in from Tania's right. She moved in close, beguiling the creature's natural instincts of how prey would fight back. The sub tried to raise its hands but Vanessa was too quick. She barred both hands with her left arm held low. At the same time she raised her right forearm up under the creature's chin, ending its effort to bite at her as she drove in. On the last step in Vanessa planted one foot behind the backpedaling creature. They were falling together, and in landing Tania imagined more than saw the result: Vanessa's knee coming down on the thing's stomach, her forearm still across the Adam's apple. Something crunched. The creature did not cry out. Its limbs jerked once, then nothing.

The immune wasted no time. She was up, turning, moving back to Tania and pulling her back to her feet. Once again her lighthouse in this ocean of terrors, pulling her toward the goal.

Tania hardly noticed. She couldn't break her gaze from the pack that converged. With each pounding pulse of blood in her temples the subhumans drew nearer. They struggled to weave through the forest as she had. Many fell, many tripped on the fallen, but despite this their numbers staggered her.

They were running again, and four steps later Tania could see the bulky shape of the *Helios* resting in the clearing where they'd landed. The sight of it brought a renewed urgency to her burning legs, and then, as suddenly as it had started, she was through the door, closing it. Vanessa had veered away and went to the cockpit without a spoken word of planning. They both knew what had to be done.

Tania pulled the door shut at the same moment a subhuman slammed into it, forcing it closed with such ferocity that she stumbled backward. She could see the being's face through the tiny porthole window. Two blue eyes, bloodshot and ragged and . . . sad. Profoundly sad.

The engines were already whirring, soon pushing to a roar that vibrated the walls.

*She'll fly,* Tania thought. The pulse that had ruined her suit had not, it seemed, extended this far.

Tania realized the light above the door showed red. No seal. Panic surged through her. Had something caught in the door? The being's foot, or hand?

She saw it then, and cursed herself. She'd simply forgotten to yank the handle into the sealed position. It took a force of will to step toward the door, toward those blue eyes and clawing fingertips that left little dirty smudges on the glass. Yet she did it, she stepped up and gripped the long metal bar with both hands and turned it clockwise. It snapped into place, the light turned green, and instantly the aircraft lurched.

Those eyes disappeared, fell down and away, as the *Helios* took flight.


Tania lay on the floor of the aircraft for a long time, the fingertips of her right hand resting gently on the triangular object. She stared at it, tried to thrust her very soul into the weave of microscopic channels that laced its surface, its beveled edges.

"Are you what saved me?" she whispered.

The emerald light that pulsed within those tiny lines did not waver.

She ran a finger over the corner of the triangle with the missing tip. "Are you what protects me now? Or am I . . . immune, after all?"

The odds of that were astronomical, she knew, and with more than a little mirth she countered that with the fact that she was an astronomer. *And, if the jury will allow, this very object came from the stars, did it not?* Tania smiled at her own wit. Astronomical odds weren't so hard to believe. Not anymore.

After a time reality began to pull her back to more practical matters. She relieved herself after first shedding the torn spacesuit and the leotard she'd worn underneath. Sitting naked on the floor, she used dry-shower wipes to clean herself, then combed her hair and tied it into a tight bun. From a locker under the bench seat she pulled a fresh set of sweatpants and light sweater, both emblazoned with the logo of some Brazilian football club she'd never heard of.

She ate a bland packet of peanut butter mixed with various vitamins and some sort of grain, the type of thing they used to drop from aircraft into starving villages. She sipped water from a stainless-steel canister. Not too much. It was room temperature and tasted metallic, and when she looked down into the darkness of the container the ripple of water there reminded her of the underground river, the cave, and Pablo.

She stared at that water for a long time, unblinking, remembering.

Later Tania pulled the hood of her sweater over her head and sat cross-legged on the floor, her arms thrown over her knees, her head bent down in something that might resemble reverence, and she cried for him. A man she'd hardly known, who died for her. Another death for her rather vague cause.

When the Builders did arrive, they'd have a lot to answer for.

\* \* \*

A few hours later Vanessa landed the aircraft somewhere in southern Mexico. She tapped the window and mouthed that she was going to recharge the caps, then stepped back in surprise when Tania yanked the handle and opened the cabin door.

"The air's already contaminated, remember?"

Vanessa tightened her lips. "Are you . . . I mean, it seems unlikely you're immune."

Astronomical odds. Tania tried to act nonchalant, and shrugged. "I don't know what happened, but when that shock wave hit the pain receded, stabilized. I think maybe the object creates a small aura. I suppose now we'll find out. Keep an eye on me."

Vanessa nodded and moved aside.

Tania stepped out into the cool evening air and inhaled the rich aroma of wild vegetation.

Vanessa had set the *Helios* down on a landing pad on the grounds of a resort or hotel. An isolated place, and despite being enveloped by the jungle around it, the grounds still spoke of immaculate, expensive landscaping. Lights were on everywhere, inside and out, but of course nobody was around.

Tania moved a step from the door. Then another. Then ten.

The ache in her skull remained exactly the same. She glanced at Vanessa and shrugged. "I have the headache, so I'm not immune. That thing must be generating an aura."

Her friend frowned, unsatisfied. "Maybe you should stay here, just in case."

"I'll help you," Tania said, smiling with more confidence than she felt. "Just . . . haul me back here if I start acting strange."

"Are you sure?"

"Yes. Come on."

Together they found, and then cleaned the charge cable, which had become home to a particularly large and hairy spider. Vanessa had recoiled at the sight of it, but Tania simply swatted it aside with one quick brush of her hand before picking away the remnants of its web. Then she carried the weight of the cord while Vanessa snapped the charge coupler into place on the receptacle near the tail of the aircraft.

"Nice strong line," the woman said. "Won't take more than an hour to ensure we can get home."

"Did you fly before . . . you know, before?"

"No," Vanessa said with visible pride. "Skyler taught me."

For a time they simply sat on benches that lined the walkway to the landing pad and listened to the sounds of the jungle. Despite the ample landscape lighting around them, the stars above still put on a dazzling display. It was a clear, warm night, and other than the occasional insect landing to snack on Tania's arm, she found the place surreal and calming.

Vanessa let out a long sigh. "I wish he was here. Pablo, I mean."

"Me, too."

The woman cast a sidelong glance at Tania and smiled amiably enough. It was clear she wanted to grieve but not in the company of a stranger. She wanted to be with Skyler and Ana, with her crew, to mourn and remember.

"What's going to happen," Vanessa asked, "when we gather all of those . . . things?"

A shiver ran across Tania's shoulders.

"I know," Vanessa continued, "I asked you before and you said you didn't know. But . . . what do you think is going to happen, Dr. Sharma?"

"All I have are lame hypotheses. Guesses, really. A hypothesis would require some concrete information at least."

Vanessa's features hardened. "Tell me anyway. I want to know."

"You want to know what Pablo died for," Tania said gently. The other woman looked away, her lack of denial serving as an answer. "I want to know that, too."

A tear slipped from the corner of Vanessa's eye and began its stutter-roll down her cheek. She swatted it away like one of the insects and took a big deliberate breath, exhaling through her mouth.

"There is some evidence," Tania said carefully, "that there will only be one more ship to arrive. An end to this . . . sequence, less than a year from now. And my guess, educated or otherwise, is that things will go very badly for us if these objects are not installed before that time."

"And if they are? What happens then?"

Tania shrugged. "No one knows. But Skyler felt strongly that simply waiting around, or ignoring this altogether, was unlikely to lead to the desirable outcome. Assuming of course there is a desirable outcome, for us at least."

"He's right. And there must be."

"I wonder sometimes." She shivered again. A few minutes later, an audible click from the cap spooler said the *Helios* was ready to go.

# 23

## DARWIN, AUSTRALIA

### 31.MAR.2285

A small waft of smoke rose from the barrel of the gun in Kelly's hand.

So swift had the motion been that Sam had no time to react. No time to dive toward Prumble and knock him out of the way, to take the bullet herself. No time even to wince or cover her ears as the bullet exploded from the barrel of the pistol and took flight, the report from the weapon a single deafening clap that echoed briefly off the walls of the crowded room.

No time, even, to curse Kelly's name once and for all. All Samantha had time for was the useless acceptance of the woman's new name, Sister Josephine, Patron Saint of Bitches That Need to Die.

Sam started to turn and saw the body topple backward, dead eyes staring straight ahead.

Not Prumble. Kip.

The frail man's stringy gray hair folded around his head like the embrace of Death's own hands and he hit the floor with his arms splayed outward.

Skadz reacted first, a split second before Prumble. He rushed sideways behind Sam and tackled the nearest Jacobite guard.

Prumble, God bless him, flung his clipboard like a Frisbee straight into the face of the guard on his left. The thin, hard object caught the man right in his gaping, surprised mouth, and when he coughed in reaction a spray of blood came out. He fell, gurgling. Prumble had already moved on. He surged forward and to the left, swinging one meaty arm like a cricket bat, his flat hand slamming into another soldier just below the ear and sending him, eyes closed, to his knees.

Kelly fired her gun twice more, dropping another guard, before the man closest to her slapped the weapon away and raised his own rifle.

The initial fog of battle melted away and everything around Samantha seemed to slow down. She rushed straight toward Kelly, heard a gunshot behind her that surely had been meant for her own heart. Had she not moved, she'd be dead, and the guard who fired would have done so again had Skadz not swept his legs from under him.

Kelly and her assailant were locked in a tug-of-war over the guard's rifle. Sam closed the distance in two wide steps, lowered her shoulder, and rammed into the man's abdomen. He grunted, and miraculously held on as Sam lifted him off his feet. When his back slammed into the vault door, though, his grip failed as quickly as his lungs lost their air. The round door might as well have been a solid wall of stone.

Sam let the guard fall. Gunshots rang out behind her. Who was shooting she had no idea, so she dove, rolled, and came up with her own weapon in hand. The former broom handle wasn't much, but the wood had a heft to it and it ended in a mess of splinters.

There was no one left to swing it at. Bodies of Jacobite guards lay everywhere. One that had fallen against the wall was in a sitting position, his brains splayed across the surface behind him in a splatter of gray matter and dark red blood. He slowly, slowly toppled to one side, the back of his skull leaving a neat curved smear on the wall.

Skadz and Prumble were eyeing Kelly, unsure if they should attack her or thank her. She smartly lowered her gun.

"Back on our team?" Sam asked her.

"Never left. But I figured this was the right time to make it official."

"You're a good actress, hon."

She smiled, a hint of sadness in the crease of her brow. "Kip sold you out. I think Grillo knew, instinctually, that he was a mole after that business over at Selby Systems. He forced Kip to turn rat or face the alternative."

Sam eyed the man's body, and once again recalled the sound of Grillo's knife plunging into that captive man in Lyons. At least this had been quick.

"When you landed, Kip called for help, and Grillo asked me to personally take care of the situation."

"Is he here? In the building?"

Kelly shook her head. "I'm not sure where he is. Is that why you came? To kill him?"

"No," Prumble said before Sam could. "We came for the thing inside that safe."

Her eyebrows climbed up her forehead and she turned— they all turned—to watch as Prumble approached the massive gleaming barricade that was the vault door.

A small panel inset into the wall beside the round portal opened with silent grace when Prumble tapped it, revealing a numeric keypad within. Above the keypad was a small black square that emitted a dull red glow.

With two thick fingers he held down the buttons in the bottom corners of the keypad. Five seconds passed, then he tapped in a series of numbers before holding the two corner buttons again. At the same time, he crouched slightly and leaned down so his left eye was level with the black square. The red light pulsed. There was soft beep from the panel, then a startlingly loud noise from the door itself that reverberated within the room.

Prumble gripped the oversized handle in the door's center and pulled. The whole thing swung outward in silent, languid motion. Inside, a series of recessed lights came on, revealing a large square room with bright white walls and a dark polished floor. The contents were haphazardly arranged. From neatly aligned lockers and shelves to disheveled wooden crates and even stacks of paper on one table. Stamped council notes, Sam guessed.

She ignored all of this. Her prize lay near the back. It looked exactly as it had the last time she'd seen it. A cube-shaped bundle of gray blankets, with rope holding them in place. Inside she knew would be a wooden crate, and within that . . .

Something else caught her eye. A familiar color at the edge of her vision. Sam glanced up and studied the small item on an otherwise empty shelf near her prize.

Sister Haley's notebook, the original Jacobite holy text, in a zipper-locked plastic bag. Funny, Sam thought, that half the city probably cared more about the scribbling of a drug-addled teenager than an object sent by an alien race. She snatched the bag and stuffed it into her vest, imagining Grillo's anger and dismay when he found it had gone missing, too.

Her attention shifted back to the bundle on the ground. Confirmation was needed, she decided. Sam untied the ropes and pulled the blankets aside, then unlatched the lid of the crate and peered inside.

Nestled within lay the alien cube. Sky-blue light still coursed through its strange geometric veins. "Found it!" she called out.

"Then grab it and let's get the bloody hell out of here," Skadz replied.

"Our chariot awaits," Prumble added.

She retied the ropes and pulled the ends tight. The object weighed less than she remembered, but it still required both hands to move. An ache began to seep into her biceps by the time she reached the massive round door.

The others were already turning to leave, except Kelly, who stood staring vaguely toward the floor with one finger pressed to her ear. Sam hadn't seen it before, but there was a small headset there, skin-pink in color. "There's a problem," Kelly said.

Sam set the heavy parcel on the floor and waited as her friend—how good it felt to use that word again—as her friend's eyes danced left and right. Sam started to ask but Kelly held a finger up.

"Something's . . ." She started to talk, then listened more. "I don't . . . something's wrong at Aura's Edge."

Sam's stomach lurched.

"What does that mean?" Prumble asked.

Kelly was shaking her head. "I can't . . . too many of them talking at once. Everyone's in a panic."

"Sounds like a good diversion to me," Skadz said. "Let's move; we still need to find—"

"Oh my God," Kelly whispered. "Subhumans. Dozens of them, maybe more. Yes, a lot more. It sounds . . . God, I wish some of these idiots would shut up, I can't hear anything. It sounds like they're rushing the barricade. Some are in as far as the Gardens."

Sam glanced down at the object by her feet. "Did it start when I picked that up?"

Kelly frowned, shook her head. "There was chatter before that, while we were dealing with these blokes. I was ignoring it."

"Where'd they all come from?" Skadz asked. "I mean, the Purge—"

"Ancient history," Prumble replied. "The survivors have been encroaching on the city ever since. You've been outside; you've seen them."

Skadz gave a grudging nod. "Spread out, though. To come in all at once and wreak havoc . . ."

"They've done it before," Sam said. "Recently. When the aura was faltering. A new breed." Her last word hung in the air.

"We have to leave," Kelly said. "Now. They aren't just wreaking havoc, they're rushing toward Nightcliff. Toward us."


Sam stood on the second-to-last step of the stairs that led back to the lobby, right behind Kelly. She held an unfamiliar rifle in her hands, borrowed from one of the dead guards below. Skadz had mercifully offered to carry the alien artifact, at least for the time being.

"Wait here," Kelly whispered. Then she darted out beyond the shadowed space. The stairs on which Samantha stood were concealed somewhat by the lobby's design. Two huge mirror-image stairwells curved up and around the slightly tilted column that protected the Elevator cord, which came up from somewhere below. This stairwell was tucked under and behind the two grand ones above, and Sam felt grateful for that. Unlike earlier, the lobby seemed to be buzzing with activity. People were shouting, barking orders. Booted feet clacked on the hard floors.

Kelly stood at the corner and studied the scene beyond, then ducked back and returned.

"The look on your face," Prumble said, "implies we are screwed."

"We're screwed."

Sam winced. "Tell us."

After a sharp, deep breath, Kelly said, "They've sealed off the building, a line of guards just outside. Your aircraft lifted off already, the pilot spooked apparently—"

"What the fuck?" Skadz asked, speaking to himself. "He couldn't wait five fucking minutes? He just left her?"

"The girl is not our concern anymore, Skadz," Prumble said.

"Like hell she isn't. We'll bring her with us."

"Forget it. Arkin made his choice. I'm sure he had his reasons."

"Maybe they found her while we were in the vault," Sam said.

Skadz replied through clenched teeth. "That's bullshit and you know it. I'll find her even if you guys won't help."

Prumble whirled on him, their faces centimeters apart. "You heard what Kelly said. The situation has changed. We need another way out of here or we're all dead."

The two men stared at each other for a long moment, Skadz biting down on his lower lip. Sam could see the titanic struggle going on behind his eyes. In the end he said nothing.

"Can we just make a run for it?" Sam asked.

Kelly shook her head apologetically. "Subs are already within sight of the gate at Ryland Square. The streets are in chaos."

Sam leaned against the wall, mind reeling. "So close already?" Assuming the lump of alien shit that Skadz now carried had somehow called them, they would have had to hitch a ride on a bullet train to get here so quickly. The animals must have started earlier, but how? *What could have triggered them? Our arrival? Doubtful.* She'd been here before. So had Skadz, and Prumble for that matter.

Then she recalled the tremor, the rattling deep vibration that had shot up and down the Elevator cord as if it had been twanged like a guitar string. That had been thirty minutes ago, roughly. Enough time for the single-minded monsters, at least those already lurking in the dark places near Aura's Edge, to rush toward the source of humanity's survival. Why now, though? She couldn't fathom what could trigger—

Yes, she realized. She could. "All five objects are in play," she said.

The others were all looking at her. Kelly, confused. Skadz, quizzical. Prumble, eyes thoughtful and narrow.

Sam pointed at the bundle Skadz carried. "They've now all been removed from their landing sites, and somehow that's signaled the subs to come. We felt the effect when we were coming in. That must have been Skyler, or Tania. The last one, picked up."

"If that's true," Skadz said, "every sub in . . . well, shit, I don't know, every sub—period—is coming for this. For us."

"Don't forget Skyler. And Tania."

Prumble made a hush sound. "Fascinating, but now what?"

Worry flashed across Kelly's face. She shook it off. "Everything's been sealed up tight, and anyone who can carry a gun is out there, watching. Shooting already from the sound of it."

"What do we do?"

Kelly opened her mouth, closed it. She held up her hands and shook her head, out of ideas. "It's only a matter of time before Grillo realizes I haven't checked in, and sends someone down to check on our little ambush. He may have already . . . *shit.*"

"What now?"

Kelly ripped the tiny radio from her ear and tossed it. "That answers that. I've been cut off. Grillo must suspect, or at least he thinks I failed and that radio might be in your hands."

Skadz laughed, incredulous. "We're sitting ducks here."

"What's plan B?" Sam asked.

"This was plan B, Sammy."

"Fine. Plan fucking C then. Just . . . a plan. Anything."

An excruciating silence followed. Four seconds, then Prumble spoke.

"We go up," he said.

Kelly shook her head. "Nothing upstairs except offices, control, and the climber port."

"The climber port, exactly. We go *up*." Under their combined stares he seemed to transform. His face hardened. His posture, which on any other day would have involved a slight stoop and a walking cane, made him seem like a wall despite being one step below Samantha. "No time to argue about it. That thing needs to get to space and we've got that capability right above our heads. Besides, my fancy suit we spent all that time on is in the aircraft. I've got no other choice."

"They'll just stop the climber—assuming we can even find one heading up—and turn it around."

Prumble shook his head. "There'll be one. The city is under siege. I guarantee there are at least a handful of people who have a sudden urge to move to higher ground. As for stopping us, we bluff. We pretend Kelly's our hostage and when that starts to lose its effectiveness we use that alien cube as our hostage."

*The book, too,* Sam thought. Grillo might at least hesitate if he knew they had it.

"Mental," Skadz said under his breath.

For her part, Kelly seemed to be considering the idea. She looked to Sam, who could think of no other option and shrugged. "If we can get inside Gateway, we can pull that same trick that Skyler used to get to Anchor."

"Too many things have to go just right—"

"If you have a better idea," Prumble said, "then go for it. But pick one now because we need to get off this damnable stairwell."

Kelly kept her eyes on Sam, eyebrows raised, and Sam realized she needed assurance not that the plan was worthy but that Prumble was someone she could trust. Prumble, who'd been nothing to Sam for years except the big man who served as fence to Skadz, and later Skyler. She'd always found him mildly disgusting. How he must sweat under that ridiculous duster, how he always spoke as if on a theater stage. Yet he'd shown a remarkable sense of loyalty, or at least partnership, with Skyler and Skadz. A kinship.

She'd also always thought of him as something of a coward, hiding down in that dingy garage. She'd assumed he'd never left the dark confines of that musty place, but he'd shown incredible knowledge of the city and its people over the last few weeks. And he'd killed. Killed with surprising efficiency for an overweight Kiwi locksmith.

Sam nodded to her friend. "Let's go up."

"Okay then," Kelly said. "On my signal."

And just like that, she crept back to the corner that looked out on the rest of the lobby. She spent perhaps a second taking in the scene beyond, then held up a hand instructing the rest of the party to wait before she vanished from view.

Sam swallowed hard, and studied the unfamiliar rifle in her hands once again, double-checking that the safety was indeed off. When she glanced back up, Kelly had returned. She wheeled one hand about rapidly, the look on her face matching the urgency of the motion.

Turning, Sam motioned for Skadz to go next. "Are you okay? Are you with us?" she asked him when he'd come to her step.

"Don't worry about me. I'm an old hand at letting people down."

"Don't. It's not like that. . . ."

"It is to me." He softened then, a little. "Look, I'm just pissed off, okay? It blows my fucking mind that Arkin lit out at the first sign of trouble."

"Me, too, but it's not our problem now. We have to look out for each other, first, and get the fuck out of here."

"I know, I know. Doesn't mean I'm happy about it." With that he continued up the steps.

Sam followed him after Prumble nodded to her his intention to come last. Around the corner she glanced briefly at the bank of windows and glass doors that fronted the lobby of the climber port. Guards, some in Jacobite regalia and some in the classic Nightcliff fashion of mismatched uniforms and maroon-painted helmets, stood in clumps near the entrances. Others ran toward, or back from, the fortress wall some distance away. Some stood casually; others were hunkered down behind makeshift barricades. It all looked very sloppy and confused to Sam, but clearly it would be suicide to make a run for it, especially once word of the theft got out.

Kelly strode purposefully up the stairs, Skadz on her heels. Sam followed a few steps behind, wishing she'd snatched a

Jacobite shift off one of the bodies in the vault's antechamber. Still, everyone seemed to be either outside standing guard against the vague threat of riled subs, or busy in other places. Only a few people moved about in the vast lobby, but they paid Kelly and her followers no heed.

A second wide flight of stairs led up to what must have once been a luxurious waiting area for passengers about to embark on the journey to space. A long window overlooked the northern portion of Nightcliff and the sea beyond. The room jutted out over a portion of the yard below, and Sam noted discolored portions of the floor where she guessed couches or chairs must have once been bolted down.

As Prumble had predicted, there were plenty of people milling about, crowded around the double doors that led to the climber boarding area. Someone Sam couldn't see through the crowd was speaking in calming tones, urging those gathered to be patient while a climber was prepped.

Kelly rushed past all this, eschewing the main doors for an unmarked side exit. Inside was a narrow, plain hallway with smudged white walls and a dull green floor. Exposed pipes lined the ceiling and darted out at odd places through flanged rings that showed hints of rust under their white paint.

There were two side doors along the hall, and one at the end, which Kelly raced toward.

Sam watched her burst through the door, rifle raised and barking commands of "Stand down!" at whoever lurked within.

Skadz pressed himself against the hallway wall so that Samantha could push past him. She did so, bringing her own gun up as she stepped into the room. Terrified eyes stared back at her from startled operators. Some stood by, a few hurling cries of surprise or even "betrayer" at Kelly. Others still sat ashen-faced at desks supporting wide terminal displays and slate data entry devices propped up on the flat areas. All this faced in on a giant screen that showed on one half what Sam knew to be a map of the cargo yard, and on the other half a chart of the space stations along the Elevator cord. Little icons moved about on the digital version of the thread.

"Everyone stay calm," Kelly said. Then she aimed at one of

the terrified desk jockeys. "You. Mark a car on the next climber reserved, then lead us to it. We'll take two of you as hostage."

Sam reached for the nearest technician and balled the collar of his shirt into her fist. She was about to hoist him from his chair when she noticed a familiar face at the back of the room. A rugged, handsome, slightly askew face. Vaughn locked eyes with her and the corner of his mouth twitched. The slightest of movements, the only hint she needed.

"You," she barked at him. "Come over here. Slowly. Hands off that billy club, eh?"

Vaughn almost cracked a smile. She could see it in the sparkle of his eyes, the slight tuck of his lower lip. He caught himself and glanced down as he crossed the suddenly silent room. When he'd come to stand in front of her she took him by the upper arm and twirled him to face away from her, then liberally frisked him. She double-checked his hindquarters just in case. "Can't be too careful," she said in a low voice.

"Uh-huh."

"Any funny business," she added, "and I'll do you up a treat."

This time he did laugh, but managed to turn it into a clearing of the throat that sounded reasonably like shock.

Kelly went on. "Anyone tries to prevent that climber from leaving, or announces our arrival to those up top, and your friends here will die."

In the hallway at her back, Sam heard a sharp whisper from Skadz. She glanced back. "Yeah?"

"Empty storage room back here. Toss the lot of 'em inside and lock it."

"You've got a key?"

Skadz shook his head. Vaughn shifted his weight, causing a ring of keys on his belt to jingle softly. Just enough. *Damn, I'm glad to see you.* She yanked the key ring from its loop of Velcro, the ripping sound sharp enough for a few of the room's inhabitants to jump. "Right," she said. "Everyone in there, except you and you." She nodded to Vaughn and the senior tech Kelly had singled out.

The group began to slowly rise from their seats. Some still held their hands in the air and moved with acceptable speed. Others, though—Sam saw their sidelong glances, their hesitation. The hardening of eyes. Thoughts of heroism finally cracking through the fog of shock and fear.

She was about to say something when Prumble came through the door, pushing her aside as if his personality created its own bow shock. He hefted a machine gun in each hand and looked like one of Darwin's ragged, dead skyscrapers in his long, straight coat. "You heard her," he said in a growl. "Rickity-fucking-tick. We haven't got all day."

As if to quash any last lingering thoughts of revolt, he simultaneously thumbed the safeties on both weapons. Total showmanship, the brilliant son of a bitch. His presence, the implied threat in his voice, had the desired effect. The stragglers were up and moving, avoiding Prumble's gaze as they squeezed past him and into the hall.

"Keep moving, keep moving," Skadz was saying as they filed into the storage area. "Get cozy, plenty of room."

"What's going to happen to us?" someone inside asked.

"Beats me. Good time for an orgy if you want my advice. Oh, blimey! Forgot who I was speaking to. Sorry, that was ruddy insensitive. Prayer circle, then? Hail Jacob and all that shit?" He slammed the door and locked it. "Tossers."

"Can we go?" Sam asked of no one in particular.

Kelly gave her captive a little shake. "Soon as this one gets to work. What's your name?"

"Miles."

"Hello, Miles," she said, tone light and friendly. "About that climber. Let's lock out the main entrance, okay? Can we do that from here?"

"Um, yes. I mean, maybe. I'm not really sure—"

"Do as she says," Vaughn said. He managed to sound drained, defeated, and stern all at once. Sam wanted to bite his earlobe, just the way he liked. "Not the time to fuck around, Martin."

Kelly's eyebrows went up. She studied Vaughn, then glanced at Sam and perhaps caught the hint of admiration in Sam's face. "Martin, is it? Well now. Better do as your friend here says and we'll all get through this with our fingers still attached. Understand?"

Prumble stayed by the door through which they'd come.

Skadz gave him a respectful slug on the shoulder as he came back in, hauling the bundle and hoisting it up onto one of the desks with an unceremonious thud.

While Kelly worked with the tech, Sam moved Vaughn over to the exit on the far wall, had him open the door, and peered out into the hallway beyond. It sloped down to join with a sparse loading area, polar opposite to the once-luxurious passenger entrance on the other side of the building. There were a few handcarts about, some crates of varying content. No workers, thankfully.

The far wall of the loading area had an open section in the middle, blocked by a half-height metal gate. As Sam took this in the building vibrated slightly and she heard the deep sound of large machinery begin to whir. Beyond the gated gap in the wall, she saw the familiar sight of a climber car rotate into place like the chamber on a revolver.

"What's in that bundle, Sam?" Vaughn asked. He kept his voice low.

"Something important."

They were facing each other now and some internal debate raged behind Vaughn's eyes. "Something Grillo's going to miss?"

"He'll be mad as a cut snake. I guarantee it."

Vaughn grunted. "You'll be stuck up there. Eventually he'll win. Starve you out, or—"

Sam heard the goodbye beneath the words. She closed the distance between them and kissed the man. She gripped his head, her thumb in front of his ear, fingers entwined within his fine brown hair. When he kissed back she let her lips part and felt his tongue dart into her mouth with a profound urgency. She pulled him away, met his gaze. "Come with us. It's too much to explain now, but there's a way out. Another Elevator. I know, it's crazy but it's there. In Brazil. That's where they went. The traitors."

"Bollocks," he said. He sounded more amazed than doubtful.

"Come with us. We need you. They don't know you and I are . . . you know, acquainted."

"Grillo does."

She smirked at that. "Then imagine how fucking surprised he'll be when he realizes you're our hostage."

Sam saw that sparkle in his eyes again, and knew she had him.

They made their way back into the control room. "All clear," Sam said.

"Just about ready here," Kelly replied.

Skadz stood in front of the big screens on the long wall, his mouth agape. Sam turned to look and felt her heart lurch. A row of video feeds at the bottom provided a live view of the loading yard. Each image seemed worse than the last. Scenes of harrowing violence rendered in cold, austere silence. Subhumans numbering near a hundred rushed in from every angle toward shell-shocked guards who stood in a rapidly folding line in front of the climber port. The creatures had the smell of blood now, and the guards, used to minimal action in Grillo's world of order and piety, were being quickly overwhelmed.

Through the walls came the distant chatter of gunfire from somewhere within the facility.

"Time we were off," Skadz said.

"Yeah. Prumble? Kelly? We need to move."

Kelly went first, her captive prodded along in front of her at an apprehensive run. He stumbled the last few steps into the climber car and yelped when Kelly yanked him back to his feet with one powerful movement.

Skadz went in next, smartly moving straight to stairs that led to an upper deck of the tall, narrow compartment.

Sam ushered Vaughn in, making little effort now to pretend he was a true captive. If the technician hadn't guessed already he was unlikely to ever figure it out, and if he knew, well, he probably also knew that would get him killed. Regardless, the man was staring at his shoes as Kelly strapped him into one of the jump seats along the wall. Vaughn glanced at Sam, then caught Kelly's eye as well and winked at both of them as he took a seat next to the tech.

"It's going to be okay if we just cooperate," he said.

The other man kept his eyes on the floor but his head bobbed in agreement. "Pray with me?" he muttered, not looking up.

Vaughn looked at the two women and rolled his eyes. "Of course, of course," he replied to the man, giving him a gentle pat on the back.

Sam grinned slightly and caught Kelly looking at her. "Old friend," Sam mouthed.

A Klaxon sounded, then an artificial voice announced the cabin door would seal automatically in thirty seconds.

Sam turned to make room for Prumble but the big man still stood at the control room's exit, twenty meters from the climber. He moved awkwardly down the sloped ramp, and still had fifteen meters to cross when the door behind him burst open.

"Go!" he shouted. Then Prumble whirled and brought both assault rifles to bear, one tucked into each armpit.

A group of Nightcliff guards piled through the open doorway at the far end as Prumble's guns began to bark thunder. Flashes of muzzle fire lit the incoming men even as the bullets tore through them. They were falling, screaming, and yet they continued to file in. Whatever came behind them, a hail of bullets was apparently preferable.

The climber door began to swing shut of its own accord. Sam stepped forward to block it. She put her shoulder into it and fought for purchase on the floor with her boots. The heavy airlock door kept moving. Silent, robotic, unforgiving. Sam shoved an arm out around the edge of the doorjamb, groaning with effort and feeling the pressure waves of Prumble's gunshots roll over her.

Kelly grabbed her, hauled her back an instant before her hand would have been crushed.

"No!" Sam shouted, pushing Kelly away and moving toward the porthole, helpless now but to watch. She pounded her fist on the thick metal. In a clearer state of mind she would have looked for an abort button, an emergency-open lever. Later that idea would hit her. Too late.

The thick door shut with an almost imperceptible sound as pressure seals connected and the motorized latches glided into place, muting the thrum of Prumble's twin rifles and the cries of the dying.

Suddenly the climber car lurched. Not up but to the side. The noise of violence faded. The last thing Samantha saw was the hulking form of Mr. Prumble, twin cannons gripped in two meaty hands, spitting fire and death. The desperate guards already lay dead. Climbing over them in a tidal wave of ragged limbs was a writhing mass of subhumans.

"Stop this fucking thing!" she screamed without turning, both fists now hammering the tiny round window.

A gibbering, feeble voice answered from somewhere at the back of the cramped cabin. "It's all automated now. Only the control room can—"

"We get it, Martin," Vaughn said. "Shut the hell up."

Sam felt a hand on her shoulder and turned to find Skadz standing next to her. His face was a grim, hollow mask. "Nothing we can do, Sammy."

Balled fists still against the door, Sam leaned until her forehead pressed against the cool porthole glass. Black cables and industrial piping slid by centimeters away as the climber went through its departure motions.

"He didn't have his suit," Skadz added, voice distant and numb. "Bought us time rather than burden us. Shit. If only I'd . . ."

Sam turned to him, anger welling up over her grief, harsh words on the tip of her tongue. When she saw Skadz's teary eyes, she bit down and kept her mouth shut. He'd wanted to stay behind. Needed to, if only to find some relief for the guilt he'd carried like a goddamn cross all these years. He would have traded places with Prumble in a heartbeat had the opportunity been there. Only it hadn't. Prumble had been the last in line, and simply did what needed to be done. Selfless in the end. A hero.

She gritted her teeth and faced the small window. "Thank you," she whispered to the glass. "We won't forget."

A stark five minutes passed in absolute silence. The climber stopped and started a few times, first turning and then lifting. Then came one final lurch upward that didn't abate as the vehicle began to accelerate and climb toward the heavens.

Last climber out.

# 24

## BELÉM, BRAZIL

### 1.APR.2285

The idea of breathing fresh air took time to settle in.

Leaving Mexico, Tania had been one foot into the rear cabin when she realized she no longer needed to confine herself to the dreary loneliness that waited within.

"Need a co-pilot?" she asked Vanessa at the cockpit just before the other woman closed the hatch. Vanessa grinned at that and let Tania inside.

They spent the three-hour flight back to Brazil in near-constant conversation. Vanessa shared a few tales of her time in Gabriel's cult of immunes, stories that involved Pablo and even young Ana and her now dead twin brother, Davi. She stuck to warm stories, and a few times let the endings fall by the wayside when Tania sensed they were drifting into darker waters.

Whenever Vanessa trailed off, Tania stepped in, happy to find someone who would listen attentively to everything that had happened since the disease first arrived. She even told her new friend about the daily life and—in hindsight—comical politics that went on aboard Anchor Station both before and after SUBS broke out. She told of how she'd only been down to Earth once since the disease confined everyone to Darwin's meager footprint, on the harrowing journey to Hawaii on which she'd met Skyler.

"Did you and Skyler have a . . ." Vanessa paused. "You know, a relationship?"

Tania felt her pulse quicken, kept herself quiet long enough to compose her thoughts. "I think we both had hopes, but circumstances . . . well, there was so much else going on."

Vanessa said nothing.

"I'm happy for him," Tania added, aware of how lame the words sounded and wishing she hadn't said them.

"He's had a remarkable influence on Ana," Vanessa said. "I guess you probably don't want to hear that."

"It's okay," Tania replied. *Please stop talking.*

"She came of age after the disease took her parents, took everyone she knew except Davi. Her brother was the grounding force in her life, you know? They grew up together, riding in Gabriel's fleet. Can you imagine going through that? At that age I was in university. You were probably studying aboard a space station, for God's sake. Those two were riding through a demolished world with a psychopath. It's amazing they both survived, much less escaped. They could have fled. But instead they brought Skyler to rescue us."

*And at the same time, I was agreeing—apparently—to give Skyler up to save the rest of the colony.* Tania felt a familiar wave of regret flow through her and this time she allowed it to run its course. The past she couldn't change. The future, though, was another matter and there was still work to do. She let the conversation drift away from the topic, and spent the last hour of the journey learning the basics of the *Helios*'s navigation systems.

Vanessa guided the craft along the coastline of Venezuela and Guyana, avoiding the mountains where Doppler indicated a vicious storm. When Belém finally came into view on the horizon, the city looked like a jagged, uneven row of dirty teeth jutting upward from low, cotton-ball clouds. It was midday, hot and rainy below.

"Weird," Vanessa said.

Tania glanced at her.

"No response from Exodus. Everyone's eating lunch, maybe."

A comment died on Tania's lips when she noticed the wisp of smoke rising up through the dense clouds below. Vanessa saw it at the same moment and immediately aborted their landing approach and angled the aircraft for a flyby.

The smoke curled upward along the path of the thin, almost invisible Elevator cord. Tania followed the line upward and spotted a lone climber high above, beacon light winking rhythmically. She watched it for a few seconds until the motion became apparent: down.

As the *Helios* drew closer the wisp proved more like a plume. Something big was burning below, and it was right where the camp should be. She dug her nails into the armrests, craned her neck for any detail that might be glimpsed through the gray and white soup. And then they were inside the clouds, her view suddenly shifting torrent like static on a dead screen. This ended as quickly as it had started, and the city came into full view.

Flames engulfed a section of slums near Camp Exodus, leaving a row of charred homes closest to the wall. The fire had started there, Tania noted, and spread north in a cone. In the heavy rain the licking tongues of yellow were almost totally obscured by thick smoke. The tendrils rose black and oily in places, paper white in others and mixing into a gray morass that seemed to become one with the heavy storm clouds that clung overhead.

Bright flashes of light caught Tania's eye, rapid winks from the perimeter of camp. A few years ago she would not have understood, but now she knew muzzle flashes when she saw them. These crackled along the wall of Camp Exodus as if someone had set off a string of fireworks.

Vanessa brought the aircraft in low over the camp, keeping the speed above 150 kilometers per hour and maintaining a safe distance from the invisible thread of the space elevator. She banked steeply as they flew over, giving Tania a clear view of the entire camp from just a few hundred meters up.

Within she saw people running, ferrying supplies back and forth to the defenders on the wall. A crowd huddled around the medical tent, another by the tower yard where Tania knew the munitions closet to be.

On the wall, every few meters, were colonists facing the erratic onslaught of subhumans that poured in from the city and even the rainforest to the east. Bodies of those shot trying to approach the camp were everywhere, and a few even lay within.

Tania craned her neck to take in more details as the *Helios* slipped out over the river and began to turn for another pass. "It's safe to land, I think," Tania said. "We've got to help them."

"Copy that," Vanessa said. "Switching to verts."

The note of the electric motors changed as thrust was redirected out the tiny vertical ports. Vanessa spun the craft about. As the camp came back into view, Tania glanced down at the swollen river below. People were swimming toward camp amid bodies floating limp, arms outward. Not people, she corrected herself. More subs. Just like in Colorado, they were of a sudden single-minded purpose, only here it seemed to be to get to the Elevator and not the alien object in the *Helios*'s cargo hold. What then? And what had triggered their sudden, all-consuming goals?

She made a sudden, frantic study of the camp, looking for the Magpie. Were they back already? Prize, or prizes, in hand? There were no other aircraft within the walls that she could see, but maybe they'd been forced to complete the journey on foot, or by truck. Tania tried the radio again while Vanessa focused on lining up the *Helios* with the colony's single landing pad. Again no response came.

"If anyone can hear me, please respond," she pled. "We need to know if the landing site is safe."

Silence. Then, a crackle. A thud. "Tania?"

"Karl," she said. Relief spilled out into the name, perhaps a little disappointment, too. She'd hoped for Tim. "Karl, thank God."

"When we saw you fly over we realized we'd left the comm room empty. Really sorry about that."

Tania gripped the transmitter tightly. "Can we land?"

"It's safe for now, far as I know anyway. I'll send a squad over there just to be sure. You saw the subs, I take it?"

"Hard to miss," Tania said.

"Fucking-A."

"The same thing happened in Colorado."

A slight pause. "Then you succeeded, too?"

"We did." She fought to keep her voice level. "Skyler's back, then?"

"No," he replied. "It's just that the Elevator did that twang-effect twice, so we knew both objects had at least been recovered. There was a weird shock wave after the second time a few minutes later. Came from the east, where Sky went. Scattered birds from every tree. I'm afraid all's quiet, otherwise."

She couldn't imagine what would cause that, but the fact that it hit here from that direction certainly implied Skyler had done something *big*. "Right, okay. We're almost down. Hold the fort, huh?"

"Count on it."

"Is Tim with you?"

A pause. "He went up, last night. Zane needed a break."

"It's okay, I understand." She clicked off and shared a glance with Vanessa. The subs were attacking despite the presence of an object. Tania felt a now-familiar ripple of fear at the thought.

"Do you think they're trying to get up the Elevator?" Vanessa asked cautiously. "To the other ones, I mean?"

"I suppose it's possible." She considered it as the landing pad began to slip below them and the aircraft started to drop the last twenty meters. "Or maybe they're wired to converge on the nearest Builder technology once all of the objects are found."

A vision exploded into Tania's mind. Packs . . . no, herds of subhumans from all over the world, making the same desperate migratory trek to the auras that humanity had. The final hint, the final push the beings needed to finish what the disease had started.

She had her harness off before Vanessa could even reach for the throttle to kill the engines. The canopy opened to the sound of roaring wind from the dwindling fans, the crackle of distant gunfire, shouts of alarm and surprise, and even, here and there, encouragement. Tania skipped the tiny steps engraved into the *Helios*'s fuselage and simply leapt to the soaked concrete below. Rain fell in a heavy vertical barrage.

A group of colonists stood nearby, armed with various weapons and varying amounts of confidence in the way they held them. She took in each person's stance and rushed up to the one with the most presence in the way he stood, the most familiar grip on the gun in hand. "They're swimming across!" Tania shouted to him. "You need to get some people covering the river entrance!"

Camp Exodus's wall left the shore open for fishing and swimming. Subs weren't known for their ability to cross water, and indeed in the two-plus years since the camp had been established Tania had never heard of a sub reaching the camp from that direction. A few snakes, sure. Even a black caiman. But no subhumans.

The man glanced that way, disbelief in his eyes.

"We saw them from above. Trust me. Many are drowning but some will make it. Take this group, find others, form a line. There's no time to debate. We'll be okay."

"Right," he said. With a jerk of his head the ragged group filed in behind him and walked toward the turbulent waters.

"Tania!" a familiar voice called out. She turned and saw Karl limping toward the aircraft. He swept her into an embrace that favored his good arm. "Are you okay?"

"We survived."

He squinted, confused. "I saw you get out of the cockpit. No suit? I don't understand. Are you . . . you're . . ."

Tania shrugged. "I don't know what happened. Started to get the headache, just like you, then that shock wave rolled past and I felt fine. Well, I felt okay."

Karl blinked at that. "Immune . . ."

"Let's figure it out later," she said, casting a glance toward the combatants on the wall.


Ninety minutes of hell served as Tania's welcome back to Belém.

She left Vanessa with instructions to guard their cargo, and dust off if necessary to protect the object. Then she went to the wall, picked up a gun from someone too tired to continue, and began to kill.

Pounding rain dropped visibility to fifteen meters, even less at times. The waters ran in milky brown rivulets along the battered roads beyond the camp's wall. Tania felt soaked to the bone, and like most of the others she'd shed much of her clothing for the simple reduction in weight.

The subs came alone, in families, and in packs. One group thundered in as if in careful coordination—fifty from the west, another thirty from the north. Many went for their general plan of scaling the walls, but a number rushed the gate and tried to shoulder it open. They were cut down in seconds by those on the wall, Tania included. She saw her own gunfire pop the blood and brains out of a child-subhuman that couldn't have been more than twelve years old. She'd turned and retched after that, and she wasn't the first nor the last to do so. After her fourth or fifth kill the revulsion ebbed as the task became less a violent art and more a chore.

A lull followed. Stragglers, here and there. Conserving ammunition was becoming the principal concern along the wall, and so colonists began to call their shots before firing. "I've got one-arm," and "Blondie on all-fours is mine." Tania took a sip of offered water from the woman who stood next to her. They shared an embarrassed laugh at the line of partially clad warriors lining the top of the wall. Flames from the fire that had blackened most of the slum north of the camp were now too far off to provide sufficient light, and the day grew darker by the minute. Torches were improvised and tossed out into the mud, but most went out upon landing, forcing a call for volunteers to go out and set them up. Tania found herself raising her hand without a second thought.

Three minutes later she stood behind the massive colony gate, half a broom handle in one hand and a borrowed pistol in the other. The meter-long stick had an old shirt wrapped around the end. It had been doused in some kind of grease or oil.

A stout, dour woman lit it for her seconds before the gates were thrown open, and Tania rushed madly over the bodies that had piled up just outside. Her feet pounded in the mud and soaked asphalt beyond. Sixteen other colonists ran with her, some carrying torches like hers, others carrying cap-powered LED lanterns that would last for weeks. The group dispersed, each running toward a spot they'd chosen ahead of time, ten or fifteen meters in front of the place they'd previously occupied on the wall. Those nearest to the gate were done quickly and, as per the hastily agreed-to plan, turned and went back to the gate. The fewer colonists abroad that might be confused for subs, the better.

A few gunshots rang out from the wall. Tania heard animal grunts from nearby, and cries from farther away. She ignored it all, focused on the stump of a telephone pole she'd picked as her landmark. Murky water splashed with every footfall, and as she lifted her feet from the ground it sprayed up her back and into her hair. Filthy, soaking wet, overwhelmed with adrenaline, Tania reached the stump of wood and leaned her torch against it. Each drop of rain that hit the fire ended with a little hiss. There was no soft ground nearby to thrust the torch into, so this seemed the next-best option to her. She'd brought no rope, though, and the torch seemed likely to fall with the slightest breeze where it stood.

A guttural roar emerged from the smoke and rain nearby. She heard fingernails scrape on concrete as a dark shape began to emerge. Tania held the torch in place with one hand, kept low, and raised her pistol. Before she could fire someone on the wall did, dropping the diseased human with one rifle round to the thigh, and a second in the center of the back when the creature had fallen.

Tania returned her focus to the torch. Other flame-bearers who'd ventured farther than her were already running back toward the gate. With no better idea, Tania set her pistol on a relatively dry bit of ground beside her and unlaced her boots. As more shots rang out from the wall, she set about knotting the two laces together and then wrapping the now-joined string around the stump and the broom handle.

More cries from the darkness. Tania swept her pistol up and managed to find the proper grip just in time. A sub had crept up slowly on the opposite side of her torch, using the flame itself to cover its approach. She registered it as two glowing eyes just beyond the flame, raised her weapon, and fired twice as the creature leapt to strike her. Her shots missed and the subhuman crashed through the flame and into her abdomen. She had the presence of mind to turn, using its momentum to send it rolling away from her toward the colony.

No shots from the wall. They couldn't see well enough to know who was friend or foe. Tania froze, caught between fighting, moving to the torch so the shooters could see her as one of their own, or running for the gate.

She had no choice. The creature came up from its fall and ran in the opposite direction from her, toward camp, toward the space elevator. Tania lifted her weapon, squeezed the fine trigger. The gun barked, slapped against her palm, and thrust a dull pain up her arm. A single, perfect red hole appeared in the center of the subhuman's back and it stumbled. One arm shot out to brace the fall, but by the time it had dropped that far the life had gone out of it. Tania lowered the gun. The flames behind her hissed and sputtered under the heavy rain. She dropped her chin to her chest and let the water cascade off the clumps of black hair that were matted to her cheeks.

She stared down between her feet, captivated by her own silhouette reflected in the dark puddle below. The wildly dancing flame behind her seemed to burn in a halo over her shadowed form. Heavy drops of rain rippled the demonic image, made it look as if she herself wavered like an apparition.

A shape rushed past her on the left. A subhuman, loping awkwardly on two feet and one hand. The other arm was tucked up against its body, an infected stump where the hand had been.

Another on the right, racing toward the wall. They were ignoring her, she realized, as the whip-crack serenade of gunfire rang out from the wall. *They see me as one of them,* she thought. *Or they don't see me at all.*

The two were quickly dispatched and then she heard the shouts from the wall, urging her to move. Move *now*. The pall that had settled on her lifted and Tania ran for the gate.

Ten meters away another subhuman came toward her. This one's single-minded drive toward the Elevator faltered when it noticed her. It slid to a stop, lost its balance, and then righted itself. It screamed at Tania and leapt, filthy hands outstretched.

Tania slid under the attack, rolled in the mud, and came up at a sprint. A chorus of gunshots rang out from the wall and Tania heard something splash into the mud behind her, heavy and final. She didn't look back.

They were ready for her at the gate, holding it open just enough for her to slip through, and as soon as she did the massive metal door slammed shut behind her.

"What's wrong?" someone asked, a person she did not know. "Why'd you stay out there?"

Tania shook the cobwebs from her mind. "They weren't after me," she said.

A dozen confused stares from the people around her.

"They're after what we stole."


The climber slid the last few meters in near-total silence, its motor column producing only a soft whir over the unrelenting storm.

Tania sat in the cargo bay of the *Helios,* the door open so she could watch the climber arrive. Vanessa or Karl, she couldn't recall which, had thrown a scratchy blanket over her shoulders and handed her a cup of hot tea. Only seconds after the vehicle arrived, Karl returned, the question she knew he would ask apparent in his concerned gaze.

Gunshots still rang out from the perimeter of Camp Exodus. Less frequent than before, the miniature thunderclaps had faded into the landscape.

"I'll take it up," Tania said.

"You sure?"

She nodded. "Vanessa can assist me. Besides, we need an immune to open the hatch."

He stood in the rain, waiting.

Tania let her gaze drift up. Belém's skyline still hid under the blanket of rainfall. Dark shapes at the edge of vision, like gigantic versions of the aura towers. The fires had finally burned themselves out.

"Load the other cars with the injured, or anyone too weak to fight." She took a sip of the scalding hot tea and winced as it singed her tongue. "Once we're above, we'll send every available climber back down and the evacuation can begin."

Even in the dim light, under the ashen clouds, she could see his face pale.

"Tania . . ."

"If they give up before then, fine," she said, "but we're going to burn through all our ammunition like this and it might not be enough. We won't even get a chance to clear the bodies, and without that task accomplished our problems here will only get worse."

His mouth tightened into a thin line.

"Don't take this personally, Karl. You've done a remarkable job holding out this long. Tell me, how well are the stations provisioned?"

He considered the question, his shame momentarily forgotten. "Melville and Platz have enough for three or four weeks. The farms a bit less. Black Level is running low."

"It's a skeleton crew there anyway. I'll call Greg and Marcus and have them move the staff down to Platz. I could use their help anyway."

"What about down here?" he asked.

"You tell me."

He frowned, but he turned and studied the place he held responsibility for. "We'll lock everything down. I suspect they'll leave it all alone except the food, most of which will spoil anyway. We'll need to secure the aura towers well. I don't think they know how to use them, but they might set them in motion by accident."

She wanted to say that might not be necessary. That what had happened to her in Colorado signaled an end to the need for the auras. She had no real proof, though, and while she had little in the way of superstition in her personality, a real fear dwelt within her that to voice the idea might doom it somehow. So she said only, "Good. Proceed."

With that he turned and held a hand out. Tania picked up the bag that held the alien object, took Karl's offered assistance, and walked to the climber. He helped usher her into the waiting compartment, already packed with the first evacuees and their belongings. The goodbye was short, too short, and she hoped it wouldn't be their last.

Vanessa came in a few minutes later. Tania offered her the adjacent seat and set the brown bag containing the relic between them on the floor.

As the vehicle rose up through the raging storm clouds that seemed almost a permanent fixture over the city, she wondered if she would ever set foot on Earth again, and what kind of place she would find if she did.

# 25

## SOUTHERN CHAD

### 1.APR.2285

Russell Blackfield stood on the rim of the pit and basked in the incredible sight of the alien pyramid below.

*I'm inside an aura.*

No other explanation made sense, despite the fact that there were no towers around. He should be dead by now, or at least completely insane. Instead he felt stable, and he was finally able to stop his feet. None of the other subs had managed to do that. They rushed forward on either side of him, tumbling over the precipice like lemmings to the sea. They rolled in the grit and sand of the steep-sloped walls, throwing up a cloud that filled Russell's nostrils and coated his throat. Some of the creatures cried out as they tumbled into the depths. Most seemed oblivious, as if caught in the grip of some ecstatic drug. He'd felt it, too, at first, during his trek through this wasteland. But it had faded.

An aura. A fucking trap just like in Darwin, only here he had no one but a bunch of subs and maybe, just maybe, Skyler and Ana. Of course, they'd leave at the first possible opportunity and had zero incentive now to cart him along. He wanted to laugh and scream all at once. How the hell had he traded the cushy, power-laden confines of Nightcliff and Darwin for this sorry lot?

He closed his eyes to the world, tilted his head back, and howled out this pathetic frustration. Mid-cry he opened his eyes to see the heavens. Might as well include the man upstairs in this curse, too, he figured.

His roar cut off, trapped in his throat as his breath caught in wonder.

A moon hung above him. Not the moon he knew, no. This was something new. Something artificial. Roughly circular in shape and . . . no, no, it was square. Rounded, yes, but no circle.

It grew larger with each passing moment, and so did Russell's awe. The surface became as big as the sun and then larger still. Not a moon at all, he realized, but something much closer. And not a single object, either. It was some time before he noticed this detail, but gradually it became clear. He was seeing dozens, maybe hundreds of objects, all floating down toward him like . . .

Yes, like climbers. He'd lain on his rooftop in Nightcliff and watched the mechanical spiders often enough to know that pace, that lazy drift.

But these numbered in the hundreds, and there was no Elevator here, much less a multitude of such devices.

Russell stared, studied, and ignored the growing knot in his gut. The objects continued to fall. They blotted a quarter of the sky now, and he could make out individual details. They were like spikes, some as much as a kilometer tall. All were hexagonal and were made of material identical to the Builders' shell ship he'd seen while aboard Anchor Station, though each of these dwarfed that object and there were hundreds.

Beside him the subhumans continued to fall helplessly into the pit. Russell, enveloped in a sudden and overwhelming desire for self-preservation, stepped backward. The spikes weren't falling at all. They were being lowered. Each had its own Elevator cord, exactly like the one in Nightcliff, only multiplied. An array. Blackfield reeled, imagining the lift capability they must have when used together. Darwin's capacity multiplied by ten and then ten again. But why? There was nothing here but sand. The whole thing would be wasted. They couldn't even anchor to the ground because . . .

He glanced down, and understood.

The columns matched the pattern of holes on the alien pyramid's surface. As this realization crept into Russell's mind, a cracking sound seemed to tear the very sky apart. He fell, ignoring the spike of pain in each elbow as he landed, and glanced up. The columns glowed with dazzling yellow energy. They rocketed toward the ground with a sudden ferocity, sizzling through the air in a concert of sonic booms. The noise overloaded his ears, shut them down, crippling his mind with a ringing unlike anything he'd ever heard before.

The mass of projectiles hit the pyramid. A strike of overwhelming force had destruction been their purpose. Russell threw an arm over his face and cowered low to the ground, expecting a massive explosion. None came. Hardly anything happened at all, in fact.

Russell sat up and crawled back to the edge of the pit.

Below, as he'd guessed, the columns had impaled themselves perfectly into their matching holes, which dotted the pyramid's surface. From the tip of each, Elevator cords stretched upward until they disappeared against the azure sky.

A fractured noise vibrated through the ground, like a mountain shattering into a thousand pieces. Russell knew then. He knew what the columns were for, what so many Elevator cords were needed to lift.

They weren't here to lift climbers full of sand. They were here to lift the entire fucking building.

The subs tumbling mindlessly into the abyss, he suddenly realized, were just trying to make the last bus home, or something. Skyler and Ana were probably inside, too, doing God-knows-what. Trapped maybe, or dead.

If Russell didn't move he'd be left behind, alone in this polluted moonscape of a place, as his last chance at survival, and perhaps redemption, was hauled away.

Fuck that.

He did as the subhumans, then, and dove into the pit, rolling in a choking cloud toward the pyramid below.

\* \* \*

Skyler lay on his stomach at the end of a trail of bodies. The dead subhumans covered every centimeter of the long, upward-sloping hallway.

His throat felt dry as the sand outside. In the lull of battle his stomach growled and twisted as if in a death throe of its own.

Ana lay a few meters away, breathing softly. Her eyes were closed but he could tell she had yet to sleep. Behind her sprawled a massive room that dwarfed the one below.

The dark walls sloped inward, soaring to a point high above that hid in shadow. Throughout the space were hundreds of erratically placed columns, no doubt matching the holes Skyler had seen in the pyramid's surface from above. Light seeped into the room through narrow zigzag lines that ran about the floor in a pattern as alien as the place itself. These produced so little light Skyler almost missed them at first. It was only when he'd lowered the intensity on his rifle's barrel light that he noticed the trace glow.

Ana stirred, shifted her weight on the hard surface. "Have they finally stopped?" she asked without opening her eyes.

"Doubt it," Skyler said. He glanced into the shadowy depths of the room. The columns, thick around as a fully loaded climber and tall as a building, stood in silent audience. Motionless, judgmental. "We should explore this room; there could be another way in. Or out."

The girl sat up. She coughed into her hand. "Did you bring any rations?"

Skyler shook his head. "Running low on ammo, too." He tried to sound casual and failed miserably.

Ana stood, rolled her head from side to side, and shook feeling back into her hands. "You go ahead and look around. I'll hold them here."

"Are you sure?"

With one hand she gave him a swat on the behind while simultaneously hefting a pistol she'd taken off one of the corpses that littered the facility. She cocked it and leaned against the wall beside the passage entryway.

"Won't be a minute," Skyler said.

He kept to the perimeter of the room as best he could. The

columns were placed randomly, as far as he could tell, and often were partially embedded into the wall of the chamber. Some were so close together he could not squeeze through the gap between and had to walk around. Without the landmark of Ana's flashlight playing against the walls beside her, he might have easily become lost in the eerie, silent forest.

Skyler glanced up toward the blackness of the ceiling. His thoughts drifted back to the first time he'd walked among the aura towers in Belém at night. This place wasn't so different, save for the scale. If he was right, each of these columns was a hollow tube that dipped down into the once-beating heart of this gigantic place. Exhaust tubes, spewing out the SUBS virus in concentrated blasts year after year, taking advantage of every dust storm and stiff wind to further the reach. Presumably each infected being became another, smaller factory, but for whatever reason the Builders had kept this initial source running all this time.

Until now, it seemed.

He yearned to leave, to find out if his efforts had indeed killed the source of the disease. Quietly, in the silent depths of the enormous room, he chuckled to himself. Would he once again get credit for saving everyone and everything? Below Nightcliff he'd been forced to flee into the deep silo, and only an aggressive subhuman's tackle had sent him careening into the strange iris at the bottom of that pit. What had happened after that he scarcely understood, much less remembered in any detail. Yet he'd done it. He'd short-circuited whatever malfunction had plagued the aura for the months leading up to that moment, and ended the sporadic incursions of subhumans into Darwin and above.

At least those who knew what had happened had the sense to keep it quiet.

More than all this, though, Skyler found in himself a strange desire to return to Darwin. To see Sam, Skadz, and Prumble again. He should have been away from here hours ago to make the agreed rendezvous.

The room began to tremble.

He felt it through the soles of his feet first, and turned to face Ana. She shouted something, a cry of alarm, as the building began to rumble for the second time. *What now?* Skyler thought.

The vibration grew more intense, producing an unpleasant tingle up his entire body and rattling his clenched teeth together.

Bits of material the size of pebbles began to fall from above, shaken loose from the columns and walls. Somehow this frightened him more than anything that had yet happened. The Builders weren't sloppy architects. It would take something mammoth indeed to shake their walls to the point of crumbling.

Skyler ran—lurching, awkward steps on unsteady feet— toward Ana. She seemed impossibly far away. A silhouette before the glowing orb of a flashlight that wavered in all directions as she struggled to stay on her feet.

A horrible rending sound built from above, and with it the very ceiling seemed to fall as large quantities of dark material crashed to the floor. Skyler threw an arm over his head, weaved to place himself at the base of a column. He glanced up, casting his light into the torrent of discharge that now fell.

The tops of the columns were twisting like trees in a gale. They slid across the surface of the ceiling, reforming and rearranging, though for what purpose he couldn't imagine. He stood frozen, staring in wonder and disbelief as the gigantic pillars, solid as marble a moment ago, thrashed like worms. Their midsections were moving now.

And then Skyler felt his breath catch in his throat as the base next to him slid away. He stumbled, caught himself. Somewhere Ana screamed, and Skyler was running.

He raced through the room, all caution abandoned. All around him the huge columns shifted along the floor as if they weren't attached at all, like the aura towers did when pushed. Only, he somehow knew they were still perfectly, inexorably stuck to the floor. For a split second he watched one move, saw it drift along the floor and saw, yes, the material that had sluiced down from above seem to absorb itself into the space left behind, repairing instantly whatever damage the moving column left behind.

His lack of attention cost him. A column lurched suddenly in his direction and slammed into him. The surface, hard as stone, clipped his knees and sent him tumbling. The pain of the impact brought tears to his eyes. He gritted his teeth and rolled, came up hobbling to get out of the way as the column barreled onward to whatever destination it sought.

Everything stopped.

The room went silent save for Skyler's own breathing, and Ana's frightened sobs from somewhere ahead.

A glow began to build above, like the sun coming out from behind a violent storm. With it came a new sound, a terrible roar that built from nothing to a crushing volume in seconds. The entire ceiling glowed, as if partially translucent.

And then the columns began to fill from the top down with that same yellow-white energy as something poured, or thrust, into them. In the span of half a second every column became a glowing rod, pulsing heat and light. The room became so luminous that Skyler had to throw an arm across his face and squint against the glow. It was no use, though. The light came from everywhere.

Ana was suddenly pressed against him, her arms thrown around him. "What is it? What's happening?"

"I don't know," he said. "But we should get out of here, now. I don't care what it takes, we have to get back to the Magpie and leave."

She met his gaze and nodded with absolute determination.

Skyler took a step and winced at the fresh blast of pain from his knees. He doubled over and tried to rub the sting away. Then Ana slipped an arm around his waist and urged him on, taking much of his weight.

They were near the center of the room when she froze in place.

Skyler glanced up, swallowing his aches. Twenty meters away, standing at the mouth of the hallway that led from the room, was a subhuman coated in black.

It stood well over two meters tall. Half a head higher than even Samantha, Skyler guessed, and despite its diseased state the being was corded with muscle beneath the black coating. Its eyes blazed yellow, like twin stars, and it stepped forward.

The glow in the room began to abate at the same time, slowly dimming back to near-total darkness.

Without thinking, Skyler pushed Ana behind him. He raised his rifle, trying to remember how many rounds were left in the magazine. Four, maybe five? Not enough, not nearly.

Ana knelt beside him and hefted her own pistol. Together they unleashed the last of their ammunition. Their guns sang, spitting plumes of fire as the bullets found their target.

The rounds rattled against the armored subhuman and ricocheted away, bouncing harmlessly on the rapidly dimming floor. If the creature had felt any pain, it didn't show it. It simply weathered the barrage and then stepped forward again, now just ten meters away.

"Ideas?" Skyler asked out the corner of his mouth.

"Split up. Maybe one of us can get out."

"I'm not leaving you here."

"Who says you're the one who would make it?"

He grunted. "Ana . . ."

She reached out and took his hand, her eyes never leaving the approaching enemy.

He didn't want to tell her that he was simply too tired to run. He wouldn't get ten steps before this augmented mass of muscle and primal instinct fell upon him.

"Plan?" Ana asked out the corner of her mouth.

Her little spark of humor in the face of the approaching monster melted Skyler's fear away. "You go low, I go high," he said to her. "Keep its legs tangled up if you can. Okay?"

"Got it."

"On three."

He counted down. Ana let go of his hand. At three they lurched forward in almost perfect unison. Skyler caught the briefest hint of surprise and confusion in the subhuman's body language as it became mentally tangled with the decision of whom to defend against.

Skyler leapt as Ana dove. The creature reacted with astonishing reflexes, kicking out even as it lifted its hands to grip Skyler. One viselike hand tucked in under Skyler's armpit, the other latched over his face, fingers digging into his temples and cheeks so tightly Skyler thought his head might pop like a tomato.

And then he was sailing through the air, tossed away like a harmless toy. He heard Ana grunt from the kick she'd received in the instant before he hit the warm floor. Skyler landed like a confused fish tossed on the deck of a ship. His chin cracked against the rock-hard material as he landed, splitting skin.

Ana grunted again, a wet sound this time as the creature kicked her once more. Skyler rolled in time to see it bend over her, lifting her by the neck. Her face contorted as the two powerful black hands wrapped around her throat. She kicked and clawed in a hopeless effort to free herself.

Skyler's vision swam. He tried to push himself up, even to one elbow, but his limbs felt sluggish and thick. He shouted, or tried to. All that came out was a mouthful of blood that splattered across the floor in front of him.

The entire room lurched, like an elevator beginning its climb. He thought it was just his shaken body at first but then he saw the creature stagger, if only for a moment. Ana sprang to life in that instant. She brought both legs up, knees to her chest, feet to the subhuman's chest, and kicked outward with everything she had.

The subhuman lost its grip on her neck and fell backward. Ana dropped like a stone, her back slamming into the now-dim floor. She cried out and rolled to one side, sucking in a lungful of precious air.

Skyler tried again to stand. The room swayed like a ship cresting a massive wave. The creature, on its feet already—*fuck it's fast!*—stumbled with the motion as well. Skyler spat the blood in his mouth aside and said, "Over here, bastard."

The subhuman whirled. Its eyes flared yellow again, and it strode forward, Ana temporarily forgotten. *Good,* Skyler thought. That was something at least.

In two powerful steps the armored creature stood before him. Skyler tried to lift his hands into a boxer's defense, but his battered, exhausted limbs hardly moved. He only had time to close his eyes as the sub backhanded him, knocking him a meter to the right and sending him sprawling in a useless tangle of limbs. Skyler felt no pain this time. His mind had somehow removed itself from further agony.

Again he tried to stand, the effort producing only a slight lift of his head from the floor that brought stars to his vision. Once again the room swayed. *That's not helping, goddammit.* He lifted his head enough to steal a glance at his attacker. The sub had almost faded into the darkness that had swallowed the room once more. It looked like a shadow made real.

"Well, well. What's all this then?"

The voice came from somewhere off to Skyler's left. He thought it a figment of his clouded mind, but there was a familiarity to it. He flopped his head to the side and looked.

Standing just inside the room's entrance was a naked Russell Blackfield.

*I've lost my mind,* Skyler thought.

The creature heard it, too, though, for it turned to face the newcomer with as much surprise as Skyler felt.

"Blackfield," Skyler said thickly. "Get out of here. There are weapons below—"

"Don't tell me what to do," Russell barked, anger palpable. "It's my turn to be the fucking hero, all right, mate?"

Skyler tried to say more, tried to tell him heroics might be more possible if he was dressed and armed to the teeth. The man's nudity suddenly registered. *He's exposed, he's been outside, and yet he's here. Immune?* The odds said no, and Skyler felt a cold flutter of hope that his theory was true, that this plague forge had been shut down. Either that, or Russell was indeed infected. Perhaps the building provided an aura and held him in stasis, or maybe the towers outside yet remained.

Skyler strained his eyes looking for signs of the rash on Russell's neck, but the light was poor, the angle all wrong.

The subhuman shifted, momentarily caught between three opponents. But it only needed a glance at Skyler and then Ana to decide Russell was the only one it had to worry about.

"That's right, mate," Blackfield said. "Let's see what you've got."

Skyler pushed to get to his elbows and felt a searing stab of pain from his chin. Warm blood trickled down onto his shirt. His arms faltered, and he flopped back onto the floor again. He rolled to his side in time to see Ana staggering to a stand. "No," he croaked. "Ana, no."

The creature took a heavy step toward Russell just as the building swayed again. It paused until the motion abated, then it continued its march toward the newcomer. Blackfield somehow held his ground as the hulking armored thing closed the distance, and whether the man was insane or brave Skyler had to respect his tenacity.

Ana found her feet and began a lurching, anguished jog toward the subhuman's back. This, Skyler thought, deserved respect as well, but he wasn't about to let her die just to buy Russell Blackfield another few seconds of life. Ignoring the white-hot lance of pain in his chin, Skyler thrust himself to his feet and surged on a path that would intercept the girl.

The creature must have seen something in Blackfield's eyes. It stopped, turned. Its eyes flared like camera flashes when it saw Ana bearing down, and it fully spun to face her.

Russell took the opening. In two quick steps he leapt onto the subhuman's back.

In that instant Skyler saw it. Just a flash, but he knew a clutched grenade when he saw one and he watched in horror as Russell's arms flew around the creature's neck. And despite everything going on—Russell's battle cry, Ana's gasp of surprise, his own boots thudding on the floor as he sped toward her—Skyler heard the pin drop. The slightest *tink-tink-tink* as it bounced on the floor.

Ana pulled up, unsure what to do, and Skyler hit her in the midsection. He wrapped his arms around her and thrust his legs with all the energy he could muster and more. She screamed in surprise, an accusation of betrayal in her cry that stung Skyler more than any of his injuries.

Even before they hit the ground Skyler glanced back.

The subhuman, large as it was, toppled under Russell's sudden weight. Its hands were too busy trying to pull Russell's aside to break its fall and it hit the ground face-first with a single, sharp crack.

The creature bucked upward immediately, somehow getting its elbows underneath itself and pushing. But Blackfield had no intention of trying to strangle the thing. He released his grip at the same moment and used the creature's own thrust to bounce back onto his knees.

On the floor in front of the creature's face lay the hand grenade.

Skyler turned away, and fought Ana, who writhed to free herself from his weight. He threw his arms over her head. "Stay down!"

The grenade went off.

* * *

Blackfield felt the pulse of raw heat, the concussive wave pound every bit of his skin. Every instinct in his head wanted to shut his eyes in that moment, but he refused. He wanted to see the fucking thing die and he was not disappointed.

The creature's head and shoulders blew apart as the explosion ripped through it. For a single glorious fraction of a second Russell saw the blood and guts and gore of the human within. The soft, sweet center inside the hard candy shell. He'd have laughed at his thought but a fist the size of a city bus punched him and sent him sailing backward.

For another fraction of a second, this one decidedly less glorious, he felt the astonishing pain of a thousand wounds delivered simultaneously as chunks of the alien's armor, shrapnel from the grenade, and bits of human flesh slammed into him.

And then, nothing. Not death, just . . .

Clarity.

In the flash of the explosion he saw the ceiling high above amid the tangle of the strange floor-to-ceiling tubes that filled the room. There, in the center of the ceiling, was a hexagonal section wholly different from the rest of the place. Symbols were engraved into the sections around it, and they glowed briefly in the flash of light, each reflecting back a different color. Then it slipped back into shadow. He felt a strange gladness at having seen it. Whatever it was, he'd fucking seen it. A little reward, finally.

Russell had a dim awareness of his body crashing into the floor. He bounced once and then slid to a stop, still staring upward. One of his legs splayed out at a crazy angle, and he saw a jagged edge of bone sticking upward from the middle of his thigh.

He lifted his head a bit higher to inspect his manhood. Despite the wounds all over his body, that bit seemed to have made it through unscathed. Russell rocked his head back and . . . stopped short of laughing. He settled for a smile instead. He'd redeemed himself, hadn't he? Time to leave his lascivious side behind.

A face appeared within his view. Skyler's ugly mug. He was saying something, but Russell's ears were ringing. Slowly the words cut through.

". . . medical gear in the ship. Just hold on."

Russell tried to talk but found his mouth was full of blood. He turned his head with an effort that almost cost him his consciousness, and spat. Dark red splatter on an alien floor. Gingerly, he turned back to Skyler. The edges of his vision were blurred now, and getting worse. Darker. "Weren't expecting me, huh?"

"We'll get you help, just hang on."

"Don't bother. I'm cooked. I did my bit."

Then Ana was there, too. Beautiful Ana. Her dark hair spilled over her face, hanging down toward Russell.

He tried to smile for her, had no idea if he'd succeeded.

"Blackfield," she whispered. "Why'd you do it?"

And there it was. There, in the small patch of his vision still clear he saw the look. The same naked admiration she favored Skyler with every time she glanced his way. No fear, no disgust or hatred or suspicion. Just pure, genuine respect. It was every bit as worthwhile as he'd hoped.

He coughed; his vision swam. It took effort to find and focus on her again. "For that," he said, voice thick and growing weaker. "It makes it . . . made it all . . ."

A tear formed on her eyelash and dangled there.

Russell found he could twitch the index finger of his left hand. Then his arm moved. Yes, he could lift it. His whole hand shook as it came into view. Blood dripped away. He couldn't quite manage the reach to Ana's sweet, innocent cheek, though. She was on the right and Skyler, damn him, was on the left. Russell tapped Skyler's arm with the back of his hand and the pilot took it in his own. Gently, as if he might cause injury.

"I ran out of air," Russell said. "You assholes left me to die."

"Sorry," Skyler replied, practically choking on a guilty laugh. He sounded sincere and humbled. "We were stuck in here. I'm amazed you made it to us."

"Yeah. Tell you all about it another time, huh?"

Skyler said something else, but Russell's ears refused to let the sound back in. A good thing, too. It was kind of peaceful in here. He rolled his head slightly to focus on Ana again.

Her lips were pressed into a thin line now. Holding back grief or something. The little teardrop had tumbled away already, leaving a thin, watery trail down her face.

"We're moving up," Russell told her. "The whole building, heading to space." *Now I'm a fucking poet, too?* He grinned as Ana shot a confused glance at Skyler.

The girl faced him once more. She took his hand from Skyler's and lifted it to her soft cheek, holding the back of his palm there and letting the warmth seep from her body to his.

He stared into those eyes, lost himself in them even as darkness began to creep into the center of his vision. Russell held her gaze as he slipped into the void.

"I bought the two of you a second chance," he said. He couldn't hear his own voice but he could tell from their expressions that they heard him despite the stutters and wet, ugly coughs. "Don't fuck it up. Vary the pattern. Finish what you came here for."

"We will," Ana mouthed.

Russell Blackfield winked at her. Then he died.

# 26

## THE KEY SHIP

### 2.APR.2285

Tania's third journey to the Builder ship began much like the first two. Locked in a tin can, with only one person to keep her company, and a hard case containing an alien object of unknown purpose at her feet.

Her companion was Vanessa again, not Skyler, and this time the object in the case had blood on it. Too much blood, Tania thought, though any amount would qualify. The image of Pablo's stony gaze seemed forever etched on the inside of her eyelids.

Tim sat above her, in the single-seat compartment where the rudimentary controls were. He'd insisted on handling the job, and she'd agreed without hesitation.

Reports came in at a near-constant stream from Karl and others in Belém and aboard Melville Station. *The exodus from Camp Exodus,* Tania thought dryly. Ammunition dwindled almost as fast as the camp's population. Every report of a lull in subhuman activity brought hope the worst had passed, a hope dashed each time with frantic and maddeningly sporadic reports of new sightings, new combat.

"We'll be fighting with knives soon," Karl said after giving his most recent report. There were still more than three hundred people in camp.

"See that you're out before that happens."

"I had a different idea."

Tania hesitated. She had only Vanessa to look at, and the woman's eyes held as much intrigue as Tania felt. "Tell me."

"We're going to form an inner wall," he said.

Tania frowned. "There's no time."

"There is if we build it out of aura towers." When she didn't shoot the idea down outright, he went on. "I figure we can make a ring with a twenty-meter radius. Plenty of room for those of us still here."

It was a good plan, she had to admit. The easily moved towers were by far the quickest way to erect such a barricade. And yet their movement might also be the fatal flaw. "You're assuming the subhumans can't push the towers."

"I am, yeah," he said. His Australian accent was softer than Neil's had been, but every now and then he said something that brought the late tycoon back to life in a way that Zane could not. "It beats a knife fight."

Tania forced herself to swallow her concerns. It was unclear if the aura towers still did anything at all, but if there remained a purpose to them, the last thing she wanted to do was have the colonists return to find them scattered to who-knows-where. Yet Karl had to do something, and she could think of no better option. "Okay. Don't waste any more time talking to me then. Report in when it's done."

"Cheers," he said, and signed off.

She'd barely drawn her next breath when Tim shouted down from the pilot's cabin. "Tania, you should see this!"

The hatch at the top of the ladder was still open, but she already had her excursion suit on and this one was nothing like the svelte model she'd worn last time. The one she'd worn to Colorado, and left in the mud at the base of Camp Exodus's wall. "Tell us, Tim. We're both suited and can't come up."

"Right, sorry." His voice had a slight quiver to it. "Remember those pointy bits that stuck out from the bottom of the Key Ship?"

"What about them?" Skyler had thought they might be a

weapon. Tania feared they were the nozzles of a massive engine.

"They're gone."

She blanched, and cursed whoever had built this tin can for not putting a vid screen down here. "Gone? As in retracted? Vanished?"

"Yes . . . Wait, No. Hang on."

Seconds passed. Tania felt subtle changes in her weight. Tim must be turning the small ship to get a better view.

"Tania, where those towers were I now see Elevator threads. Hundreds of them, stretching down."

She tried to absorb the ramifications of this and rammed into a mental stumbling block that went part and parcel with anything the Builders did: Why? Why so many in one place? Why put one in Darwin, one in Belém, then concentrate orders of magnitude more on a third site so late?

Perhaps the other two sites were just test locations, or outposts, in their eventual colonization of Earth. And this site represented what would become their hub. A capital city, or something like it.

"Skyler and Ana," Vanessa said. Her voice shattered Tania's mental picture like a rock through a window. "They're down below, somewhere, aren't they?"

Tania shook her head. "They should be in Darwin by now, or even on their way back to Belém." She didn't feel the need to correct her by adding Russell Blackfield's name to the list.

"They should be, yes. But maybe not. And we can go check."

"Hmm?"

Vanessa spread her hands. "Bring a climber over here and go down. They might need our help. They might . . . if they failed, we could still finish the mission."

"We finish our task first," Tania said, more stern than she'd intended. "After that, it's worth preparing for, at least. Tim?"

He answered instantly. "I already asked them to prep a climber and send it over."

"Good man."

"Thanks. But Tania?"

"Yes?"

"The door is tucked in the middle of that maze of Elevator threads."

She hadn't considered that. On the first visit, Jenny had had the decency to position their craft directly over the hexagonal door before unleashing her betrayal. That maneuver would be impossible now. The graphene cords were thin to the point of being invisible, so piloting into that mess was out of the question. The threads were so strong that a solid impact would likely slice the vehicle in two without leaving so much as a scratch on the exotic material. Either that or the tiny ship would be flung back from the thing like an arrow off a bowstring. "Get us as close as you can," Tania said. "We'll wiggle through somehow."

Another shift in weight as Tim corrected their course. Ten minutes passed, long enough for Tania to cycle twice through feelings of fear and resolve. The only thing that remained constant, through everything that had happened, was the doubt. She couldn't shake the idea that all of this, the installation of these objects, amounted to the digging of one's own grave. It made no sense to her, of course. Certainly there were much easier ways to wipe out a planet with minimal effort, so she concluded there must be some other purpose. She simply doubted that the purpose the Builders had in mind would be a desirable outcome for humanity.

"Patching Karl in," Tim said.

Tania flipped her comm on. "Karl, I'm listening."

"Bad news," he said. He was practically shouting, the sounds of battle heavy in the background. "The towers refuse to move."

"What?"

"They won't budge, no matter what we try. Ammo is low—"

"Get out of there," Tania said. "Leave now."

"It'll be eight hours before the next climber returns." Somewhere near him a woman screamed.

"Karl, listen," Tania said. "I didn't want to say it before because I didn't want to be wrong. I think the auras are gone."

"Gone? Wait, you *think*?"

"I was in the Clear in Colorado, just like you when you first set foot in Belém. I had the headache, so I'm not immune. But then it stopped. It stopped right before the subhumans started this assault. I think SUBS has switched off, and the auras, too."

"I . . . Tania, Christ. I think I get what you're suggesting, but I don't know. . . ."

She tried to fill her voice with a confidence she didn't feel. "You can't hold out there any longer, correct?"

"That's an understatement."

"And the subhumans only want to reach the Elevator. So let them. Move into the city and wait it out. Take the comm, and tomorrow or the next day we'll coordinate a plan to retake the camp. Understood?"

"Okay. I read you," came the stiff reply. "Signing off; it's getting ugly down here."

"Be safe," Tania said even as the connection closed. She leaned back and shut her eyes, wondering when the time would come when all crises were behind them and some actual progress could be made. Years away, she suspected.

"Okay," Tim said from above. "This is about as close as I'm willing to go. Nearest thread is ten meters away."

"Nice flying," Tania replied. "Seal your hatch; we'll get our helmets on now."

A second later Tim's face appeared over the hatch. He motioned for Tania to come, as if he wanted to tell her a secret. His expression was strange. Not worried, but still somehow nervous. Tania glanced at Vanessa, who busily inspected the grooves of her helmet's seal. Shrugging, Tania allowed herself to drift up to the hatch. "What is it?"

He leaned in to say something, and when Tania turned her ear toward him she felt his lips press against her cheek. The kiss was brief and warm and sent a tingle along her spine. "Come back in one piece, okay?" he said as he moved away.

"I . . . I'll do that." His action took her off guard. Belatedly, she added, "You'd better be here, waiting."

"Count on it."

Tania favored him with a smile and Tim responded in kind.

"Sealing the hatch," the man said. He caught Tania's eye one last time before the metal door closed with a deep twang. Tania waited for the small indicator light next to it to turn green, indicating a good seal. Then she drifted back down and helped Vanessa get her helmet on. For a few long minutes Tania felt a warmth on her cheek and a smile playing at the corners of her mouth. If Vanessa noticed, she said nothing.

* * *

The older, bulky spacesuits were not equipped with the fancy conveniences of the kind she'd worn on her previous visit.

Instead of a wrist-mounted thruster, Tania had to make do with a box-shaped device that hung from a strap on her forearm. It had a nozzle on the front, and a handle on either side, which meant two hands were needed to operate the thing. Easy enough when moving alone and unhindered, but Tania had both the alien object and Vanessa in tow. The immune was a quick learner, but she'd only spent a scant few hours in zero-g. Her movements were still too jerky, too abrupt, for her to be set loose in open space.

So Vanessa clutched the case containing the object with both arms and legs as if trying to merge with it. Tania couldn't see her eyes through the reflective gold visor, but she suspected the woman had taken her advice and closed her eyes to ease the sense of vertigo. Per Tania's instruction, Vanessa made no movements at all so as not to throw off Tania's aim.

For her part, Tania decided not to attach herself to the case or her companion at all. To navigate she needed to be able to propel them in any direction, and that would be impossible if she was stuck on one side of the package. It was a risk to spacewalk without any kind of tether, but risk somehow felt normal to her now after Colorado. After everything, really.

So Tania put her back against the combined mass of Vanessa and the case, and pulsed her thruster just enough to push them all into the strange forest of Elevator threads at the pace of a slow walk.

The individual cords, illuminated by sunlight reflected off the blue and white marble of Earth below, looked like strands of spider silk. With each thread so impossibly thin, this gave the illusion of each being equidistant if she looked directly toward her destination. So Tania looked down instead. Nearer the planet the hundreds of cords blurred together into something like a single, dark column. From this perspective, individual strands closer to her would separate from that mass as she approached or passed by, making it possible—only just—to spot them in time to avoid an impact. The lamps mounted to either side of her helmet provided the second line of defense, illuminating those portions of thread very close by with a different sheen than the rest.

Above her, a scant fifty meters away, loomed the underside of the Builder ship. Where before there had been hundreds of long "spikes," as Skyler had called them, now there were shallow indents with irislike centers from which the Elevator cords emerged. Somewhere, a few hundred meters ahead, lay the hexagon door. Or so she hoped.

Despite this being her third visit, the size of the vessel still left her breathless. She could not imagine what purpose a ship of this size might serve, though she could venture a guess at the reason for such dimensions: storage. Storage for what, she had no idea, but Tania thought it a reasonable assumption that no space-faring species would bother to accelerate such mass between the stars unless they had a damn good reason.

A thread loomed directly ahead. Tania quickly, carefully, shifted herself to the right side of her combined cargo. She aimed the thruster, pulsed it for one second, then again when she felt the shift in trajectory might not be enough. Mentally she started counting seconds. The package now moving both forward and to the left, Tania gingerly climbed over to the opposite side, going underneath so as not to paw at poor Vanessa. Once the thread passed harmlessly on the right, Tania pulsed twice more to straighten their path. She stopped counting; eleven seconds. She pulsed twice again to send them back toward the original course, moved once more to the right, and after eleven seconds pulsed two final times. She felt the tingle of sweat along her spine when the maneuver finally ended.

"I felt that," Vanessa said, her voice surprisingly even and calm in Tania's ear.

"It's a lot of work for one simple course correction."

"I can only imagine."

Tania found herself smiling. "Do you want me to talk you through it? Would that make it easier?"

"No. It's hard not to look, and that would make me want to even more."

"Okay." Tania was about to say more, to try to strike up some trivial conversation, but another thread loomed. This one was off to one side but still appeared to be in their path. Tania moved to the left side again, then, at the last second, ducked underneath the case. The thread passed by harmlessly on the left, less than a meter away. She exhaled a breath she hadn't realized she was holding and forced herself to look down and forward again.

Six more corrections were needed, one of which left her stuck in a pocket of three cords that required a careful retreat. But finally, after an hour, she saw the hexagon door. At almost the same moment, the cords began to thin out, clearing the rest of her path.

"We're here," Tania said.

Around the hexagon door were five sigils, one each for the objects scattered across Earth and their matching receptacles inside. Only three of the symbols were illuminated now, however: the oval with its wavy side, the cube with a notch on one edge, and the triangle with the missing tip that matched the object within the case Tania now pushed. Just like on her previous visits, as soon as the case was within range all but the matching symbol faded. With only the triangle lit, the door opened, revealing the long tunnel within.

"Tim? We're going inside."

"Copy that. Keep talking. I'm on pins and needles out here."

"Will do," Tania said. She turned the case so that Vanessa's back pointed toward the door, which now looked like a gaping black pit. Then she tapped Vanessa's shoulder. "You can open your eyes now. I need some help."

Vanessa relaxed her grip and drifted a few centimeters off the surface of the case. Unlike Tania, she had a belt tying her to the object. "What do I do?"

"Turn yourself around. Nice slow movements, remember? Face the opening and once I start moving, just be ready to adjust our path if we veer toward one of the walls."

"Just use my hands and feet?"

"Exactly. Nice slow movements. Keep repeating that to yourself." The immune had struggled with keeping herself oriented in the lack of gravity on their first visit together, and Tania thought she had enough rapport with the woman now to offer some simple, if condescending, pointers.

A moment later, Vanessa had herself in position. Tania turned, again putting the hard, flat surface of her suit's backpack against the case. She aimed her thruster toward Earth. The Elevator threads, all around her now, formed an ethereal tunnel that converged below in the haze and blur of clouds and atmosphere.

She turned, focused. A good five-second blast from the thruster and they were inside, moving at the equivalent of a brisk walking pace. The interior held a strange comfort to it now, on her third visit. Compared to the missing spikes outside, and the crowd of Elevator cords left in their place, the tunnel beyond the hexagon door looked exactly the same.

*Stay sharp*, she said to herself even as she added on another few seconds of thrust. She climbed around to the front of the case now, where Vanessa waited. Together they used their fingertips to push off the ceiling in a slight trajectory correction, and when the time came, they both put their legs and arms forward to take the brunt of the impact with the end of the hallway.

After a brief pause the wall at the end of the tunnel separated into angular sections, divided by bright lines of light. The lines grew into gaps as the sections of wall slid away to reveal the room beyond.

"We're at the key room," Tania said for Tim's benefit.

"That was quick."

"This place feels like a second home. Perhaps we should furnish it."

Tim laughed. Vanessa did not. She'd flipped her gold sun visor up and Tania saw her eyes grow wide. "It's changed," the immune said.

Her tone ripped Tania's attention from wrangling the object. She spun, and the room beyond sent a chill down her spine.

The ten-walled "key room" was gone. Instead she looked in upon a nearly spherical space, ten meters in diameter. Uncharacteristically for the Builders, the material was white, and it glowed with a faint luminance that seemed to come from everywhere and nowhere. The light, so dim it would have been hard to perceive had it not covered the entire interior, was alien in its flawlessness. A perfect, unwavering, evenly distributed light that constituted the white material's only visible feature. Tania found herself wondering what it felt like. From appearance alone she could not tell if it was solid, or if her hand would pass straight through it.

Nestled within the glowing white sphere were two strips of metallic gray, each a meter wide and spanning the circumference of the room. The bands were perpendicular to each other, and met on the far side to form an X, exactly opposite where the door was.

Tim's voice came through the speaker in her helmet. "Say something."

"I'm not sure what to say," Tania replied. "The key room is not here. We're seeing a sphere. More in a second."

She glanced at Vanessa and nodded once, a gesture the other woman returned. Tania pushed off gently and drifted toward the opening, wrapping one hand around the edge.

The gray material felt hard as steel through the glove of her suit. She moved her hand farther, then touched the white portion. To her surprise it had a spongy feel, like a firm cushion. Tania moved all the way inside and glanced around. Her first impression proved correct. Other than the two light gray bands, the room was completely featureless.

"What do we do?" Vanessa asked. She still floated in the hallway, next to the bagged object.

Tania continued across the space, then pushed off with her feet to drift back. She turned at the midway point to face Vanessa, and shrugged. "Bring it in, I guess. Let's see what happens."

Vanessa urged the bag forward and kept with it, matching the pace perfectly with slow, precise movements. Tania couldn't help but smile at the immune's progress. Soon she'd be bouncing about in zero-g like she'd lived in orbit for years.

Tania drifted out to meet her near the center of the room, not wanting to be near the wall if something happened. She'd barely moved a meter when the two bands began to move. They spun like wheels, independently of each other, and in doing so the opening they'd framed vanished. Tania's breath caught in her throat. The rings, still spinning, began to tilt wildly, spinning on their axis now as well. Their motion revealed the portion of the sphere where the hallway had been just a second before. Tania saw nothing save for the pure, spongy white surface of the sphere where the only exit had been.

"Don't panic," she said, realizing a second later she'd said it aloud. "Tim, can you hear me?"

All she received in answer was a faint hissing sound from the speaker inside her helmet.

Vanessa tried. "Tim? Please respond."

A few garbled words came through in bursts now.

"Some kind of interference," Tania said.

Vanessa sucked in her lower lip in concentration. "Maybe this room is meant to sever our communication."

Tania considered that. She wondered what would have happened had they come in here on some kind of umbilical or guywire. The motion of these two rings, she thought, would have severed it like a piece of string. The thought worried her.

The two metallic rings continued to rotate around the room, silent and ominous. *Decelerating now,* Tania thought. She studied them closely. "They're slowing down."

The two rings settled into a new position, forming X's once again on opposite sides of the room. Different places than before, Tania thought, though she couldn't be sure in the otherwise featureless bubble of glowing white.

The rings stopped rotating axially but still rolled along their own length. Tania watched, fascinated despite the sense of being trapped, as each ring began to slow to a stop. When they did, a new opening appeared where their surfaces met. In a perfect reversal of the exit hallway's closure, panels slid apart on each band.

Tania felt the tension within her melt. The key room lay beyond. Only the entrance this time was in the middle of what she had considered the floor. She exhaled slowly as she took in the sight, looking for any other changes since last time, and saw none. Still the ten walls that rose a hundred meters above. Five were empty, just spacers really. Between each of those were the five that had receptacles for the objects, each wall alive with the color that matched its "key."

"Didn't we come in from the side last time?" Vanessa asked. "Why would they move the door?"

"A very good question."

Through silent agreement, Tania pushed off to the new doorway and stopped herself at the opening. She took quick stock just to be sure nothing here had changed.

"Come up here," she said.

A moment later Vanessa joined her, the object still expertly placed in front of her for easy guidance. "What do you suppose that new room is for?"

Tania thought about it. "Some kind of junction, maybe? One that can reconfigure itself?"

The immune started to speak, stopped herself, then met Tania's gaze. "I was going to ask why, or why now, but I'm not sure I want to know."

"It would only be speculation," Tania said. "I vote we call it the Lobby for now, and not worry about it. We're here; let's do what we came to do."

Vanessa nodded. Together they turned and took in the alien majesty of the key room. Only the purple and red walls had exposed sections where their keys had been inserted. The objects themselves glowed with hues that matched their respective walls, only much brighter.

"There, look at the green," Tania said, pointing.

Halfway up on the wall of emerald light patterns, a circle appeared as a section of the flat surface recessed into a half-dome cavity, just as before. Tania didn't wait for the process to finish this time. Instead she set to work removing the wedge-shaped object from its case.

"This will be trickier than last time with these awful old thrusters," Tania said.

"What can I do?" Vanessa asked.

Tania propelled the object in front of her with one hand and glided to the base of the green wall. Vanessa joined her a moment later, using Tania's offered arm to stabilize and orient herself. They looked up in unison. The circular cavity was about fifty meters above, and hard to see from this vantage point.

On a whim Tania glanced back toward the room she'd dubbed

the Lobby and saw no sign of it. No hint at all. Where a passage had existed moments before, she now saw only the perfect flat surface of the key room's floor, and she found strangely enough that she felt completely at ease. It would open again, of this she felt absolutely sure. The idea carried a strange comfort she didn't quite understand but also could not deny.

"You okay?" Vanessa asked.

The immune had noted the lack of an exit, too, Tania saw. She nodded to her. "Just like last time, okay?"

"Okay."

"Right, then." With a slow, careful movement, she set the object in Vanessa's hands. At the same instant a scramble of static came over her headset.

"Are you read— me?"

"Tim? Go ahead. You're breaking up a bit."

"Something's coming up the —vator."

"A climber, you mean?"

His response came through as a garbled mess. "Repeat," she said, moving back toward where the door had been. Memory of the spinning of Belém's Elevator came to her. Once again she saw the mysterious dark "blobs" that had raced down that new cord, demolishing a supply climber as if it were a mere insect. Those shapes had become the aura towers, of which there were numerous examples directly below this ship, theoretically at least. Perhaps they were coming back? Her mouth went dry at the thought of forty of those dark masses hitting this ship with the same ferocity that single one had when it took out the climber.

Tim's voice came through a bit clearer now. "I don't — what it is, but it's huge. The cords are lifting it."

She tried and failed to imagine what "it" could be. What would they need to raise from the ground that required so much lifting power? There was simply nothing to relate such an action to, no analogue. She'd studied the early history of human space exploration, and the only thing she could think of was the soil return missions from Mars. Could this be the same, only on a scale that simply defied human imagination? "How quickly will it arrive?"

"It's moving pretty slow. Faster than a climber, but not —. A few hours?"

"Okay," Tania said. "Any change, you let us know. We'll make sure to be out before it arrives, just in case."

"Understood."

Tania propelled herself back to Vanessa. "I guess we'd better hurry."

"I'm ready."

"Don't forget," Tania said. "Once we install it, there will be an energy buildup, and that bright flash. Remember? Okay. We'll need to push off for here as soon as the object is inserted." *And hope the door reappears.*

Vanessa signaled affirmative and got into position.

As per their plan, Tania pushed off from the floor and drifted along the wall. She had to force herself not to become mesmerized by the glowing green patterns along its surface. At the inside-out dome she stretched out her arm and, once on the far side of it, gripped the edge and stopped herself with ease. She turned and sat on the rim, mentally forcing herself to think of this as the new "floor." "All set," she said, and dug in the thick heels of her boots.

Vanessa pushed toward her, a clean and slow trajectory that was only a little off in aim. She was within arm's reach by the time she got to Tania, and after a bit of awkward reorientation, the two women sat on either side of the cavity.

"Tim," Tania said. "If you can hear us, we're inserting the object now." He made no response. Tania glanced at Vanessa. "On three—smooth, fluid movements okay? We push it into this bowl and it'll take over. Then we push for the Lobby. I'll guide you."

At Vanessa's nod Tania counted. At three she pressed her heavily gloved fingertips against the object, her eyes dancing between it and Vanessa to make sure they were in synch. As soon as the object broke the threshold of the cavity it began to glow more brightly. Then it started to turn, moved by an unseen force. It oriented so the corner with the missing tip pointed at the far end of the room. Tania gripped the edges of the indentation and pulled her legs free of it, crouching on the green-patterned wall.

Vanessa mirrored the action, moving a bit more confidently in the lack of gravity now.

Tania moved across the circular cavity, ignoring the mind-boggling display of materials science as the cavity began to reshape itself once again. She'd seen the process twice before and knew they had to move quickly, and yet she still found herself fighting the temptation to study the process. She gripped Vanessa by her forearm and felt the woman's hand clasp around her own. Tania made eye contact with her. They knelt in unison and turned their bodies to face the "bottom" of the room where they'd entered.

"Visors down," Tania said.

Vanessa swatted hers into position, leaving Tania looking at a gold-tinted reflection of herself. She flipped her own visor down an instant later, plunging her surroundings into near-total darkness. This did not last, though, as the extraordinary burst of light from the object they'd inserted continued to ramp up.

"Now," she said, "jump!"

They pushed off in unison, or near enough. At the same instant the room began to glow with an intense emerald green. Tania felt the vibrations begin and hoped she'd pushed off hard enough.

Forty meters to the floor. She doubted they'd be in any kind of danger when the energy release occurred, but she didn't want any residual shock wave to send them tumbling, either, or their landing might be nasty indeed.

Thirty meters. The vibration grew. She stole a glance at the readout inside her mask, sure enough there was nothing but vacuum outside her suit, and yet somehow pulsations that went along with the brilliant glow buffeted her. The suit's external microphone picked up no sound, so everything she was hearing must be simply her own suit, her helmet, being shaken by subsonic vibrations.

Twenty meters to go. Despite the distance, the visor, the fact that she wasn't looking directly at it, when the light peaked and cascaded into a burst of white-green energy Tania found herself momentarily blinded.

Ten meters now. Her vision began to return. Her legs caught

a wisp of momentum, but nothing more than that. Not enough to drastically change their path toward the bottom of the room. Only . . .

"What's happening?" Vanessa asked.

Everything looked blurry all of the sudden, as if condensation had suddenly formed on her visor. She swiped a hand across it, to no avail, and realized the room had filled with something. Smoke? Steam?

She glanced at her HUD again. The red text VACUUM DETECTED no longer floated there.

"We've stopped moving," Vanessa said. "No, wait—"

Tania felt the tug then. The inexorable pull of gravity.

She was no longer drifting toward the floor; she was falling sideways toward the wall that glowed blue.

In the miserable tin can of a ship, Tim watched the suit telemetry indicators wink off again. They'd done this six times in the last few minutes, leaving him holding his breath for the handful of seconds that elapsed before the connection reestablished.

This time, though, the seconds ticked on.

"C'mon, goddammit," he muttered. "Come back to me, Tania."

The display remained blank.

"Tania, Vanessa," he said into the microphone. "Please, say something. Can you read me?"

No response came. The indicators remained blank. No EVA suits detected in range.

He had no suit of his own. There wasn't room in the tiny ship for three. Besides, someone needed to remain in the sealed cockpit to fly the thing.

Tim wiped a bead of sweat from his brow and dialed the cabin temperature down. "Keep calm, keep calm, keep calm," he whispered.

Movement out the window caught his eye. He glanced up and stared once again at the object being lifted up from Earth. From this distance and angle, it looked like the tail of a wasp, yanked from the body proper. He'd seen footage of such a thing once, in the sensory chamber on Anchor Station. The insect would sting its target and then pull away, leaving both stinger and a good-sized chunk of its own body behind. Little glistening wisps of bodily fluid would stretch between the two sections as they pulled apart. What he saw now resembled that process, only in reverse. The Elevator cords spanned the gap between the Key Ship and this new component. They were attached to protrusions of varying height—the spikes that had been on the bottom of the larger vessel originally, he guessed, though clearly they'd sunk most of their length into the gigantic object they lifted.

He felt helpless, parked like a chauffeur at a polite distance. He couldn't go outside, he couldn't go in, and he damn well wouldn't leave. He'd rather suffocate on his own stale air than abandon Tania to this place.

So Tim settled in, ground his teeth, and waited. Every time he glanced at the object coming up from Earth, it seemed a little closer, a little larger, and a little more terrifying.

# 27

## ABOVE DARWIN, AUSTRALIA

### 2.APR.2285

Between the three of them the box of crackers vanished almost instantly.

Skadz kicked aside the formerly locked door of the emergency supply cabinet and rooted around some more. "Blankets? Moist towelettes? They must be fucking joking."

Sam couldn't bring herself to smile. Instead she forced herself to chew the last bite of her cracker. It tasted like salty cardboard, with the familiar sour aftertaste of Preservall. Unfortunately there was no alcohol to wash it down, much less to offer a toast to Prumble.

"At least he went down fighting," Sam mumbled to herself. No one responded. She'd said the same line three or four times since they'd lifted from Nightcliff. She and Skadz had reminisced a bit. It felt forced, though, and neither of them had the appetite to go on for long. What they both wanted was to raise a glass to their fallen friend and then raise a few more to dull the pain of leaving him behind.

She glanced at Kelly. The woman had discarded her Jacobite robe not thirty seconds after clearing the tower at Nightcliff.

Underneath she wore a black bodysuit, just like the kind she'd favored when sneaking about Gateway. In fact, it might well be the same one, Sam realized. Kelly had probably hidden it somewhere in those early days of captivity under Blackfield. The fact that she wore it now spoke volumes about how successfully she'd conned everyone in Grillo's organization over the last two years. As good a ruse as Prumble's bum knee, really.

Kelly stood, as she had been, near the car's single terminal screen, monitoring their progress. If her manipulation of the climber's programming held, they would pass right through Gateway at a speed high enough to obliterate the station should anyone try to get in their way, and continue on up to Penrith Assembly. That station, she'd explained, had been all but abandoned a long time ago when raw materials became scarce. By her reckoning there should be ample shuttles or ERV-type vehicles parked there, any one of which should support an escape.

"Ah," Skadz said. "Not a total bust. Chocolate."

Sam held out a hand. "Gimme. Anything to drink?"

"Negative. We'll have to wait to toast our fallen brother." He handed her a thick square of chocolate. Sam couldn't read the label, but she knew the Preservall logo well enough to assume the treat would taste like wax on the finish. To her surprise, it wasn't half bad.

Skadz passed a portion to Kelly, who took the chunk without looking. "Almost to Gateway," she said.

"What's the plan?" Skadz asked.

"Well, if we start slowing, then our control of the climber is gone and we get ready to fight our way out. If we don't slow, we either sail through Gateway as I hope, or we crash into something, in which case we won't have to worry about a plan."

Silence greeted the comment. They were working on the assumption that the security forces aboard Gateway, as well as Grillo, knew about their heist and subsequent climb. The question was, would Grillo order everyone to back off due to the presence of the object, or would he sacrifice it rather than let some nonbelievers take the thing?

No attempt had been made to contact the climber, not even a cursory call from the control center on Gateway to inquire about their excessive speed.

Sam took another hunk of the chocolate bar and gave it to Vaughn. He'd been mostly quiet during the climb, recognizing that the others might not trust him the way Sam did, even though she'd done her best to convince Skadz and Kelly that he was on their side. The thing was, she couldn't quite decide why she accepted his defection so readily, other than the simple fact that she wanted it to be true.

"Thanks," he said, taking the candy. He gave half to Martin, the poor climber control operator who'd also been dragged along.

"Five," Kelly said, "four, three, two . . ."

Sam braced herself against the wall. If the climber slowed then gravity would shift from below her feet to above her head.

But nothing happened. The climber kept going, accelerating toward Gateway at more than 200 kilometers per hour. Then it passed the station. No catastrophic impact occurred, in fact not even a wobble to mark the event. The climber sped past the station's closed docking rings and out the other side.

Kelly turned from the display and cracked a grin at Sam, and she returned it. Maybe this was going to work, after all. Skadz let out a little whoop.

The screen mounted on the wall next to Kelly did something odd then. The image flipped upside down. Sam saw this, blinked. She had time to think it would be good to point this out to Kelly, who was looking at her instead of the display. But before she could even open her mouth, gravity flipped.

In a split second Sam went from standing on the floor to falling from the ceiling, headfirst. She managed to get her hands over her head just in time to break the fall. Skadz landed next to her with a grunt, and Kelly fell on top of both of them, one elbow slamming into Sam's stomach like a well-aimed punch. Vaughn and the other captive landed somewhere behind her, both crying out in surprise.

Sam tried to stand and found she couldn't. She felt as if a blanket made of lead had been thrown over her. Above her came the whirring sound of machinery. She looked up and saw the couches, mounted on one wall, moving down toward the new floor on tracks, their cushions reconfiguring as they descended. "Vaughn, head down!"

He curled up, chin to chest. The couches moved into their new position just a few centimeters above his head. Had he not moved, the metal frame would have given him one nasty bruise.

"What the hell is going on?" Skadz asked. He'd come to a sitting position and made no attempt to stand. Sam did the same, and then the others followed suit.

"Deceleration," Kelly said. "Two times Earth norm."

"Passengers put up with this shit?"

The woman shook her head. "Normally it's gradual, with a period of weightlessness and lots of charming bells and soothing voices explaining the cabin will realign for the new 'down.'"

"In other words," Sam said, "the jig is up."

"'Fraid so. We're too far from Penrith or even Hab 2 to be slowing for them, and we've passed Hab 1 already. My guess is they are turning us around, back to Gateway."

"Or back to Nightcliff," Skadz said.

Sam thought not. "Why didn't they just stop us when we went through the first time? Or turn us around well before we passed Gateway?"

Kelly considered this, then shrugged. "Whatever the case, we've lost control. They can take us wherever they want."

"Or," Vaughn said, "just let us sit out here until our air runs out, then reel us in."

Skadz wheeled on him, an awkward move in the press of double gravity. "Bloody hell, mate. Thanks for the downer."

"Take it easy, Skadz," Sam said. "He's right. They don't have to do anything but wait us out."

Skadz grumbled something, then nodded at Vaughn in a silent apology.

After what felt like an eternity, the blanket of weight began to lift. An easing back to normal weight, then further still until they were floating about like balloons. Floating meant stopped, Sam knew. She glanced at Kelly. She and Skadz both were looking up at the ceiling, waiting to see if their direction would change again, back toward Earth.

The climber car reverberated as something clanged against the airlock door.

"Fuck," Kelly said. "I've no idea where they brought us, but we're docking. Get ready, just like we talked about."

Skadz pushed off for the door, while Kelly tugged herself along the wall to a position on the opposite side. Sam moved near the back, taking a position behind the couch with Vaughn and the other prisoner, Martin. There'd been considerable debate about how to use the prisoners. Skadz had advocated lining them up in front of the door in a situation like this, forcing Grillo's people to have to shoot some of their own just to get inside. Sam had been emphatically against this, though, and not just because of her feelings for Vaughn. She also knew what Grillo was capable of; she didn't think he'd have a second thought about giving the kill order.

So the prisoners would be used only when the situation called for it. Traded for a resupply of air, or more likely water, given the climber's dry state. Sam wasn't sure what she would do if the time came to trade Vaughn away for a damn drink. She wasn't sure what he would do, either.

A hiss of pressure equalization from the door killed her line of thought. Sam hunkered down as best she could in the lack of gravity and checked her weapon. Mentally she recounted their supplies. Six bullets in her gun, five in Skadz's. Kelly had twelve, and of a different caliber or else she would have divvied them up. A dire situation by any measure, so they'd all agreed on the tactic required should a shooting scenario come up: Let them get close, drop the front line, and scavenge.

*It all comes back to being a scavenger,* Sam thought.

Another thought came to her, like the first flash of lightning on a night about to turn stormy. *Scavengers. Could the Builders be looking for that trait? Is that what this has all been about? To find out if our species can dawdle on by picking at the remains of our cities?*

She grimaced. *So what if we can?* She couldn't imagine how that would matter to a bunch of aliens who could travel the cosmos, gift space elevators seemingly at will, and engineer pandemic diseases as well as magical fucking force fields that defend against them. What the hell would they gain by finding out if a species could rummage through its own garbage?

The hatch opened and intensely bright light flooded the cabin of the climber car. A crumpled white umbilical tube surrounded the perimeter of the door, leading straight off, though to where Sam couldn't see from her position. She watched as Kelly stole a glance, leaning out and then whipping back into position. She repeated the motion a few times, careful to time her looks at random intervals. After four looks she turned and whispered. "The tube leads out of a cargo bay, and there's a spotlight at the end. Can't see anything else."

"There's no rush," Skadz said. "Sit tight; let's wait and see what they do."

"What if they toss some tear gas in here?" Sam asked.

"That would change the equation."

Kelly turned back toward the door, using a handle on the wall to keep herself from floating into view of anyone outside. "I say we shoot out that light. We're blind otherwise."

"Agreed," Sam said.

Skadz shook his head. "Bad idea. Not until we know who we're dealing with. They could be friend—"

A whirring sound cut him off. It sounded like an electric desk fan, and Sam braced herself. Fans moved air, and air was something they couldn't afford to lose or have contaminated.

Seconds later an object floated up to the open climber door. It propelled itself on a half-dozen small fans mounted off a central truss, aimed in each direction to give it a full range of movement. In addition there were two glass domes, one on top and one on the bottom, with glowing red cameras mounted inside. They swiveled, taking in the scene within the compartment, and almost immediately they focused on the package beside Sam.

"Drone!" she shouted.

Skadz swung the butt of his weapon down toward the thing. Its fans ramped to full power in a millisecond and on a burst of speed it avoided his attack neatly. The cameras had not swiveled toward him, so it must have sensed the impending strike with some kind of proximity detector. He swung again, to the same result, and with each motion to avoid attack the little automaton moved farther into the cabin. The two cameras jumped from one angle to the next, taking in everything. One stopped on Samantha's face for a half second, and she did the only thing she could think to do and extended her middle finger at it.

Then Vaughn was next to her. He'd taken his jacket off and simply floated over to the thing and gently lay the garment over the top of it. Only when one of the cameras became occluded did the robot try to lurch away, fans screaming, but Vaughn pulled the sleeves of the jacket together at the bottom and held on tight. He pushed off toward a corner of the cabin and managed to wedge the bundle between himself and the spot where the walls joined. The robot squirmed inside his coat like a trapped cat.

Sam turned back to the door and her eyes narrowed. A welcome rush of adrenaline coursed through her. Whoever was out there knew much about the contents of the climber, including that Vaughn wasn't exactly a cowering captive. But she thought perhaps it hadn't seen Kelly.

"How about we talk," a voice called from somewhere outside.

In the darkness Sam couldn't see Kelly very well, but she looked at her anyway. Their eyes met, communicating the same thing: *That is Grillo's voice.* "Skadz, kill that fucking light," Sam said. "Ours, too."

Beside the door, Skadz aligned himself and then leaned out, gun aimed. He fired once, a deafening single clap that made Sam jump despite herself. The light went out as he pulled himself back out of view.

"Suit yourselves," Grillo said. He did a good job of sounding bored.

With sudden, nauseating motion the climber lurched. Sam felt the meager contents of her stomach churn as her mental perception of up and down changed almost instantly. Suddenly the door of the climber was down, and she was falling toward Skadz. She managed to reach out and grab one of the couch's support legs, which were bolted to the movable base. She slipped her feet in to rest against another and found she could stand like that.

The bundle containing the alien object slid down what was now a wall, bumped against something, and went tumbling into the air.

"Catch it!" Sam said.

Kelly reached but missed, and their prize fell down the umbilical tube. Sam realized then with cold certainty that the tube hadn't moved away when the climber lurched into motion. They'd moved together. *The whole station is being moved.*

A shape on the periphery of her vision dashed the thought as the captive Martin fell past her. Or maybe he'd jumped. Either way, Sam watched their last true bargaining chip plummet through the door and into darkness. She glanced back and up. Vaughn had managed to stay wedged into the corner, his back against the couch on the opposite side of hers. His face was strained from having to support his own weight and the still-struggling camera drone.

"Just drop it," she said. She doubted the little propulsion fans on the thing could actually support its weight in gravity, and anyway it had seen everything.

Vaughn took her advice and practically threw the thing toward the door, along with his jacket. The whole package fell like a stone, and a few seconds later she heard someone, probably Martin, grunt as the little robot crashed on top of him at the bottom of the umbilical.

"That was Grillo talking, wasn't it?" Skadz asked.

"Yeah," Kelly said.

"Fuck. He picked a bloody convenient time to be in orbit."

She nodded. "Options?"

"I say we go now," Skadz said, "guns blazing. We're sitting ducks in here, and just giving them time to plan. Plus they've got the object and our one real captive now."

"I agree. Let's go."

"Hold on," Sam said. She fixed her gaze on Kelly. "I don't think the drone camera saw you. Skadz distracted it when it came in, and it never looked your way after that."

"So? He'll know I'm with you."

"But he doesn't know you're *with* us. So when we go out, turn on us, say you planned the whole thing. We wanted to flee on foot, you suggested orbit where you knew he'd be."

"To what end?"

"He must want us alive, or he would have just left the climber sitting outside for a few days. So you present us, take credit for bringing us in, and when he's mulling that over you pull the same move you did in the vault."

Kelly bit in her lower lip, thinking it through.

"It might work," Skadz said. "Sounds plausible. Too plausible, if you ask me. Sorry, Kelly, I don't know you too well."

"Plausibility is why it might work," Sam said. "And there's no time for another plan. Let's go."

Reluctantly, Kelly nodded.

"Your move!" Grillo shouted. "No rush, we've got plenty of time."

Kelly frowned. "We're coming out. I've disarmed them."

"Is that Sister Josephine?"

"It is, Father." She rolled her eyes at the title. "Can you kill the gravity?"

Within seconds the press of acceleration faded and weightlessness returned. Sam tucked her pistol into the back of her pants and floated over to the door next to Skadz.

"You'd better be right," he said under his breath. "That he wants us alive, I mean."

"Who wouldn't want us alive? We're so much fun to be around."

Sam went first, bracing herself in the door and pushing off gently to float down the white tube that had been attached to the climber. Without the blinding spotlight she could see the tube ended at a normal hallway about twenty meters away. That hall in turn continued much farther, ending at a T intersection a good hundred meters distant. There were people down there, waiting. Four or five, at least.

She glanced back and saw Skadz was right behind her. Kelly had pushed out, too, and floated a meter back from him, her gun trained vaguely toward his back.

"Keep your hands visible," Grillo called out.

Sam turned back as they crossed the threshold of the umbilical and into the hallway. A series of red ladder rungs lined the wall on her right, and she recalled a similar layout in Gateway's cargo bay exit, though this tunnel was narrower, and bare metal instead of painted. A door drifted by on her left, with signage next to it:

## MIDWAY STATION—AUX. CLIMBER CONTROL

She'd never spent much time studying the various space stations and their places along the cord, but she remembered Midway simply because it sat alone at the very center of the cord, with nothing on either side of it for thousands of kilometers. Sam recalled something about it being the smallest station, an outpost really, serving merely as an emergency stopover for climbers on their way to points much farther above or below.

But they hadn't traveled nearly far enough to reach it. Sam pondered this as she floated toward Grillo and a handful of tough-looking Jacobites.

Grillo eyed her with casual interest, like a surgeon analyzing a patient. He'd ditched his usual business suit for a uniform of sorts. Black shoes, khaki pants, and a black sweater open at the neck to reveal a white turtleneck beneath. Almost priestly. Almost.

He must have moved Midway Station down, near Gateway. But why? There wouldn't have been time to do it simply to capture her climber. They would have had to start moving it days ago.

*Of course,* she thought. *Kip. He told Grillo everything. Grillo had been planning this all along. Not our presence, but moving the object over to the Key Ship. And we brought the fucking thing right to him.*

The thugs at the end of the hallway pushed back to give her a wide berth as she reached the wall. Sam stopped herself with her hands and feet, and used a rung on the wall to move aside so Skadz could land. For the moment she decided to avoid Grillo's gaze, which she felt hot on her like the glaring spotlight before.

Instead she scanned the faces of the men with him. Jacobites, she assumed, but they wore none of the usual garb. These men were dressed instead like Gateway Security. Sam flicked her gaze across each, sizing up their weaponry and anything else useful she could glean. The problem with zero gravity, though, was getting the measure of a man. How he stood, what kind of confidence wafted off his posture.

Two of them, she realized suddenly, she knew. Alex Warthen himself, along with his right-hand man, whose name she'd forgotten. They'd interrogated her after Skyler fled Gateway what seemed like a lifetime ago. Platz and council allies once, then Blackfield's, and now Grillo's. Some people never change, though neither man looked terribly happy to be here.

One of the others looked familiar, too. Had she stalked him in the halls of Gateway? Perhaps stolen from his quarters while he slept? That had been a favorite game of Kelly's. Swap two guards' shoes around, or steal the caps from their flashlights and earpieces. But no, Sam knew where she'd seen this one.

*Hightower. Bonaparte.*

Weck was his actual name, if she recalled, and she'd floored him with a kick, starting the brawl that ended the lives of Angus and Takai. The brawl that sent Skyler fleeing the station. And all because Sam had drunk a bit too much. He was staring at her, his head tilted to one side, brow furrowed. Sam looked down. He recognized her, of course, but she didn't want him to see the wrath in her own eyes. Her gaze found his weapon, a snub rifle like one she'd seen on Gateway, just before the fight in that tavern. What had her guard said? Something about an electric shock . . . No, a toxin.

Skadz landed next to her, moved, and then Kelly arrived.

"Get us moving again," Grillo said under his breath. A few seconds later Sam began to feel the press of gravity again. The wall she'd landed on became the floor, and once she felt firmly held to it, she stood and mentally reoriented herself.

"I caught them at the vault," Kelly said. "But they killed the others and so I pretended to be on their side. They were after the object, of course, and I couldn't let them walk out into the city with it. The confines of a climber seemed—"

A sharp crack cut off her words.

Sam felt a warm spray across her face.

Kelly dropped to her knees and toppled over, blood seeping from the back of her head.

"I'm so very tired," Grillo said, "of liars in my presence."

Samantha reacted without thinking. She pulled the gun from her belt and aimed for Grillo even as tears welled into her eyes and rage flooded her mind. She fired once, but no one was there. The fucker had moved.

Something bit her in the neck. Two fangs, sharp as needles. Sam swatted at it and found a cord that stretched from her to Weck. He held his weapon, the toxic whatever-the-fuck, like a shotgun, and had a satisfied grin on his face.

A mass slammed into her legs. One of the thugs. Men around her were shouting; orders were being barked. She tried to turn the gun downward but another body crashed into her, and before she knew it her face met the floor and there were three people holding her down. Something drew around her wrists and tightened. She felt no pain from any of this. Her body felt like it had melted into a nerveless mass as the chemicals from that damn weapon seeped into her brain.

"Keep an eye on them until we reach the temple," Grillo said. "I only need one alive, so if one resists . . . I don't know, shoot the other."

A knee kept Sam's face pressed to the floor, not that it mattered. She couldn't move a muscle. She doubted she could even blink. All she could do was stare into the dead eyes of Kelly Adelaide. The woman who'd freed her from her cell on Gateway. A woman she'd fought with, killed with, hidden with, and in that time learned from. Learned when to leap back into shadow instead of forward into the fray. Learned the true meaning of loyalty, no matter the cost. Kelly had feigned conversion to that sick cult and lived under Grillo's thumb for two years just to keep Neil Platz's vision of the future from being perverted.

She deserved a hero's death. To go down fighting like Prumble or Jake, not halfway through some bullshit line. Samantha gazed deep into those cold, unmoving eyes and made a silent promise. *Not like this. Not like this.*

Grillo's face filled her view. He'd crossed to her and knelt down, his eyes looking at her chest with a perplexed expression. He reached out and began to fiddle with her vest, Sam helpless to stop him. Finally his hand pulled back, a bag clutched between two fingers. His lips curled back in a smile and he began to laugh at the sight of the notebook. The Testament. "Oh, Samantha," he said, still laughing. "You really have made this far too easy."

He stood and walked away, his laughter fading in synch with her senses.

# 28

## THE PLAGUE FORGE

### 2.APR.2285

Skyler lowered Russell Blackfield's head to the floor, slid the dead man's eyelids closed, and sat back on the floor with a grunt. He felt twice his normal weight, like he was seated on the floor of an aircraft making a hard climb. Russell had been right: Not only was the facility being lifted off the ground; it was accelerating.

Across from him, Ana gazed blankly at the body of their former captive. At the man who'd . . . who'd what?

Seated here, staring at the man who'd just saved his life, and the life of the woman he loved, Skyler couldn't recall exactly what Blackfield had done wrong. Sure, he'd been a womanizing asshole, and he'd confiscated scavenged cargo without much in the way of evidence, but what else beyond that? He'd held Tania against her will, but never laid a finger on her. He'd used his position in Nightcliff to gain a seat on the Orbital Council, which was probably within his right. It wasn't Russell's fault that this happened to coincide with Neil Platz's efforts to figure out the next Builder visit, a situation that forced everyone to choose sides.

So what had Blackfield done? Destroyed Prumble's garage? Yes, though in the lawless confines of Darwin this wasn't exactly outside of his right, either. Prumble hadn't even really argued the move.

Granted, he'd sent numerous spies over to Belém. Yet Skyler doubted he'd have done differently had he been in Blackfield's shoes. Tania, and Skyler to a degree, had stolen the primary source of food for Darwin. It wasn't a situation that could be allowed to linger on.

And in the end Blackfield had been betrayed by Grillo, a much more worthy recipient of Skyler's hatred, in hindsight. Blackfield had fled to Belém, brought an entire station as his ticket for entry. And what had they done? Assumed a trick, thrown him in a cell. Skyler had pressed Tania to put the man out an airlock, advice that, if taken, would mean Skyler would likely be dead right now.

A tear rolled down Skyler's cheek. "Dammit," he growled, wiping it away.

"What's wrong?" Ana asked.

He laughed, embarrassed. "The bastard can't even die without doing something to get under my skin. How can I hate him now?"

Ana raised an eyebrow, confused.

"After everything that's happened," Skyler said with a reluctant grin, "in the end I'm the one who feels like an asshole."

Ana smirked. "He was arrogant and cruel."

"True, but our treatment of him was rather out of proportion for it, don't you think?"

"Maybe," she admitted. "Caution was necessary. He was dangerous. Erratic. Everyone said so."

"Erratic, yes," Skyler said. "Vary the pattern indeed."

The press of acceleration made him reluctant to move. In a strange way he envied the peaceful expression on Russell's face. Skyler hadn't known rest like that in a long time. And he suspected his turn was still a ways off. "I don't know where this place is going," he said, "but I think we'd better prepare ourselves."

"I can hardly move," Ana said.

"I know. Still, we're low on ammo, not to mention food. Lots of bodies down below to search. Soldiers, medics, et cetera."

Ana looked at him closely. "We need to do something about your chin."

Somehow he'd managed to bury the constant hot pain there. At her mention he almost, almost reached up and touched the wound, then thought better of it. "It's okay as long as I don't smile."

"It's bad, Skyler. Worse than that." She seemed in pain just staring at the cut.

He struggled to a standing position, wincing at a spike of pain from his knees. In his years as a pilot he'd often accelerated at a pace like this, or even faster, but always it had been in a cushioned seat. Trying to stand, much less walk or fight, while weighing twice the normal amount, felt like an unnecessarily cruel joke. What could the Builders be doing with this damned pyramid that required such a pace?

*Getting it off Earth as quickly as possible,* he guessed. *But why?*

"I guess we won't be making our rendezvous in Darwin," Ana said. The defeat in her voice stung.

"Nope."

"Will your friends be okay?"

He considered that. "They'll think of something. Get in touch with Belém at least, and come up with a new plan."

"You don't sound convinced."

"I'm trying." Skyler lumbered to the tunnel that led back down. "What about the . . . thing?"

"Leave it. It's not going anywhere." The last thing he wanted to do was lug that block around when it weighed twice its normal amount. He took stock of the rest of his possessions on the way to the tunnel. One Chinese assault rifle, no ammunition. He almost tossed it aside when he realized it would make a passable walking stick, so he kept it. Remembering his manners, he held it out to Ana.

She waved it off. "You're the old man with bad knees."

He groaned. Dammit if she didn't always know how to dispel a bad mood. "Any weapons left?"

"Just my wicked tongue."

"No wonder they've all run away."

At the tunnel Skyler paused to let his ears adjust. They still rang from the grenade blast, but the sensation had faded to a background din. Plenty of other sounds reached him, but what their sources were he couldn't know. A creaking noise, like pack ice settling, he guessed came from whatever lifted the facility to space. Another space elevator, he wondered? Surely this building weighed far too much.

Beneath that, a sound he knew well and dreaded now more than ever before. Mumbling. Shuffling of feet. The occasional hiss or snarl. He glanced at Ana and could tell from the tired look in her eyes that she heard it, too. Fighting them hand to hand was bad enough; to do it when he felt like he wore a suit made of sandbags would be something else entirely. Suicide, he guessed.

"Change of plan," he said.

Ana stood next to him now, a hand on his shoulder for support, her gaze fixed on the dark tunnel.

"This pace won't go on forever. We'll either slow down, in which case the floor will be up there," he said, pointing, "or we'll reach a cruising speed. If we're high enough at that point—"

"We'll be weightless."

"Yes."

Her brow furrowed. "So?"

"I'm guessing the subhumans aren't very adept at moving in zero-g."

Ana grinned at that. "Neither am I."

"You know how to swim, though." When she nodded he went on. "It's similar to that. You'll get your bearings fast enough. So, let's wait a bit."

"Okay." She sounded skeptical. "But, Skyler? Let's wait in the tunnel."

"Why?"

"If the floor and ceiling swap roles," she said, glancing up, "that's a long way to fall headfirst."

Whether due to the added illusory gravity, or from a shared exhaustion, the subhumans below did not climb the steep hallway. Whatever drive they'd been possessed with to reach the oval-shaped object had vanished either with the defeat of their armored friend, or perhaps simply with the facility's lift from Earth.

Skyler let Ana dab the blood from his chin. She had nothing to stitch the cut with, so she held a patch of cloth torn from her shirt to it. After a time the simple act of keeping pressure on the bandage became too tiring, so Skyler lay on the floor and Ana rested her head on his chest. She kept the fabric in place with the back of her head. She slept after a time. He lost himself in the smell of her hair, still a wonderful comfort despite the hints of smoke and blood that mingled there.

He felt as if aboard a great ocean vessel, rocked gently by unseen waves. The motion pushed him toward a trancelike state that he fought at first, then gradually welcomed. Time began to slip by in blurred moments of clarity and fog.

A sensation of falling jerked Skyler awake.

Ana drifted a few centimeters above him, arms splayed out like a spirit.

"Wake up," he said, careful to keep his voice low. "Ana, wake up." He reached up and tugged at her.

Her body spasmed and she let out a frightened gasp. Skyler tried to pull her back down, but his action only succeeded in propelling them toward each other. His own body off the floor now, too, he realized a critical flaw in his plan: Unlike the stations built by Platz, this place had no handles or ladder rungs on the walls by which to control movement. The floors, walls, and ceiling were smooth for the most part.

"What's happening?" Ana asked, still groggy.

"We're in space, that's what's happening." *And it's a damn lucky thing we can still breathe.* He wondered if this fact meant the Builders breathed the same air as humans. More likely the structure had simply sealed itself, including whatever air had been inside at the time. Air that would no doubt run out eventually, but he guessed it would be a long time given the sheer volume of open space within.

Skyler clutched at the fabric of Ana's shirt and turned to face the nearby floor, still in arm's reach. The motion sent them both spinning like figure skaters. "I'm not setting a very good example, am I?"

"Either that or you're a terrible swimmer."

The rotation stopped. Ana managed to wedge her fingertips into the space between two of the large hexagonal tiles that made up the floor of the tunnel. Moving with dreamlike slowness, Skyler tugged gently on her shirt to get his own momentum moving toward the same surface, and then let go and allowed that motion to carry him without putting any more pressure on her.

A few more seconds of floundering and Skyler found himself perched next to her and even facing the same direction. "The fact that neither of us has vomited means this is going rather well."

She scrunched her face at him. "Your chin looks better. The bleeding's stopped at least."

Skyler resisted the intense urge to probe the wound with his fingertips, partly because of the pain it would bring and partly so he wouldn't wind up drifting about like a fish with no fins. He focused instead on the tunnel. "Right. Let's get moving before gravity changes again. One of us moves at a time, agreed?"

"Sure."

He nodded and pulled himself forward. The motion sent him drifting just centimeters above the floor. As he flew along he wondered if the building had reached orbit and stopped, or merely had reached a cruising speed at an altitude beyond Earth's gravity well. For the first time the idea crept into his mind that they might be stowaways on a departing starship.

At the first corner he stopped, righted himself, and waited. This part of the hall hid in darkness, with dim light coming from behind drawing Ana in profile. Below, a warmer glow crept into the hall. The light remained constant as Skyler watched. No signs of movement or the shuffling of bodies. Yet he sensed they waited down there. Cut off from food, how long would the subhumans wait before they turned on one another? Not long, he thought. If they retained anything from their former human instincts it was the will to survive. The question was why they weren't searching the facility now, exhausting all other possibilities.

Ana arrived and flashed a thumbs-up. Skyler pushed off again. He held his breath as he reached the junction at the back of the first room they'd found upon entering the structure. Drifting along in total silence, Skyler glanced sidelong as he passed.

Subhumans, perhaps ten of them, huddled in groups of two or three in the corners. Their motion must have naturally clumped them there, he thought. Their heads were down out of boredom or simple exhaustion. Some slept, adrift in the open space. Perhaps they were dead, but somehow he didn't think that to be the case. Their faces were too peaceful and he saw no signs of injury.

The whole scene was too peaceful. *It's like all of their aggression has gone.*

He wondered if they'd been ordered, or compelled somehow, by the armored creature to stay below while it took on the human stowaways. Maybe these subs assumed their superior had won, and they were now awaiting new orders. Cut off from the ground, perhaps they thought their purpose for existence had run dry.

The bodies left behind from the earlier battle here had been removed, though by what means Skyler had no idea.

He drifted past without being noticed. The tunnel continued down, but he stopped himself midway by brushing his hands lightly against the stonelike surface. Any farther and he'd be out of Ana's view. He turned and motioned for her to come.

The entrance to what Skyler considered the basement was a misshapen, bandaged wound. Ana had fired numerous grenades into the opening out of sheer terror and desperation. Only one of their armored pursuers had made it through that. As for the others, Skyler could only hope her blind firing had been effective. Where her explosives had hit he expected to see rubble, charred debris, bits of sparking wire poking out of the walls and ceiling. He found none of that. But the floor, the walls, the whole perimeter of the entrance had dents and irregular lines, as if the damage done had been hastily covered by duct tape and painted over. Skyler touched the wall, ran his fingers along one of the odd bends. Hard as stone. Vibration tingled his fingertips, as if the very wall coursed with energy.

"It's repairing itself," Ana said.

He felt his mouth go dry, wondering if the coated subhumans could do the same. It had been one thing to fight them when armed to the teeth, but now he suspected the outcome would be vastly, horribly different.

Skyler poked his head inside and glanced around. There were bodies floating about. A few, black-clad, sent his heart hammering, but on closer inspection he saw them for what they were: Chinese paramilitary, dead for years.

He let his vision relax and took in the entire space. Inside he found a maze of semitransparent columns not present before. The vast circular room now looked like a storage area for black cylinders that stretched floor to ceiling, not unlike the room above where Blackfield lay. Many of the mummified corpses had vanished as a result of the appearance of the pillars. Impaled or subsumed into the floor, never to be seen again. A burial of sorts, and perhaps that was where their armored foes had gone. The rest had drifted off the floor in the lack of gravity, settling in corners or simply adrift.

A soft pulsing glow came from the interior of the columns, the only light in the room now. Ana right behind him, Skyler drifted slowly between the columns until he came to the center of the chamber. The platform where the oval object had been was gone. Collapsed or perhaps simply retracted. The deep silo beneath it remained, however, and he could still see a bright glow coming from the very bottom, nearly a kilometer distant. He wondered if the platform had fallen down there when the building rose, and shuddered. If he and Ana had waited here instead of fleeing, they'd be down there now, too.

"Look," Ana called out.

He glanced where she pointed and saw the body of a long-dead soldier. Choosing his angle carefully, Skyler pushed off from a column and floated over to it. The dead man wore the same black Special Forces outfit as the one Skyler had searched earlier. If he'd carried a rifle it had floated away already, but he might have ammo that would fit the empty one Skyler carried. Skyler rummaged through the corpse's pockets, found nothing in that regard. But there was a Sonton pistol holstered at the belt. Skyler took it, as well as two clips of ammunition from an adjacent leather container. He let his own empty rifle drift away in the process. A walking stick wouldn't do much good in zero-g.

On a whim he took the man's jacket as well, a surprisingly frustrating task in zero-g. By the time he'd wrestled the garment away he was spinning wildly, and drifting toward the open maw of the silo. "A little help?"

Ana pushed toward him and her momentum carried them both off toward the room's sidewall. When they were at rest, Skyler handed her the jacket and the pistol. "If we're in space, it may start to get cold in here," he said.

The jacket had bits of Kevlar sewn into it, but on the whole it wouldn't provide much warmth. Ana shrugged it on anyway, not questioning his motivation. She checked the pistol like a seasoned expert and placed the two extra clips in a zippered pocket on her pants. Then she took a long breath. "Skyler . . ."

"Hmm?"

"We might be in here a long, long time, right?"

"It's possible."

She left her next thought unsaid, but Skyler could see it in her expression. *No food, no water.* "We'll figure something out," he said.

Ana looked away. He could see the gleam of tears in her eyes even in the darkness.

# 29

## THE KEY SHIP

### 2.APR.2285

She stared up at the strange room, using every mental trick she could think of to ignore the large crack that spidered across her visor. There was numbness in her right calf, too, and a lingering pain in her right wrist where she'd broken the fall.

The room, which she'd mentally thought of as a tall cylinder, lay on its side now. Tania lay flat on a dark surface that had been one of the ten walls before. The three lit walls—red, emerald, purple—were above her, forming an almost cathedral-like curved ceiling that ran a hundred meters end to end.

Next to her, Vanessa sat up. She raised her arms over her head and, before Tania could caution her against it, the immune removed her helmet and tossed it aside.

Vanessa inhaled, a full breath as if she'd just entered a busy kitchen on a special occasion. Tania could only lay still and watch out the corner of her eye as the woman stood and shrugged out of the rest of her bulky suit. The process took some time, and Tania, despite knowing she should help, did not lift a finger.

By the time Vanessa freed herself from the legs of the bulky suit, Tania's pains had mostly faded, as had her mortal fear of the hairline crack across her vision. She'd come close to suffocation twice in recent weeks, and thought if that fate approached her again she'd find some quicker, more palatable way to die.

The immune stood and stretched her arms, wincing briefly from some injury. Then she hopped up and down from her toes, testing the gravity. What she found pleased her, from the grin she flashed down at Tania. Standing there, wearing only an athletic bra and tight exercise shorts, and illuminated by the green, purple, and red glows coming from the soaring walls of the room, she looked like a goddess.

She said something, but without the intersuit comm system Tania heard only a muffled voice. Then Vanessa held out a hand and Tania, growing less wary by the second, took it.

In a matter of minutes Tania had her spacesuit off and breathed fresh, oddly fragrant air. It held none of the rich, bright smells that Colorado had, nor even the pungent, slightly moldy aromas of Belém. Yet it had no sterility to it, either. Tania was used to processed air to the point that setting foot on Earth had been like a slap across the face in its intensity. This air was somewhere between the two.

She took a few tentative steps and found she agreed with Vanessa's expression of delight. The gravity felt like Earth normal. Either the ship had begun to spin or the Builders had some means of generating their own gravitational force. Before Skyler's visit to the time-compressed dome in Ireland she would have discounted that possibility, but not now.

The third option, acceleration, she pushed out of her mind.

She walked gingerly to the room's former floor, now an endcap wall, where the door had irised open upon their arrival. She feared it would not open as it had before, in order to keep the room's newly earned atmosphere from escaping. Worse, what if it opened and she was sucked out into space before she had a chance to curse her own curiosity?

Instead the iris door simply pulsed open, right in the center of the wall. With atmosphere present the mechanism made a sound like two panes of glass sliding against each other.

Tania stared at the opening for a long time. Even if the passage represented a way out, she couldn't go. The web of cracks across the glass of her helmet would prevent that. "We have to contact Tim," she said, her eyes never leaving the portal in the middle of the wall. "He'll have to try to get the ERV to the exterior door and . . ." She left the rest unsaid. She would have to risk vacuum exposure in order to board the vessel, and hope they could seal it in time. Thirty seconds at most.

Vanessa brushed Tania's elbow with her fingertip, drawing Tania back to the moment. "He said something was coming up from the ground, Tania. What if it blocks our way out?"

The thought left Tania Sharma numb. "We'd better hurry, then." She picked up her broken helmet and moved to stand below the exit.

"I'll boost you up," Vanessa offered. She cupped her hands together and, when Tania stepped in, hoisted her until she could reach the rim of the door. Tania tossed her helmet inside before gripping the edge with both hands.

Grunting with effort, she hauled herself up and straddled the edge. The spherical Lobby on the other side had not changed, though the faint glow from its spongy interior surface could not be seen, overwhelmed as it was by the brilliant colors coursing through the surfaces within the key room.

"Maybe I should stay with the suits," Vanessa said from below.

Tania thought about it, then shook her head. "I'd rather we stay together. Besides, odd as these doors are they do seem to be reliable." She gripped the edge of the portal with one hand and reached down with the other.

Vanessa jumped, grasped, and together they pulled until the immune's fingers found the edge. She hoisted herself the rest of the way with ease.

Tania slid down the inside of the sphere until she could get her feet under herself. The slide turned into a running fall before she found herself at the base of the Lobby room. Vanessa joined her a second later.

Above, the portal to the key room remained oddly open. Cut off from much of its light, Tania's eyes began to adjust until once again she could see the glow emitted by the spongy white material of the Lobby sphere. It took Tania a moment to realize the light no longer had a uniform brightness. The intensity now coalesced at her feet, leaving the portion directly above her head in almost total darkness.

The two metallic bands came to life. With a deep, faint grinding sound they began to rotate on their axis and then, gradually, tilt as they sought new positions. The portal to the key room, Tania noted, remained open, as if the ship somehow knew they'd left their suits in there and would need to return.

With gravity, Tania couldn't simply drift and watch. She had to leap over one of the bands as it slid across the surface of the sphere. The band slapped her broken helmet and sent it tumbling like a piece of clothing in a dryer.

After one revolution the bands began to slow down in flawless unison, and then they stopped. Each band had a patch that, before, had aligned with the other before forming a portal. This time the patches were in mirror positions, low in the room and separated by perhaps three meters. One ahead, one behind.

They both opened simultaneously, and Tania found herself dropping into a combat stance on pure instinct. Vanessa did as well, she saw, and they were both facing a different door.

Tania did not see a long tunnel leading out to the ship's hull. Instead what lay before her was a curved hallway, with a glowing floor, leading gently upward and out of sight. Other than the material, it reminded her of Anchor Station. Clean lines and soft light along that graceful upward curve of the floor.

*Curved floor. We're under spin, then. But why?*

Somehow the use of spin to generate a gravity-like force made the Builders a little less impressive, a little less intimidating, and Tania felt the tension within her unwind if only slightly.

She turned then to look out the other portal, the one Vanessa silently faced. Years of life aboard space stations gave Tania the automatic expectation that the curved hall would simply continue in an unbroken ring. Instead she saw a perpendicular corridor, leading off into darkness on both the left and right.

"What the hell's going on?" Vanessa asked, her voice barely more than a whisper.

"It seems the Builders have done some remodeling."

"Why?"

"I wish I knew. More important, why did they provide us with gravity and air? And how did they get it so perfectly matched to our needs?"

Vanessa frowned, then shrugged. "Maybe it's just proper etiquette."

Tania snorted a laugh, despite herself. "Right. Sorry we killed nine billion of you. Please, come in, make yourselves at home."

"You sound like Skyler," the woman said, laughing herself. The moment passed. "Perhaps it's just some automated process then."

At that much more plausible answer Tania nodded. Still, she couldn't imagine why it hadn't happened on the previous two visits. She knelt and glanced in both directions. "I wonder if the ship looks the same from outside," she said. "Shit! Tim!"

While Vanessa looked on, Tania picked up her cracked helmet and tried the comm. "Tim, are you reading this? Are you there?"

Silence.

"Tim? Come in, please."

No response came. Not even static. She swallowed. Perhaps the curved hallway was an architectural feature after all, and they were under acceleration. For all she knew Tim was already a million kilometers behind them and fading by the second. Tim, Skyler, Earth . . . Everything.

Tania felt suddenly buried under the arrogance and the lack of scientific rigor that marked their forays into this place. In urgency real or imagined they'd acted no better than the explorers who'd entered so many sacred tombs in Egypt hundreds of years earlier, tracking in sand and grime, grabbing at every shiny object with their bare, sweaty hands. *We're fumbling about here, proving ourselves idiots.* She recalled Skyler's sarcastic remark that the Builders were playing some kind of elaborate hoax out of sheer intergalactic boredom, and suddenly she could imagine it, too. Imagine them snickering somewhere behind these walls.

"Is he gone?" Vanessa asked.

The words snapped Tania back to the present. The sounds of alien laughter in her mind faded. "We need to get closer to the hull. But which way?"

"I've no idea," Vanessa admitted.

Tania considered the choices. "The curved hall would keep us at this position on the length of the ship," she said. "But it might get us away from whatever is causing the interference. Closer to the hull, away from the key room. I say we try that first, then come back."

At Vanessa's emphatic nod, Tania tucked her damaged helmet under one arm and stepped into the curved tunnel.

The walls and ceiling resembled what Tania considered "classic" Builder material: dark gray, nonreflective in the extreme, and laced with a fine pattern of geometric grooves. The floor differed only because its grooves shimmered with a dim white light. Tania recalled her theory that the lit floors marked the direction of apparent gravity, and started to like the idea more and more. Given that this direction would change often in a mobile starship as it accelerated, decelerated, or cruised, she could see how such an indicator would be useful.

The illusion of gravity via spin became evident when the curved hallway always seemed to be curving upward at the same gentle pace. Had they been under acceleration, the hall would have quickly become a slope impossible to climb. For this at least Tania felt grateful. She mentally rendered the image of Earth floating off to one side, just where it would have been if she were aboard Anchor Station, and found surprising comfort there. "So we've spun up," she said, ostensibly for Vanessa's benefit but mostly because she found it easier to think if she talked aloud. "We're at Earth-normal gravity it seems, breathing air that approximates our planet's atmosphere. Even dressed as we are, the temperature is comfortable. The odds are astronomical that the Builders live by the exact same parameters we do, so I think we can assume they're doing this for us."

Vanessa said nothing. They strolled along in the near darkness, barefoot and dressed in wholly inappropriate fashion for first contact. Tania suddenly recalled a campy movie poster from the presensory Golden Age, *Earth Girls Are Easy,* and could not suppress her smile. *Sorry, Mom. You always taught me to rely on my mind and yet, alas.* "Decorum and modesty will be your greatest ally in staving off those drawn only to appearance," her mother had said on Tania's sixteenth birthday, forcing her to wear a simple blue sari instead of the short gold dress she'd pined for. It hadn't helped. Tania knew even then why boys and even most men looked at her the way they did, and the blue sari if anything heightened their lustful stares. Only the loose jumpsuits worn in space ever seemed to dampen such looks, though she liked to think that had been due to the company of scientists and thinkers.

"The question I have," Tania went on, "is why now? Why not spin up when the first object was installed? Or when all five were present?"

"Maybe it has something to do with what Tim saw. The thing those Elevator cords were lifting."

Tania hadn't considered that and she liked the theory instantly. Whether Skyler played a role in it or not, whatever those cords were lifting to space had come from the ground. A synchronization of air and gravitational needs made at least some sense. "We'll know soon enough, I suspect, but I'd sure like to hear from Tim first." *If anything just to know he's still there, waiting.*

She tried the comm again, heard nothing, and kept walking.

Ahead an intersecting hallway came into view. Tania slowed and strained her senses. It took a moment to be sure her eyes were not playing tricks, but soon she felt sure there was a dim pulsating light coming from within. A glance at Vanessa indicated the same realization in her eyes. Tania took the lead and crept until she could peer around the corner.

The tunnel spanned only a few meters before exiting into a larger space. Much, much larger. One slow step at a time, Tania crept forward until she stood on a pathway within a place that defied explanation.

"My God," she whispered.

Nothing in human experience could have prepared her for the scale of it, much less the contents.

She stood on the floor of a gigantic cylindrical room. Not a room, she corrected herself: a world. Multiple worlds.

Tania closed her eyes and forced herself to look again as a scientist, taking in details with clinical detachment.

The far end she guessed was at least two kilometers distant, and the diameter must be at least five hundred meters, meaning it represented a significant portion of the Key Ship's length.

There were two distinct halves, split lengthwise down the center of the cylinder by no physical barrier Tania could see. On the bottom half within which she stood were hundreds of aura-tower-like structures protruding upward. Their positions seemed to be wholly random, though there were square areas every hundred meters or so that were completely devoid of the structures.

Snaking throughout this forest of dark sentinels were thousands of conduits, varying in size from perhaps a meter in diameter to as thin as a space elevator cord. Cables or pipes she couldn't be sure. Multicolored, though all muted, and some glowed faintly. Most protruded from the same floor as the towers, and weaved around the silent obelisks, reaching upward like tentacles until they touched that invisible yet starkly obvious barrier that separated this side of the space from the other.

*The other.*

Tania swallowed. In the other half of the space, starting a few hundred meters above her head and continuing all the way to the far end, was what appeared to be cotton clouds. A hazy murk of swirling white fog, filling exactly one-half of the cylinder as if someone had inserted a glass sheet down the center and flooded one side with a thick mist. The cloud was not, she noted, an even and organic thing, but rather a segmented construct. Each segment spanned a few hundred meters in length, marked only by the perfect point of division between one and the next. A thick white cloud here, a thinner gray cloud in the next section down. Farther off, toward the far end of the massive space, Tania could see one section that appeared to have no clouds at all.

She glanced straight up and watched the cloud above her swirl like smoke against a pane of glass.

"Tania," Vanessa whispered. The woman had come to stand next to her, and Tania realized belatedly they were holding hands, the pair of them subconsciously seeking something familiar in the face of such an alien view. "Tania," the immune repeated, "what is it?"

"I've no idea."

"It's like those towers are holding up a ceiling of clouds."

Tania's view still remained held by the chaotic cloud pattern directly above her head. She was about to say something, but before the words formed she glimpsed something through the mist, and paused.

She knew, then, and smiled. "Not a ceiling," she said, and tilted her head on one side. "We're spinning, remember? Think of the entire outer edge as a floor."

Vanessa mimicked the tilt of Tania's head, and gasped as realization dawned on her, too.

"Those clouds aren't being held to a ceiling," she went on, "they're pools. I think the towers, and all those pipes, are what created them. *Are* creating them."

"Incredible," Vanessa whispered.

"And look there." Tania pointed directly above them, and kept pointing until the mists parted again, just enough to reveal small disks of green.

"What are those?" Vanessa asked.

Tania squeezed her friend's hand. "Treetops."

The mists grew and receded, sometimes revealing as much as half of a grove of tall, dark green pines.

A minute passed in near-absolute silence. Tania gradually became aware of a constant background noise that reminded her of the air processors on the Platz-built space stations.

Abruptly Tania remembered their pressing need. "Let's go back," she said. "This clearly leads toward the nose of the ship, away from Tim. And I suspect it would take weeks to explore."

"I agree."

Tania took the lead again, ducking back into the ring hallway and continuing onward. The passage curved along for another twenty meters before she spied another junction. This one ran aft, toward Tim.

She pulled to a stop before the corner and leaned to peer within. Disappointment registered first: The passage spanned only thirty or forty meters before ending at a blank wall.

Tania almost jumped out of her skin at the sudden hand on her shoulder. Vanessa pressed in behind her, taking in the view as well. "Perhaps there's one of those hidden iris doors—"

Tania held up a hand. "Shh . . ."

Motion, a shift in the shape of the walls at the far end of the tunnel, became evident. Then a sound, too. She couldn't place it at first, couldn't relate it to anything she'd ever heard before, but as it grew louder the noise reminded her of the sudden expansion of elastic material, like a balloon being inflated, only a much deeper note. The motion grew and pushed toward Tania like a slow-moving wave.

"What is that?" Vanessa took a step back, fear in her voice.

Tania stood frozen, her fingertips white as she clutched at the corner of the wall. She could see it now. Depressions formed along the length of the short tunnel, like the half-dome cavity that had appeared to accept the objects they'd brought, only these were deeper, more complex. Portions of the wall simply recessed, creating new spaces.

Vanessa retreated as the wave finally reached their end of the hall, but Tania couldn't bring herself to look away. Not three meters from her she saw a portion of the tunnel sink inward. A square section, albeit with heavily rounded corners, stretching almost floor to ceiling. A few dozen similar openings ran the length of the hallway.

Whatever the purpose of all this was—these newly formed rooms, the gigantic biome chamber they'd just left—she had no doubt the alien mass within which she stood was altering itself, preparing itself, for something big.

New light began to fill the hall. Purple in hue now, and again starting at the far end and slowly marching toward her. The glow came from within the newly formed spaces along the hall. Some were more intense than others, and some shifted more to the red.

The space nearest her began to emit a bright, pure purple light.

Despite every instinct she had to flee, to hide, to escape, Tania Sharma crept forward and glanced in. The opening recessed only a few centimeters before expanding into something like a room. The space was egg-shaped, three meters in radius and perhaps five meters tall.

Inset within the floor sat a shimmering purple orb. Stared at directly the pearlescent surface looked as solid as marble. When Tania shifted her gaze to the walls or floor of the room, though, the glowing object seemed almost liquid.

"Tania," Vanessa called out, her voice at once a whisper and a shout. "I hear something."

"I know. That stretching sound. Come see this—"

"No, behind us. I hear voices."

At first he'd thought his own little craft had started to move. Tim had panicked, groping wildly for the attitude controls, only to find everything in place, all systems nominal.

The motion that had caught his eye was the Key Ship itself, rolling like a basking whale. Under spin.

All he could do was stare at it in disbelief. Why under spin? Why now? Had Tania found a control of some sort, a way to turn on some gravity?

From what he knew of the key room's layout, gravity would be something of a burden. He glanced down at his feet and closed his eyes, grappling with all the puzzle pieces that faced him, frustrated that they seemed to be piling up faster than he could wrap his mind around them.

Five more minutes passed. Once again, and with a growing dread for the task, Tim flipped on the microphone.

"Tania, come in. Please respond. Please, I . . ."

He clicked off, hating how feeble his own voice sounded.

In the miserable silence that followed he passed his time entertaining options. One of the displays in front of him indicated the tiny ERV had another sixteen hours of air, but that didn't matter much. Tania and Vanessa would surely run out sooner, and he'd be damned if he was going to sit out here while they suffocated.

Asking for assistance felt like admitting to his own helplessness, but there seemed no other choice. A sigh escaped his lips as he tapped the comm's shortcut link for Black Level. Above him, the craft's tiny reception dish swung away from the hulking mass of the Key Ship and began to seek out a signal from the former endcap of Anchor Station. He wouldn't hear Tania now unless she managed to get outside.

The twenty-second wait felt like a lifetime, and then the speaker crackled.

A flat, monotone voice came through. "Please state the nature of your emergency."

"Huh?" Tim said.

"Please state the nature of your emergency, *hu-man*."

Tim shook his head. "Is this Greg?"

"Please. Greg is not this good at voices. I'll fetch him if you want, um, think he popped off to have a wank."

"Marcus, listen—"

"At your service. What do you need? Pizza? We do deliver but there's a minimum—"

"Knock it off," Tim growled, surprising himself at the anger in his voice. "It's an emergency. Stop goofing around and get Zane on the line."

The scientist's voice became serious. "Are you okay?"

"Tania's in trouble," Tim said. Just voicing the words twisted his gut into all kinds of knots.

"Give me a second. Link's up, they're paging Zane now."

"Thank you."

"Sure," Marcus said. "Sorry for, you know . . . it gets boring up here."

"It's all right. Look, stay on the comm when Zane gets here. I'd like your input as well."

"Sure. Greg's back, by the way."

Tim heard a rustling of chairs. "Hello, Greg."

"*Greetings, humanoid*—Ouch! Don't hit me, ass."

"Tania's in trouble," Marcus said.

"Well all right . . . No need for violence."

A blip on the screen caught Tim's eye, a third connection established, linked through the first.

"I'm here, Tim," Zane said. "What's the situation?"

"They're still inside, and I'm unable to raise them on the comm." He quickly explained about the array of Elevator threads, the huge object being lifted from the ground, and how the whole mess had suddenly come under spin. "I'm worried that object being lifted will block their exit."

"How long before it reaches the ship?"

"Not long," he admitted, suddenly wishing he'd made this call much sooner. "And I don't have a suit. I can't go in and help."

"I'm talking to the dock chief, just a second. I'm told we can get another ERV over there in five hours. Four if some precautions are skipped."

Tim swallowed. "We don't have anywhere near that much time."

"Can you fit your ERV inside the hex door?" Marcus asked. "At least get a look; maybe they're stuck just inside for some reason."

"Maybe, but all those cords are in the way. Navigating through there would take time and . . ." His voice trailed off. He'd waited too long, that was the truth of it. He'd sat here when he should have acted. "I'd never get there in time, guys," he said, brutally aware of the defeat in his voice.

"ERV prep has started," Zane said, just to break the silence, Tim suspected. "We'll have a couple of suited walkers over there as quickly as we can."

"Thank you," he replied. In truth, not that he'd ever admit it, he didn't want anyone else to be the one waiting for Tania when she emerged from the vessel.

"What are you going to do, Tim?"

*There's nothing I can do,* he thought. "Keep trying to raise them," was what he said. "And hope there's another way in."

The others were silent now.

"Going to swing the dish back," Tim said. "I'd hate to miss their call."

"Tim," Zane said.

"Yeah?"

"Don't beat yourself up. You've done everything you can."

Tim clenched his fists again, to stop their shaking. *Have I?* "I'll talk to you soon," he said, and cut the link.

He watched, helpless, impotent, and aggravated as the gigantic mass continued to rise toward the Key Ship. All of his hopes hinged on what would happen when it arrived. Either the hexagon door would be covered, forever lost to him like the woman he loved within, or perhaps, just maybe, a new entrance would present itself, and Tania would find it. They would find it and come back to him and Tania would get that look of delight in her eyes at the sight of him still waiting.

"That's me," he said, floating in the void while others took action. "Always waiting."

A blip snapped his attention to one of the displays at the center of the console. The radar, which mapped his surroundings in simplistic form. The alien vessel, being an unknown entity to the computer, was drawn in depth-coded wire-frame, as was the object being lifted from Africa, though at this distance the display had not resolved any fine detail on it.

Something new had appeared at the edge of sensor range. Something marked with a designation that meant the system recognized its transponder. Tim stared at it, in the same moment realizing it had come from the direction of Darwin.

His heart began to pound. "No, dammit. Not now. Not now!" He tapped the microphone again, intent to alert Tania, not that she could hear him, but he held his tongue. Would these newcomers be able to hear him, too? He had no idea if the frequencies used were common across all Platz equipment, or had been changed.

He clicked off again, watching the dot on his radar drift ever closer. It seemed to be decelerating. He glanced up, looking out his tiny window, but he was too close to the gigantic alien vessel to see much of anything, and besides this ship was on the opposite side.

"Perhaps they're friendly," he said aloud. "Maybe it's Skyler." The thought filled him at once with hope and more than a little dread. Of course, Skyler would be the one to swoop in and save Tania *again. Stop thinking like that, Timmy. Just be yourself. Relax. Think.*

He decided to work under the assumption that they were not friendly. If they were, he suspected he would have heard from them by now. On a whim he searched for and found the switch that controlled his external lights, and flipped them off. *Let them assume everyone's gone inside.*

Tim tapped the newcomer's icon on the radar display and was happy to find additional details appeared on the right side of the screen. Velocity. Yes, they were indeed slowing, and rapidly at that.

Dimensions. That was odd. This was no ERV. Not even close. The width spanned more than two hundred meters.

Below these stats a designation number filled in, and then below that, a name.

MIDWAY STATION.

# 30

## MIDWAY STATION

### 2.APR.2285

Samantha lay curled in a fetal ball, her wrists and ankles bound. She ached all over and felt grateful for it. The toxin had worn off. No longer would she have to suffer the indignity of complete immobility. The guards, Weck especially, had been cruel while moving her helpless form to the cell she now lay in. They'd let her slam into walls, they'd dragged her along the floor by her feet, her face scraping along the rough irregular surfaces of the utilitarian station.

The room they'd placed her in had been someone's sleeping quarters, but because of the way the station was moving—decelerating now, she thought—one of the walls had become her floor. It had taken her mind awhile to not let this little illusion mess with her. Only when she'd imagined herself on an ocean liner that had sunk, impaling itself upright on the ocean floor, did the bizarre angle make sense enough to keep her stomach from fluttering.

No one spoke to her, and she made no effort to draw them into conversation. She knew where they were taking her, and because of Grillo's comment, she knew why: An immune had to place the object inside the Builders' ship. The temple, Grillo had called it. At the very least he knew an immune had to be present for entrance to be possible.

The fact that they had Skadz, too, complicated her situation and restricted her options immensely. Grillo was a clever bastard in saying that if one of them resisted his men should kill the other one. Sam would gladly die rather than help these people, but she doubted Skadz shared the same conviction. So her resistance would only result in both of their deaths. Better to wait, she thought. Be passive, go with the flow, and take her opportunity when it came.

And then there was Vaughn. She wondered if they'd dispatched him with the same lack of emotion that had ended Kelly's life. Grillo, of course, knew of her relationship with the man, and she knew he wouldn't hesitate to use that against her. Not that this had done Kelly a lot of good. Sam wrestled for a long time with that, trying to remove her tumultuous emotions from the equation. Kelly had at least done some real damage, actively worked against all the various regimes that sided opposite Platz. She'd made herself dangerous and cunning enough to warrant a swift execution.

Vaughn had merely been used by Sam, and perhaps helped in a marginal way in this latest gambit. It was surely evident Sam had a soft spot for the man. And Grillo, she knew, would not hesitate to exploit any angle he could, which left her in a catch-22. If she acted as if Vaughn were nothing more to her than a simple hostage, Grillo would likely kill him immediately. His loyalty was surely in doubt, so there would be no point in risking his presence. But if Sam showed concern for the man, Grillo would know he had something and use it against her. And this, she felt, had the potential to be far worse for Vaughn than a quick death.

Yet any moment he remained alive was a moment that could lead to freedom, or a turning of tables.

She'd lost Kelly. She decided she would not lose Vaughn while she still lived and breathed.

After what seemed like hours the press of deceleration that held her to the wall began to dwindle. A minute later she floated within the room, anchored by her wrist binding, which had been tied to a cabinet's handle.

One of the three men watching her left, moving awkwardly in the lack of gravity. A few minutes later he returned. "Bring the prisoner," he said, a note of anticipation in his voice.

Of course they would be excited. Grillo probably hyped the living shit out of this place, this temple, to them. The morons probably thought they were about to meet God himself.

She let them guide her through the curved hall of the station. Midway had only one ring, as far as she could tell anyway, and then the spoke hallways that led inward to the central docking and cargo area.

To her surprise, when they entered the cargo area she was tied down again, this time to a rung mounted on the floor of the space. There were rungs mounted everywhere on these stations, in neat little rows that ran along recessed channels. They reminded her of train tracks. The rungs she knew allowed people to tug themselves around in the lack of gravity, but mounting them in recessed channels confused her until she imagined this place full of crates and workers. It wouldn't do to have equipment and packages constantly snagging.

Skadz was brought in as well, of course tied off on the far opposite side of the bay. He met her gaze and offered a single, confident nod, which Sam returned.

When Grillo appeared from one of the access halls, she kept her eyes firmly on him, hoping to catch some hint of his intentions. Her opportunity would come, of this she felt sure, but only if she saw it in time.

Grillo called some of his men over and huddled with them. His most trusted or most capable, she assumed, and she tried to remember their faces. Mentally she gave them names: Mustache, Longhands, Hightower, and Commander Cocksucker. The last nickname brought a laugh to her lips when it came to her. Of the four only he had a military air about him, and yet his soft face held a vague resemblance to one of the pretty boys she'd seen at Madame Dee's.

Of the four, she'd only seen Hightower before. Weck, his actual name was Weck, but Sam would not use it. She'd seen how he reacted to being gibed once before and figured if she egged him on again, perhaps he'd make a mistake.

The conference broke up after Grillo spoke pointedly to each man in turn. They immediately fanned out to tackle whatever tasks he'd given them. She muttered a silent thanks when Hightower headed in her direction, the hint of satisfaction on his face.

Unfortunately, Grillo came with him, flanked by Alex Warthen, and his second in command. Larsen, she thought, unable to recall his first name. They'd questioned her briefly during her imprisonment on Gateway Station, and then lost her when Kelly broke her out. She and the Ghost had killed some of their men, sabotaged systems across their station, and even played a few practical jokes just to keep them on edge.

"I'm tempted," Grillo said as he strode up, "to mark you, Samantha."

From the inner pocket of his blazer came a carbon-black rectangular object he clutched between two fingers. He twirled the thing with practiced familiarity until he had the right hold in his palm. Then he squeezed.

Sam recoiled reflexively as the blade sprang forth.

Grillo leaned in even closer until she could feel the warmth of his breath on her cheek. He smelled of mint and anesthetic, his gaze flitting between her cheek and her eyes. He wanted a reaction, and she refused to give it.

His normally smooth voice became a rasp that leaked out between clenched teeth. "I believe a pound of flesh is the going rate for a betrayal such as yours. Your second, if I'm not mistaken? And I let you off so easily last time, didn't I?"

The tip of the knife pressed against the skin over her cheekbone. Sam felt a little sting, then something warm rolling downward, tracing along her chin, then her neck.

"I won't make that mistake again." He whispered now, his lips brushing against her cheek beside the pinprick wound. "Still," he said, rocking back onto his heels, "a whole pound of flesh . . . I wouldn't even know what to do with that much. So! A marking, I think. A cross on your forehead? I don't have time to carve a ladder so a simple cross will have to do. A scar for you to wear until you draw your last breath. Which, by the way, dear girl, might be only an hour or so from now."

"Just get it over with, you fucking psychopath."

He smirked. "Sam, Sam. Don't confuse conviction with crazy. I thought you more wise than that."

"Conviction?" she asked. A rage, simmering from the moment he'd walked in, finally boiled and spilled out in her voice. She let it. Fuck it. "I'll tell you who's crazy. All these Jacobites who think you actually believe any of their bloody nonsense."

"Sam . . ."

"You're a slumlord," she spat, "nothing more. A common criminal, a murderer, a—"

He slapped her with the back of his hand, a move so quick and powerful she felt it before she even realized he'd swung. The knife clutched within his fingers added a weight to the blow that drew even more blood from her cheek, along with a blinding ache. She worked her jaw, tasted a warm copper flavor.

"Do not," he raged, "question me or pretend to know what I believe! Do not!"

The room had fallen silent, she realized. Everyone stopped mid-task, staring. This marked the first time she'd ever seen Grillo lose his composure, and she suspected the same was true of everyone else in the cargo bay.

"Hit a sore point, did I?" she asked, feeling a drop of blood enter the corner of her mouth. "Sorry."

He raised his hand again and somehow turned the motion into a controlled gesture. The naked wrath in his eyes melted away in the same instant. His hand, instead of lashing out as she'd expected, kept rising until he touched it to his own forehead. He brushed back a single strand of hair that had fallen out of place. Then he raised his chin slightly, and exhaled. "You'll get two chances at redemption, child. First failure, Vaughn will lose his, er, manhood. Second, he will die and, as you can surely imagine, it won't be pleasant. After that you will go from helper to hostage, and your friend Skadz will be given the chance to perform the tasks I require and save your life in the process."

"You'll just kill us all after that."

"On the contrary," he said. "You'll be free to go. You see,

Samantha, other than the specific task I need, you're no longer special. Your immunity to the disease means nothing now because the disease has vanished."

He paused and let the words settle. "In a few hours you'll just be Samantha Rinn again. The tall, mannish brute who will probably have to beg for the clumsy pawing of men like Weck here."

Bound and helpless as she was, Samantha leveled a steady gaze on Grillo and spoke with as much defiance as she could. "And what will you be? Ruler of an empty city? Because you know, nobody's going to stick around in Darwin if they're not held in by the aura."

The smile that crept across his face tore her confidence to shreds. "Many will leave, yes. The ones I allow. My flock, ready to rebuild the world anew." He leaned in close. "They think I'm God's chosen one, you see. Lunacy, yes? But then sometimes I think, maybe not. Maybe they are right about me. Maybe I was chosen for what these so-called Builders intend. A reset. A resettlement. A chance to build a new society that can actually make proper use of the gifts they have given us."

She wanted to spit in his face. She wanted to exact her revenge right here and now. Instead she sat still and let her rage return to a simmer. Her lower lip trembled uncontrollably.

"I know it in my heart, Sam, in my *heart,* that whatever is waiting to be unlocked inside that ship is the key to this metamorphosis they wish us to undertake. And you're going to unlock the door for me." He shrugged. "Well, you or Skadz. One of you will cooperate, given enough proper motivation. I don't care much who. Neither you nor he is the tool I would have chosen, but who am I to judge the wisdom of our benefactors, hmm? That's all right, though. All that will matter is what the history books say, and it will be me wielding that pen, won't it?"

He leaned away, sensing she must be at the breaking point. *Good,* Sam thought. *Harbor some fear. I promise it's justified.* "Right, then," he called out to the room. "Places, everyone."

A flurry of activity followed. Gravity faded, something that Sam noted didn't seem to bother Grillo or his men very much. They knew in advance, of course, but they moved about with practiced ease. He'd been planning this for some time, she realized. How much did he really know?

Station crew and Grillo's guards alike cleared space around the central hub of the room where, on a normal day, climbers would dock inside a sealed central shaft and then await umbilicals to link them to the cargo bay. Sam watched with mild fascination as a barrier rose from the floor, creating an extra buffer area between the docking shaft and the bay proper. Two people wearing spacesuits drifted into the bay and entered a door on this new wall.

More chatter followed between Grillo and others, and then lights around that same door flipped from green to red. Sam felt it a safe guess that the two suited people were going outside. The purpose eluded her. Hightower lingered nearby, waiting for some order that had yet to be given, fighting to keep himself planted on the floor next to her with varying degrees of success. Given his behavior earlier, she couldn't understand why he didn't just grab on to her for an anchor point. He'd been happy to grab whatever pleased him when she'd been immobile an hour ago, but not now. Either the presence of so many other people had tempered his behavior, or Grillo had said something about it. Believer or not, the Jacobite leader did have a code he lived by.

A tech drifted across the room to Grillo and spoke quietly with him. The leader listened, nodded. They were pointing as they conferred, toward the ceiling. Then Grillo turned and addressed the room again. "Another shift in gravity, I'm afraid. Remember your training, and we'll all be fine. The floor will be there"—he pointed upward—"in a few moments."

Sam glanced up. Floor and ceiling mattered little in zero-g, but she imagined that a reversal of the most recent state would mess with even the most experienced crew.

Three Jacobites drifted into the room, each carrying a section of ladder. They took positions by the far wall and secured the parts with little metal handles on the wall that could be twisted to act as bracing.

Hightower used a pair of wire-cutters to release her from the handhold to which she'd been tied. Why Grillo needed three extra ladders brought in, when there was probably a kilometer's worth of rungs embedded in every surface of the room, she had no idea.

The way the three men who'd carried the devices waited around, she suspected the answer would present itself soon enough.

For a brief second she thought she could have pushed off with both legs and propelled herself rapidly across the room, but there were too many guards hovering around. Besides, her aim would have to be perfect. She'd wait for gravity, she decided, and play the defeated-hostage role as best she could. Hightower moved her to the exact same position on the room's "ceiling" and secured her with a fresh set of ties.

*Wire-cutters, right front pants pocket. Toxin gun, holstered under left arm. Brain, missing, presumed dead.*

Gravity returned, first gentle as a bedsheet, then a blanket. Sam closed her eyes as the ceiling became the floor over the course of thirty seconds. The transition was easier for her, tied down as she was. Around her she could hear Grillo and his men settle to their new "down" and then flounder as they rose to stand from whatever pose they'd found themselves in. When she let her eyelids lift, a sense of normalcy had returned.

"Get her ready," Grillo said to Hightower. "Her suit should be here any minute."

"Suit?" Sam asked.

Grillo ignored her. He turned back to confer with the technician. The pair now stood at a terminal screen mounted on the wall of the inner barricade.

The binds holding her down were cut once again. Sam immediately began to flex her fingers and massage her wrists as best she could, rubbing away the soreness generated by the tight cuffs.

Hightower knelt down and cut the strap at her ankles. The deed done, he made a show of returning the wire-cutters to his pocket and then stared at her as if waiting for some kind of thanks. Sam said nothing. Instead she bounced on her heels to force blood back into her feet. Something felt wrong about her body, a lethargy that had not been there on the ground. An aftereffect of the toxin dart, perhaps. Or her muscles had gone slack in the absence of gravity. Whatever the case, she felt like she'd put on ten kilos since arriving. She wanted to shadow-box, to better understand her current capability.

"Want to spar?" she asked Hightower.

"What?"

"I need to hit something. Friendly match?"

"Shut the hell up. No talking."

He'd unholstered his weapon after cutting her free, and hefted it in her general direction now. But Sam watched his face, not the gun, and written plain as day in his eyes, in the slight snarl of his mouth, was the truth. He wouldn't use it. He'd been ordered not to. Sam added this to her growing list of chinks in Grillo's armor.

She glanced at the former slumlord. He and the tech were smiling, broadly. After a minute of conversation Grillo turned in her direction and snapped his fingers at Hightower. "Time to go," he said.

"What about the suit?" Hightower asked, his voice loud in the enclosed bay.

"We won't need it. It seems they've rolled out the welcome mat. Bring her. You're coming, too."

The guard nodded and moved in behind Sam. He gave her a push by the elbow.

"Looks like your star is rising," Sam said.

"Shut up."

"The sky's the limit, Bonaparte. You'll reach heights I'm sure you've only dreamt of."

"I mean it, bitch. No talking."

The airlock door on the inner barrier hissed as pressure equalized. Grillo turned to the men who carried in the spare ladders and motioned. They came forward and followed him inside. A minute or so passed in near-total silence. Sam took the time to scan the room, hoping for some sign of Skadz or Vaughn and finding none.

Eventually the ladder carriers filed back out. Grillo emerged last, smiling. "Bring the holy relic," he said to someone behind her. "Time to make yourself useful, Samantha. Come and see what the Creator has delivered us."

She thought of refusing, of making a show. Maybe she could say something that called his piety into question, but words had never been her gift. No, she'd just make a fool out of herself and bring death or worse upon one of her companions. This gave her one idea, though. A small one, stupid, perhaps. "I want to see my friends first. Make sure they are okay."

He'd been one step through the portal already, and paused. His shoulders heaved visibly with a sigh. "Really, Sam? Now? I give you the chance to set foot inside an alien craft and all you can think to do is resort to petty delaying tactics."

"I've seen your sermons; that's alien enough for me."

He frowned, like a father displeased with his snot-nosed toddler's behavior. "You should know me well enough by now to avoid goading me, Samantha. Especially with a pathetic line like that. I won't allow you under my skin, not today. This is far more important than a little wounded pride."

*Not you, no. But Hightower . . .*

"And more to the point," he went on, brightening, "you should know me well enough to trust my integrity. Your friends are fine, and will remain so as long as you are cooperative. Which, I might add, you're dangerously close to not being."

In all this he'd never turned to look at her. When she didn't reply, he took her silence as the answer he needed and stepped through. Sam filed in behind him, at gunpoint now, she realized. An entire squad of armed guards brought up the rear. Fifteen, maybe as many as twenty, she couldn't be sure. She wondered if they were Grillo's men or, like Weck, had come from Alex Warthen's staff. Then she wondered if it mattered.

Beyond the door, a white umbilical tube had been stretched out to where a climber, her climber, had arrived earlier. The climber was gone, and the tube extended all the way into the central hub where the Darwin Elevator's cord had been before the station was moved. The tube turned here and went up. Sam could see the bottom rungs of one of those ladders hanging down.

The men who'd installed the climbing gear were waiting at the upward bend of the tube. Sam glanced behind, past Hightower and the other guards filing in behind them, all carrying compact machine guns rather than the toxin-dart weapon that Hightower held to her back.

Grillo reached the ladder and wasted no time in climbing it. His speed and dexterity always came as a surprise no matter how many times Sam saw him move, and this instance was no exception. The slumlord messiah clambered up the rungs two at a time. Two of the ladder bearers followed him up with similar enthusiasm.

Alex Warthen went next, and then Larsen, moving with the same nimble quickness.

By contrast, Sam suffered through one awkward half step at a time. Hightower neglected to cut her wrist bindings, leaving her no choice but to climb by her elbows. The ladder rose ten or fifteen meters, attached via metal clips to the skeleton of the umbilical. The tube itself fanned out near the top, ending at a ceiling of material unlike anything she'd ever seen before. Sam knew instantly it was alien in origin. The hull of the vessel Skyler had described, no doubt. Inset within the visible portion was a section with different coloration, hexagonal in shape. Next to each edge was a symbol, one immediately recognizable as a match for the object they'd stolen from Nightcliff's vault.

Grillo and his two henchmen stood on a small round platform that had been bolted to the ladder a few meters below the alien hull. They were all watching her, and waiting.

Sam continued to climb. Elbow, elbow, foot, foot. Repeat.

Nearer the top, sweating and breathing hard, she began to feel like herself again. The exertion had brought some life back to her limbs.

With four rungs left she paused and contemplated—

"If you're thinking about suicide," Grillo said, "I'd advise against it. A fall from here might only break a few bones and we'd just haul you right back up again."

Sam finished the climb, wheezing by the time Grillo and one of his goons hauled her on to the temporary platform at the top. "I wasn't thinking that," she said between breaths. "I was just getting used to the change in gravity."

"Noticed that, did you? I'm impressed. Yes, the ship is rotating at just the right speed to provide us a familiar gravity, it seems, but since we were parked just beyond that . . ."

"We were heavier. I get it. Can we just get this over with?"

His lips pressed into a thin line, remarkably similar to a smile. "That's the spirit," he said. Then he glanced upward.

Sam followed his gaze. She'd been so focused on the climb she hadn't bothered to glance at the hexagon patch. It was gone. Or, at least, it had moved out of view, revealing a dark interior space that extended off in two directions diagonal to her point of view.

The cube symbol on the hull glowed with a fine white light. Sam swallowed and stole a glance at Grillo, who, with a boost from Larsen, was pulling himself up into the alien vessel. Without realizing it, she'd just opened the damn door for him.

Tim sat in the cold silence and watched events unfold, waiting for his chance to do something and wondering if he would have the nerve to take it.

Three things had happened after Midway Station arrived.

First, most perplexingly, he'd seen the reemergence of the hexagon door. No longer nestled on the bottom of the giant craft within the maze of Elevator cords, the patch of hull had somehow moved to the Key Ship's side. He had to assume this also meant the interior layout had changed, and he wondered if that was what kept Tania from leaving.

He should have moved then, and thought he would have if he'd had an immune aboard to open the hatch. He waited instead, hoping he'd see the portal open from within, a hope dashed by the second event.

Midway Station, in a maneuver he couldn't help but admire, suddenly appeared, drifting in perfect synchronization with the Key Ship. The single-ring space station had parked itself directly on top of the hexagon door and matched the rotation of the Builders' vessel flawlessly.

He'd wanted to scream then. To warn Tania that her exiting would only open the door for the enemy.

Unsure what to do, or even what he could do, Tim watched until the hulking mass lifted from the ground finally arrived. The thing looked like a ziggurat, reeled in by a thousand cables. The pyramid tucked perfectly into the tail section of the Key Ship, cutting off his hopes of entering there, too.

He found himself wondering what Skyler would do.

"Dammit to hell," he whispered.

# 31

## THE PLAGUE FORGE

### 2.APR.2285

They sat in silence together for a long time, drifting in the mild air within the alien chamber.

Waiting seemed to be the only thing to do, and in that lull Ana withdrew deeper and deeper to a place within herself that Skyler could not reach. She was thinking of Davi, he knew, and the childhood they'd lost together.

With each passing moment her words pulsed through his mind, an echo that grew instead of waned. *I wish I could have said goodbye.*

Despite all the Builders had done, this possibility, this robbery of closure, seemed the final twist of the dagger. Pulled into space and taken who-knows-where, never to see his friends again, never to know what happened, what it all meant.

He almost chuckled at the thought. Almost, but Ana's stark expression killed the ironic mirth before it could spill out.

Skyler placed his hand on her chin and ran the tip of his thumb across the soft place below her eye where a tear might have been. Only there were no tears to wipe away. Her skin felt warm, smooth as a newborn babe's, defiantly unaffected by the harsh life she'd found herself in after the collapse. In that sense her skin matched the absolute determination in her eyes. "Hey. We have each other, at least."

Ana fixed a gaze on him that could have started a fire in the rain. "Just like that? You can put it all behind you so easily?"

"No. It's just not in my nature to lament the past."

Her brow furrowed. "On to the next adventure, then? 'Oh well, no big deal'?"

Skyler grimaced. "Not quite that callous, I hope."

"No, not quite." She tried to smile, failed, and sighed.

The tear he'd been waiting for welled in the corner of her eye and slid languidly down her cheek, pooling against the end of his thumb. Skyler let the droplet rest there. On the verge of wiping it aside he realized it had fallen. Down her cheek. Gravity.

"We're slowing down," he said. He'd been so focused on her he hadn't paid any attention to their position. They'd been drifting toward the ceiling's center, a gradual migration unnoticed in the darkness. Skyler could do nothing, adrift as they were, until the new floor came within reach. When his fingers could brush the surface he pushed to the right, rotating them so their legs pointed to the new down. Ana had remained wrapped about him until that instant, and now she released him and came to stand. The press of gravity increased rapidly.

"We're stopping?" she asked, whispering despite the empty room.

Skyler nodded. "When we do we'll be back to floating. Get ready."

He'd barely spoken the words when he suddenly felt as if he were floating in a pool, only the floor hadn't moved.

"This is giving me a headache," Ana said, her feet coming off the floor.

"Maybe the constant shifts make the subs more docile," Skyler said, belatedly realizing he only half meant it as a joke.

As if the room had heard them, Skyler's internal compass shifted once again. The pull came on rapidly; the recently christened floor began to slide away and tilted sickly.

The roughly circular perimeter wall of the room became the floor, and Skyler understood. They weren't falling—they were being thrown outward. The pyramid had started to spin.

Skyler's feet hit the new floor with a thud and he tucked into a roll. Somewhere behind him, too far behind him, Ana grunted. A bad landing.

He pushed himself to a kneel, ignoring the stabs of pain in his shins. Viewed from this perspective, the room took on a different feel entirely. Skyler stood on a narrow floor that curved rapidly upward ahead and behind. To his right, a solid wall shot straight upward all the way to where the circular floor reached its apex directly above, broken only in the center where the segmented shell ship still sat suspended in the middle of a gaping hole. Only now the ship appeared to be floating in midair, on its side. What before had been an abyssal pit now stretched sideways into darkness, out of view.

What before had been a high conical ceiling now served as the strangest wall Skyler had ever seen. Compared to the broad, flat disk to his left, the wall on his right was a dark, deep cone studded with huge pipes that shot out from seemingly random positions and extended across his view to the meet the left wall.

"Ana," he said, scanning the ground for her. "Ana!"

"Here," she called out. She'd landed surprisingly far away, almost a quarter of the curved floor's circumference. He spied her between two of the pipe pillars and his heart lurched. She stood at a perpendicular angle to him. His mind wanted, demanded, that she fall on her face and tumble down the floor, but she just stood there. He closed his eyes and forced himself to accept the geometry of the room, the physics at work. She was being thrown outward, same as him, due to spin.

Skyler opened his eyes and saw the room fresh. It was no different than the ring of Black Level, other than the lack of a ceiling. *Okay,* he thought, *okay*. He moved toward Ana, a jog at first that quickly became an awkward, bounding sprint. The force wasn't quite Earth normal, at least not here.

She sat on the ground now, back propped against the flat wall.

"Are you all right?"

Her hands gripped her left ankle. "It's just twisted, I think." She tried to stand and winced. Skyler stepped in beside her and slipped an arm under hers, felt her weight shift onto him instantly.

"Could they make up their mind on which way is down?"

"I think they have."

She glanced at him with more hope than he expected to see.

"We're under spin," he said, "and if I'm right, the gravity, or illusion of it—whatever the hell—at the outermost point is just like being on Earth."

"Why?"

"Let's go find out. Lean on me until you can walk on it."

There were two ways to leave that he could detect. The original entrance, which Ana had warped with four grenades, had become a slightly askew pit in the gravity shift, dropping ten meters off into a faint yellow glow. Skyler decided to try the other option, first.

"Come on," he said, giving the girl a little tug to compel her into motion. "Let's try to find out why we're spinning."

Ana took her weight completely off the bad ankle and hopped along next to him as he took a lap around the curved floor. The dim light in the room was something of a blessing, he decided. Otherwise the place would have resembled a carnival merry-go-round turned upright, all the merry riders thrown outward to their deaths. The mummified bodies of the original explorers of this place littered the floor. Some were draped over the large tubes that spanned the room. It took willful imagination to erase the morbid display from his mind and focus on the geometry of the room itself.

He kept his attention to the left, toward the conical wall. When it had been the ceiling, a squad of armored subhumans had dropped in through iris portals spaced evenly around the perimeter. He looked for these first, as they would be hallways now instead of chutes. The irises remained firmly closed, though, no matter how hard he tried to pry his fingers into the hair-thin grooves where the plates met. Whatever triggered their opening, it had happened once and that was likely that. Skyler sighed and looked to the middle of the huge conical wall instead. There had been a hole in the very center high above, impossible to reach. But now, with the world flipped ninety degrees, it would be a simple hike up the slope of the cone.

Two-thirds of the way around the curved room he spotted a clear path. "Think you can climb this?"

Ana frowned.

"We'll be weightless by the time we reach the top, getting lighter the whole way."

Her expression brightened. "Sure, then."

Five steps into the climb, Skyler's knees howled at him. If anything Ana had to feel worse, but she made no complaints. Her mouth became a tight thin line, almost suppressing the grunts she made with each difficult hop up the steep incline. A quarter of the way up Skyler paused and let her rest, sitting her atop one of the huge pipes that crossed the room. With a few minutes' rest, they went on, and soon the drop in centrifugal force became noticeable. Before long, Ana extracted herself from Skyler's helping arm and they were both doing a spider crawl toward their goal. Near the end, Skyler could propel himself with just his fingertips.

The hole in the wall spanned five meters across at the mouth. Skyler glanced in the opposite direction, following the clear path the shell ship had followed upon entry. A perfect shot, dead center, with a bullet that had crossed perhaps light-years of space.

"What could a race with this kind of ability possibly need with us?" he mused aloud.

Ana ignored the unanswerable question. Instead she drifted around the perimeter of the hole, studying the ragged edge carved by the ship's entrance. The hole extended off in a perfect tube, into absolute darkness. But it couldn't go far, Skyler knew. The room above, where Blackfield lay, where the alien object hopefully still sat waiting for them, couldn't be more than twenty meters off. Skyler shuddered at the idea of Blackfield's peaceful body being flung to the outer edge of that room, along with the remains of the fallen enemy.

"Crap," Ana said.

He glanced at her. She was fishing around in a pocket on her pants. "What's wrong?"

"I totally forgot," she said, producing a thin metal tube. She clicked one end of it and a bright white LED bloomed to life. "Sorry," she said.

"Don't be. I'm just glad you remembered now."

She aimed the beam into the depths of the tube. Skyler expected it to run straight to the chamber he still thought of as "above," perhaps ending at a flat wall that would be the underside of that chamber's floor. What he saw instead was a confluence of tunnels, all channeling together roughly ten meters inside. There were eight, evenly spaced, all coming in at nearly oblique angles forming a needlelike protrusion where they ultimately joined into one.

The layout didn't match his mental picture of how the shell ship had entered. The tube should extend all the way to the point of entry, not separate out like this. Then he recalled how the structure had repaired itself elsewhere. Perhaps the same thing had happened here. The ship had crashed, or maybe more accurately, had landed, in a straight line through the very center of the building. Later, somehow, the structure altered itself into the configuration Ana's light now illuminated.

She drifted across the opening to him, grabbing his outstretched hand to stop herself. "What do you think?"

"It's still better than dropping down that chute back there. But if these tunnels extend outward very far, we'll be back to walking. Can you handle it?"

"I want to get out of here Skyler, so yes. I'll make it."

Together they drifted into the tube.

Skyler selected one of the splinter tunnels at random and led Ana down it. The tube narrowed, curved outward until the illusory gravity felt almost Earth normal, and then curved back again slightly before a yellowish glow ahead became apparent. He tapped Ana to get her attention and pressed a finger to his lips. Then he took her hand, the one that held the flashlight, and thumbed the end to click it off. He hadn't quite realized until that moment just how quiet the ship had become. The simple tick-tick of the flashlight's switch cracked like a twig under foot. Skyler winced, waited, heard nothing more.

He crept on, Ana subconsciously allowing him to take the lead. The glow came from a long oval gap in the tunnel's floor.

Skyler stepped close to the opening, drew his pistol on instinct, and looked down.

A few meters away he saw what had previously been the outer wall of the room where Blackfield had died. This tunnel, apparently, constituted one of the many pillars that had spanned that place. If this opening had been there all along, Skyler hadn't noticed it.

He lay on his stomach and gripped the edge of the gap, intent to look into the huge room and see how far they were from the original floor, perhaps also to spot Blackfield's body or the alien artifact.

Just before he peered inside, though, the yellow light danced and shifted.

Skyler froze. He heard voices. Not the animalistic grunts of subhumans, but actual conversation. He glanced back at Ana and saw her wide eyes. When he held up a hand, instructing her to stay back, she quickly nodded.

The voices continued. They were distant, perhaps on the opposite side of the cavernous space. The light, clearly not a glow from a room but from a carried lantern or flashlight, moved about in bursts of activity.

One of the voices erupted into a cackle of a laugh. Skyler held his breath and strained his ears. He moved and poked his head into the oval gap. From this vantage point he couldn't see anything but a section of wall—or, floor now—and a half-dozen of the pillars.

More laughter. Animated conversation, and a single word Skyler recognized plain as day. "Blackfield," someone said. *Blackfield*.

Skyler narrowed his eyes. He didn't recognize the voice, not specifically. There was a familiarity to it, but he couldn't place it. He needed to hear more, or better yet, to see.

He moved farther, pushing his head fully into the room, and glanced around. The floor was a three-meter drop away. It was sloped, which made sense given that the room had been the inside of a pyramid now turned on its side. But it was also curved. Not smoothly like the space they'd just left, but segmented. He knew the room to be the same one where Blackfield had died, yet the geometry had changed. From four sides to hundreds.

The light, and the voices, were fading.

Skyler glanced all about, and saw no way down to the floor short of a drop. He thought he could make it but knew Ana could not unless perhaps he broke her fall. That would make far too much noise, though. He turned to her and whispered. "I'm going inside. I need to see who is in there. Wait here, and when it's safe I'll catch you when you drop down." He saw the objection in her eyes and added, "It's too far for your ankle to take."

"Okay," she whispered back, sounding anything but convinced.

Convincing her would take time he did not have. The light, the voices, dwindled with each second. Skyler turned and lowered himself through the oval opening. The walls of the pipe were shockingly thin, a few millimeters. This would have amazed him had he not seen tons of equipment and supplies, even his own bulky aircraft, climb up the thin space elevator cords. If anything the thickness of the walls here was generous.

He lowered his legs, eased himself down, gave one last affirming look at Ana, dangled from his fingertips, and dropped. As landings went it was a pretty good one. The Builders' ubiquitous material did not clang or clack like metal or tile. Skyler thought it more like stone.

He landed in a crouch and paused, listening. The voices had faded completely now, and the light was nearly gone. Skyler pushed himself to a jog, ignoring a few splinters of complaint from his shins and knees, and the dull ache that clung to his split chin like some tenacious insect.

Ahead he saw an opening in the floor, the same one he and Ana had floated through after leaving Blackfield and the object. Yellow light glowed weakly from within. He dropped to his knees and leaned his head in. If this was indeed the same tunnel they'd used before, the configuration had changed. It should angle sideways in the new gravitational context for ten meters to meet the room they'd originally entered the pyramid through. That span of passageway was gone now, vanished. Either filled in or simply sealed off. Instead a new tunnel presented itself, running straight for a long, long way. A hundred meters away, perhaps more, he saw a pocket of yellow light surrounding human forms. Two were silhouetted against the light, blocking the three or four others from view.

Skyler watched them fade into the distance. How far the tunnel went he had no idea. Hundreds of meters easily, and without curving. That meant it ran lengthwise, parallel to the axis upon which the whole structure spun. That could only mean one thing. He'd suspected it all along, somewhere in his mind, and was only now admitting it to himself. They'd docked with the Key Ship. They'd linked up and someone else was already here.

Skyler swallowed. Blood drummed in his temples, adrenaline building within him. Someone else was already here, and they'd simply picked up the object and left. Headed to the key room, he had no doubt. They didn't call out for him or Ana. They'd laughed upon discovering Blackfield.

It could only be Grillo. Anyone else—Tania, Sam—would have expected Skyler to be present, would have looked for him.

He rocked back on his ass and let the adrenaline course through him, focusing his thoughts. He glanced back, toward the tube where he knew Ana waited. She sat there in the dark, at once terrified and anxious, awaiting him. And injured.

*You'll have to forgive me later. I will come back. When it's safe.*

And with that he turned, dropped down into the connecting tunnel, and began the hunt.


Skyler kept his pistol pointed dead ahead.

The tunnel seemed to go on forever, collapsing to a pinpoint of fuzzy darkness that did not grow bigger as he walked. How big had the Key Ship been? He tried to recall Tania's words. Five kilometers at least, and with a feeling that settled like a stone in his gut he began to think this passage might span the entire distance.

The people he'd heard had turned, but as of yet Skyler had seen no connecting halls or rooms. He kept his flashlight off just in case. Once his eyes had time to adjust, it became clear the long hall was not totally dark. A ghostly purple glow seemed to span its length. Somewhere very far off there had to be more light, for the tunnel seemed to end at a pinpoint of white, like a night sky where only one star existed.

He glanced back, saw darkness. Paused, heard nothing. *Please stay put, Ana.* He tried to imagine her walking this distance on her ankle, or making the two three-meter drops necessary to get here at all, and couldn't. And as much as he hated to admit it, he couldn't picture himself tugging her along, one arm constantly around her for support. She'd become a liability.

A hissed voice shattered the silence. "Now!"

Blinding light hit Skyler from the left. He whirled, swinging his pistol in one outstretched hand. A shape flashed, something cracked into his forearm. The pistol clattered away as pain exploded above his wrist.

On instinct Skyler ducked, felt the whoosh of another blow pass over his head. He surged forward and hit something, someone. After the long darkness his eyes were useless in the sudden glare. Whomever he'd hit turned with his rush, threw him. Skyler's momentum sent him skidding on the floor. He blinked, tried to push himself up, but his right forearm wailed in complaint, sending him back to the floor. Commotion all around him.

Boots thudding as his attackers surrounded him. Shouts of alarm and, chillingly, orders to halt.

Then he felt the cold metal of a gun barrel against his temple.

"That will be quite enough," a voice said. A knee, not the speaker's, pressed down on the center of his back, crushing his abdomen painfully into the hard deck.

Skyler kept still, staring at the floor until his eyes could handle what must be the combined light of four or five flashlights.

"I thought we heard a rat," someone said.

"Yes," the first speaker replied. Skyler had heard Grillo's voice only once, a long time ago, but he recognized it instantly. Too calm, too even, like an emotionless fucking robot. "The question is, was he one of Blackfield's, or was Blackfield doing the following for once."

A hand gripped the back of Skyler's head, clasped around his mess of sweaty hair, and lifted.

"Ah, of course. I should have guessed. Skyler, right?" Grillo asked. "I hardly recognized you under all that grime."

He said nothing. Could see nothing but boots around him.

Four pairs. No, five. One of them stood remarkably close behind another. Hostage and guard? Skyler tried to mark their positions before his head was cracked back against the ground with a wet smack. Someone slapped a binding across his wrists and tightened it until the tie dug into his skin.

"My, my," Grillo said. "Pray for one immune and they practically rain from the sky. So many options."

A chill rippled down Skyler's spine like cracking ice and settled in his anguished gut. *Had they found her, so soon? Ana. Dammit.*

Grillo wouldn't know her, though. Then the epiphany hit him. They were all headed here, weren't they? Grillo could be talking about anyone. Hell, every last one of them. Skyler let the cold ball of ice in his gut fracture and expand, filling him from head to toe. "The plague source is dead, Grillo," he grumbled through lips pressed half against the ground. "Everyone's immune now, though obviously it didn't cure every sickness of the brain."

Stark silence. Skyler hadn't thought of it until this moment but Darwin without the prison walls of the aura would no longer be the tidy little play kingdom Grillo—and Blackfield before him—had enjoyed. People would flow back out into the world, and a ruler without subjects—

"Bring him," Grillo said. "One of them will cooperate. One will surely see the light." A dry laugh tumbled from his mouth, no humor in it whatsoever.

Someone hauled Skyler unceremoniously to his feet. The gun at his temple moved to the small of his back and jabbed.

"Thank you, by the way," Grillo added, already ten paces off and not looking back, "for bringing the last of these relics. You people couldn't have made this any easier."

Skyler ignored the lunatic and glanced over his shoulder, hoping to size up his captor.

Instead he saw Samantha's familiar blue eyes, a mixture of hope and justified disappointment there. A short man stood behind her; judging by his posture he had a weapon pressed to her back as well. A strip of duct tape had been slapped over her mouth, and before Skyler could utter a word he heard the grating tear as another length was shorn off the roll and pressed across his own.

Fresh pain at his chin, chased with the chemical reek of industrial glue from the tape. He ignored both and stared at Sam. He winked at her, the only communication he could offer. Before he could gauge her reaction, Skyler's own escort gripped the hair at the back of his head again and forced him to look forward and down.

Compelled by the gun, Skyler trudged forward along the gradually curving side hall, with nothing to look at but the back of Grillo and his two flanking guards. One looked familiar. Skyler had seen him when he'd snuck through Gateway. One of Alex Warthen's senior men, if he recalled. The man carried the oval object, wrapped in a thin blanket, with two reverent outstretched hands.

# 32

## MIDWAY STATION

### 2.APR.2285

Handle gripped loosely between forefinger and thumb, he tilted the lever downward and winced in anticipation.

The click as the shitter-coffin door unlatched sounded as loud as a gunshot after all the quiet. Its hinges, at least, were blissfully silent as he pulled the segmented folding door open and out of the way.

"Say what you want about the old goat," the big man said under his breath, "but he built these damn things to last."

He inhaled first. The air outside the tiny head was only marginally fresher than within, remarkable given that he'd been stewing in that dim box for days now. Still, it came as something of a relief.

Ignoring another growl from his empty stomach, Prumble sucked his belly in and *sat up* out of the bathroom to a darkened, empty climber car apparently turned on its side.

It had been a miracle of sorts that his stomach had been empty; otherwise he could have added one more bodily fluid to the stench within his miserable hiding space. It had never occurred to him when choosing the spot that up and down were not tried-and-true constants where he was going. Indeed, all directions seemed malleable, given that he'd entered the closet of a room standing, spent hours weightless, then briefly pressed on his aching neck and hands before the final, coffin-like state of sideways seemed to win the which-way's-up battle royale.

*Could be worse.* He'd said that to himself half a hundred times since his questionable decision to hop inside the climber car next up in the revolver queue behind the one Sam and the others had chosen.

He kept expecting someone to open the fucking bathroom door and shriek at the fat, wild-haired man stuffed within, but no one had. Whoever had searched the climber had done a pathetic job. Head poked in, ridiculous question asked. "Anyone in here?"

"I'm trying to take a shit thank you oh so very much!" Prumble had only mouthed that, and fought a deep rumbling laugh when it had worked and the cursory search had ended. That had been hours ago. His brief flirtation with joy had fizzled as the aches and pains in his body grew to the point of intractable agony. A cabinet knob gouged into his shoulder. The water faucet pressed in uncomfortably close to his anus. *And, God, the smell.*

Prumble stood and stretched, ignoring the oddity of standing on the goddamn wall. Anything ranked above the shitter-coffin at this point.

His stomach growled once more, the final call to action he needed. Emergency rations aboard the climber were long ago consumed. The gun he'd used to fight off the subs he'd thrown at them in one last effort to stall their advance. It had worked, too. Three of the crazy bastards had tripped over the spent rifle. Tangled scrawny limbs were the last things he'd seen as he'd pulled the climber door closed.

There was simply nothing left to do in here, and clearly everyone else had moved along. He'd have to explore. Find Sam, if she lived. Kill a few more subbies—

The last foggy remnants of bloodlust coalesced and swirled through his mind at the thought of all that killing. A sharp taste of copper in his mouth brought back the memory bright and clear. He must have slain twenty. The carnage hadn't slowed the others down. They'd vaulted and climbed over the corpses to reach him.

The odd direction of gravity probably meant his climber now languished in a storage facility somewhere. Gateway or Penrith, maybe Newcastle if they were doing their jobs right. He'd heard of the station called Newcastle Storage before, firsthand, from a cargo worker taking shore leave deep within the thighs of one of Madame Dee's nubile escorts. Prumble thought the station sounded rather like his former garage, only a few orders of magnitude larger and, at least during Prumble's boom years, holding a mere fraction of the goods.

Yet the details didn't add up. The man had said Newcastle did not spin like most of the other stations. Storage turned out to be a whole different beast in space, and the lack of gravity made the full use of all three dimensions possible.

But perhaps more damning than that was the fact that Prumble could breathe. That he hadn't become a Popsicle inside that bathroom. That his custom environment suit they'd gone through all that bloody trouble to procure was now only fit to propel a small yacht. Newcastle was kept cold, airless, so that mold and microbes and rust would not pose a problem.

"So where the hell am I?" he muttered.

At least the exit was near enough to reach. It could have been ten meters above his head on the opposite side, forever unavailable to a man of his generous girth. Instead he only had to deal with the indignity of hoisting himself through the horizontal portal. *First things first,* he thought, and yanked the handle. It didn't budge. Fear rose like bile in his throat at the prospect that this whole damn climber was indeed a coffin. Then he pulled it the other direction and the handle turned smoothly. Terror receded. He did a little jig.

When the door swung open—turning out and down as if he were emerging from a giant oven—Prumble saw part of a darkened, vaguely circular room of which he appeared to be very near the center. The space was turned on its side, of course. His stomach seemed to love to point that fact out. But in this case that minor detail mattered little. The room was a climber hub, he assumed; a cylindrical space roughly equal in depth and width. The direction of gravity mattered little as a result. Walls, floor, ceiling, all looked basically identical, and one such surface was just a few meters below him.

He pointed at it. "I dub you Sir Floor. World, start making sense."

And it did. A bit. It had an up and a down, at least.

Small point lights illuminated the perimeter, creating little pockets of white in the otherwise dark room. A few spoke hallways radiated outward, with similar sparse lighting. Terminal panels inset in the walls beside these glowed with text and iconic graphics that probably indicated Very Important Things. Lots of green there, at least. He took that as a good sign and shifted his focus to the more immediate concern: What the hell now?

*Find a friendly face. Find a gun. Find a bag of crisps. Any of the above.*

Somewhere someone laughed. The sound echoed slightly through the large empty room. Another voice followed with a hoot. Prumble strained his ears and, just at the edge of perception, heard conversation.

"That's a start," he said under his breath, and shambled down from the climber as quietly as his hulking form would allow. He paused long enough to shake some feeling back into his swollen feet, then walked toward the voices.

His foot caught on something and he nearly fell. Glancing down, he saw the floor or wall or whatever had a shallow channel running off in two directions, with what looked like ladder rungs bolted within. His brain drew a picture of floating workers, hoisting themselves along the guides with expert—

*Stop that.* He snapped his eyelids shut and shook his head. When he opened them again, he focused on the simple task of traversing Sir Floor, everything else be damned.

The voices grew louder. Prumble moved over to what seemed to be a temporary barricade—thick square sections of the floor that had rotated up on heavy hinges to block off a portion of the room for some reason. He sidled along the partial wall until he came to the corner, a good five meters still from the perimeter of the room. Leaning out slowly until he could see with one eye, Prumble noted two Jacobite guards seated on the floor about five meters away. They were facing each other. Between them lay the telltale signs of discarded Preservall packaging. Both men were chewing at their rations now, conversation apparently on hold.

On the floor next to one of them lay a compact assault rifle. If the other was armed, Prumble couldn't see the weapon.

He leaned back, weighed his options. Clearly they weren't expecting trouble. They'd been left here, as backup perhaps in case a need did arise elsewhere. Good.

Prumble turned the corner and walked casually to the men. With each step he expected them to turn, to stand and challenge him. With each step that this did not occur, a smile grew on his face.

One finally turned when Prumble was just a step away. The man's cheeks looked like they held a week's worth of food. He tried to say something but only cracker crumbs fell out. Prumble kicked him in the mouth. Bits of beige cracker and perhaps a few teeth exploded outward, propelled by a muffled cry of agony.

The other guard sat frozen, eyes wide with abject disbelief. He was staring at Prumble as if the Lord himself had appeared. Prumble slugged him twice with one meaty fist. First punch bloodied the nose, second one broke it. A low whimper gurgled up from somewhere deep in the poor bastard's gut as his brain finally caught up with what was happening. He tried to stand but Prumble kicked his legs out from under him, sending him down hard on his back. Another kick to the abdomen left the Jake a sniveling, writhing mass. Years as a bouncer in Christchurch's shittiest clubs still paying dividends, Prumble knelt beside the bloke, held him down by the shoulder, and hammered his thorax three times with his right fist.

The man stared up vaguely at the ceiling, limp, trying to breathe in sharp little motions and probably realizing somewhere in the fog of pain he lay in that breathing wasn't something he'd ever do again.

Prumble whipped his focus back to the first man while simultaneously reaching for the sleek rifle that still lay forgotten on the ground. He leaned over the guard, and ignored the horrid mush of blood and cracker being forcibly coughed from the wreck of the bloke's mouth. The man stopped his sputtering when he felt the cold metal of the rifle's business end press up under his chin. His tear-filled eyes searched, found Prumble's, and froze at the deadly gaze they found there.

"Take me," Prumble said, "to my friends."

Tim swallowed hard.

The alien ship, all six kilometers of it, suddenly beginning to rotate was one thing. To see Midway Station attached to it like a barnacle frayed the last of his nerves.

Tania was not alone in there now. Her oxygen reserves would be uncomfortably low, too. A decision had to be made.

He could wait. Wait for the backup ERV and the strength of a couple more people to enter with him. It would only be—he glanced at the timer—four hours.

"No," he said. His voice sounded feeble, a squeak. Tania would be so impressed.

He cleared his throat and tried again. "No," he said. "No." Conviction now. "No." There. Force, drive.

Tim pulsed his thrusters and headed for the emergency docking ring on Midway Station.

"Which friends?" the guard sputtered. He coughed, and groaned with pain for the effort. Cracker crumbs stained red with blood sprayed out in a cone on the floor in front of him.

Prumble gripped the man's shirt and hauled him to his feet. "You know who I mean."

Nose broken, the man had to speak and breathe through his mouth, forcing him to talk in short, nasal bursts. "There's two groups. Some went inside the . . . ship. The rest are still here."

"Where's here?"

"Midway. Midway Station."

He knew of it from an occasional spec-list request and the odd glimpse of a Platz Station map, but nothing more. "The group still here: How many guards?"

"Uh," the man said, "six."

Prumble frowned. "I'm going to start breaking fingers in a second here, mate. How many?"

"Two . . . two."

"That's better. Which way?"

The man gestured off to his left, and started to turn.

"Sorry, friend. You're a liability now." Prumble raised the compact rifle.

The guard began to whimper and slid down to his knees.

"I'm not going to shoot you, mate. I just can't have you shouting a warning. This way." Prumble guided him to the vacant climber and, after a few more threats of bodily harm, stuffed the man inside the shitter-coffin and tied the door closed, securing it with a length of cable ripped from behind a nearby access panel.

The spoke hallway leading away from Midway's cargo bay hid mostly in shadow, and this suited Prumble just fine. Halfway to the far end he began to wonder if he'd made a mistake leaving the guard alive. He thought not. The door was well secured and besides, the poor sod was in a living hell now, as Prumble well knew.

At the end of the hall he paused long enough for his breaths to come at a normal rate, and the steady drum of adrenaline at his temples to recede. Then he listened.

The outer ring led off in each direction, to his left and right, each bending backward in the current setup instead of up as they would under normal circumstances. His brain desperately wanted to make the carpeted side the "floor" instead of the outermost wall and it took an effort of will to keep his bearings.

He waited for a long moment, the only sounds coming from hidden fans and plumbing behind the thin walls. Ventilation ducts were everywhere.

Voices to his left.

Prumble moved instantly in that direction, keeping close to the wall, his stolen gun pointed at the floor a few meters ahead. The passage was lit by one long, contiguous LED strip along the curved wall to Prumble's left, normally the ceiling. The band of light zigzagged from top to bottom in a pattern that didn't help his mixed-up internal compass at all.

Worse, the surface upon which he walked normally served as a wall, and had been designed as such. Half of it was removable ventilation plates, forcing him to keep to one side. And every three meters or so he had to step over a raised support truss.

A new sound caught his ear. A metallic thud, like a heavy door closing. The voices, closer now, responded.

"Who's there? Identify yourself!"

Prumble pressed himself against the wall and froze. The thud had sounded even farther away than the voices, and he knew he'd made no noise at all. They were responding to the door. Maybe Skadz or Sam had escaped. Maybe they were closing in from the other side.

Time to act, he decided.

He moved forward at a jog, drawing confidence from the rifle in his hands.

Two guards came into view, creeping in the opposite direction, guns sweeping the hall before them. One, clad in Jacobite garb, carried a Sonton pistol like he knew how to use it. The other, a Gateway regular, had a weapon exactly like the one Prumble had picked up from the cargo bay floor.

They heard him before he could close sufficient distance to get an effective shot. The guards whirled in unison and raised their weapons.

Prumble did the same, dodging right at the same time. His finger squeezed on the trigger even as they fired.

Something smacked into his foot. A bullet, his mind concluded as he fell. He realized the truth before he hit the ground. He'd tripped, caught his foot on a blue placard stenciled with a stick-figure man and the word RESTROOM next to it. It would have been wall signage had the station been in its normal configuration.

The sign probably saved his life. Bullets sailed over his head. Prumble hit the floor awkwardly and, relying on the theory that neither guard would put a second bullet in his back, went limp, sliding to a stop. The gun clattered away.

His theory proved accurate. Neither man fired again. One of them even barked a nervous laugh after a brief, shocked silence.

"Where the hell did he come from?" one of them said.

"Beats me," the other replied. "What do we do?"

"What do you mean?"

"We can't just leave the body lying there."

Prumble fought to keep his breathing even and slow. After the run, the burst of adrenaline, this proved near impossible. If they came closer . . .

"Search him at least. Check for a pulse," the first said.

*Shit.* He weighed his options even as he heard footsteps coming toward him. Mind racing, he decided to try for time and perhaps a bit of distance. He let out a long, feeble groan.

From the sound of it, the approaching guard almost fell himself in surprise. He scampered back a step or two. "Don't move!" he shouted.

Prumble hadn't moved, and didn't now. Instead he groaned again.

"What the heck do we do?" the nearer guard said. "There's no medic around."

"Shoot him again."

Prumble tensed.

"You fucking shoot him!"

"You've got the darts. Knock him out for a while until Grillo—"

A sudden clang reverberated down the hallway, loud and deep. Prumble flinched on reflex, felt nothing. Something heavy hit the floor.

He rolled and came to a knee in one motion.

Ahead of him, one of the guards lay prone on the floor. The one near Prumble was whirling to face a third man. This one wore a blue jumpsuit and wide, terrified eyes. In his hands was a red fire extinguisher.

The guard raised his pistol.

The newcomer threw his fire extinguisher as the gun went off.

Prumble surged forward, saw a bright spark as a bullet hit the metal cylinder and ricocheted harmlessly away. The guard managed to fire again, but he was also trying to lean away from the meter-long red tube sailing toward his face, wrenching his aim. Prumble went low, aiming his shoulder at the man's thighs, and at the moment of impact, he swept his arms forward and up and heaved.

Another clang followed by a muffled yelp as the fire extinguisher took the bewildered guard full in the face. Prumble lifted him, adding to the momentum and sending the body in a heels-over-head flip.

The guard cried out as he landed.

Prumble kept moving straight ahead, diving for his own gun, which lay two meters away at the base of the wall. He grabbed it, spun about, and saw the overturned guard extending his pistol in a desperate blind-fire move. Prumble ignored the two booming shots and took his time. When he fired, a single red dot appeared on the guard's forehead. Blood sprayed along the floor and wall behind the man as he slumped, dead.

Lowering his weapon, Prumble leaned back against the wall and turned to look at the newcomer. "Nice timing," he said.

"You shot him," the man stammered.

"Uh-huh. And you threw a bloody fire extinguisher at him."

The man looked down at his own hands as if he'd never seen them before. "I . . . I guess I did."

"Like I said, nice timing. Who are you?"

"I'm Tim," the man said, as if that explained anything.

"Prumble. A pleasure."

Hearing the name seemed to pull Tim out of the well of bloodlust he'd apparently fallen in. He blinked and faced Prumble now. "Skyler mentioned you. I . . . Are you hurt? They shot you."

"No, I just tripped, though I'd appreciate it if you kept that detail to yourself."

Tim nodded, then drew a deep breath. "I have to find Tania."

From somewhere nearby Prumble heard a new sound, like someone screaming into a pillow. Multiple people, he realized.

"First things first," Prumble said. He hauled himself to his feet and lumbered over to a door, which, given the layout, was on his floor. He crouched and tapped a button, smiling as the barrier slid aside.

Skadz stared up at him, eyes wide. The guard named Vaughn sat next to him. Both had tape across their mouths.

Prumble grinned. "You didn't think you could ditch me that easily, did you?"

# 33

## THE KEY SHIP

### 2.APR.2285

Skyler's body teetered on the verge of giving up. He felt like someone had hot-glued a line of pure fire to his chin, like a hammer had been working at his shins, his knees. Worst of all, each step they forced him to take brought a pinpoint of white agony from somewhere deep inside his gut, as if a razor blade banged and clattered on one long, lazy journey through his intestinal tract.

Something was wrong in there; something had popped or torn when Grillo's men had held him to the floor and cuffed him.

*Cuffed. Shit.* He'd almost forgotten the hard-edged nylon straps about his wrists, so tight his hands had become two nerveless oven mitts attached by a ring of biting teeth where his arms ended. He willed his fingers into a little tap dance against one another, cursing himself once again for failing to flex as the binding ties were zipped. Relaxation brought no marginal relief, much less a looseness that could be exploited.

The hallway curved upward ahead at an almost imperceptible slope. Given the enormous size of the ship—ship, station, whatever the hell it was—Skyler guessed the circumference must be three times that of Black Level or any of the other Platz-built stations.

Every twenty meters or so a perpendicular hallway jutted off to Skyler's right.

Only one hallway went left, back toward Ana, though it ended only forty meters in and glowed faintly purple.

Purple. A hue he'd seen before, a hue he'd been enveloped in. The shade sent a chill through him that temporarily masked every ache he felt.

The sight of that glow triggered something in him. The barest whisper of a plan. It trickled in slowly, his brain under siege from seven other directions. If he could somehow shove Grillo inside one of those purple fields, maybe Warthen and Larsen as well, then he'd have hours to finish the task he'd come here to do before they could even turn around and run back out. Assuming, he admitted to himself, the glow came from a field similar to the one in Ireland—

Something smacked into his shin. He'd been so laser focused on Grillo's back he hadn't realized they'd come to some kind of room, the portal to which was raised like a bulkhead. A faint white glow came from within the spherical room beyond. Skyler glanced inside as he stepped through, assessing the situation out of a mixture of instinct and habit. He discarded the alien oddness of the place and focused on details. An exit, directly across. Another, to his right, halfway up the sphere. Someone had placed a metal ladder diagonally from the floor to the lip of that portal. Beyond he could see enough hints to know that the key room lay within. He turned, focused on the people present. His gaze swept past the head of Grillo and his elite guards, past a crowd of armed Jacobites who stood within, and into the terrified eyes of Tania Sharma.

She should have lost all hope right then and there.

The sight of Skyler, bound, chin and neck caked with blood and sand, hair matted and wild, should have extinguished the candle within her. That flame did flicker, dipped precariously to the barest whisper of blue flame in an endless void.

But then she saw his eyes. Had he simply stared at her, she would have abandoned the few fine shreds of optimism within her and let the candle wither, sputter, die.

He did not stare at her, though. As he stepped into the room, urged forward by the nudge of a gun barrel, his gaze leveled toward her, yes, but it stopped only for the briefest of instants, then continued on. He noted the tape across her mouth, her seated position on her hands. Vanessa, next to her, in the same state. He studied, with almost callous calculation, each person in the room. Grillo, the guards. Their faces, their weapons, their postures. She could see it in his stony expression. That analysis. His apparently innate hardwired ability to take in a scene and digest it with all the warmth of a computer algorithm. Tabulating options, building a mental hierarchy of anything and everything available to him.

The scavenger.

Another captive marched up the stairs behind him. Tania expected, even here, even now with a twinge of disappointment, the diminutive form of Ana. Or worse, Blackfield. Yet neither appeared to be with him, a detail she forced aside. For now all that mattered was who did stand behind him.

Tania saw a woman who stood a head taller than Skyler and towered over Grillo. Despite the short dyed-black hair, Tania recognized her instantly.

She would have smiled if the duct tape smashed across her mouth would allow it. Her candle danced back to life.


Skyler had no fucking clue what to do.

Tania and Vanessa, bound and gagged as he was. No sign of Pablo, which gnawed at his already-stressed gut. Pablo would never have willingly left Vanessa's side. Either they held the man elsewhere or something much worse had happened.

Samantha, behind him, also bound and gagged. No sign of Skadz, though Skyler wasted less worry there. Skadz might simply have decided to stay in Darwin with Prumble.

Given the sorry state of things, only one path seemed the reasonable choice: Do whatever the hell Grillo wanted.

Buy time, for himself as much as Ana. He almost chuckled at the sudden realization that the girl was, in the end, still the wild card.

He buried with extreme prejudice the wave of delight and relief that swept through him when Tania's face appeared before him. It simply would not do to give Grillo any more buttons to push in order to secure cooperation. The slumlord had plenty of those already, whether he knew it or not.

"I assume you all know one another?" Grillo asked, gesturing vaguely with his left hand at the space between Skyler and Tania. He'd pulled a pistol from his jacket and held it lightly against his right thigh.

No one replied. No one could, mouths taped. Grillo went on. "Good. Now, one of you immunes better volunteer to finish this job, or I'll have no choice but to implement some population control measures."

Skyler felt his own weight shift to one foot, his body deciding before his brain, ready to step forward before anyone else could. Nobody moved, though, whether of their own volition or taking a cue from him. A heavy silence settled in the long room and Skyler kept his foot still.

Grillo's right arm raised with mechanical smoothness, the pistol pointed toward Tania, seated a few meters away. She recoiled, shrank away. Vanessa, next to her, remained still, her face a mask.

Skyler stepped forward and grunted as loudly as the tape on his mouth would allow.

The gun lowered.

Skyler felt Tania's look like the heat of a spotlight on his skin, but ignored it. He took a full, slow stride toward Grillo, placing himself between the man and his two seated captives.

A thin, satisfied smile tugged at the corners of Grillo's mouth. He stepped up to meet Skyler, then reached and yanked the tape from his mouth in one swift motion. The pain across Skyler's lips barely registered, masked by the renewed gritty burn across the gouge on his chin as the skin was tugged and separated yet again.

Skyler couldn't help but wince. Couldn't help but notice the flicker of sadistic ecstasy in Grillo's otherwise placid face. Skyler met the gaze, stared it back into the dark corner it had emerged from. "This isn't going to work, you know," he said.

"Your problem, Skyler, is that you lack faith."

"Not true. I have faith this isn't going to work."

Grillo clacked his teeth together. "A comedian, are we?"

"You've got me there. I'd probably make a great zealot if it weren't for my sense of humor."

A crease formed across Grillo's forehead, halfway between his eyes and his greasy, perfectly combed hair. A flash of redness on the skin there, too. "You don't know me very well, Skyler. Miss Rinn does. She could have warned you against talk like that if she hadn't been censored herself." He let the words settle, then lifted a radio to his lips. "Shoot one of them," he said. "Skadz . . ." He trailed off, looking for some flicker of recognition in Skyler's face.

Whether he found it or not, Skyler couldn't tell. The news that Skadz was here somewhere almost didn't register, not right away. When it did click into place, Skyler had no idea what information, if any, his expression had given away.

Grillo nodded. He'd learned something. "Belay that," he said. "The other one. Vaughn."

The name meant nothing to Skyler, but Samantha suddenly howled beneath the tape on her mouth and thrashed against the man holding her. Another guard had to step in and help restrain her.

"That's not necessary," Skyler said.

"Oh it is, it is. I don't make empty threats. Ever." He spoke into the radio again. "Once in the heart, then dispose of the body. Confirm, please."

The sounds of Samantha's anger-fueled struggle filled the stark silence that followed. Eventually she stopped.

Grillo held Skyler's gaze for a long moment before that worry line appeared across his forehead again. "Confirm, please," he repeated into the radio.

No response came. One of the Jacobite guards shifted uneasily in the otherwise absolute stillness within the room.

Grillo dropped the radio to the floor and stamped down on it with one swift strike of his heel. Bits of plastic and metal skittered across the floor. A strand of hair drooped across the man's forehead. He brushed it back with the side of his pistol with only partial success, some composure returning to his face in the same motion, as if a switch had been turned off. Still, he drew his breaths through clenched teeth, eyes fixed on the broken remnants of the radio.

No one spoke. They were, Skyler realized, as shocked at the outburst as he was. Grillo teetered on an edge.

"You," he said evenly to one of the guards not shadowing a prisoner, "go check on them. And you, follow him. Pull the ladder in and only lower it if he returns. Clear? Go right now, quick as you can. The rest of you hold this room at all costs. No one gets inside the temple, understood?"

The men nodded in unison and began to spread out, taking cover positions on both doors.

"Enough conversation," Grillo said. "Any more distractions and Dr. Sharma here will join Kelly Adelaide in the afterlife. Do I need to prove my mettle in this regard, Sam? Or will you vouch?"

Skyler glanced over his shoulder at Sam. Her gaze met his, and she nodded once. Kelly was dead, and apparently for the simple reason that Grillo had needed to prove his sincerity.

The ball of ice inside Skyler's chest turned into an avalanche, spreading through his veins until his entire body seemed to realign into a machine finely tuned for one single purpose.

*Kill. This. Man.*

Grillo shrugged. "Now that we're all on the same page, it's time. Warthen, Larsen, you and your men with me. Weck, organize the female prisoners in the center of this chamber. Let them shoot through that if they want to reach us."

He turned then, and climbed the ladder to the portal high on the side of the room. Alex Warthen followed, robotic in the way he shadowed his new boss.

The younger guard, Larsen, fell in behind Skyler and helped him up the steps. At the top, Skyler found another ladder leading down. Warthen waited there, and with a strong grip at Skyler's elbow, helped him through and down to the key room floor, which rippled with lines of cold, blue-white light.

Beside the base of the ladder lay a pair of nylon sacks. Skyler could see hints of shimmering light through the material. One blue, one yellow.

"Bring those," Grillo said, then turned and strode purposefully along the immense, cylindrical room without looking back.

In zero-g, Skyler had thought of the room as a tall silo, with ten sides. But the spin-induced gravity forced him to shift his perspective once again. The room had become a long tube, at least a hundred meters from tip to tip, and twenty meters in diameter.

Skyler, guided solely by the viselike grip Alex Warthen had on his elbow, fell in step behind Grillo. The floor—perhaps coincidentally, perhaps not—was one of the two sections that still awaited a corresponding object to be installed. Directly above him he saw the purple, vaguely hourglass-shaped object recovered in Ireland, still resting in its form-fitted receptacle. Following the circle clockwise, Skyler noted the red object, circular with a half-moon-like chunk missing from the top, found just east of Belém. Counterclockwise, he saw a new object. This one had a triangular shape, one tip squared off. It glowed in a soothing emerald. The object that Tania, Vanessa, and Pablo had gone after. He wondered where they'd found it, and where Pablo was. Awaiting their return in Belém, most likely. Bringing him along here would have been logistically difficult, no doubt, and really, why would they have?

Skyler pushed the thoughts away and renewed his focus. Two objects still needed to be installed. Grillo had both, and the majority of known immunes at his disposal to do the work. Refusal would serve no purpose. Skyler would say no; Grillo would shoot Tania. Then Sam. Then Skadz, if Skadz yet lived and was still captive. Then Vanessa. By then he'd probably find Ana, too. One of them would speak up, offer to do the deed, for the simple reason that none of them had any bloody clue what was going to happen.

As far as Skyler was concerned, whatever the Builders had to offer might well be something he'd gladly let Grillo have all to himself. A case of the clap if there was any justice.

Grillo stopped a half-dozen meters short of the bowl-shaped depression in the middle of the long floor. He motioned and Skyler was marched to stand beside him, a few meters between them for safety. The bindings at Skyler's wrists were cut, bringing a sudden rush of blood to his numb hands. He immediately began to massage feeling back into his fingers.

Two more guards—no, workers, Skyler decided—carried one of the rucksacks up and set it on the ground. At Grillo's nonverbal order they pulled the bag open to reveal the object within.

A cube nestled within the folds of the cloth bag, blue-white light rippling along inset geometric grooves in its sides. Like all the other objects, one side had a difference—a feature, not an imperfection—to indicate "this way up." In the case of the cube, a channel was etched along the length of one side.

"Leave us," Grillo said, to no one in particular. Alex Warthen opened his mouth to object but stopped at Grillo's raised hand. "It's all right. This one won't try anything with all of his friends held captive."

"He fled Gateway Station while his crew was—"

"He can't flee now, though, can he?" Grillo let a few seconds of silence follow. "There is nowhere to go. He'll have to look into their dead eyes this time and know he brought it upon them."

Alex seemed on the verge of speaking again. He changed his mind, cast one doubtful glance at Skyler, and clambered back up the ladder. Larsen followed, and Skyler and Grillo were alone.

Oddly, Skyler felt more unease alone with the deranged man than when his guards had been present. He steadied himself, then turned to face the slumlord.

"What happens when it is inserted?" Grillo asked.

"The ship has an orgasm," Skyler said. "Lower your gun. I wasn't joking."

"Skip the salty language then and explain, quickly."

*Orgasm, salty? Maybe he really has bought into all this Jacobite nonsense.* "There's a lot of light, and warmth, and if you want my opinion the ship's response is vaguely akin to ecstasy." *Never mind that the pulse of light will knock you straight across the room if you're standing too close.* A good orgasm would, too, but Skyler guessed Grillo had never experienced such a thing. He seemed like the type of man who had to wear surgical gloves just to take a piss.

"All right then. Proceed." He kept his gun trained on Skyler now, aim steady.

"Ladder's up!" a voice shouted from the far end of the room. "No sign of them."

"Remain vigilant," Grillo called back. "Shoot on sight."

"Understood."

Skyler glanced back. The spherical lobby chamber was fifty meters away. Inside, Sam, Tania, and Vanessa would be sitting in a line now, between the two lower doors. A human shield. Hands bound, mouths taped.

He'd failed to count how many guards were with them. Six or so, he thought, plus the two who'd left to check on the other prisoners. If Skadz or Ana tried to approach that room they'd be gunned down instantly.

Best to hurry, Skyler decided. Get everyone's attention on the relic, wait for that flash of light, then act. Hopefully the others would get the hint. He'd need to shout something, just to be sure.

"Now, Skyler," Grillo said.

Skyler nodded, shifted his focus to the relic on the ground before him. The blue-white light rolled through the fine grooves with a liquid pace, inviting scrutiny, demanding it. Skyler forced himself to blink and break the spell, then deliberately blurred his vision as he knelt and lifted the cube.

He struggled under the weight of it. The strain brought fresh pain from his shins and knees. Even his chin bloomed with renewed heat as his grimace stretched the skin there. But it all felt distant now, as if he were just an observer studying the injuries from the other side of that sheet of fallen ice brought on by the news of Kelly's death. The cold thirst for revenge numbed his mind better than any painkiller ever had.

Skyler crossed the distance to the socket indent on the floor and knelt. He heard Grillo gasp as the indent sucked inward as if the floor were made of nothing more than plastic wrap. The area grew, forming a pitch-black half-dome almost three meters deep and wide in the floor.

"This was easier in zero-g," Skyler said, shimmying his legs over the edge of the enlarged bowl.

"No talking. Finish it." To hammer home the point he pressed his gun to the back of Skyler's head.

Skyler perched himself on the edge and lifted the cube object out over the middle of the depression. The weight of the relic melted away, yet simultaneously it seemed to tug against Skyler's grip, pulled downward into its designated slot.

The glow began to build, starting from the grooves along the object's surface and then spreading like spilled laser light into the bowl. The center of the receptacle bulged outward, reaching and taking on the same shape as the object.

Skyler pulled his feet out of the pit and lifted his arm across his face, ready to shield his eyes.

Object and floor met. In that instant a blue-white flare seemed to come from everywhere at once. He pressed his arm over his eyes. Felt the heat of the energy release on his skin, the pressure pushing him backward like an expanding bubble of force.

Someone cried out in alarm. A yelp that was instantly cut off.

Skyler felt his feet slip. A centimeter skid, then more. Then he was falling sideways.

The entire room *rolled*.

# 34

## THE KEY SHIP

### 2.APR.2285

Tania clamped her eyelids down when the eruption of blue light began. It flooded through the key-room portal like a searchlight. Soon even through shut eyes the world seemed as bright as a summer day.

She coiled in anticipation of the pressure wave that would follow, and hoped the guards would be thrown off balance.

The wave came, like an inflating balloon of pressure building at her back. And then, abruptly, it vanished. The light blinked out as well, plunging the room into darkness.

Tania opened her eyes and registered the faint glow the room emitted. Anyone who hadn't shut their eyes would be all but blind for a few seconds. She glanced back and saw that the high portal that led into the key room had vanished.

An initial confused chorus of puzzlement welled up from the guards. A few urged calm. She heard something else, too. A sound like stone gliding against stone.

Tania knelt and pitched forward, knowing what was about to happen. She could only hope Vanessa understood, too, and that Sam would take the hint.

The gray bands lurched into sudden motion, turning and rolling at once this time. Confused shouts burst out from the guards as their feet were swept out from under them by the thin, flat rings. Arms bound as they were, Tania could only roll with the motion as one band slid under her like a spatula.

The men were falling sideways, backward, pitching atop one another into a tangle of limbs in the basin of the room.

The bands stopped as quickly as they'd started, and once again light filled the room. Yellow light.


Prumble's heart had dropped through his stomach when the door ahead irised closed.

He'd been seconds from sending Vaughn in as a distraction, when the light from that space had winked out, leaving him staring at a dark end to a featureless tunnel. Sam and the others cut off from view. Skyler, likely somewhere beyond, hopefully alive, a distant unknown.

Prumble had acted without thinking. He'd rushed forward, past Vaughn, leaving Skadz and Tim hissing his name in a mixture of surprise and warning. They hadn't seen the door vanish, the route to their friends disappear.

He'd rushed, howling and full of blind anger, to the tunnel end, intent to slam into the wall with the butt of his gun and every gram of his weight.

Intent to, but the wall pulsed open when he still had a half step to go.

Beyond he saw writhing bodies. Armed men and prisoners alike, struggling back to their feet after some kind of massive and total upheaval of the spherical space.

Prumble did not break stride. He couldn't have, and didn't want to. He kept going, full steam, straight into the crowd, and slammed the stock of his gun straight into the face of the first Jacobite he reached.

\* \* \*

When the room settled, Tania rocked onto her back, pulled her knees to her chest, and swung her arms under and around herself to get her hands in front of her.

A guard began to rise in the same instant, and she kicked her legs back down hard, catching him on the shoulder and sending him sprawling on top of the others still struggling to get up.

Somewhere, someone was howling. A battle cry.

She rolled to her stomach, pushed up to a coiled crouch, and found herself staring into Vanessa's eyes. The immune had indeed acted. She'd managed to get her arms in front of herself, too. Her hands came up and gripped the tape at Tania's mouth, tearing it away in one brutal motion.

Tania ignored the sting across her lips and performed the same favor for the other woman. "Hands," she said, trying frantically to rip the duct tape away from Vanessa's wrists.

"No time," Vanessa said. "Duck!"

Tania did, diving sideways in the same motion into the torso of a guard who'd come to one knee beside them. The guard grunted, fell away. Tania rolled and looked back in time to see Vanessa, hands bound, block the swing of one of the uniformed men, the one called Larsen. His swing was meant for Tania and would have knocked her senseless had Vanessa not warned her. The other woman whipped her hands back up to slug him in the jaw, then she dropped her fists to the neck of his shirt and grasped, pulling him down toward her. In the same motion she thrust a knee upward into his groin. Larsen groaned, face contorted. Vanessa didn't stop. The immune dropped her knee and coiled her leg into a full-blown kick. She let go of the man's shirt as her foot connected with his abdomen. The kick lifted him off his feet and sent him toppling backward into the confused tangle of bodies behind.

Others had entered the room. A huge man in a leather overcoat and a Nightcliff guard who seemed to be fighting his own people. She saw a third person bolt in from the entryway, just a shadow, but the dreadlocks gave Skadz away. She'd heard enough stories from Skyler to know the man instantly. He held a pistol, smoke curling from the barrel, and raced through the chaos of the room to the side opposite her. In two quick steps he was up the curved surface and vaulting himself into the thick of the melee with an almost acrobatic grace, shooting as he flew.

Tania lurched to her feet, driven by a sudden flood of newfound hope. The whip-crack sound of Skadz's gun echoed strangely within the sphere, replaced instantly by a bright ringing and the labored sounds of her own breath. She whirled, saw a guard rise before her with a snub rifle in hand. Tania swung her bound hands at the weapon and knocked it free.

The guard reacted with a quickness that surprised her. He pulled a knife from a sheath at his calf and swiped it at her face. Tania recoiled, felt the whoosh of wind as the blade missed. He jabbed next, sending her back a step on the steeply curved wall. Her foot slipped and she fell back onto her elbows, her bound hands over her chest as if clasped in prayer.

The guard grinned and managed to raise his blade before a pair of thin arms enveloped him from behind. Tania recognized the blue jumpsuit before she saw Tim's long, usually kind face over the surprised guard's shoulder. That kindness hid now beneath a mixture of desperation and rage.

Confused, angered, the guard shifted his blade and sliced wildly across Tim's forearm, producing a dark red gash across the blue sleeve. Tim didn't scream, didn't make any noise at all. He just tightened his grip and stared into Tania's eyes as both he and the guard began to topple forward toward her.

She did the only thing she could think to do. She reached up, grabbed the falling guard's wrists, and twisted.

The man groaned as his body collapsed onto hers. She felt a sudden warmth at her breast as blood began to ooze from around the buried blade.

With a force of will she tore her gaze away from the dying guard's eyes and sought Tim's instead.

Somehow he managed a smile.


Skyler thrust himself up into a ready stance, fists up, ignoring the searing heat of torn skin at his chin, and the deep new ache that had exploded in his gut when Grillo's first kick had landed. Tears welled in his eyes, blurring his view.

He shook his head violently. Grillo stood before him. Half turned in profile. Knees slightly bent. Hands low and coiled. He shifted his weight rapidly from foot to foot, ready for anything.

Skyler spat blood and moved in, his head swimming from pain and the constant upheaval the Builders' ship kept putting them through. He managed to keep his fists in front of him but felt none of the lightness Grillo seemed to be enjoying.

Gritting his teeth, Skyler stepped in and threw a left jab that Grillo sidestepped easily. Skyler followed with his right, putting everything he had into the haymaker blow, anticipating where Grillo's head would be as he returned from his sidestep to counterattack. But Grillo didn't return. He didn't answer Skyler's left jab at all.

Instead he'd kept moving, ducking low and sliding past Skyler altogether.

Skyler whirled to find the slippery bastard, stepping back at the same time to stand where Grillo had been. He felt the fist against his cheek before he saw it. And then another, rocking his head in the other direction. Skyler sputtered as a third blow took him in the stomach, filling his entire gut with a heat unlike any pain he'd known before.

And he knew he'd lost.

"Put the fucking yellow key in," Grillo rasped.

Skyler blinked. He heard the sounds of fighting, desperate and violent, from the other room. It killed him not to be able to see. Not to know who lived and who'd fallen. He'd heard the distant, abstracted sounds of people falling in panic even through the closed wall when the key room had rolled. There'd been no chance to find out what happened. Grillo had been on him from the instant the cylinder stopped, relentless and stunningly adept in combat.

The slumlord stood before him now, not a single mark on him. Not a goddamn hair out of place. The polar opposite of Skyler's litany of cuts and bruises.

Worse, Grillo had finally found a gun and held it in one unwavering hand aimed directly at Skyler's forehead.

"I've no more patience," the man said, his voice high and bristling with pure contempt and frustration. "Not for you, not for your damned friends, not even for those pathetic Jacobite twats. I simply want what is beyond that wall down there, Skyler, and you will open it for me. Do it now, or I'll kill you and drag one of your friends in here to do it."

Skyler opened his mouth, something clever on the tip of his tongue about false gods, when Grillo fired the pistol. The bullet made a *thawp* sound as it sailed through the fabric of Skyler's shirt at the neckline, harmlessly and yet perfectly full of the promise that harm would come, and soon.

Nodding, bewildered and fighting pain from a half-dozen injuries, Skyler lumbered toward the last key.

Samantha kicked the hand away that gripped her boot. She thrust herself to a stand in one surge of strength that came from God-knows-where.

There was fighting around her. The other immune, the one Tania had been here with, lay on the ground, her hands flailing at Alex Warthen, who straddled her. His hands were wrapped around her neck, fingers white with the force of his choke hold. She'd be unconscious soon. Sam lurched toward them.

A guard suddenly rose from the floor in front of her, blocking the way.

*Hightower.*

The short man raised his toxin gun, his lips curling into a vulpine, shit-eating grin.

Sam kicked, her foot a blur. The gun went sailing straight up, leaving his hand empty as his stupid fucking smile slid right into a pathetic, shocked, utterly wonderful O-shape.

"Bitch—"

She high-stepped in, planted her left foot squarely on his chest even as her right came off the floor. Sam cartwheeled, kicked upward with all the strength she could muster and a whole lot more. Her boot met chin. Bone cracked, loud enough to echo off the walls of the vast room, loud enough to drown out all the commotion for one single, perfect instant.

Weck tried to scream through his ruined mouth. Spat teeth and blood instead, backed with a sloppy gurgling sound that rang like music in Sam's ears. She didn't even feel the floor as she hit it. She'd flipped completely over and, hands bound as they were, landed poorly, and did not care. Hightower collapsed to his knees next to her, choking on his own blood. She thought she might have driven his lower jawbone through the roof of his mouth and could not—would not—deny the satisfaction that brought her. Instead she rode that like a surfer on a wave.

She rolled to her back, brought up her knees, kicked up and forward. The momentum brought her off the ground and into a coiled stand.

A huge, hulking form barreled past her, leather jacket trailing behind. The sight of Prumble brought tears of raw joy to her eyes. She tried to shout his name, to sing it like a battle cry, but the tape on her mouth prevented it.

He said nothing as he passed, moving straight to the hunched form of Alex Warthen, who still gripped the now-limp woman's neck with both hands. Prumble stepped in behind the man, grasped his face with two meaty hands, and twisted. Sam winced at the horrible sound that followed. It was a sound she'd heard before, a sound she'd caused on more than one occasion. The sudden grind of bones that were never meant to touch. The tearing of veins and muscle.

Prumble shoved the lifeless form of Alex Warthen aside.

A hand gripped Sam's upper arm. She whirled, coiled to strike, and stopped when she saw Vaughn next to her. He had blood on his face, and one eye half closed where he'd taken a punch or six. His fingers came to her face and gripped the tape. At her nod he tore it away.

"Thanks," she blurted, working her jaw.

"Later," he said, and pulled her aside.

Sam whirled with the motion and found three Jacobites still standing. Two carried guns, and were leveling them.

"Come on, pilot," Grillo said. "One last task and it'll be over."

"What do you think is going to happen, Grillo? I mean really going to happen, when the last one is put in place."

The slumlord hauled Skyler to his feet and nudged him toward the oval object, which lay on the floor a few meters off, having rolled like a cheese wheel when the room tilted.

"I have no idea," Grillo said, sounding genuinely sincere. "What's that old saying? The Lord works in mysterious ways?"

Skyler managed a thin laugh. "You don't actually believe all that shit, right? I mean, you can't tell me this isn't all just an act." Skyler bent down and lifted the oval object. The shimmering traces of yellow light on its surface matched those on the floor below it, albeit on a smaller scale.

"I believe there are powerful forces at work here," Grillo said. "A plan that is beyond our comprehension."

"So that's a fucking no then?"

He prodded Skyler again with the gun, hard this time. The bowl-shaped receptacle for the oval object loomed only a few meters ahead now. "I suppose you think we'll get answers."

"They have a lot to answer for," Skyler shot back over his shoulder. "The disease—"

Grillo threw his head back and cackled at that. "Oh, of course. You're here to make them apologize, is that it?"

Skyler felt his own composure slipping. "They wiped out—"

"We were the fucking disease, you fool! An infection. An infestation! What they brought was the cure. Our salvation, if you want a word that turns those Jacobites into weak-kneed, drooling sheep."

It was Skyler's turn to laugh. "So you're here to shake their hand. How's that any smarter than me?"

"The point is, pilot, I don't know what will happen. All I know is, for better or worse, I will be the one standing there when it happens. I'll be the face of humanity."

"Suppose it's just confetti and balloons?"

Grillo said nothing.

"Suppose it's a weapon that fires on Earth, destroying it utterly?"

"I'd say it's a good thing we're safely up here, then. I've enjoyed this conversation, Skyler, but it's finished now. Put the object in place."

This time he loomed close, one hand on Skyler's shoulder, body wound like a spring. The gun remained firmly planted at the top of Skyler's spine, pressing in as Skyler knelt and then sat on the rim of the depression in the floor.

*He's going to kill me,* Skyler realized. *The moment this thing clicks into place, my job will be done. The others won't get here in time.*

Yet he saw no way out. The sounds of combat still wafted in through the room's only entrance. He had no idea which side prevailed, but odds were on those with guns and unbound hands.

He couldn't turn and fight. Grillo had already demonstrated his speed. Skyler could maybe, maybe get a grip on that wrist above the hand that gripped his shoulder—

"*Quickly,*" Grillo hissed.

Skyler leaned over the pure black bowl and, straining his muscles, held the glowing oval object over the center. Again he felt that conflicting sensation of the object shedding its weight while simultaneously being sucked downward through some invisible attraction.

This time Skyler kept his hands on the relic, as if he were helping to lower the thing into place. The geometric lines laced along the object, the floor, the inverted dome, all began to flare up, coming to life in a synchronized swell of energy.

The receptacle began to bulge and take on a complementary form to the object approaching it. It seemed to reach out, hungry. A physical force, pressing against him, warming his skin.

Light, unbearably bright now, heat like standing beside a roaring bonfire. The gap between object and holder dwindled to less than a meter, then half that.

Something unexpected happened. A gift. Gravity in the room began to melt away.

Tania clawed her way to Vanessa's side, terrified of what she'd find, or wouldn't find, when she pressed her fingers to the woman's neck.

She did it anyway, dropped her head, feeling nothing.

And then a faint twitch pushed against her fingers. A pulse. Weak, but there.

Fighting tears, numb from exhaustion, Tania turned to study the room. Sam grappled with a guard for control of his gun. The giant in the leather duster was facing off against two others.

A strange glow began to fill the room.

"Get to Skyler!"

The voice sounded distant. Tania sought the source and saw Skadz trying to pull himself out from under a fallen soldier. "Someone . . . get in there."

Tania glanced up at the portal high on the curved wall just as brilliant yellow light began to pour through. She understood the urgency, then. The last key had been installed. Grillo had no more need of his captive.

As she tried to stand, a new sensation enveloped her. An easing of pain, of weight, of . . . everything. Gravity fading.

"Get in there!" Skadz roared, pointing.

Tania heard the scraping sound as her weight began to melt away. Stone on stone. The portal would close again, perhaps forever.

Movement caught her eye. Someone running in from the side. A girl.

*Ana.*

Tania could see her eyes clearly in the growing yellow light. And in them she saw the same calculation that Skyler could exhibit. In the span of a heartbeat Ana took in the scene, and without breaking stride she ran up the wall opposite the portal, her weight—everyone's weight—dwindling to nothing with that last step.

And then she jumped.

She pushed off and raised her hands straight above her head like a diver off a cliff and flew. Flew across the blood-drenched lobby, sailed by the sudden flotilla of dead and dying bodies. Ana torpedoed herself straight across that space and through the portal a split second before the hole irised closed.


Skyler let go of the relic. He planted his feet on the dome's edge, reached back with both hands, and clasped down on Grillo's wrist. In the same instant he jerked his upper body sideways and forward. Felt the barrel of Grillo's gun slide across the skin of his neck, felt the scorching line of pain across his skin as Grillo finally reacted and fired.

The man's reflexes kicked in then. He swung the gun instead of firing it again, the handle cracking against Skyler's cheek. Twice. A third time. It was all Skyler could do to hold on as their bodies twisted and floated free.

Something hit Grillo then. Someone sailing through the room with remarkable speed.

Ana, Skyler realized.

The impact was glancing. A shoulder to Grillo's waist. He grunted but could do nothing about the sudden change in rotation.

Through sweat and blood and tears Skyler caught a glimpse of the glowing oval key swinging into view behind Grillo. He pushed against the man with every bit of strength he could muster. Hands and feet, shoving out in unison, breaking the man's hold. Grillo shouted in surprise as his body flew backward, his head slamming into the cavity that had formed to accept the final key at that exact tipping point where the two objects overcame all other forces and clapped together with magnetic finality.

Grillo screamed. A scream cut short as the Builder relic slipped home. A scream that ended with a soft pop like a melon under a car tire. Skyler slammed his eyes shut, couldn't look if he wanted to given the final burst of yellow light that erupted from the object.

Already moving away, the pulse of energy shoved him like a giant fist toward the far wall. Skyler wheeled uncontrollably and did the only thing he could think of by tucking himself into a ball. At least his arms might protect his head.

He heard shouting, nearby and from the far side of the room. The scorched line on the back of his neck that marked the bullet's trail suddenly burned with unholy pain.

His body thudded against a solid surface—the opposite section of wall, he guessed—and bounced away. He opened his eyes, blinked away the lingering brilliance of the flare, and glanced around for Ana. She drifted near the side wall that glowed red, her hands trailing along the surface as she fought to slow herself.

Skyler cast a gaze in the other direction, hoping for some sign of the others, but the portal at that end of the room had vanished again. Ana must have jumped through at the last possible second.

A new sound began to fill the space. Like slabs of polished stone sliding against each other. Skyler looked straight up—it felt like "up" again—toward the source. The huge iris door there, its thousands of facets sparkling with a rainbow of reflected hues from the five lit walls within the room, was opening.

Pure white light streamed through. The beams pulsed and flickered like a living thing.

Skyler spiraled, bleeding, suddenly feeling the weight of all his wounds. He felt near death and chuckled. To die, just before the wizard finally pulls back the curtain. He stared into the beautiful pearlescent glow and grimaced, suddenly humbled and awed all at once. The light really was heavenly, in perfect contrast to the hellish sounds of fighting that had preceded it.

Then Ana was next to him. She'd pushed out to meet him, and her momentum added to his took them inexorably toward the light streaming in through the now fully open disk.

He could do nothing to stop them, and deep down he didn't know if he would have had the possibility existed. Instead he simply held her, and gazed into her gold-flecked brown eyes as the light blotted out everything and consumed them.

# 35

## LOCATION UNKNOWN

## DATE IMPRECISE

Skyler woke up in someone else's head.

His eyes opened to a white void that stretched to infinity.

His body was alone. He knew that without looking, not that he could. He felt . . . detached. Like a visitor. Physically he was alone, lying on his back on some invisible cushion of air and floating in an endless, abstract void. Mentally, though, something else was going on. Someone else was here with him, running the show.

And what a show.

It was like sitting in a sensory pod, a film of his life coursing through the emitters. Only the frames, the visuals, noises, smells, and touches were all jumbled, all far too fast. Comprehension of any single thing was impossible, yet taken as a whole he knew this was his life on display.

*I must be dying. Or dead.*

The thought brought immeasurable comfort. The first chip of stone off a prison wall. *He thinks, therefore he is.* Isn't that what the philosopher said?

*Good, I exist. That's a start.*

The erratic replay of his life ended, and real memory flooded in to fill the space left behind. Memory of pain, of a glancing gunshot wound to his neck and a deeply cut chin, among a thousand other smaller aches, crashed into his brain like snow through a brittle roof and . . . and, vanished. Just memory, he realized. He reached up and touched his chin. No pain. Just stubble and irregular patches of caked blood.

"You are suitable," a voice said. It came from everywhere and nowhere, as if he'd said it himself. Only the voice had a feminine quality, and something else. Something artificial. Haunting and synthetic.

"Ana," he said, voice hoarse. "Ana?"

"She rests," the voice said, clear and yet ephemeral. A girl's voice, young woman at best. Strangely accented. No one Skyler knew.

He looked around. A pointless effort and yet he found comfort in the fact that his head did not ache. White stretched off in every direction as if he were inside a vast . . .

Bubble.

Skyler stretched his hand out, felt a pressure, a bulging. *This is familiar. This I know.* He pressed harder and the void seemed suddenly very much finite. A cocoon or egg, centimeters from his body.

"What did you mean? Suitable for what?"

"You are suitable."

"Can I leave?" he asked, unsure whom he was speaking to.

"If you're ready."

He swallowed, not expecting that. And, worse, realizing with a sudden crystalline clarity that the voice was the other entity in his head. The one who'd been watching his life. "What will I find out there? Bullets already in flight? More death?"

"A decision."

"Is that all?"

"All that matters."

He grunted. "Will you be out there?"

"Yes."

"So you don't matter?"

"I'm the decision," she said simply.

A chill ran the length of Skyler's body, bringing gooseflesh to his arms and legs. He shivered, and realized suddenly that he was alone in his own head again.

"Are you still there?"

"Yes." Yet detached now. Separate.

Skyler pushed his other hand against the milky white void. "What do I call you?"

A slight hesitation. "Eve."

He waited, digesting the name. He didn't know anyone named Eve, and yet somehow he'd known she would say that. As if no other name would match.

The void began to stretch around his hands, pushing outward.

A nervous energy began to build in him. "Aren't you going to ask what to call me?"

"I know what to call you."

# 36

## THE KEY SHIP

### 2.APR.2285

Fear and desire propelled Skyler forward through the malleable void. Desire to find Ana, or Tania, or anyone. A familiar face, a real face. Then a way out.

*Eve.* Of course it would be that. The name hung in his mind like a black hole, daring him to move toward its inescapable grasp.

His whole body began to shake. Then the bubble of white that was his world shattered and collapsed around him. He fell forward on his hands to a cold floor, hard as stone.

He found himself alone in a dark circular room. The bubble had been perched on a raised dais in the center, and there was an exit directly in front of him. He paused only long enough to bring his breathing under control. Quietly he stepped through into a hallway and glanced left. The passage extended forty meters or so, ending at a T intersection. He walked that way, the female voice ringing in his mind like a church bell with every step. *You are suitable. . . .*

At the first portal he slowed, held his breath, and leaned in to look.

A dome rested on a dais in the center of the space, two meters high and wide, made of pearlescent white tinged blue at the edges. He thought of breaking it, or stepping into it, and thought better of the idea. He continued down the hall, instead, and found more identical rooms.

Save for one, near the end, with no white dome. The dais was empty, like the one Skyler had left. Ana?

He swallowed, continued to the T intersection at the end. A soft yellowish light lit the walls from one direction.

He expected a long hall with a gentle upward curve.

Instead he saw a moderately large room, hexagonal in shape. The far wall was clear, revealing a stunning view of Earth and space. The room reminded Skyler of the one where he'd encountered Neil Platz.

Ten seats dotted the floor of the room, facing one another in a rough oval. Not red couches like Platz had, but simple platforms with low backs that seemed grown out of the surrounding floor.

Two were occupied.

Prumble sat in one, relaxed. Almost jovial, as if this were just another meeting at Clarke's. He was talking in a low voice, his fingers drumming on his knees like they did when he was spinning a whopper of a story.

In the other occupied chair, across from Prumble, sat a girl. Twelve or thirteen years old, Skyler guessed. Light brown hair that fell in long wavy locks over her shoulders and down to her waist. She was perched on the edge of her seat, leaning forward and listening intently as Prumble spoke to her in a low, casual voice. Her hands were folded in her lap, her legs crossed. A graceful pose, sincere and very *adult*. She wore a white dress that Skyler thought looked familiar.

Her face was at once exotic and yet bizarrely familiar, like seeing a distant, long-lost relative after decades apart.

Skyler stepped into the room and withered under her gaze when she noticed him. There was no mistaking the resemblance. Part of him was in that face.

Prumble turned and grinned broadly. "There's our man now!" He stood with an effort and met Skyler near the entrance, hauling him into a hearty embrace. "It's good to see you, my friend."

"Uh, likewise," Skyler managed. "Sorry, I'm a little . . . out of sorts."

"Come sit with us! This is—"

"Eve," Skyler said.

Prumble's gaze swung between the two of them, then settled on her. "I thought you only had a title?"

The possibility that Skyler's earlier discussion had been a dream suddenly dawned, then vanished when the girl nodded.

"Eve," she replied. "I found my name, just a moment ago."

"Oh," Prumble said. "Excellent choice. Much better than Emissary, if you want my opinion."

"Thank you. I agree."

"Emissary?" Skyler asked, baffled.

The girl nodded again, and smiled.

"I'm afraid I don't understand," Skyler said.

Prumble spoke out of the corner of his mouth. "Roll with it, my friend." He turned toward the girl. "Do that thing you did a minute ago. You know, the—"

Eve vanished. A ghosted afterimage remained, like a frozen projection of light onto some impossibly fragile lattice. This vanished, too, a second later.

Too stunned to move on his own, Skyler allowed Prumble to guide him to a chair. "She's not real?"

"Amazing, isn't it? Some kind of hologram, although it has a physical aspect."

"Please," Eve's haunting voice said from all around them, "sit. Another is waking, I must attend."

The urge to argue, to demand answers immediately, rose and then bled out of Skyler with the realization that time to think would be welcome. He scanned the empty chairs and took the one next to Prumble.

The big man threw an arm over Skyler's shoulder as soon as they were seated, fingers gripping tight. It should have been painful, given everything Skyler had been through. Yet it wasn't. He wasn't sore. He wasn't tired, or hungry, or thirsty. In fact, aside from his state of confusion, he'd never felt better.

Prumble leaned in. "Did you see the room?"

"What room?"

"Oh," Prumble said, "you're in for quite a treat. They have a whole world in here, Skyler."

Skyler ran his hands over his face. Too much was happening at once. He heard a soft pop accompanied by a change in the room's lighting. When he glanced up, the girl—the projection—had returned.

"Look at her, Skyler," Prumble said quietly.

He did.

"Can't you see yourself in her face? Can't you see me? Tania? Sam, even? We're all there."

Eve sat unnaturally motionless, oblivious to the scrutiny or simply expecting it. She smiled warmly when Skyler began to really study her face.

Prumble had it right. They were all there, something from each of them. In the turn of her mouth, Ana. The eyes had Tania's shape yet all the bright luminosity of Sam's. Vanessa's hair. Each time she moved he saw something new.

Motion in the hallway caught Skyler's eye. He turned and saw three familiar faces. Tania, with Tim next to her, his arm around her waist. Vanessa walked behind them, and when she stepped into the light of the room Skyler let out a breath he hadn't realized he'd been holding. None of them appeared to be injured.

He locked his gaze on Tania, watched her expression of relief and joy when she saw him, and then the confusion at the stranger.

Eventually they all looked to Skyler for guidance, and he nodded at the chairs across from him and Prumble, the chairs at Eve's right hand.

"Pablo?" Skyler asked.

Vanessa's gaze dropped to the floor like stone. The color drained from Tania's face.

A far-too-familiar tightness pressed in on Skyler's gut. Another of his crew gone. An immune, a good man. *Will it end now? Do they have their pound of flesh yet?*

Vanessa raised her chin. "Later," she said, "we'll raise a glass for him."

Skyler nodded, blinking away the moisture clouding his eyes. He leaned toward Prumble. "What were you and, uh, the Emissary talking about when I came in?"

Prumble smirked. "She had a lot of questions. She . . . knows, Skyler, things she shouldn't know. Everything about humanity. And I do mean everything. But it was like she had none of the context to stitch any of it together. She sounded like a computer at first, though that's almost gone already."

"How long were you talking to her?"

"Hours," he said, with noticeable pride. "Heard some crazy things, my friend. Did you know the Elevator wasn't the first ship they sent?"

The words stung like cold water. "What?" he and Tania said in unison.

"There was some kind of, I don't know, she called it an exhibit, but I think she's still figuring out what words mean what. Apparently it explained all this up front, like a map or blueprint or something, but it would seem we destroyed it."

Skyler considered this. Something Tania had said tugged at his mind. Neil Platz had known. *Interesting*. Skyler filed that. It was water under a bridge, unimportant now.

There were footsteps in the hall. Skyler turned and saw Skadz. He stood and walked to his old friend, pulling him into a soldier's embrace that felt as familiar as an old coat.

"Good to see you, Sky."

"Likewise."

"What's . . . uh . . ." His gaze went past Skyler. "Am I supposed to believe they just happen to fucking look like us?"

"Do not be alarmed," Eve stated.

Skyler gripped his friend by the shoulder. "She's not real, Skadz."

"I'll say. I suppose speaking English isn't real, either?"

Eve tilted her head slightly. "I speak two hundred and thirteen of your languages so far, and more are coming online. This one seemed appropriate, though."

"Do me a favor," Skyler said to Skadz in a low voice. "Keep quiet, keep alert, all right?"

"Yeah. Yeah, okay. Kinda at a loss for words anyway."

"I don't blame you. Take a seat; we'll talk later."

Samantha came next, with a man Skyler didn't know. She took in the scene with a quick glance and grunted, unimpressed. She acknowledged Skyler with the briefest of nods and tilted her head to the room beyond. "Are you the girl who's been talking in my head?"

"Yes," Eve replied.

"Neat trick. I hope you have a good fucking explanation for all this."

"I hope so, too."

Sam's eyes narrowed. "How long were we in those freaky healing whatever-the-fuck egg things, anyway?"

Eve tilted her head, her brow furrowed just like Sam's did. "Sorry. My understanding of time differs from yours."

"How fucking long?"

A hesitation, again. Then, "Thirteen point six-seven-five fucking minutes have passed in this, well, this context. I think minutes is a scale that is applicable here?"

Prumble erupted into laughter. "Oh, I like you. Oh yes. We'll get along fine."

The Emissary smiled at him, then glanced back at Sam.

"Good enough," Sam said, all the gusto suddenly drained from her voice.

"Not good enough," Tania said suddenly. She leveled a gaze on Prumble. "I'm sorry, but there is nothing to joke about here. Our planet is a ruin. Our species on the verge of extinction. Billions have died. Billions. And you sit here and laugh?"

"Forgive me," Prumble said, "but it was pretty funny."

Tania's expression flashed to disgust. "I don't think you understand—"

"Can we let her talk?" Skyler said. He hadn't intended the words to plunge the room into silence. They did. He ran a hand over his face. "Let's hear her out first."

"Thank you," Eve said. "There's just one more . . . ah, here she comes."

Skyler turned.

Ana stood at the corner of the intersection, one hand resting lightly on the wall.

"Skyler," she whispered, tears on her cheeks. "I don't understand what's happening."

"Me neither," he said. "Come sit," Skyler said. "She's about to explain."

\* \* \*

Eve looked at each of them in turn, framed by the view of Earth outside the window behind her.

"For lack of a better term," she said carefully, "I am an Emissary."

"For the Builders?" Tim asked.

Eve shook her head. "For this vessel." Her eyes went up, looked around, implying the ship around them. "And, yes, perhaps for who you imagine the Builders to be, in an indirect way."

"Skip to the part where you make sense," Sam said.

If Sam's tone bothered the girl, she didn't show it. Eve looked at each of them in turn. "Technically speaking, I am the projected visual representation of a simulated mind."

"Like a robot," Skadz said.

"No. More like an artificial intelligence."

Skadz nodded as if he understood. "Respect."

"I am activated by this ship whenever we meet a candidate that is suitable."

Skyler lifted a hand to stay the question poised on all of their faces, the same question he wanted to ask.

"And, in a sense," Eve went on, "I am all of you, compiled from what you've taught me. My visual appearance is an amalgamation of all your features. We find this makes first contact . . . easier."

Silence settled over the room. Skyler felt Ana's hand tighten around his.

"You were each placed into a kind of stasis. Thirteen minutes passed out here, but the flow of time inside your spheres varied depending on your injuries, or simply how much you wanted to teach me."

"Sorry," Tania said. "*Wanted* to teach you?"

Eve nodded, visibly gathered herself. "I suspect your minds interpreted this as dreams. That's one area where your species is still somewhat primitive."

"Excuse the fuck out of us," Sam said.

Skadz leaned forward. "Will you let it talk?"

Sam folded her arms.

"Dreams," the Emissary went on, "are easily forgotten, but

some of you may recall portions. Raising me. Teaching me. As Nigel . . . Prumble, indicated, I hold copious knowledge but little wisdom. You've all helped me understand."

Skyler glanced at Tania, saw her face flush, her eyes close, as some recollection crossed her face.

"So you've been in our heads," Skyler said. "You know everything that we do."

Eve turned to face him. She shook her head, her expression almost sad. "Each of you taught me, but in terms of information I have access only to some of Tania's mind and, to a much lesser extent, Prumble, in that regard."

Skyler shot a glance at Tania. Her face had gone white and utterly still.

"Why me?" she whispered. "Why not the others?"

Eve's eyes flickered from side to side, as if searching for words. "Tim and Vaughn were never in contact with the gleaners. And the rest of you are immune—a mystery to us in every sense, I'll admit. But you, you and Prumble, though in his case only for a few seconds, were exposed to the . . . the disease known here as SUBS. 'Disease' is not quite accurate, though."

"It is from where we're sitting," the man named Vaughn said.

"What would be accurate?" Tania asked, nonplussed. "You said 'gleaners' a second ago. It's an uncommon word."

"I will share details in time," Eve said. "Suffice to say, I am able to draw upon the memories, thoughts, and feelings of all those who contracted the disease you call SUBS. The two of you, and approximately nine billion others."

The words, the number, sent a pall across the room like a curtain drawn. Skyler kept his gaze on Tania's stony face. Anger, or something like it, simmered just beneath the surface. Gradually it melted.

Tania blinked and spoke very quietly, barely a whisper. "My mother is in there?"

"She is."

At that Tania's eyes closed. She sat very still.

Skyler slumped back, the chair morphing to support him. His thoughts turned back to his fall into the aura generator below Nightcliff, how it had felt like all of his memories had been laid out on a table, and yet he could focus on no specific one. Immunity had been a surprise to them, and still was, apparently.

The silence went on a long time before he realized that everyone, save Tania, was looking at him. He met Eve's gaze and took a long breath before he found the nerve to speak. "What do you want from us, Eve? Why are you here?"

"I represent the race you think of as the Builders. And we need your help."

# EPILOGUE

TAKEN FROM
*THIS DIRE EARTH: A MEMOIR IN LETTERS AND SPEECHES*

## TRANSCRIPT OF A SPEECH TITLED "THE TRUE GIFT," GIVEN BEFORE THE ONE EARTH ASSEMBLY ON THE FIFTIETH ANNIVERSARY OF THE DEPARTURE, APRIL 2, 2335

It's odd to think, now some fifty years since we met the Emissary, that for Skyler and the others only a few minutes have passed.

By the time they arrive Skyler will only be a few hours older, perhaps just starting to get hungry. Back here, though, Earth will have celebrated the year 3000, and I'll be long dead. My ashes, which I've asked to be scattered into the Pará upon my passing, will have long dispersed into the currents of the Atlantic and beyond, eventually perhaps consumed by the distant descendants of our resettlement colonies.

Or maybe we'll have long since failed, and Earth will finally get some rest, waiting for a new species to rise and try again. Perhaps a Builder ship will come for them, too, if Skyler and the others fail at their task like so many apparently have before.

I digress. To be quite honest, I'm stalling. The Emissary, and the entirety of what it told us, is the information I wish to finally share with you today. It has been fifty years, after all, and I'm an old woman now.

I'm still not sure I entirely understand or forgive their tactics. Their motives. Nevertheless, it should not die with me, and I hope this information helps those who may one day welcome Skyler and the others home.

I've tried before to document this. Three times, actually, but each time I could not bring myself to do it. Time may have clouded some of the details, but it's also given me the chance to distance myself from the emotional aspect, and the farewells I had to say. Besides, I'm the only remaining witness to what was said in that alien place. The only Earthbound witness alive, I mean, now that Skadz has passed. The others all agreed to help them, a decision many of you have openly questioned and, until today, I have stayed mostly silent about. This was selfish of me, and unfair to those who left as well as all of you. Still I cannot bring myself to regret not sharing this sooner. I hope you will understand.

So, the Builders . . .

First, I should get the confusing part out of the way. We always assumed that the "Builders" were an alien race sending automated ships to Earth. This is not exactly true. The "Builders" *are* the automated ships. They are a collection of intelligent machines that have scoured our galactic neighborhood for millennia, searching for the help they require.

To use the Emissary's choice of word, the "Creators" are the species behind these robotic vessels. Only, these Creators did not send the ships to Earth. Indeed, they have no idea their creations came to us, or the hundreds of other subject worlds that were tested.

Perhaps I should back up a bit.

The Creators are a species from a planet orbiting the star known as Kepler-22. Their recorded history spans at least one hundred thousand years, and as we know, their technology far exceeds ours.

For much of that history they've been a space-faring race. One technological hurdle they could never get around, however, was the distances involved. Visiting other worlds in person proved a ridiculous waste of resources, and machines were the answer. A machine does not age, can easily build copies of itself—even improve on its own design. Software can be installed and reinstalled again and again, and the size and shapes that machines can take on are, well, limitless.

So they created, and dispersed, machines. Machines we call the "Builders." These ships ventured out, multiplied, even evolved. And every now and then, they would converge back on the home world to report what they'd found. They were explorers back then, nothing more.

On one such convergence a surprise awaited the machines, however. Their home world had gone dark, and upon arriving the Builders found that their Creators had fallen to an invasion. The entire planet, indeed their solar system, had been captured and cut off from the Universe. Many Builder machines were destroyed in their attempts to assess the situation there. Every attempt to physically approach the blockade resulted in destruction. Sure, some defenses were bypassed, but never all of them, and whoever these invaders were, their ability to reconfigure their traps and barriers was, we were told, remarkable.

The Builder ships discovered certain weaknesses, though. Chinks in the proverbial armor. Chief among these was that the invaders assumed that only machines would attempt to penetrate their blockade. A few probing tests with some primitive life-forms showed something of a blind spot, though the Emissary was vague on any specifics. Suffice to say, the machines realized they needed to find biological life that could aid them.

They needed to do something, and so they did. They sought help. Being machines, they went about this in a systematic way. They developed a sorting algorithm.

What the Builders did to Earth, to humanity, is unforgivable. Deplorable, disgusting, heartless . . . all this is true, and yet seen from the context of an emotionless *machine* just trying to filter target species through a list of selection criteria, it oddly makes sense.

When I think now about all the billions of humans who died here, and couple that with the realization that the same thing has probably happened on hundreds of other worlds, I must admit it gives me a strange sense of peace about the whole thing.

It took me many years to reach this understanding. Skyler and all the rest of them only needed a few minutes of discussion before they all agreed to go. All except Skadz, I mean. He said it then and repeated it to me, many years later. "I had enough of wandering, and I had promises to keep. Besides, someone has to stay and tell people what happened."

Only we didn't tell you. Not everything. We both pretended not to know certain details. We were worried, quite frankly, about what humanity would do with the . . . with what they've given us. I hope you will understand, or at least find a way to forgive us.

The machines needed to find a species that could bypass the defenses that keep their Creators imprisoned, and so they devised a series of tests that would help weed out unsuitable candidates. The Emissary told us, almost as a side note of inconsequential interest, of life's incredible abundance in the Universe. Their problem was not finding life, but that they found too much. They needed a way to whittle down the list.

They altered their tactics. Joined together and began to launch preprogrammed vessels in a carefully designed sequence to as many stars as possible, all searching for a target species with the capabilities they required.

Unfortunately for us, we fit the profile.

The Emissary did not explain, at least when I was present, what the various stages of their actions against Earth were designed to test. All I know is they've spent thousands of years perfecting this sequence of trials, and that insertion of the five keys into the arc ship before the date of the final event signifies, to the Builders at least, that they've finally found their best chance at breaking the siege of their home world.

And that was it. She asked us to decide, right then and there, if we would go. The test was over, we'd passed. Their plague forge was shut down. Our planet—what was left of it—given back.

I must admit, I was livid. I tried to point out that in order to end the siege of their home they'd laid siege to hundreds of other planets, probably wiping most of them out in the process. In hindsight, I was too harsh. The Emissary—Eve, she named herself—was truly an emissary, innocent in all of this.

What galled me then, and still keeps me up at night even now, was that the others agreed to go so readily. And for it to all start with Skyler, agreeing to go practically the instant the Emissary agreed to his single demand.

Everyone else fell in line pretty quickly. Everyone but Skadz and me.

Since then, many have vilified Skyler and the others for choosing to help, given the immeasurable damage the Builders inflicted on our world. Those same people have often tried to turn us into some kind of heroes. They said we put Earth first, that we stayed to help rebuild and renew our own world rather than dash off across the cosmos to assist our enemies in some kind of bizarre Stockholm syndrome scenario.

So for the record, helping Earth was the furthest thing from my mind in that moment the offer was made. I simply knew I couldn't help them. I couldn't forgive. They took everything from me: My parents, my aunts and uncles, my friends. My childhood, and Davi's.

The fact remains that it's Skyler and the others who are helping Earth. This cannot be understated, and I should have said it before. I should have explained. Instead Skadz and I agreed to wait. We wanted to see what happened in the aftermath, to make sure the survivors on Earth were ready for what Skyler negotiated on their behalf.

I've never spoken of this to anybody until now. Nor did Skadz, as far as I know, before he passed away. Before I do explain, however, allow me to review the considerable gifts bestowed on us in exchange for the sacrifice Skyler and the others made:

Two space elevators, plus the ships needed to construct three more whenever we wish.

Two hundred mobile towers, reconfigured to produce unsynchronized pockets where time runs at speeds ranging from a virtual standstill to almost a year per second spent inside, the possibilities for which we are still dreaming up even now. Someday these will be what allow us to reach the stars ourselves.

Knowledge of how to reproduce their remarkable building materials as well as their energy sources. Granted, it will still be many years before we have the resources and manufacturing capability online to make use of this, but it's coming. Last year's restart of Penrith, Brisbane, and Newcastle stations is an incredible start toward this goal.

Honestly, if or when Skyler ever returns, I wonder whether he will recognize our planet. Despite everything, even I can admit that the chance to have a fresh start, backed by all these marvels, makes me tingle with excitement. There have been mistakes and missteps, sure, but on the whole I think everyone agrees we are doing it right this time. We're building a utopia.

But there is something you're not aware of. Something else they left behind, and it was Skyler who thought to ask for it. To demand it, rather.

There is a machine in orbit above us. Dormant as of yet, but there. Ready and waiting to act as guide, tutor, friend. We only need visit the place, and ask. I'm telling you now because I think we are ready. And I think we need the help.

It has been five decades, after all, and our progress, while admirable, is slow. By most estimates it will take another six hundred years to repopulate the cities we've designated as resettlement candidates. Six hundred! With the intelligence they left us, and the information it contains, we could reduce that figure significantly.

This brings me to the true gift they gave us. The grand apology.

What we knew as SUBS, the virus that took so many from us through the systematic dismantling of the human mind, was in fact an information-gathering network. A vast swarm of machines, built to seek sentient minds and harvest from them the information they carry. Thoughts, memories, perhaps even personalities.

They collected it, all of it, in a trove of information almost beyond comprehension. Nine billion minds, cataloged and stored. It's all there, waiting for us to access it. I now believe we should do exactly that, despite some inherent dangers I'm sure you can all imagine. We need to be careful who is allowed inside, but if we do it right then it's possible all of the knowledge lost to that terrible disease can be regained.

It was Skyler who spoke up. He's the one who demanded they leave this treasure behind, and provide us a method to interact with it. This morning I've shared the details regarding this with the Science Committee.

Hindsight is a wonderful thing. No matter the Builders' motivations, the fact was that Earth lay in ruins and likely would have collapsed entirely without these gifts. My stubbornness, if shared by the others, would have left us with nothing. And for all I know they would have just taken us against our will and left Earth to die. They are machines, after all, following a core set of principles they cannot break, including the simple instruction at the very center of their programmed souls:

Protect your creators.

Something I think we humans can understand.

Ana Vielma
Speaker, One Earth Assembly

# ACKNOWLEDGMENTS

This novel would not have been possible without the help and support of the following:

My endlessly patient wife, Nancy.

Sara Megibow, my agent and champion.

My editor Mike Braff and his assistant, Sarah Peed. Their insights and thoughtfulness constantly amaze me.

All my family and friends, and notably: the Brotherhood and the Cosmonicans.

The tremendously talented Kevin Hearne, my first and biggest fan, and someone I now call a friend.

I also extend my heartfelt thanks to all the people at Del Rey who helped bring this series to life. You're one hell of a talented bunch.

# THE DIRE EARTH CYCLE

## JASON M. HOUGH

The automated alien ship came and built us a space elevator—an impervious thread connecting Darwin, Australia to the heavens. We took advantage of the Builder's gift and established orbital colonies along the cord. Then, years later, a plague almost completely obliterated the world's population...

**BOOK ONE: THE DARWIN ELEVATOR**

**BOOK TWO: THE EXODUS TOWERS**

**TITAN**BOOKS.COM

# THE WITHOUT WARNING TRILOGY
## JOHN BIRMINGHAM

### WITHOUT WARNING

When a wave of inexplicable energy slams into the United States, America as we know it vanishes. From an engineer in Seattle who becomes his city's only hope, to a war journalist trapped in the Middle East, this is a story of survival, violence, and a new, soul-shattering reality.

### AFTER AMERICA

While the United States lies in ruins and a skeleton government tries to rebuild the nation, swarms of pirates and foreign militias plunder the lawless wasteland, where even the president is fair prey.

### ANGELS OF VENGEANCE

With a conflicted US president struggling to make momentous decisions in Seattle, and a madman fomenting rebellion in Texas, three women are fighting their own battles—for survival, justice, and revenge.

"A seamless fusion of alternate history, post-apocalyptic fiction, and espionage-fueled thriller... Birmingham's story is tightly woven and deeply considered." *Publishers Weekly*

# THE CLONE REBELLION
## STEVEN L. KENT

Earth, 2508 A.D. Humans have spread across the six arms of the
Milky Way galaxy. The Unified Authority controls Earth's colonies
with an iron fist and a powerful military—a military made up
almost entirely of clones...

### THE CLONE REPUBLIC
### ROGUE CLONE
### THE CLONE ALLIANCE
### THE CLONE ELITE
### THE CLONE BETRAYAL
### THE CLONE EMPIRE
### THE CLONE REDEMPTION
### THE CLONE SEDITION
### THE CLONE ASSASSIN (October 2013)

"A smartly conceived adventure." SF Reviews

"Kent is a skillful storyteller." *Science Fiction Weekly*

"Offers up stunning battle sequences, intriguing moral quandaries,
and plenty of unexpected revelations." SF Site

## TITANBOOKS.COM

# THE LOST STARS
## JACK CAMPBELL

For the first time, the story of the *Lost Fleet* universe is told
through the eyes of citizens of the Syndicate Worlds as they deal
with defeat in the war, threats from all sides, and the crumbling
of the Syndicate empire. In the Midway Star System, leaders
must decide whether to remain loyal to the old order or fight for
something new.

### TARNISHED KNIGHT
### PERILOUS SHIELD (October 2013)

"Campbell maintains the military, political and even sexual
tension with sure-handed proficiency... What emerges is a
fascinating and vividly rendered character study, fully and expertly
contextualized." *Kirkus Reviews*

"As can be expected in a Jack Campbell novel, the military battle
sequences are very well done, with the land-based action adding a
new dimension." SF Crowsnest

# THE GAMES
## TED KOSMATKA

In a future where the most popular Olympic event is a bloody gladiator competition that pits genetically engineered life forms in a fight to the death, Dr Silas Williams is the brilliant geneticist tasked with creating the US entrant. But when the creature demonstrates monstrous strength, speed and—most disquietingly—intelligence, Silas's scientific curiosity soon gives way to sheer terror.

"An outstanding debut novel." *Booklist*

"Exacting science and meticulous attention to detail provide the backbone for this thriller, which blends the best of Crichton and Koontz." *Publishers Weekly*

"Kosmatka successfully captures the thrill of groundbreaking technology characteristic of Michael Crichton's technothrillers... The pleasure of his polished, action-packed storytelling is deepened by strong character development." *Library Journal* [starred review]

# TURBULENCE
## SAMIT BASU

When Aman Sen gets off a plane from London to Delhi, he discovers that he has extraordinary abilities corresponding to his innermost desires, as does everyone else on the flight.

Aman wants to heal the planet, but with each step he takes, he finds helping some means harming others. Will it all end, as 80 years of super-hero fiction suggests, in a meaningless, explosive slugfest?

"You'll laugh, you'll cry, you'll gasp and you'll demand a sequel." Ben Aaronovitch (bestselling author of *Rivers of London*)

"Solid writing, great character development, humour, loss, and excellent points to ponder in every chapter." *Wired*

"Snappy and clever." *Publishers Weekly*

FOR MORE FANTASTIC FICTION, AUTHOR EVENTS, EXCLUSIVE EXCERPTS,
COMPETITIONS, LIMITED EDITIONS AND MORE

**VISIT OUR WEBSITE**
titanbooks.com

**LIKE US ON FACEBOOK**
facebook.com/titanbooks

**FOLLOW US ON TWITTER**
@TitanBooks

**EMAIL US**
readerfeedback@titanemail.com